THE DEVIL IS IN THE DETAILS

A NOVEL BY LAKEISHA LAKAY

The Devil is in the Details
© 2021 by LaKeisha LaKay
All rights reserved

ISBN: 978-1-7371723-9-0
ISBN: 978-1-7371723-2-1

Library of Congress Registration Number: TXu 2-259-305

Printed in the United States of America

I GIVE THANKS...

To God for my ability to write. It is from Him did I receive the gift to express my thoughts in a creative way;

To the host of family and friends that encouraged this project to its end, particularly my parents (who took away my books and writing materials as a form of discipline when I was a child; you helped foster my enjoyment of and appreciation for reading and writing) and my inspiring four siblings (Clayton, Evelyn, Janay, and Natalie);

To my dedicated primary readers: Natalie Jones, Corin Miller, and Celeste Gantt (who was first my high school English teacher and is now my amazing book editor); and

To you who have supported my endeavor with the purchase of this book.

None of this would be possible without the community of love that surrounds me.

I thank you, I love you...

Things are not always what they seem; the first appearance deceives many; the intelligence of a few perceives what has been carefully hidden.

-*Phaedrus*

*** *ONE* ***

"Damn."

The word involuntary slipped past his tongue and escaped his mouth as if it were powered by the same electrical impulse that prompted his heartbeat.

From the top floor of the garden-style condo, he watched from his sliding glass door as her toned legs, broad hips, and small waist moved in sync with the arm that massaged soap onto the hood of her car. The oppressive Florida heat had glistened her caramel complexion with perspiration, and the thin fabric of her tank top cleaved to her full breasts.

Stifling his impish grin, he sipped his hot coffee and continued to look on until he believed her eyes caught his. When she smiled then waved, the meeting of his gaze was confirmed.

"Damn," he uttered again—this time in embarrassment.

He returned the wave and contemplated a formal introduction. Failure to offer one would force him across the line that separated spectators from voyeurs, and ruin the prospects of being cordial neighbors. Breathing deeply, he begrudgingly placed his cup on the marble end table and exited his front door.

"You missed a spot," he teased, descending the final steps.

"Excuse me?" She asked, lifting her head to meet his light

brown eyes. He stood approximately 6'3 to her 5'8.

He cleared his throat and repeated, "I said you missed a spot."

She shook her head and chuckled at his wit, "Really?"

He privately thanked the designer of the denim shorts she wore before he responded knowingly, "Yes, and it's on the other side of the hood. You may have to reach a little further to get it."

She took in his casual Sunday dress: khaki slacks with a plaid, button-down shirt faultlessly tucked behind the light brown belt that paired with his shoes. "You're something else. You know that?"

"I have been told." He paused. "Do you need any help?"

She retrieved the hose from the ground and proceeded to rinse the soap off her black Camry. "I'm finished now." She looked up at him and added, "But, I could have used the help earlier."

He blushed at the innuendo and shamefully lowered his eyes.

She laughed at his coyness then extended an olive branch. "Thanks for the offer though, Mister..."

"Russell. Bryan Russell," he finished, meeting her eyes again.

She released the pressure on the lever to stop the water and dropped the hose to the ground. After wiping her wet palms on her ribbed tank top, she held out her right hand. "Pleased to meet you, Mr. Bryan Russell. I'm Saamyah Cambell."

Bryan took her soft, manicured hand and shook it. "Please call me Bryan, and the pleasure is mine, *Mrs.* Cambell."

Tickled by his poor attempt at subtlety, Saamyah released his hand, retrieved her hose, and corrected, "I'm not married, Bryan."

He nervously shoved his hands in his pockets. "I'm just batting a bunch of fouls with you, aren't I?"

Saamyah's face contorted and shoulders shrugged at the question. "Looks like." She rinsed the soap from her legs and then asked, "Are you married?"

"...I'm sorry?" Bryan asked.

Saamyah's eyes caught his gawking. "Don't hurt yourself trying to answer the question."

"I didn't hear you," he defended.

Saamyah scoffed. "I'm bet." She slipped off her sandals, rinsed her feet, and then covered her soles again. After placing items in her bucket, she readied herself to return to her ground level, summer-lease condo.

Bryan stepped in her path to halt her step. "Yes," he replied although uncertain of what he was answering.

Astonished by his response, Saamyah took a moment to recover before she met his stare and advised, "You should really consider spending the time you waste surveying women with your wife."

Perplexed by her comment, Bryan stated, "I'm not married...I mean I am—*was*." He stopped to let his anxiety subside; something about her made him increasingly nervous.

He inhaled a relaxing breath and clarified, "I *was* married is what I meant to say."

Saamyah gave him a blank stare.

"I'm sorry, it's just that..." His voice trailed off.

She waited for him to complete his thought. When he failed to, Saamyah offered, "thanks for the introduction," and walked to her unit, dropping the bucket and hose outside her door.

Bryan sighed in frustration and followed. "Saamyah, wait...You don't understand."

Saamyah stepped past her threshold and held the door ajar. "You are right. I don't understand and, frankly, I don't care to." She closed and secured her door. Unfavorable occurrences, such as this, made her regret not selecting the second floor unit sans washer and dryer. The top floor always provided her with a greater sense of security.

She moved to watch through the vertical blinds that covered her sliding glass door Bryan walk away. Exhaling in relief and disappointment, she spoke to herself, "Second day in the community and you're already making enemies with the neighbors. Good job, Saamyah."

Saamyah rotated the blinds closed and then walked over to a group of boxes that her earlier procrastination kept her from unpacking.

Hours later, Saamyah had organized her home office and master bedroom. Though the home décor she purchased added life to the rented furnishings, she regretted heeding her brother's advice to be frugal during her temporary duty assignment. She loathed the choice they had made and hated more that she alone had to live with it.

"Get over yourself, Saamyah," she finally muttered as she released her dark brown hair from the clip that held it on the top of her head. She tousled her tresses until they fell down her back and walked toward the kitchen for a glass of water. A hard knock on the door stopped and pivoted her step.

She squinted through the peephole, then unsecured and opened the door. "Bryan, I thought I told you tha-"

The tall, muscular man turned to face her and pushed himself past the door. He closed and secured it then watched her regain her bearings on the floor.

"Patrick?" Saamyah whispered in confusion as she looked up at her intruder. She rose to her feet and ogled the haunt from her past.

He stepped into her personal space. "It's been a while...Hasn't it, Saamyah?"

She did not respond.

The back of his hand grazed her soft cheek. "Just as aesthetically pleasing as I remembered."

Saamyah nudged his hand from her face. "What do you want, Patrick?"

His solid weight maneuvered her into a wall. "What I've always wanted." He clawed at her bare, outer thighs and breathed on her neck. "I spent three years in prison dreaming about this moment...dreaming and plotting."

Ignoring her stinging flesh when she tore his fingers from her legs, Saamyah asked, "What are you talking about, Patrick?"

"Pain," Patrick answered. He looked deep into her gleaming brown eyes and continued, "I want you to experience it in the same fashion that I did."

Saamyah swallowed the swelling knot in her throat and held each of his hands that rested at her side. She kept his grief stricken gaze as she confessed, "I miss him, too, Patrick?...I loved h-"

Patrick gripped her jaw and held it tight. "DON'T."

Saamyah clasped his grip with both her hands and recited, "I'm sorry. I'm sorry."

He shoved her head into the wall as he released her face.

Saamyah winced at the pain and fought the tears that swelled in her eyes.

Glowering with disdain, Patrick confessed, "I want you dead...I really do, but a part of me won't allow you the satisfaction of emotional freedom."

"So what? You've come to bind me in my own purgatory?" Saamyah cried. "What sense does that make, Patrick? I'm already tormented by the choice he made."

He clenched her throat. "It should have been you...It should have been." Ignoring the hurt and fear that trickled from her eyes, Patrick lowered his mouth to hers.

Saamyah pushed at his chest and broke their kiss. "Stop...please, just go...I don't know how you found me, but please...please just leave."

Patrick yanked her arms from his chest and pinned them against the wall above her head. His lips brushed her wet cheek, pecked at her lips, then traveled down her small chin and narrow neck.

Her skin burned from the friction caused by her twisting wrists in his firm grip. "Patrick, stop!" Saamyah yelled in frustration, finally yanking her wrists free.

He grinned at her fight and met her eyes.

"I'll call the police," she warned. "I swear to it, I will. And, believe you me, the state penitentiary is not as luxurious as federal prison."

Patrick chuckled at her warning before he struck her face with the back of his hand. "Don't humor me with your idle threats."

More tears fell from her eyes as Saamyah held her warm cheek.

Patrick stepped from her personal space and started toward the door. He stopped partway to face her and revealed, "Your brother is the true reason I went to prison."

Oblivious to what he spoke of, Saamyah repeated what came natural to her, "I'm sorry, Patrick."

Patrick shook his head in disbelief and uttered, "No, you're not. If you were, you wouldn't have left me in prison to rot for three years."

She wiped her face and cried, "That's not true, Patrick. I am sorry...I'm so sorry for everything."

"You're not, but you will be."

Before she could abscond down the hall, he lunged and grabbed her forearm.

Saamyah screamed as he pulled her down to the floor and tore the thin fabric of her top. She wrestled with the weight of his body and strength of his arms until the fight in her extinguished.

"Patrick, please," she breathlessly panted when his body moved further down the center of hers. "Please don't do this to me."

Their eyes met and he kissed the tears that fell from hers. He then gently wiped her face dry.

Saamyah said in a whisper, "I don't want my first time to be this way."

Patrick gazed into what use to be their past, then took her wrists and pressed them deep into the carpeted floor. His cool mouth touched her lips, neck, and finally the black lace that covered her nipple.

Saamyah's legs grew weak struggling against the relentless might of his knees that forced her legs further apart. She released a relentless cry, but instantly quieted when a knock at the door gave hope to the end of her nightmare.

"Saamyah, it's me." Bryan knocked again.

Patrick unhurriedly dismounted her. He met her stare and instructed, "Answer it."

Saamyah staggered to her feet and quickly wiped eyes. As she walked to the entrance, she adjusted the torn pieces of her tank top, and smoothed her hair.

"Hey," Bryan lowly breathed in astonishment after she cracked the door open in his mid-knock.

"Hey," she replied avoiding his eyes.

"I uuh…I uuh…Are you okay?"

She quickly met his eyes, "Yeah, fine. Why?"

"Because you look like sh-"

Saamyah glanced over her shoulder and then looked back at Bryan. "I'm just feeling a little homesick—that's all."

Bryan recognized a quiver in Saamyah's voice. "Homesick?"

She simply nodded and wiped the fresh tears that fell from her eyes. Bryan noticed her discolored cheek and neck.

"Well, listen, I need your help with something. Do you mind if I come in?"

"Now is not a good time, Bryan. Maybe later?"

"It will only be a minute," he pressed.

Patrick widened the door and stated, "It's fine, sweetheart. I am on my way out." He touched Saamyah's lips with his and whispered, "I'll be back."

Bryan acknowledged Patrick with a simple nod and side-stepped to allow him to exit the unit. He then entered, locked, and chained the door behind him. Saamyah dropped to a seated position on the floor, brought her knees to her chest, and cried uncontrollably in her hands.

"Are you alright?" Bryan asked, kneeling in front of her.

She did not answer.

"Saamyah, did he hurt you?"

She shook her head and wiped her eyes.

"Why don't you go fix yourself up? I will wait for you out here."

Bryan rose to his feet and then helped her to hers.

"Thank you," she murmured avoiding his eyes before walking to her master bedroom's shower.

Bryan sat on her sofa with a cup of coffee in hand when Saamyah returned to the living room. She was dressed in grey leggings and an oversized t-shirt that fell off her right shoulder. Her hair was wet from the shower and face dewy, but Bryan still noticed that she had been crying.

He handed Saamyah a cup of coffee when she took a seat next to him.

Saamyah shook her head and said, "I don't drink coffee."

Bryan returned the cup to the coaster on the coffee table in front of them and replied, "That would explain why I couldn't find your coffee or a coffee maker for that matter...I just grabbed the instant from upstairs—not as good as my expresso, but it does the job when I need it to...I'm actually trying to cut back though. The caffeine is wreaking havoc on my body."

Saamyah nodded, appreciating the hollow talk that lessened the awkwardness between them. When the room finally fell silent, Saamyah spoke, "Thank you, again."

"For what?" Bryan asked before sipping from his cup.

Saamyah met is gaze. "For coming to my aid."

Bryan lowered his beverage and shrugged. "I actually came for another reason, but-"

"Just receive my appreciation..." She looked down at her hands and rubbed her palms into her knees. "...especially since I was abrupt with you earlier."

Bryan shrugged and responded in jest, "Just due for time wasted surveying you." When she failed to share his humor, he sipped from his cup and asked, "Do you know him?"

Saamyah respired aloud as she contemplated the best description of their relationship. She finally responded, "...Patrick is an old friend…His older, twin brother and I were engaged to be married before he died."

"I'm so sorry to hear that, Saamyah. What happened to him?"

She felt his inquisitive eyes burning in her and she avoided them like an infectious disease. "Killed in the line of duty…We were…We were both of The Federal Bureau of Investigations and he was shot during an undercover operation."

Bryan placed his mug on the coffee table next to hers. "Wow…I can see how that can be a devastating loss for the both of you."

Saamyah inhaled deeply and exhaled loudly. She wiped her eyes and confessed, "More so for Patrick—I suppose. Identical twins share an unfathomable bond." She briefly reminisced on the day of the raid and shared, "The bullet that David took was marked for me."

"A bullet never has a name attached to it, Saamyah. It just lands its designated target in a good shot."

She feebly smiled and responded, "That is kind of you to say, but I know I am to blame and Patrick never lets me forget it."

"He is just hurting, Saamyah. Loss, especially that of a sibling, is difficult." He took her hand in his and lightly squeezed it. "In any event, he shouldn't be hitting you."

Saamyah turned her face to his and slowly closed her eyes when his free hand tenderly wiped away her tears. Her cheeks flushed when he placed a lingering kiss on her lips. Saamyah gently pushed him away.

"Your wife," she simply said looking into his eyes.

"Rachel?" Bryan asked.

"…You are married?"

"I was. Rachel died a little over a year ago."

Saamyah dropped her head in ignominy, embarrassed by her inaccurate assumption of him. She eased her hand out of his and offered, "I am so sorry."

"Thank you."

"How did she…" Saamyah voice trailed off unable to complete the question.

"Ovarian cancer."

Saamyah looked up at his solemn face and repeated, "I'm so sorry."

Bryan merely shrugged. "Life does not guarantee us a happy ending."

Uncertain how to perceive his callous statement, she attempted to soften his tone by asking, "Did you at least have children?"

Bryan looked away and shook his head. "No."

Saamyah admired Bryan's muscular physique as well as his radiant, copper skin; brown, curly hair; and faultless, white teeth. All of which told of his good health absent the unknown impact of his excessive caffeine consumption.

Bryan caught her eyes when he felt them watching him. "Do you like what you see?"

Saamyah smiled. "Aren't we full of ourselves?"

"Just answer the question."

"Do you?"

"I do, and that actually brings me to the point of my visit." He cleared his throat and offered, "I want to start again, perhaps over dinner."

Saamyah was taken aback by his forwardness. The confident man that now sat next to her was different from the earlier one knotted with nerves.

"Bryan, I…I can't. I-"

"Sorry—is this too soon for you? I didn't mean to-"

"No, no. It's okay. It's just that…" Her voice faded. "Look, it's getting late and I have to report for duty in the morning."

Bryan nodded. "Good night, Saamyah."

"Good night."

With that, Bryan left and Saamyah rose to secure her door.

*** *** ***

LAKEISHA LAKAY

"Detective Cambell, it is so nice to finally meet you," a short, husky man greeted Saamyah the next morning. "I am Lieutenant Duncan." He extended his right hand for Saamyah to shake. After she did, he instructed, "Please, come with me."

"This," he began while en route to his office, "is the infamous Miami Police Department." He glanced over his shoulder at her and warned, "I could tire you with statistics, but I will leave that for you to investigate—if you haven't already."

Saamyah gave him a bogus smile and retorted, "You mean there is more to know than what Hollywood depicted in *Miami Vice*?"

Lieutenant Duncan stopped outside his office as he chuckled halfheartedly at her jest. He opened the door and motioned for her to enter first. "Yeah, Marshall was right about you." He closed the door behind him and gave her permission to take a seat in a chair in front of his desk as he took the seat behind it.

"And how is that?"

"Lieutenant Marshall shared that you are a force to be reckoned with."

"I'm not sure how to respond to that," Saamyah confessed.

"You don't. You just let your work speak for itself."

Saamyah nodded.

"So, we are Miami's Special Crimes Division (SCD)— investigating crimes against children, the disabled and elderly, as well as all sex-based offenses."

"Is this entire building the-" Saamyah started perplexed.

Lieutenant Duncan interjected anticipating her question, "No, this place is three stories up with a basement that houses our records and a lower level parking facility. So, there are many divisions within this fortress."

Saamyah nodded.

He observed her for a brief moment and then said, "Tell me about yourself," before the room grew too quiet.

"You mean Lieutenant Marshall has not told you all there is to know about me?" She taunted with a smile.

"Not anything concerning why you requested this TDY."

Saamyah pushed back the hair that had fallen out of her French braid and said, "This temporary duty assignment is merely time I need from San Antonio."

"And you believe that 90 days will suffice?"

"I don't, but I do believe it is what I need prior to stepping into my new role as sergeant and...and forever being anchored in San Antonio."

Her vagueness made him uncomfortable and he began to regret honoring the request of Lieutenant Marshall—his longtime friend. Lieutenant Duncan loosened his tie and leaned forward into his desk so that he could peer deep into Saamyah's eyes. "Detective Cambell, I will not lie to you. You are only here as a favor to my college friend and academy brother."

Unsure of what he was alluding to, Saamyah swallowed the knot in her throat and replied, "I understand."

Lieutenant Duncan relaxed in his chair and said, "Good, then I expect to have no problems during your tenure."

Saamyah feebly grinned and nodded in accordance.

"You have an impeccable resume: double major in criminal justice and biology at both the undergraduate and graduate levels of education; quite a few internships and volunteer work—all very commendable."

"Thank you."

"So, why did you leave The Bureau?" Lieutenant Duncan bluntly inquired, no longer able to contain the question that burned within him the moment he received her credentials.

Taken aback by the unexpected question, Saamyah responded defensively. "It is not uncommon for a fed to resign and work among state or local law enforcement."

"I understand that, but that wasn't my question."

Saamyah exhaled loudly and finally answered, "A supervisor was killed in the line of duty and I had problems coping."

"I'm sorry to hear that."

"It's fine—I'm fine," she assured him.

Lieutenant Duncan nodded and slightly changed the subject, "Well, by your credentials you are more than qualified for a position here if you decide to make Florida your home after three months. We can always use a LEO like you on our force."

Saamyah shook her head in dissent. "No, thank you. I am not interested in a new law enforcement officer opportunity; I am just here for the change in scenery. That's all." His empty stare compelled her to further justify her response. "Absent training in Quantico, San Antonio is all that I know…I need this sabbatical before career advancements anchor me in Texas."

"And this TDY is your idea of a sabbatical?" The lieutenant asked with skepticism.

"Well, I suppose if I were sane I, would backpack through Europe. But, who is truly sane among us?"

Lieutenant Duncan nodded, smiled, and accepted her argument. "I'll show you to your office and introduce you to your partner. He will take you for your credentials and firearm as well as show you around. Any questions?"

Saamyah shook her head.

"Welcome aboard, Detective Cambell. Come with me."

They walked up a third flight of stairs, down a long hallway, and through a door with a frosted glass window that read *Detective Bryan Russell and Detective Saamyah Cambell.* Saamyah did not notice the window.

"This here is your office and that opening over there is your partner's. Come, I'll introduce the two of you."

When they walked through the door Bryan was at his desk reviewing documents.

"Detective Russell, this is your new partner," Lieutenant Duncan announced.

Bryan looked up and recognized Saamyah.

"You've got to be kidding me," Bryan said then laughed.

Saamyah shook her head dismay. "You are kidding, right?"

"You must know each other," Lieutenant Duncan assumed.

"Yes," Saamyah answered. "I mean no…Well, we met yesterday…by happenstance…"

"Great, no need for drawn out introductions…I received a call about an attempted rape on Miami Beach. It is believed to be linked to a few other rapes across Miami-Dade County, but we won't know until the Sheriff transfers the case over. I want the two of you working it."

Lieutenant Duncan walked out of Bryan's office and Saamyah followed. She walked to take a seat at her wooded, L-shaped workstation.

"Lieutenant, may I have a word with you in my office please?" Bryan asked.

Lieutenant Duncan turned on his heel and walked back into the office.

"Lieutenant," Bryan began, shutting the door behind him, "I know that Washington's departure a couple of months ago was untimely and we are operating with a skeleton crew, but I don't want a woman to look after."

Lieutenant Duncan took a moment to calm his natural reflex to ignorant talk. "…So, this is what you want to talk about? The fact that she's a woman?"

When Bryan did not answer, Lieutenant Duncan continued, "Russell, might I remind you that we have several great, female law enforcement officers that work in this department—our captain being one of them."

"I know that and I didn't mean it that way. It's just that-"

"Russell, I don't have time for this and your toxic masculinity. The decision has been made; for the next 90 days you are partners. Cambell will keep watch over you and you will keep watch over her." He turned to leave, but stopped to add, "And maybe, just maybe, you can now tame that trouble in your pants that makes it such a challenge for you to work with women."

Bryan's response was stifled by the allusion to his rumored sexual history that swarmed the department. In discontent, he watched Lieutenant Duncan walk out of his office and into Saamyah's, then listened to him say, "See you around, Detective Cambell," before leaving.

Saamyah was unmoved by the remarks she overheard. Law enforcement was, is, and most likely forever will be a male dominated field. Fortunately, her many ill-encounters throughout her career developed her thick skin. As a result, smug remarks from male chauvinists lost their damaging affect on her years ago.

Saamyah was, however, perturbed by Lieutenant Duncan's comment concerning Bryan's inability to work with women.

Bryan sat on his desk and contemplated all that Duncan had said. The more he thought, the more he grew frustrated at his failure to pinpoint the source of his irritation. At his core, he did not mind working with women or even having one as a partner. Bryan just did not want Saamyah. He was uncertain as to why, but assumed it to be that trouble lie ahead. Resentfully accepting his fate, Bryan grabbed his keys and exited his office. He saw Saamyah sitting behind her desk scrolling through her cell phone.

"Are you wearing that all day?" Bryan asked her.

Saamyah looked up at him and then down at her tailored, black suit and stiletto pumps. "Well, I wasn't anticipating a day at the beach." She took off the jacket and unbuttoned then rolled the long sleeves of her light blue, collared shirt. After pushing back loose hairs into her French braid, Saamyah said, "I have a change of shoes in my car."

"Have you signed for a laptop?"

"No, not yet," Saamyah answered.

"What about your credentials and firearm? Have you picked them up?"

Saamyah shook her head.

"Checked out the sights?"

Another head shake.

Bryan exhaled loudly and instructed, "Follow me." He swung the door open and immediately noticed the new labels on the door. "Did you see this?"

"I do now," Saamyah responded cavalierly.

Bryan shook his head then led Saamyah out the office, down several flights of stairs, and towards the records department. He waited on Saamyah as people stopped, introduced themselves, and engaged in small talk en route.

"Hey, Carol," Bryan said when they finally walked into the records department.

"What's up, Bryan?" The grayed hair, Caucasian woman standing behind the high counter greeted.

"The usual."

"Sugar honey iced tea?"

Bryan chuckled at her aversion to vulgarity. He thought to simplify her inquiry, but was reminded of her explanation that the use of crude language conveyed a limited vocabulary and exhibited low class.

In an effort to set the tone for a conflict-free Monday, he heeded her advice and simply replied, "You know it."

"So, who's that you've got with you?"

"Saamyah Cambell, my new partner."

Carol's face beamed at Saamyah. "You made it!"

Saamyah smiled back and confirmed, "I did."

Carol extended her right hand across the counter and shook Saamyah's when she took it. "So very nice to meet you, Detective Cambell. I'm Carol Lee, but please call me Carol or by my alias 'Wonder Woman.'"

The three of them laughed.

"Well, this is your multifunctional records department. And, because of the city's budget cuts, I mean that literally. Here we store and manage a large number of case files and evidence—both hard and soft copies in most cases. Don't ask me why...We now also house firearms and ammunition in this department."

"Yes, the reason we are here," Bryan stopped her. "Carol, Saamyah is here to sign for her credentials and firearm."

"Yes, yes, perfect timing too because I was heading upstairs soon." She looked at Saamyah and explained, "From time to time you will see me upstairs assisting with booking, registration, visitors, mail, et cetera, et cetera."

Saamyah smiled and said, "Wonder Woman, indeed."

"Indeed, I am." She winked at Saamyah and handed her a clipboard of documents. "Please review and sign while I go to the back for your new toy."

Saamyah skimmed the familiar, standard language typed on the forms before scribbling her signature on them. When she had finished, Carol had returned and placed the badge and gun on the counter. Carol retrieved the clipboard from Saamyah, recorded the serial numbers on the forms, and then gave Saamyah the items.

Saamyah signed and dated the tags and then removed them from the credentials and then the weapon. Handing them to Carol, she asked, "Anything else?"

Carol shook her head as she took the tags and placed them on the clipboard. "The gun is already loaded, but, of course, the safety is on. In the bottom left hand drawer of your desk is a box of bullets. If you run out, come back to sign for more, okay?"

Saamyah nodded as she said, "Thank you."

"You're welcome, sweetie." She paused to place a set of keys in her hand. "These are the keys to your government ride. Be careful, though, because that one there," she pointed at Bryan, "has a reputation of bullying people out of the driver seat."

Saamyah chuckled and nodded avoiding Bryan's gaze. "Thank you for the warning."

Carol smiled and winked at her. "I.T. should have your laptop ready for pick-up sometime this afternoon."

Saamyah nodded.

At last, Carol wished, "good luck out there," before she disappeared with the clipboard.

"Are you ready?" Bryan asked.

"Yes," Saamyah answered clipping her badge at her waist. She then eased the firearm behind her back.

"Good. We will do the tour later," Bryan assured as he held out his hand.

"What?" Saamyah asked.

"The keys," Bryan answered.

"What?" She asked again in dismay.

"You heard me. Give me the keys to your g-ride."

"No."

"Yes, I know the Miami area better than you do."

"I don't-"

"You have to change your shoes anyway, Saamyah," Bryan interjected. "I will meet you out front."

Unable to contest his point, she shoved the keys into his palm.

Bryan smiled knowingly and glanced at the key tag. "The navy Dodge Charger. That's new to our fleet...I'm jealous."

Saamyah rolled her eyes and walked past him to the door. "I will meet you out front."

In the sedan, Bryan broke their silent ride by asking, "Why didn't you tell me that you were here for a Miami PD TDY?"

Saamyah looked at him as he made a right turn towards the beach. "I suppose for the same reason you didn't tell me that you are a detective for the Miami PD."

"Well, at the time I didn't think it was important for you to know," Bryan responded.

Saamyah reflected on their meeting the day before and silently agreed. His advances provided no segue into conversations about their careers. "To the right," she commented, changing the topic after returning to the present moment. "There is police activity to the right."

Bryan followed her directive and parked as close as he could to the crowd. Saamyah was the first to exit the vehicle as well as the first to greet law enforcement officials. "I'm Detective Cambell and this is my partner Detective Russell. We're with the MPD's Special Crimes. Can any of you tell me what is going on?" Saamyah quickly shared her credentials.

"Everyone keep calm, MPD's finest has just arrived," a sheriff deputy smugly remarked, offended by her commandeering air.

"Excuse me?" Saamyah asked.

"No pardon necessary. I will clear out my men to allow your division to do what they do best."

Saamyah lifted her sunglasses to the top of her head and read the name on his uniform. "And what is that Deputy Connor?"

"Waste taxpayers' dollars." He signaled for his deputies to vacate the scene. "I will see to it that this report is added to the others that are being transferred to your department. Let's not let this perp fall through the cracks like the others." The deputy walked off and a group of concerned citizens followed, shrieking questions at him.

Officers first on the scene provided details of the incident and recapped the summaries of witnesses. They then offered a loose link between the current incident and a string of similar incidents that had occurred on the beach and surrounding areas within the past month. To their knowledge, the present victim was the only who got away relatively unharmed.

Saamyah thanked them for the debriefing and requested their aid in dispersing the crowd. She then took the towel offered by the lifeguard who shared that the victim refused medical treatment or a visit to the hospital.

"Are you alright?" Saamyah asked slowly approaching the victim. She wrapped the towel loosely around her close-to-bare body and took a seat next to her on the bed of the lifeguard truck. After noticing the surreptitious eye contact that she made with Bryan, Saamyah requested that he walk the crime scene.

The woman brushed a strand of hair out of her face and gave Saamyah a disturbing look. "I'm fine, Detective…I'm one of the lucky ones that escaped intact."

Saamyah nodded. "I'm relieved to hear of it…Do you-"

"Detective, I have provided my statement already." She stood and returned the towel to Saamyah. "If you don't mind, I would like to go home now."

Saamyah nodded, mindful not to push. "Would you like an escort?"

The victim shook her head and walked away.

"Any luck with Kimberly James?" Bryan asked Saamyah when he returned to the car.

"So, you do know her?" Saamyah asked as she watched him lean his back against the vehicle next to her, adjust the sunglasses on his face, and fold his arms across his chest.

"I guess you can say that."

"She wouldn't talk to me," Saamyah confessed.

"No surprise there."

Saamyah exhaled loudly and pushed back the hair on her face "Thanks for your help back there—by the way."

"Of course. I wouldn't have it any other way."

She looked at him in antipathy. "I was being facetious."

He glanced over to her. "And I was being supportive."

Saamyah laughed halfheartedly. "Supportive? By not being present, you were supportive?"

"I witnessed your entire showdown with MDPD; rest assure, I was present." He turned to walk away, but stopped to add, "I don't know what they teach you feds at Quantico, but, with local law enforcement, we don't make it a habit to disparage fellow LEOs, especially those here in Miami."

"Really, Bryan? Now is that all law enforcement officers or just the ones with penises dangling between their legs?"

Without waiting for a response, Saamyah nudged Bryan away from the passenger door and climbed into the car.

Saamyah gasped after opening the door to her office. She slowly walked through the threshold and took in the several boxes that were aligned against the walls and the many more that were placed in front of her desk.

"You have got to be kidding me," Bryan muttered, walking in behind Saamyah and closing the door.

"This cannot all be related to this current case. There is just no way," Saamyah spoke in disbelief. She quickly scanned the number of boxes and counted 37. "This has to be every single sex crime reported to the county since…" Her voice trailed off as she continued to speculate in her mind.

Bryan exhaled in frustration. "This would be laughable if there wasn't bad blood between the county and the city."

Saamyah scratched her head in confusion and asked, "About that, what's the back story?"

Bryan watched her maneuver around boxes to the get to the chair behind her desk. "No more than your typical rivalry between agencies that I am sure you are privy to."

Saamyah fingered the post-it that read *Delivered: June 3 at 2:17 P.M.* She glanced at her wrist watch and saw that is was almost 5 o'clock. "Yes, but I feel that this rivalry is different,"

Saamyah shared while peeling the note off of the manila folder. She crumpled and tossed it in the wastebasket under her desk.

Bryan moved the boxes that barricaded the chair in front of her desk and sat in it. "Special Crimes is a fairly new division. It was implemented following a public outcry for more police scrutiny of crimes that almost always fall through the cracks."

"That's not atypical of law enforcement. Homicide and narcotics have their own task forces for that very reason."

"But," Bryan continued, "this task force was not the first choice of the Sheriff, especially since many of these special crime cases stretch across the county. Instead, he advocated for increased funding for more deputies, equipment, and training. He believes that the use of tax dollars on a specialization such as ours only exacerbates the issues we are currently experiencing with silos."

Saamyah nodded in agreement. "Information sharing is a long standing issue across all law enforcement agencies. The fact that we continue to operate independently and struggle to work together only hurts the public." She contemplated her earlier spirited exchange and declared, "I understand now why Deputy Connor stated that this division is a waste of taxpayers' money."

Bryan nodded. "I have been on the task force since its inception two months ago, and I have been hearing it ever since."

Saamyah opened the manila folder and skimmed the sexual assault report. When she recognized the name, she extended the report to Bryan. "Ms. Kimberly James."

Bryan took the sheet and read it as Saamyah reviewed the witness statements.

"So, what can you share about Ms. James?'

He avoided her eyes and handed her back the report. "Not much," he answered.

"Do you think we can get anything more out of her?"

Bryan shrugged his shoulders and then rose from his seat. "She is pretty private." Changing the subject he offered, "I am going to call down to Records and see about getting some of these boxes moved downstairs."

Saamyah nodded and watched as Bryan walked into his office. After he closed the door behind him, she walked to a group of boxes and began to sift through their contents—organizing the files the best she could prior to their delivery to the basement.

Saamyah hurried through the front door of her condo to grab the shrilling cordless phone ringing in the dark. "Hello," she answered.

"Hey, babe sis."

"DeVaughn." Saamyah rolled her eyes in annoyance. She returned to the door to shut, chain, and lock it. "I can't believe that you are calling me again. You can't-"

Her brother chuckled and assured her, "I am not going to call every day of your TDY, Saamyah. I'm just calling to hear of your first day—that's all."

Saamyah turned on her table lamp, kicked off her shoes, and settled into the sofa. "It was fair. Not much more to report."

"And the department? Any similarities with San Anton-"

"DeVaughn, I literally just walked through the door. It's been a long day and I am tired…Can we do this another time, preferably in a week?"

"Yes, but no. I will call you in a couple days."

Saamyah rolled her eyes.

"I saw that," her brother warned.

"You always do," Saamyah retorted.

"I love you; be careful out there."

"Me too and I will." She disconnected the call and sank further into the cushion of the sofa. Just as her lids lowered to cover her eyes, the phone's ring shrilled again.

Saamyah's body flinched at the sound and her eyes wearily opened. She begrudgingly answered, "DeVaughn, I told you that-"

"Good evening, Detective Cambell," a male voice greeted.

Saamyah sat up in her seat and inquired, "Who is this?"

"I would be insulted if I weren't already disappointed by your inability to recognize my voice," he taunted.

Saamyah released a sigh of relief after recognizing Patrick's voice. "And I would ask how you obtained this number if

I weren't already privy to your ability to get everything you want," she responded.

"Not everything, Saamyah...At least not yet."

"I'm hanging up now."

"There is a French café a block north of the police station. Meet me there in the morning at 8 for breakfast."

"No," she simply replied.

Patrick laughed half-heartedly. "You respond as if that was an invitation that could be declined, Saamyah."

Saamyah said nothing in response. Instead, she listened to Patrick bid, "see you in the morning," before he hung up.

Saamyah's racing thoughts were halted by the busy tone that pulsed in her ear. She ended the call and then lowered the phone to the cushion next to her. Refusing to give Patrick another thought, Saamyah stood to double check the security of the door. She then turned off the table lamp and walked toward her master bathroom for a hot shower.

*** *** ***

"And here I thought I was the only detective in SCD that start the days early," Bryan announced after walking into the office the following morning. He closed the door behind him and glanced at his watch. The time was quarter after eight.

Saamyah turned from her whiteboard and greeted, "Good morning."

"Good morning." He met her at her side and gazed at the whiteboard. "What is this?"

"It's a victim chart," she began to explain. "I compiled the most recent victims in hopes of building a perpetrator profile."

Bryan looked on as Saamyah described each victim. He took in their photos, names, ages, and dates of victimization. "Are there more?"

"Several, but these are the ones that I believe are related to the," she stopped to emphasize with air quotes, "'Miami Beach' case."

Bryan nodded. "And all these assaults actually occurred on the beach?"

Saamyah shook her head. "Just the first three and the last," she pointed out.

"How do we know these women are the only victims?"

"Well, we don't, but these seven have all occurred within the last five weeks in this geographical location." Saamyah stepped to the Miami-Dade County map that she taped next to the whiteboard. She used her index finger to trace the red circle she drew around the location of interest.

Ignoring her observations, Bryan asked again, "So, there could be more victims?"

"The victim count is not the focal point, Bryan," Saamyah stressed with annoyance. "Finding a common link between these women and building a perp profile is."

"I understand that," Bryan began. "I just think-"

His justification was interrupted by the ringing phone on Saamyah's desk. "You should probably get that," he encouraged when her disposition suggested that she otherwise would not.

"This is Cambell," Saamyah announced as she watched Bryan walk into his office and close the door.

"Detective Cambell, this is Carol. You have a Mr. Patrick Barnes signed in to visit you."

Saamyah glimpsed at her watch and exhaled loudly. "Thank you, Carol. I will be down in a moment."

"I'm actually on my way up so I can escort him en route."

"I appreciate that," Saamyah replied prior to hanging up.

Minutes later, there was a light tap on the door and Saamyah reluctantly answered it. She thanked Carol again, widened the door for Patrick to enter, and immediately closed it behind him.

"I waited a half hour for you," he informed her, taking a seat in front of her desk.

"I don't know why. Patrick, I told you that I was not coming." She sat behind her desk and asked, "What do you want?"

"Do you have a problem with me being here?"

Saamyah took in the tall, brown skinned, low-cut, black haired man and broke the gaze she held with his brown eyes. Seeing him, she saw David and a host of past memories. "I have a problem with you being anywhere that I am," she responded.

A brief silence fell in the room and it made Saamyah uneasy. When she heard faint shuffling in Bryan's office, she was reminded that she was not alone. She met his eyes and asked again. "So, what do you want?"

Patrick chuckled. "Let's not waste time playing games, Saamyah. You know what I want."

Changing the subject, Saamyah asked, "So, when did you get out?"

"Why do you want to know?"

"My brother helped you didn't he?"

Patrick smiled at her and answered, "It's one of the perks of knowing people in high places."

"Does DeVaughn know that you are here?"

"You already know the answer to that."

"Well, he will after today," Saamyah assured.

Patrick grinned and grabbed the family photo she had on her desk. He looked upon the three familiar faces of Saamyah's brothers and then began tracing hers with his fingers. "I am sure that you are aware of this, but, in the state of Texas, there is no statute of limitations for murder or manslaughter."

"I did not kill your brother," she quickly asserted.

"No, but your brother killed several of his patients...I was almost one of them."

"Get out," Saamyah ordered.

"Have I again tainted your glowing perception of the good doctor?"

Saamyah did not answer.

"Wake up, Saamyah, your brother was not and is not who feigns to be...He is the opioid crisis—he and his fellow medical practitioners."

Saamyah looked at him with disgust. "Get out, now."

"No," he replied. "Three years in prison is the price I paid for my silence. I'm here to collect on the balance owed to me…And you, Saamyah," he lustfully licked his bottom lip and completed, "are the appeasing cost."

"Get out, now!"

Patrick leaned back in his chair and chuckled.

Saamyah rose to her feet and yelled, "I mean it, Patrick! Get the he-"

Bryan swung open his office door after hearing Saamyah's shouts. "Saamyah, what is-"

Patrick eyes met Bryan's and a harsh silence fell in the room. Patrick stood and stared at Saamyah then Bryan. "Is this some kind of joke?" Patrick asked referring to their working partnership.

"If it is, then you're the only one humored," Bryan told him walking further into Saamyah's office. He looked at her and asked, "What is the problem?"

"You interrupted our private discussion," Patrick answered for her.

Bryan looked at him and said, "I believe that private discussion ended when she told you to leave."

"I believe-" Patrick began.

"Just leave, Patrick," Saamyah interjected.

Patrick looked at her and then Bryan. He tossed the photo he held onto her desk. It knocked over a second family photo and tipped over a paper cup of tea.

Saamyah jumped back to keep the warm liquid from soiling her navy pants and pale pink, portofino shirt. With Bryan's help, she quickly moved files and used several facial tissues to soak up the tea. Immersed in the unexpected clean-up, Saamyah did not break focus to respond to Patrick's admonition, "At least have the courtesy to show your face the next time I invite you to dine with me." He walked out the office and closed the door behind him.

Saamyah exhaled loudly and tossed several wet tissues in the wastebasket. She yanked more from the square box and dropped to her knees to mop up the substance from the wood floor.

She rose to her feet, tossed the tissues in the wastebasket, and shoved a lock of hair behind her ear. "I'm so sorry about this, Bryan."

He nodded and tossed the wet tissues he held into the wastebasket.

"Thank you…by the way."

Bryan did not respond. Instead, he handed her the partially wet folders, walked into his office, and closed his door.

Saamyah looked down at the cracked glass that sat in the frame that Patrick had tossed on her desk. Fixated on the now distorted view of DeVaughn, she sunk into her chair and sobbed.

"I brought you something to drink," Bryan announced later that afternoon, walking into Saamyah's office. She stood in the same spot as she was when he left.

Saamyah turned from gazing out of the corner window and watched Bryan set the Starbucks cup on her desk.

"I told you that I didn't want anything," she whispered then turned back to the window to watch the rain.

"It's green tea to replace the one you didn't get to finish."

Saamyah rested her head on the window pane and began to race her pendant along the sterling silver chain around her neck. "Thank you."

He took the seat behind her desk and swiveled it to face her. "Are we going to address the elephant in the room?"

Saamyah did not respond.

"Saamyah."

His calling of her name pulled her out of her trance. She looked at him and answered, "No."

"Why?"

Saamyah exhaled loudly and looked out the window. "Because it's hard to discuss what happened when I don't even know myself."

"What does that even mean?"

She walked toward him and motioned him out of her chair. When he rose from it, she sat down and took a sip of the tea he had purchased for her. "It means," she took another sip before placing the cup back on her desk, "that my eldest brother, who has played the role of my father since I was seven years old, may not be the man I believe him to be."

Bryan took a seat at the corner of her desk and offered, "We all have skeletons, Saamyah."

She agreed in a whisper, "Don't we all."

Before she slipped into another daze, he gripped her armrest and turned her chair to face him. "Go to him and talk this over. Find out the truth for yourself."

"It's too soon for me to go back home to San Antonio."

"Then call him."

She broke his gaze and simply said, "...maybe," despite her belief that the conversation was better had in person.

Bryan opened his mouth to speak, but stopped short when Saamyah looked up at him and shook her head. He understood her silent request not to press the issue.

"We should create an interview plan for the seven victims," he suggested, changing the subject as he rose from his seat and walked around her desk towards his office. "Perhaps two a day and then we can move on to the witnesses?"

Saamyah nodded. "Sure."

"Tomorrow morning?"

She turned to look at him and weakly smiled. "Sure."

Bryan walked into his office and closed the door.

Saamyah stared at the phone on her desk for several minutes prior to reaching for the handset. After placing it to her ear, she slowly dialed 9, 1, and the ten digits of DeVaughn's cell phone number. She subconsciously counted the five times the phone rang before the generic voicemail greeting announced his unavailability. Without leaving a message, Saamyah placed the handset back in the base.

For a moment, several thoughts plagued her mind and Saamyah pondered whether the truth was something she really wanted. Knowing the truth would mean that her whole life post her parents' death would not have only been a lie, but ill-gotten. Blinking back the tears, Saamyah opened her bottom desk drawer and retrieved her cell phone from her tote. She composed a brief text message requesting that he call her. Afterwards, her index finger nervously hovered over the send icon.

Cowardice overcame her and Saamyah deleted the message. She then tossed her phone back into her tote, grabbed her tea, and sipped on the beverage. Reclining in her chair, she reflected on Patrick's earlier comments.

*** *** ***

"I don't believe the victims were entirely truthful during their interviews today," Saamyah shared as she pushed around, with her fork, the uneaten portion of her kale salad.

Bryan swallowed a mouthful of chicken alfredo pasta before asking, "And why do you believe that?"

She shrugged her shoulders, leaned back in her chair, and took in the quaint restaurant. "No definitive reason...I just believe that they are withholding information."

He exhaled loudly in annoyance. "Saamyah, it's not uncommon for victims of sexual violence to forget details of their attack."

Saamyah shook her head and opposed, "No, this is more than the victims' failure to recall details of their attack. This is...This is just different..." Her voice trailed off as she contemplated the words to adequately express her thoughts.

"Well, before you devise a plan to victimize, again, our already broken victims, let's wait and see what the other five have to say," Bryan urged, taking his napkin from his lap to wipe his mouth and placing it in his plate. "Right now, I think your assessment is a bit premature and insensitive."

Saamyah blankly stared at him, taken aback by his comment. "That was harsh."

Bryan drank from his glass and smugly replied, "That wasn't my intent, so I'm not sorry."

Livid, she retrieved her wallet from her handbag and placed cash on the table. Saamyah then grabbed the car keys off the table and walked out the restaurant.

"You are un-fucking-believable," Bryan scolded, walking into the office and slamming the door behind him.

Saamyah was unmoved by his anger. "Such language. I pray you don't kiss your mother with that mouth."

Bryan leaned over her desk on his hands and responded, "Every damn chance I get."

She met his eyes and retorted, "How common."

"Common?" He inquired in disbelief. "You leave your partner stranded in the middle of nowhere and I am common." Bryan stood erect and started towards his office. "Un-fucking-believable."

"You weren't stranded in the middle of nowhere, Bryan," Saamyah called out after him. She rose from her seat and walked to stand at the threshold of his door. After resting her shoulder on the door pane, she taunted, "As I recall, you know the Miami area...I believe your exact observation was that you know the Miami area better than me."

Bryan sat behind his desk and looked at her with derision. "Do you have any idea the challenge it is to open carry while walking the streets of Miami?"

"Don't know and don't care," she answered, turning to walk away. "Next time travel in your own g-ride."

Bryan paused to consider his response knowing that his enraged temper, combined with her haughty attitude, made for an explosive end. While he allowed his anger to subside, he weighed his options. To remain partnered with Saamyah would subject him to infinite, and, possibly painful, unknowns. To separate from her would prove that he was indeed incapable of working with the opposite sex. Comfortable with his decision, Bryan stood and walked out of his office.

"Where are you going?" Saamyah asked.

"To Duncan...This working relationship is not going to work."

Immediately alarmed by the ramifications of his actions, Saamyah asked, "Are you seriously going to rat me out?...All because I took back possession of MY government ride."

"We traveled in the same g-ride, Saamyah!" He turned and shouted at her. He moved toward her and then added, "I don't know how the PD in San Antonio operates, but in this department we come and go in the same vehicle and we always stick together."

Saamyah swallowed the lump in her throat and considered the unwritten office policy. Refusing to admit wrongdoing, she simply responded, "If that were the case, each detective would not have their own."

Bryan shook his head in dismay and retorted, "You are such a bitch." He then walked out her office and slammed the door behind him.

*** *** ***

"Good morning," Saamyah greeted when Bryan entered the office. When he attempted to walk past her desk without responding, she asked, "How did it go with Duncan yesterday?"

Bryan's hope to pass her without a word diminished when the question that followed her greeting compelled him to stop and face her. He asked, "What do you think?"

Saamyah shrugged her shoulders and responded, "I don't know. You left without notice yesterday and-"

"And why would you need notice, Saamyah?"

"Because we are paarr…" Her voice trailed off after realizing the point he just made. She dropped her eyes to avoid his stare.

"What? Partners?"

Saamyah did not respond.

"Because I am starting to think that I am just the mere jester among your highness's court." He moved in her direction until the desk and the box on it were the only things that separated them.

"Don't be so dramatic," she looked up and replied.

Not surprised by her indifference, Bryan struggled to hold his tongue. He finally breathed, "And you…you…" He exhaled loudly feeling defeated. Bryan could not look past the softness of her face to exclaim what he really felt in the language that he wanted to express it."You just be you, Saamyah."

Having already prepared her ears for a vulgar tirade, Saamyah was astonished by his concession. "…Thank you…Not that I need your permission to be who I am, but thanks."

Bryan shook his head and turned to walk away. "You're looking for a fight and I am not interested."

"The fight is within yourself, Bryan, not with me," she acknowledged, fulfilling her need to have the last word.

"No, Saamyah, it's actually with you." He faced her. "You have been a pain in my ass from the moment I met you. And the pain grows a little more each day."

Saamyah chuckled and stood clapping her hands at the arrival of the brute she was expecting. "And there he is, right on cue."

Bryan exhaled in frustration and said, "Saamyah, Duncan has given us two options. We either work together or we work together. "

She placed her hands at her waist and took a moment to digest the ultimatum. "Well, how well we do that is up to you."

"Us," he corrected. "Up to us. This is supposed to be a partnership."

Saamyah dissented shaking her head. "No, it's not, Bryan…But maybe it would be if I had massive amounts of testosterone pumping through my veins."

Again, Bryan exhaled in frustration. He recognized more at that moment that his chauvinistic comment struck a chord that Saamyah could not move past, and it was hindering their working rapport.

"So, I don't care to work with women. Big deal! GET-O-VER-IT…We all have our preferences."

"THAT is not a preference, Bryan. It IS a prejudice."

Bryan took a deep breath in an effort to calm himself and deescalate the tension in the room. "Saamyah, just let it go."

"It's easy for you to recommend that I let go. It's not your competence under attack."

Having grown tired of their confrontation, Bryan turned to retreat to his office.

Saamyah hurried from behind her desk and grabbed his arm. "Don't walk away from me."

He snatched his arm from her grip. "And don't put your hands on me."

She winced at the pain in her fingers and shoved his shoulder. "You hurt my hand!"

Bryan instinctively shoved her back shouting, "And you hurt my ass!"

Saamyah lost her footing and fell on to her desk. The box and other items on it dropped to the floor with a loud *thud, crash,* and *clatter.*

Rolling on her side, Saamyah groaned at the sharp pain that shot through her lower back. She then pushed at the hands that tried to help her to her feet.

"Saamyah, I'm so sorry."

"Get away from m-"

Lieutenant Duncan pushed open the door and stood at the threshold in a stiff rage. "What the hell is going on in here?!"

Saamyah and Bryan looked up at him. Confused in how to respond, neither of them spoke. Instead, Bryan helped Saamyah to her feet and then they both watched the lieutenant step into the office, slam the door behind him, and walk to inspect the room.

A sea of folders and papers covered a portion of the floor and an array of office supplies scattered about it. Drops of tea rolled off the desk into the large puddle underneath it and were the only thing that could be heard in the silent room.

"Lieutenant, I can explain," Saamyah finally muttered. She stopped short of her explanation when his frown quieted her. Lowering her eyes to avoid his, she began to massage the pain in her lower back.

Lieutenant Duncan breathed deeply through his nostrils and exhaled slowly out of his mouth. As he paced the floor in front of them, he considered the punishment that would best fit their misbehavior. Distressed, he uttered, "I can't believe this." He stopped in front of the both of them. "The two of you acting like children."

"Lieutenant, I told you that I could not work with her," Bryan reminded.

"Shut up, Russell," Lieutenant Duncan ordered.

Bryan turned his head away like a scolded child.

"The two of you are together for a reason," Lieutenant Duncan elucidated. "Believe it or not, you need each other."

Both Bryan and Saamyah stared at Lieutenant Duncan perplexed.

Lieutenant Duncan peered in Bryan's eyes. "You have never partnered with a woman." He then peered in Saamyah's eyes. "You have never partnered with a man who has never partnered with a woman." His eyes dashed between the two of them and instructed, "Learn from each other. Grow in your craft together."

Bryan parted his lips in protest, but arrested when the lieutenant raised his hand. "You have two options." He looked at Saamyah. "You work together…" He looked at Bryan. "OR you work together…For your sakes, I really hope you choose to work together…" His voice trailed off and the room fell to a brief silence.

"5 A.M., The Trail," Lieutenant Duncan finally reprimanded.

"Oh, come on," Bryan groaned in contest.

"Want to make it 4?" Duncan asked.

Bryan folded his arm across his chest and looked away. "For how long?"

"Until I grow tired of looking at your pitiful faces," Lieutenant Duncan answered.

Afraid to ask, Saamyah kept her inquiry about The Trail to herself. She thought it better to ask Bryan later than to take a chance of being further berated by Lieutenant Duncan.

"Clean this place up," Lieutenant Duncan commanded to no one in particular. He turned to leave, but remembered the element of office decorum that Saamyah violated. The lieutenant turned toward her and started, "And, Cambell."

Saamyah looked up from her feet. "Yes, sir?"

"In this office, when we leave together, we return together."

Saamyah swallowed the knot in her throat, nodded, and recited, "Yes, sir."

Bryan dropped his arms and exhaled loudly after Lieutenant Duncan exited the office and closed the door. He ran his fingers through his soft curls and walked around the office to fully assess its disarray. When his eyes caught Saamyah's, he glared, contemplating how one woman could cause such a ruckus.

"Bryan, I-" Saamyah started.

"Don't," Bryan interrupted, irate at the idea of being forced to work with her.

Before leaving for a walk to cool his temper, Bryan took in the modest, casual business attire that hugged her curves. He then considered the one thing that would make the trouble worth his while—her body.

*** *** ***

"It's nice to see the two of you arrive when it is convenient for you," Lieutenant Duncan announced, referring to their late arrival.

"Thank Mr. Sleeping Beauty," Saamyah said after getting out of Bryan's personal silver Lexus and walking over to Lieutenant Duncan. Bryan followed.

Lieutenant Duncan looked at Bryan and repeated, "Thank you, Mr. Sleeping Beauty."

Bryan shook his head and rolled his eyes.

Lieutenant Duncan smiled and taunted, "You know the drill. I want my time back at the end."

"Lieutenant, I really wish you would reconsider this whole thing," Bryan beseeched.

Lieutenant Duncan glanced over his glasses and spotted Saamyah completing warm-ups in her black leggings, sports bra, and shoes. He then looked at Bryan and scrutinized his white tank top, grey jogging shorts, and shoes. "Start running, Russell."

Bryan cursed under his breath, careful not to have Lieutenant Duncan hear him, and started toward the mountainous trail.

"You, too, Cambell," Lieutenant Duncan commanded.

Saamyah came out of her leg stretch and nodded in acknowledgement. She tightened the armband that held her phone, placed her earphones in her ear, and started after Bryan.

A few minutes shy of an hour, Bryan scanned his phone at the box of their final checkpoint.

"So, what now?" She asked him after removing the earphones from her ears and hanging them around her neck.

Bryan used his tank top to wipe the perspiration from his face and answered, "We take a minute to recover and then head back down."

"So, we don't keep heading up?" Saamyah inquired as she stretched her legs.

"Not for our first fight," he responded as he shamelessly watched and clandestinely appreciated the bends that unveiled her body's flexibility.

Saamyah did not entertain his gawking. Instead, she asked, "And for your tardiness?"

Bryan shrugged. "Probably a few laps around the park or calisthenics for the amount of time that we were late."

"We?"

"We...Us-"

"You," Saamyah interjected. "You made us late and you have us here at 5 o'clock in the morning."

Bryan bypassed the confrontational bait and asked instead, "Are you always this bitchy? Because it appears to be something that comes so naturally for you."

Saamyah rolled her eyes as she tightened her ponytail and gave them the space they needed by walking away. Observing her surroundings, she noticed on the left side of the dirt trail miles of trees and, on the right, miles of metal railing. She slowly walked to the railing and peered over it to see a canyon hosting a flowing river of water.

Bryan slowly crept behind her and pushed her leaning body.

Saamyah quickly jumped back and turned around to face him. "YOU BASTARD!" She screamed while pushing and striking him in his arm. "I could have fallen," she added after she calmed herself.

Bryan laughed at her reaction. "No, you wouldn't have." He caught her eyes and assured, "I wouldn't have let you."

Saamyah shook her head, rolled her eyes, and attempted to walk away in disgust. She was stopped when Bryan grabbed her arm and pulled her into him. He gently wiped the perspiration from her face with his hands and pushed back the hairs that had fallen on her face.

Bryan caught her gaze again and held it. He whispered on her lips, "I'm sorry." He cupped her face and lowered his mouth on hers.

Saamyah raised her hands to push him away, but his strong hands held her face close to his.

"Bryan," Saamyah managed to say through his overbearing lips. "Bryan, stop," she ordered, successfully pushing him away.

"What?...So, now you're too good to be touched?" Bryan asked coldly, angered by a concept that he was unfamiliar with—rejection.

Saamyah looked at him in abhorrence. "No. Just too good to be touched by you," she confirmed, placed her earphones back in her ears, and started back down the trail.

"What?" Saamyah asked in annoyance after sensing his presence.

Bryan took a seat in front of her desk and watched as she tapped at the keys of her laptop. She had positioned it on the stem portion of her L-shaped desk.

Saamyah quickly glanced at him over her shoulder, then back at her screen, and, finally, back over her shoulder. She abruptly stopped typing. "What? What is it?"

"Our one o'clock cancelled."

Saamyah glimpsed at the hands of her wrist watch and saw that it was quarter to eleven. She dropped her hands in her lap and exhaled in frustration. Re-interviewing the rape victims was more challenging than she had anticipated. Many refused to relive the horrid event and others failed to recall pertinent details.

"What now?" Bryan asked.

Saamyah swiveled her chair in his direction and used her legs to move herself to the leaf portion of her desk. She peered at the whiteboard and quickly scanned the photos and notes she had made. Lynne Grimes, the cancellation, was one of the earlier victims of the Miami Beach case.

She looked at Bryan and responded, "I don't know."

Bryan handed her a post-it note.

"What is this?" Saamyah asked taking the note.

"Kimberly James's business contact information. If you want her to talk, harass her at work."

"And that works?" She asked in disbelief.

He shrugged his shoulders. "It hasn't failed me."

Saamyah rolled her eyes and pressed the note on the folder in front of her. "Our ram in the bush," she muttered under her breath.

"How did your phone interview go?"

Saamyah took a moment to ponder the question before remembering her earlier call with a victim that vehemently declined to speak in-person. She exhaled loudly and opened the folder of her notes. "It went as expected."

Bryan leaned back in the chair and listened as Saamyah recounted the details of Blythe Collin's attack. As she spoke, he sifted through the hodgepodge of information and attempted to piece together the likenesses.

"So, each victim was attacked from behind?"

Saamyah flipped through her notes and answered, "...Yes. Well, at least based on the statements we have thus far. Initial reports corroborate the same...Unfortunately, though, none of the women can positively I.D. him."

Bryan nodded and began thinking aloud, "So, he approaches them from behind, commands them to undress, and then sexually assaults them."

"And graciously thanks them after."

Bryan met her eyes. "He thanks them?"

"Every single one of them."

"What a fu..." He stopped short of his offensive rant.

Saamyah grinned at his well-bred efforts. She cleared her throat and added, "A latex condom was used in each case. So, we have no DNA...And none but Ms. James physically resisted."

Bryan nodded. "Hence, the reason she got away unscathed."

Saamyah twisted her face. "Uuumm, I don't think she would agree with that observation, Bryan...She may have gotten away without being sexually assaulted, but not unscathed."

He shrugged his shoulders. "Semantics."

Saamyah allowed his cavalier comment to dissipate before concluding, "To date, we have no skin or hair to run through the system."

"So, what do you do think?"

"What do I think about what?"

"About the perp? Have you built a profile?"

She closed her folder and rolled her chair back to her laptop. "I'm still working on one."

Bryan stood and advised, "Call Kimberly James. If anyone could help you build a criminal's profile, she would."

Saamyah nodded. "Off to lunch?"

Bryan nodded. "Coming with?"

Saamyah shook her head. "I have plans, but I will be back in time to sit in on the hearing with you."

"No need. The case pre-dates you. So, you go and get a head start on your weekend."

"No, I want to…We're partners."

Bryan smiled. "We will leave for the courthouse at three."

"Detective Cambell, I am glad you were able to steal away from the office."

"You called, I came…Just trying to avoid another office mishap," Saamyah assured Patrick after joining him at his table. He had opted for a table on the outside deck.

"And here I was thinking that you've finally come to the realization that you are mine."

"Thank you," Saamyah spoke to the host that escorted to her seat. After she sat in the chair that he had pulled out for her, she took in the stellar view of the water.

"I'm not yours, Patrick—never was." She caught his gaze. "And, so that we are emphatically clear, I was your brother's and even then he did not own me."

He snickered at her feministic vigor, sipped from his wine glass, and inquired, "No shadow today?"

"Detective Russell has better things to do with his lunch hour…Just be thankful that I am here."

Patrick returned his glass to the white linen table covering and fingered the stem. "This new partner of yours has the potential to become a thorn in my side."

Saamyah did not respond. Instead, she observed, and, secretly envied, the happy couples enjoying their lunch together.

Taking notice of her voided stare Patrick said, "You know, Saamyah, we could be just as happy."

She looked at him. "I despise you and you want me dead. Trust me, it will never work."

"Now, that does not sound like a mouth that reflects the heart of a Christian woman."

Saamyah did not respond.

The attendant arrived to refill Patrick's wine glass and, at Patrick's direction, he left the bottle. When he offered Saamyah a menu, she politely refused and assured him that she would not be staying much longer. The attendant shot a glance at Patrick and then left them to their private conversation after Patrick nodded in deference to her.

Patrick watched Saamyah watch the water and asked, "DeVaughn—when was the last time you spoke with him?"

"Why? Should I call home?"

He lifted his glass, swirled his wine, and sipped it. "It would be nice to know if you have to prepare for a funeral…or not."

Saamyah looked at him with contempt and repulsion. "What happened to you?"

"Prison does have a way of changing a man."

Saamyah shook her head. "No, you had already changed—prison just exacerbated it."

"Life is a series of natural and spontaneous changes," Patrick quoted prior to taking a long swallow from his glass.

Saamyah ignored the wisdom of the ancient Chinese philosopher and asked, "Does my brother know that you are here?"

"Staying away from his family was one of the many stipulations I agreed to when he spoke at my parole hearing."

Saamyah huffed incredulously. "You're paroled and you still left the state?"

Patrick took another leisure sip of his beverage before responding, "The conditions of my parole leave geographic location open for broad interpretation."

She shook her head in disbelief and replied, "You truly are a glutton for punishment."

"No, Saamyah, I believe your brother is if you don't play your cards right…A wife and unborn twins are a lot to leave behind." He caught her gaze and held it while asking, "Don't you think?"

"What do you want, Patrick?"

"It depends. Are you referring to the pain of my past or my hope for the future?"

Saamyah shrugged her shoulders and shook her head. "What does it matter?"

"Well, the first, to avenge my brother's death. The second," he leaned to gently move the loose hair that fell over her eye, "you."

When his hand dropped to palm her cheek, Saamyah pushed it away. "My life is not a chip to be bargained."

Patrick centered himself in his chair and moved the items on the table to the side so that the server could set his plate before him. Patrick thanked him and waited for him to depart before he responded, "You are absolutely correct about that, Saamyah…You are not a chip, you are the prize."

Saamyah watched him lower his head to silently rehearse his grace and then grab his fork and knife to slice his asparagus and roasted potatoes. He switched to his steak knife and began cutting his meat.

"And what about my pain or, better yet, that of your mother's…For crying out loud, Patrick, she lost her husband in a senseless war and then her eldest son in the FBI." She paused to calm her nerves, closing her eyes to take a deep breath. When she opened her eyes she warned, "If she loses you, that's it. That is literally everything she has, and that kind of pain is insurmountable."

Patrick slowly chewed to savor the morsel in his mouth. After he swallowed, he swirled his wine and then sipped from the glass. "You know, you can tell a lot about a man in the way he prefers his steak." He took another morsel in his mouth, chewed, and swallowed. "A man that prefers his steak rare has an appreciation for things in their natural state. A man who prefers his steak medium rare is a perfectionist and won't accept anything less than the perfect steak…Then you have the man who lingers in the safe-zone; he is mild-mannered, so a medium steak suits his palate."

He paused to fill his wine glass. "And, finally, you have men like me." He set the bottle back on the white linen, and peered deep into Saamyah's eyes. "I demand that my steak is well-done…Straight to the point, no bullshit."

Saamyah broke their gaze and took a moment to contemplate the subliminal message he was trying to convey. She looked at her watch. "I've got to go." She stood, but was yanked back to her seat by Patrick's forceful hand. The clatter drew attention, but Saamyah avoided the stares. When he released her forearm, she brushed the long bang from her face, and looked straight ahead to avoid his burning eyes.

"You don't inflict hurt without the expectation of being hurt in return."

She faced him and asked, "And what gives you the right to hurt because you have been hurt?"

"I lost my identical twin… I believe that makes my pain insurmountable."

"And I lost my fiancé," Saamyah reminded him before she rose from her seat a second time and departed.

*** *** ***

Sleeping comfortably on her abdomen, it seemed as if she had just settled into bed when the phone rang in the dark. Saamyah glanced at the clock on her nightstand and groaned when it read 2:42 A.M.

"Hello," she managed to whisper after fumbling with the cordless phone.

"Hey, babe sis," a deep male voice greeted her. "How is it going?"

"DeVaughn?" She cracked. "Do you know what time it is?"

"Yeah, I know. I am on my way to the hospital; working a split shift this weekend."

"And you couldn't wait until the second half of your split-shift?" She rolled on to her back and exhaled in frustration.

DeVaughn laughed. "This is the second half, Saamyah...Anyway, I have some time now while I am driving. So, catch me up. How are you? What's been going on?"

"Fine...nothing," she simply responded, drifting back to sleep.

"You know, Saamyah, these 3 A.M. calls wouldn't happen if you knew how to call your family...There always seem to be some challenge with you."

"...I know...I know and I'm sorry...I've just been really busy." She yawned into her phone and diverted the conversation. "How's everyone?"

"Good, good. Simoane looks like she is ready to drop, but we have about ten more weeks...She is so miserable."

"Is she still working?" Saamyah muffled.

"No, she started her maternity leave a few days ago. The OB/GYN stated that her working was too much stress on the babies."

"Mmm." Saamyah began drifting again.

"How is work? What's your assignment?"

"...It's okay...I'm in the special crimes division working on a potential serial rape case... Slowly progressing though."

"I am sure you will crack it, Sherlock. You always do."

Saamyah smiled at the familiar encouragement.

"And your partner? What is he or she like?"

"His name is Bryan Russell...Cocky, strong-willed, and aggressive."

"Sounds like your match."

Saamyah rolled on her side and fluffed her pillow under head. "I'm not cocky."

He laughed loudly in her ear. "I know my child and, Saamyah Anne Cambell, you are cocky."

Saamyah did not have the energy to fuss with the man that raised her since their parents' deaths twenty years ago.

"We have been reprimanded for fighting," she hesitantly disclosed.

DeVaughn sighed in disappointment. "Not again, Saamyah…You requested this TDY for renewal—a break in monotony—and you are still exhibiting the exact behaviors you did while here—capricious and irascible…So, what's the point? What's the ultimate goal here?"

"DeVaughn, please, I can't do this now. It's 3 o'clock in the morning…This is not how I want to start my Saturday."

He contemplated her request and reined in his frustration. "I have always told you that you have to learn to work with-"

"People that you do not like," they narrated together.

"Don't be smug, Saamyah Anne. I just worry about you."

"You always worry," she muttered under her breath.

"I heard that."

"You always do," she reminded him.

DeVaughn exhaled loudly. "Look, this is not how I pictured this conversation going. I definitely did not call before sunrise to pick a fight."

Saamyah said nothing.

"Let's just talk again later this weekend. What's your availability?"

She turned on her back, stretched, and yawned. "I have a list of errands and a host of to-dos today, and church and possibly a few hours at the office tomorrow."

"Okay. I'll call you tomorrow."

"Fine," she finally conceded rolling her eyes. Saamyah loathed when her eldest brother did not hear her.

"I love you, babe sis."

"Me, too."

Saamyah pressed the end button on the phone and struggled to place it on the base. When it fell to the floor, she groaned her aggravation and made the decision to leave it there. She then rolled to her abdomen and fell back to sleep…

"…Saamyah!" David yelled as he ran toward her.

Gunshots fired and David's body collided into Saamyah's after she turned to face him. Hitting the ground, she groaned her pain and struggled to lift David's heavy body off her.

Saamyah ignored the revving engines and squealing wheels that indicated the culprits' departure. She shook David's body and pleaded, "…David…David get up…I can't breathe."

Laying her head back in the dirt, Saamyah rested for a brief moment then used her might to roll David's body off hers. She sat up and discovered the blood that covered her shirt.

"David!"

David slowly opened his eyes and coughed up the blood that rose in his throat. "Saamyah."

"Shhh, don't talk. Don't talk."

"How bad is it?" He whispered.

Saamyah touch the wound in his chest and added pressure in an effort to slow the bleeding. David hollered in agony.

"You're going to be okay."

"…I don't think so, Saamyah."

Crying she argued, "Don't say that. Don't you dare say that…I am going to call for help. Just hang in there."

Saamyah rushed to their unmarked car and made her call. When she had returned, David had his eyes closed. He groaned when she shook him.

"Saamyah," he whispered.

"Help is on the way, but, you have to keep your eyes open." Her tears dropped on his face and she gently wiped them away. "You have to stay awake. Okay?"

"I'm so sorry, Saamyah." He touched her face with his trembling fingers and smiled weakly when she kissed and held them close to her cheek. "I…I love you so much, Saamyah."

He coughed up more blood. "It's…it's getting harder to breathe." The tears rolled down his face. "…Say it, Saamyah…"

"No," she cried, slowly shaking her head.

"Please...I..." He coughed up more blood and grimaced his pain. "Saamyah, I don't have much time." He started to close his eyes, but opened them when she nudged him.

"Don't you dare die on me, David Barnes!" She screamed. "We've got to get married and have babies," she added in a whisper.

He smiled weakly. "How many?"

"A boy and a girl."

"And a girl," he reaffirmed.

Saamyah laughed through her tears. David loved little girls. "Okay, two girls." When she heard sirens in a distance she assured, "They're coming. Just hang in there."

"Please...Say it, Saamyah." He coughed. "Just this once."

Saamyah looked into his eyes as she gently stroked his face. "On our wedding day."

David felt himself fading as his eyelids grew heavier. "I love you s-s-so much, Saamyah...Remember that. No matter what, always r-remember that." He closed his eyes.

Saamyah cried profusely when David ceased responding to the calling of his name or the shaking of his body. Fulfilling his last wish, she lowered her lips to his ear and whispered, "I-

...A hard knock on the front door startled her awake from the familiar nightmare that relived David's demise. Saamyah glanced at the clock on her nightstand and saw that it read 4:30 A.M.

"You have got to be kidding me," she groaned, pulling the comforter over her head in a poor attempt to return to sleep.

When the knock graduated to banging and the calling of her name, Saamyah threw the covering off her and started towards the door in anger. After she confirmed the offender through the peephole, Saamyah unsecured the door and swung it opened.

"What do you want, Bryan?!"

He surveyed her pajama shorts and matching camisole. "I knew you wouldn't be ready."

"Ready for what?"

Bryan pushed past her, inviting himself in her unit. "The Trail."

Saamyah closed the door and secured it. "On a Saturday?"

He glared at her. "It wouldn't be punishment if it wasn't on a Saturday."

"And Sundays too?"

"Saamyah, enough with the questions. Get dressed and let's go. We are already going to be late."

She begrudgingly walked toward her bedroom to change.

Saamyah sluggishly ran several feet behind Bryan. Her exhaustion was greater than his encouragement and she struggled to keep his pace.

"What is with you today?" Bryan asked, jogging back towards her.

Saamyah slowed to a walk and snapped, "I'm exhausted, Bryan."

He stopped in front of her and retorted, "As am I, but I don't want to spend all damn day making it up this trail. So, move your ass."

"Don't make this about my ass, Bryan," Saamyah huffed. "We both know this is about all of the asses you had to forego to be here with me."

Saamyah attempted to walk around him, but Bryan grabbed her elbow and held it firmly before she could. "I don't know who the hell you think you are, Saamyah, but you don't know me well enough to speak to me like that."

She snatched her elbow from his grip and raised her hand to strike him. He instinctively caught her wrist and warned, "Never strike a man without the expectation of being struck back."

Saamyah yanked her wrist free and growled through her clenched teeth, "You're no man; you're an animal." She stomped his toes with the heel of her foot and stepped around him to continue up the trail.

Bryan flinched at the pain in his foot and walked in small circles to ease it. When the pain finally subsided to a pulsating throb, he kicked his sore foot in the air multiple times and deeply inhaled. It was not until the throbbing ceased, that he took off in Saamyah's direction to catch her.

Saamyah gasped at the sudden tackle from behind. She fought to turn and rest on her back before wrestling with the strength of Bryan's arms.

"Get off me!" She commanded as their bodies twisted in the dirt.

Bryan ignored her demands and continued the fight to pin her arms down.

"Get off me!" Saamyah kneed him in the groin and shoved his leaning body. She quickly rose to her feet and started back down the trail.

Lieutenant Duncan glanced at his watch surprised by the record time Saamyah made it back to the mouth of the trail. He eyeballed her appearance and said nothing until Bryan arrived with the same soiled and disheveled look. Without asking, he discerned that they had been fighting.

"Car detail, tomorrow morning at 7." Lieutenant Duncan walked away before either of them could protest.

*** *** ***

"What a way to spend a Sunday," Saamyah bemoaned. She rubbed soap onto the final section of the patrol car, tossed the sponge into the bucket, and grabbed the water hose to rinse.

Bryan moved onto the next car, ignoring her complaint and dismal effort to engage him in conversation. Anger overwhelmed him and he used silence to contain it.

"Are you not speaking to me the whole day?" Saamyah called out to him.

Bryan continued to rub soap on the patrol car and answered, "We have a lot of ground to cover. It will go a lot quicker if we don't talk."

Saamyah looked around the enclosed parking garage and exhaled loudly at their plight. They had until noon to wash all the marked vehicles in the fleet.

Bryan looked up to see Saamyah staring at him. He was unmoved when she smiled and teased, "Do you see something you like, Detective?"

"I'll let you know when I do," Bryan smugly responded, dropping his sponge in the bucket. He conducted a quick rinse, gathered items, and walked over to the next car.

Saamyah cleared her throat and called out, "You know, this is your fault that we are here."

Bryan shook his head and rolled his eyes at her sanctimonious air. "Yeah, and I am sure that you had not a blame in this."

Transfixed by his retort, Saamyah reflected on her contribution to their plight. When feelings of guilt grew, she suppressed them and lauded, "What a smart man you are," as she walked to help with the car that he moved to.

Bryan shook his head and rinsed his side of the vehicle. "Sorry," he offered when the water splashed her. When it happened a second time, Saamyah threw a sponge at him.

"What you do that for?" Bryan asked.

"I know that you are doing that on purpose."

"Doing what?"

"Doing this." Saamyah took her hose and sprayed Bryan.

"What the fu-" Bryan dropped his hose and blocked the water from his face. "Saamyah, stop. STOP, Saamyah."

Saamyah laughed as she moved toward him determined to power-wash his discontentment. When within arm's reach, they fought for the hose bending the spray of the water that ultimately soaked them both.

Bryan freed the hose from her tight grip and dropped it to the ground. He stood before her in silence and took in her wet, tantalizing skin. Her thin t-shirt and jersey shorts left little to the imagination now that they dripped with water. After he closed the gap between them, he pulled her in for a kiss.

Saamyah cupped his face, closed her eyes, and returned the kiss. When she opened her mouth, Bryan accepted the invitation to taste it. Their fervent kisses led to the hood of a wet sedan, and Bryan lifted her on to it. Saamyah felt his hands drop to her firm breasts and fingers to her hardened nipples. A soft moan escaped her.

"I want you, Saamyah," Bryan confessed in whisper on her lips before kissing them, her chin, and down the center of her neck. He brought his lips back to hers and dipped his tongue into her mouth. His hands gripped her thighs and pulled her body closer to his pulsating manhood.

Saamyah felt his hand move to the drawstring of her shorts and tugged it loose. When his fingers pulled at the elastic band, she dropped her hands to his. "Bryan, stop." She opened her eyes to find his lustful ones peering at her. "Someone could be watching."

"So what," he dismissed.

She gently pushed him away and slid off the hood of the car. "I am so sorry."

Bryan shook his head in dissent. "Don't give it another thought. I'm the one that's the animal—remember?" He collected his bucket and hose and moved to another vehicle.

*** TWO ***

Bryan blocked her office door before she could walk out. "Saamyah, we can't keep working like this."

Saamyah met his eyes for the first time that Monday morning. "Working like what?"

"Like this. You running out when I walk in, pretending to be so consumed with work that you can't have a conversation with me, or stalling this morning by talking to Lieutenant so that you could jog the trail far behind me."

"Your case is circumstantial, don't you think?" Saamyah turned from his eyes and started back to her desk.

"No, I don't and-"

"My guilt got the better of me," Saamyah admitted in her interjection. She then looked at him and beseeched, "So, let's just act as if yesterday never happened...Please?"

Bryan nodded. "Fine."

Saamyah lowered herself into her chair and dropped her head in her hands. "I'm so exhausted." She looked up at Bryan and asked, "How long are these 5 A.M. runs are going to go on?"

"Until Lieutenant gets tired of seeing our pitiful faces," Bryan reminded her walking to the whiteboard to make notations.

"Aaarrrrgh—I am a work hazard in this condition... Workplace hazing is typically reserved for disorderly officers."

Bryan rolled his eyes and unsympathetically muttered, "Then the punishment suits you."

Saamyah ignored the slight that she vaguely heard and bemoaned, "Back home I wouldn't have to do any crap like this."

"You're not in Kansas anymore, Dorothy."

"Why aren't you bothered by this, Bryan? Are you accustomed to this form of discipline?"

Bryan failed to dignify her inquires with a response and simply encouraged, "Just take it one day at a time, Saamyah." He picked up and flipped through a folder then added more notes to the whiteboard.

Saamyah swallowed the last of her tea and tossed the cup in the wastebasket. She stood and walked to Bryan's side. "What are you doing?"

"I'm trying to create a criminal profile."

"And?"

"I believe we are looking for a male with medium stature and average height...Because the victims reported that his body was heavy, but firm, I believe he may be muscularly lean."

Saamyah quickly summed his observation and knowingly stated, "So, someone physically fit like you."

Bryan chuckled. "Sure."

Saamyah rolled her eyes at his aim to be coy. "That's pretty much two-thirds of Miami's male population when you consider the slothful, the moderately active, and the athletes."

"Okay...Now, narrow those two-thirds by the typology of a power rapist."

Saamyah reflected on her knowledge of the matter, "He is a man that seeks power and control."

"Exactly," Bryan concurred. "That's why his victims survive unscathed."

She shook her head at his insensitivity, and reminded him, "Victimization by rape cannot be considered unscathed."

"That's not what I meant, Saamyah.

"Then what did you mean, Bryan?"

"I meant that these women survived their sexual assaults without being victims of excessive violence. The perp does not need it to manipulate and control his victims."

Saamyah pondered the offender profile for a moment and the characteristics of the victim. "But these victims do not strike me as physically and emotionally vulnerable. They don't fit the typical mold of a power rapists' victim...There has to be something more."

"Maybe, but this perp's goal is not to assert power over these women."

Saamyah looked at him and asked, "Then what?"

Bryan shrugged. "Some other element of his life."

"Okay. So, these women are connected in such a way that raping them allows him to feel empowered...What is the common link?"

Bryan surveyed the seven faces. "Now, that, I don't know," he whispered under his breath.

A light tap on the door interrupted their quiet, contemplative thoughts.

"Come in," Bryan commanded.

When the door opened a pair of cerulean eyes met Saamyah's hazelnut ones. They belonged to a sun-kissed, Caucasian man typical of Miami Beach—lean, muscular, and well-groomed. In his black t-shirt and denim jeans, he was the ideal demonstrative for a police academy billboard.

"I'm sorry. I don't mean to interrupt." He walked into the room adjusting the badge around his neck and then the gun at his waist.

"No interruption at all," Saamyah assured. She extended her right hand. "Detective Saamyah Cambell."

He pulled his glasses to rest on top of his dark hair, took her hand, and gently shook it. "Detective Andrew Bryce—homicide."

"Pleasure is mine, Detective Bryce."

"Please, call me Drew."

"Saamyah and I were just putting together a criminal profile of our perp in the Miami Beach case," Bryan announced, interrupting their introduction.

"I wasn't aware you had a new partner," Andrew stated. He then gazed at Saamyah and added, "A woman at that."

Saamyah dropped her eyes and grinned. "Apparently it is quite the shock to most."

Agitated, Bryan asked, "Did you need something, Bryce?"

Andrew handed Bryan a manila folder. "This is the information you requested on that rape-homicide."

Bryan accepted the folder and offered a mere thanks. Afterwards, the room fell uncomfortably silent until Andrew scanned the faces on the whiteboard and lauded, "Looks like you are close to achieving your goal...Let me know if homicide can be of any assistance." He looked at Saamyah. "Let's do lunch some time."

"I look forward to it," she responded.

Saamyah waited for Andrew to exit the room and close the door behind him before she turned to Bryan and stated the obvious, "You two have quite a history."

"Just two lions battling for kingship in the same jungle," he simply dismissed.

"I-" The phone rang and Saamyah's thought was cut short. She walked to her desk and grabbed the head piece. "Detective Cambell," she greeted.

"Hi, Detective," a soft voice responded. She cleared her throat, "Detective Cambell, my name is Alexandra Corbin." She nervously added, "You don't know me and we never met, but is it possible that you and I can meet to talk...privately?"

"In regard to what?"

She hesitated. "Not over the phone, but could you please meet me?...Alone?"

Saamyah pulled her hair from one shoulder to the other and bit her bottom lip. Though a series of what-ifs plagued her mind, she exhaled loudly and asked, "Where?"

"Thank you for coming," Alexandra spoke after opening the door to her beach-front home.

"Of course," Saamyah said stepping past the threshold.

"I'm out back, if you don't mind."

"No, not at all."

Saamyah followed the barefooted woman wearing heather grey leggings and a white, off-the-shoulder top down the hallway. She was mindful of her steps so as not to scratch the polished, wooden floors with her heels.

Alexandra stopped in the space that separated the living area and open kitchen. "Would you like something to eat?"

"No, thank you."

"Something to drink?"

Saamyah shook her head.

Alexandra nodded then walked to the sliding glass door, opened it, and stepped out onto the deck. She waited for Saamyah to do the same before sliding close only the screen door to allow the ocean breeze into her home.

"Please have a seat," Alexandra directed as she resumed her seat in the wide, cushioned bamboo chair. She lifted her white wine to her lips, sipped it, and placed it back on the glass top of the bamboo table.

Saamyah watched the beautiful woman nervously fiddled with the base of her glass. Her smooth skin was the complexion of wheat and her coily hair, the color of honey. Her lips were full, her nose was broad, and her figure slim, but shapely. In many ways, she favored the seven women on Saamyah's whiteboard at the office.

Alexandra finger combed her fly-away hairs back into her thick bun. "You've probably pieced together the reason why I asked you to come here."

"I have an inclination."

"I learned of you from the 5 o'clock news…when I also learned of the other victims." Alexandra met Saamyah's eyes and confessed, "I couldn't come forward with what happen to me." She looked out at the ocean waves. "At least, not publically, anyway."

"I understand," Saamyah whispered.

"I knew you would, Detective Cambell...You, too, work in a field dominated by men." She sipped from her glass and elucidated, "I'm a sports agent for the NFL."

"That's admirable."

Alexandra drew her knees to her breasts and rested her bare feet on the soft cushion. After taking another swallow, she concurred, "Considering there are less than five percent of us registered with the NFL Players' Association, I would like to think so." She huffed and added, "I won't begin to bore you with the minutia of minority statistics."

Saamyah gave her a moment then asked, "What happened to you, Ms. Corbin?"

"...I was preparing for a bath, he came in from behind, told me to remove my robe, and within minutes it was over." The tears that she allowed to run freely down her face were the release she desperately needed.

"Are there any details that you can provide? How did he enter? Where did the assault occur? Height? Weight? Smell?"

Alexandra shook her head. "I don't know. Maybe average height, muscularly built. We—I was upstairs...He must have come in from the sliding door. I tend to leave it unlock and the glass open for the breeze." She swallowed the last of the wine and set the glass on the table. "He was very stealthy. I had no idea he was in my house."

"Did he say anything to you?"

After wiping her face, Alexandra answered, "Uuuumm...Don't move, don't scream. Do as I say and I won't hurt you."

"Anything more?"

She pondered Saamyah's question. "I don't know. This happened over a week ago—a lot I have repressed and a lot more I have tried to force out of my mind... I need to or else I cannot function...I return to work on Monday. The competition won't allow more than two weeks before rumors start to surface."

Saamyah nodded. "Do you mind if I take a look around?"

Alexandra shook her head. "Don't bother. I had my housekeeper scrub this place clean several times since the incident. Nothing but the memory lingers here."

"I would still like to, if you don't mind," Saamyah urged.

Alexandra nodded and then hesitantly started, "He..."

Rather than rush her to finish, Saamyah gave her a moment to continue in her own time.

"...He was incredibly tender. The assault was nothing like you hear of most forcible rapes...It was almost as if it was something that he himself was being forced to do." She scoffed. "...He even thanked me afterwards...There was something so familiar about him...Something that I can't seem to place."

"Something like what?" Saamyah asked, careful not to unveil her enthusiasm by the new revelation.

Alexandra lowered her feet to the wooden deck. "I don't know—maybe a past lover, client, colleague...acquaintance at the grocery store...Someone I may not remember well, but he remembers me. Or at least has been watching me..."

Saamyah nodded and allowed all that she shared resonate. She then beseeched, "I know that you want to deal with this in private, but please don't cope alone."

Alexandra shook her head in dissent. "No, no one can know. I only shared this with you because I want to help...It wouldn't sit well with my spirit if I didn't." She caught Saamyah's eyes and pleaded, "Please, don't make more of it."

Saamyah smiled, reached across the table, and touched her hand. "I'm a detective, Ms. Corbin. I make more of everything."

Alexandra laughed in spite of her tears.

"But your experience is safe with me," Saamyah assured. "Thank you for sharing."

Alexandra covered Saamyah's hand and gently squeezed it. "Thank you, Detective."

Saamyah nodded, slid her hands from underneath hers, and stood to scrutinize the home prior to departing.

Saamyah pressed the button on the door handle to secure her car. She then struggled in the night's darkness to find her keys in the tote that hung from her shoulder as she walked to her condo.

"Saamyah."

She jumped at the abrupt calling of her name and the keys fell from her hand before she could place it in the lock.

"...Patrick?" She inquired after retrieving her keys and turning to face him. The dim lighting of the lamppost offered only a silhouette of the man walking towards her.

"In the flesh."

"Have you lost your mind? You scared the crap out of me."

A short silence fell between them.

"It's late. What do you want?" Saamyah asked.

"We need to talk."

"It's been a long day and I am exhausted, Patrick. Can we not do this tonight?"

"This won't take long." Patrick caged her between his long torso and muscular arms that stretched forward until his palms pressed flat against the door. "Invite me in."

Saamyah backed as far from him as the barricade would allow. "What for?"

"Just let me in, Saamyah," he breathed on her lips.

She met the whites of his eyes and replied, "No."

Patrick grinned at her stubbornness. "You know, you are making this a lot more-"

A vehicle pulled into the parking space next to Saamyah's and she peered over Patrick's shoulder to see Bryan exit his car.

Bryan started up the stairs, stopped, and walked back down.

"Saamyah, is that you?" Bryan asked, walking toward her.

She met Patrick's eyes and knowingly answered, "Yes, it's me."

"What are you doing out here in the dark?" Bryan stopped in mid-step when noticed the second person. "Are you okay?"

Patrick lowered his hands, turned to face Bryan, and slowly walked towards him. "Why is it when I'm around, you pride yourself with these annoying appearances? Can't Saamyah and I work out our differences without your interference?"

When Bryan finally recognized Patrick in the shadows, he chuckled. "You would have to be the last man on earth and the probability would still be a snowball's chance in hell."

Bryan brushed past him, but staggered forward when Patrick shoved him. Bryan quickly recovered withdrawing his firearm.

Saamyah rushed to grasp Bryan's free arm and urged, "Don't."

"He's a bad man. Let him," Patrick taunted. He peered deep into Bryan's eyes, and encouraged, "Shoot me."

Resting his index finger outside the trigger, Bryan clutched tighter the gun's grip. "Don't fucking tempt me."

"Bryan, please. Let's just go inside." Saamyah beseeched. "Please."

Bryan slowly lowered his weapon and returned it to the holster at his waist. After shoving Saamyah's hand off his arm, he slowly walked past Patrick in the direction of the stairs.

"Just as I thought—another town clown that is all juggle and no jab," Patrick arrogantly mocked.

Bryan spun with his fist tightened and struck Patrick's jaw. When Patrick retaliated, they both stumbled to the ground.

"Stop!" Saamyah yelled, struggling to separate them as they rolled in the grass grabbing, pulling, and punching each other. "Stop it!"

Neighbors emerged in their bathrobes and pajamas and Saamyah's anxiety grew. She was certain that such a brawl in their esteemed community would have a flood of law enforcement officers at her door in little time. In desperation, Saamyah retrieved her weapon and fired a single shot into the ground next to them.

Bryan and Patrick abruptly halted their tussle and gazed at her in astonishment. She pointed her firearm at the two of them: first Bryan, who was seated on Patrick's abdomen with his fist ready to strike his face; and then Patrick, who lay on his back with a grip on Bryan's clenched hand and another on his shirt.

"I said stop," she calmly repeated. After watching them slowly untangle each other, Saamyah lowered her weapon, revealed her badge to the onlookers, and assured that everything was copacetic. She then apologized for the late night ruckus and encouraged them back into their homes.

Saamyah gawked at Bryan and then Patrick. Exhaling, she spoke, "Let's call it a night, gentlemen."

When neither of them moved, she turned to Patrick and commanded, "Go home."

Patrick remained steadfast. So, Saamyah walked to close the distance between them and muttered, "I may not kill you, but I will shoot you so many times that you will wish I did...Now, go home."

Patrick gave Saamyah a hard stare and she returned it while tightening the grip of the weapon at her side. She exhaled loudly in relief when he pivoted and began the slow walk to his vehicle.

Saamyah looked at Bryan, his busted bottom lip, and torn shirt. She shook her head and asked, "You just couldn't let it go, could you?"

Aggravated by Saamyah's tone, Bryan forewent the opportunity to share what he really felt and simply said, "You're welcome."

"Bryan, wait," Saamyah pleaded as he started to walk past her. She reached to touch his arm and insisted, "Come inside."

After fumbling with her lock and entering her unit, Saamyah asked, "Do you want something to eat or drink?"

Bryan slowly lowered himself to her sofa, groaned in pain, and responded, "No."

"Do you need a physician?" She asked as she walked to the kitchen.

"No."

Saamyah returned with her first aid kit and knelt down in front him. "Do you feel more of a man now?"

Bryan rolled his eyes at her and then replied, "Fuck you." He squirmed in the seat and winced in pain.

"Nice. Real nice." She dabbed a cotton ball in peroxide and touched his lip.

He pushed her hand away. "That burns."

Saamyah exhaled in frustration and attempted to touch his lip again. "It's just peroxide."

"Don't," he forcefully said, pushing her hand away a second time.

Saamyah gave up. "Fine, let it get infected."

Silence fell in the room and the only thing could be heard was Saamyah throwing items back into the first aid case. She then rose from the floor, went to the kitchen, and returned with a glass of water and ibuprofen.

"Here, take this. It will help alleviate the pain."

Bryan did as he was instructed.

Saamyah sat next to him and whispered. "Thank you."

Bryan winced at the pain triggered by her seat next to him. "No, problem. It's what men do." He paused and suggested, "I should get going."

He rose slowly and walked to the door. "See you at the park," Bryan confirmed before walking out.

*** *** ***

"Come in," Bryan said.

Saamyah opened the door and saw that Bryan was at his desk looking through a folder.

"Hey," she said after she walked in.

Bryan looked up for only a moment. "Hey."

"So, what's up with the silent treatment?"

"Silent treatment?" Bryan asked confused.

"You haven't spoken a word to me all morning outside of 'hey' and 'good morning.' For a minute I thought I was jogging the trail alone until I heard your steps every now and again." She paused. "What's up? Are you pissed at me or something?"

Bryan held his pencil in his mouth and fumbled through his desk drawer. "We don't have much to discuss, Saamyah...When we do then I will let you know."

Saamyah placed a FedEx envelope on his desk. "Carol said that this came this morning for you."

"Thanks."

"Yeah…" Saamyah turned to walk out of his office.

Bryan took the pencil out of his mouth and exhaled loudly. "Saamyah, wait." He paused when she turned to look at him. "You're right, we should talk. How about lunch?"

"I already have plans for lunch."

"Oh?…With who?" Bryan inquired.

"That isn't important," Saamyah quickly answered and walked out his office.

Bryan rose from behind his desk and followed her. "It's with Patrick. Isn't it?"

"Bryan-"

"Isn't it?" He paused and waited for an answer when none was given he stated, "You are not going to meet him, Saamyah." He stood face-to-face with her.

"You can't stop me, Bryan."

"The hell I can't. Why are you meeting him?"

"There's a lot about me that you don't know."

"Are you out of your damn mind?"

"Are you out of yours?" She asked him in return.

"With a partner like you, I am starting to think that I am."

Silence fell in the room. Frustrated, Bryan ran his fingers through his hair.

"Saamyah, this man is psychotic."

"I can handle him."

"Like all the other times you handled him?"

Saamyah glanced down at her watch. "Bryan, I am going to be late."

Bryan blocked her from moving. "Saamyah-" The phone rang in Bryan's office. "Wait here. Don't go anywhere."

Saamyah waited for Bryan to walk into his office and answer the phone before she grabbed her tote and left.

Bryan quickly hung up the phone and hurried into Saamyah's office. When he noticed she was gone, he punched the closest wall and cursed.

"So, how was your lunch with Patrick?" Bryan asked walking away from the whiteboard to take a seat at her desk. He grabbed a pen from her supply cup and scribbled text in his notebook.

Saamyah slowly closed the office door as she grew weary of Bryan's interest. "...It was everything I expected."

Bryan ceased writing and rested his back in her chair. He then picked up the handcuffs on her desk and whirled them around his index finger. "Well, I hope that it was, because if you meet with him again alone, I will report it to Duncan."

Saamyah chuckled as she walked to the front of her desk. "You're not serious because you cannot stipulate what I do with my personal time."

"Oh, but I am, and Duncan can. In fact, I have already discussed the reoccurring safety hazard with him. I am sure he will be talking this over with you." Bryan tossed Saamyah the handcuffs and she caught them.

"Safety hazard? Really?"

Bryan shrugged. "Shit happens when you act irresponsibly."

Saamyah walked around the desk to meet him when he stood. "Acting irresponsibly?" She asked in disbelief. "You lock fists in the middle of the night and I act irresponsibly! Kiss my ass, Bryan!"

Bryan smirked at her crude language use. "Maybe another day, Saamyah." He nudged her out of the way to move past her and walked towards his office. "I've got my eye on that Patrick. Be sure to let him know of it."

He closed his door and was not surprised when the handcuffs Saamyah held hit the frosted glass.

"Come in," Saamyah commanded the owner of the knock at the door.

Andrew opened the door to see her standing in the familiar spot in front of the whiteboard. "You are here later than I expected."

"Hey, Drew. I could say the same for you. How are you?"

"Exhausted, but such is the life of a crime fighter." Andrew crossed the threshold, closed the door, and walked to stand at her side.

Saamyah feebly grinned. "Touché."

"Is Russell in? I need that file that I loaned him."

Saamyah shook his head. "No, but he'll be back."

Andrew glanced at his watch; it was almost 9 P.M. He opted to wait the final twelve minutes of the hour before he left for the day. "How is the case developing," Andrew asked peering at the more elaborately decorated board than he last remembered.

Saamyah exhaled and answered, "Into one big conundrum."

"No new leads?"

"No new leads…And it's not because we don't have a strong case. We just have 'indisposed' victims."

Andrew empathized with her frustration and offered, "It will come to you, Saamyah. Just keep in mind that sexual assaults are always under-reported and when they are reported, the reports are often deficient."

Saamyah contemplated his advice and took solace in their achievements to-date. "Well, I have been able to compile his style."

Intrigued, Andrew inquired, "His style?"

"His style of attack."

"Really? With minimal information?…That's quite some detective work, Detective."

Saamyah laughed. "Nothing to write home about just yet, but I have concluded that-"

Her office door opened and Bryan entered, engaged in a conversation on his cell phone. "We're still on for our annual date, right?" Bryan asked. He laughed at a response and then said, "I love you…I will call you when I get home…Okay…Alright…Surprise me…I love you, too. Bye." He ended the call.

Bryan looked at Saamyah, then Andrew, and his smiled faded. "What's going on?"

"Nothing," Saamyah answered. "Drew and I were just reviewing the details of the case while he waited for you."

Bryan met Andrew's eyes. "Waited for what?"

"The file I loaned you."

"I'll get it." Bryan left the room and quickly returned with the folder in hand. He extended it to Andrew and, in lieu of expressing gratitude, Bryan spoke, "Enjoy your evening." He then walked back to his office and closed the door.

Saamyah was paralyzed by the tension in the room. "I-I'm sorry, Drew," was the only thing she could offer.

"Don't be," Andrew assured. "The rift between us began way before you and it will continue long after. Just be mindful not to get caught in the middle of our cross-fires…Have a good night, Saamyah."

"Good night," Saamyah whispered as she watched him walk out the office.

*** *** ***

The next morning, Saamyah opened her office door and was immediately mortified by the visitor sitting in front of her desk awaiting her arrival. "Patrick, what the hell are you doing here?!" She crossed the threshold, closed the door, and walked to him. "You can't be here. Bryan will be in within the hour."

Patrick smirked and answered, "I was told to wait here after I signed in and was escorted up. I mentioned that I had pertinent information that may prove vital to an SCD matter."

Saamyah shook her head in dismay, walked behind her desk, and dropped her tote in her chair. "This is not a game,

Patrick. This is my career." She took a deep breath to calm her nerves before asking, "When have I ever popped-in on you during your stint with the Wranglers? I've always respected your boundaries."

Patrick snickered and responded, "One, those boundaries where set by David, not me. And, two," he salaciously eyeballed her shape in the black sheath dress she wore, "I would have gladly welcomed the pop-ins." Patrick leaned back into the chair and added, "I would not have made the mistakes I did with women had you did."

Saamyah huffed. "When will you ever take full responsibility for your own demise?"

"When will you, Saamyah?" He retorted.

She ignored the hostile inquiry and clarified for him, "Your mistakes were not restricted to women."

"You're right. I was a semi-pro ball player with a bad jump shot and a bum knee," he confessed.

Saamyah dissented, "No, you were a great semi-pro athlete with a major chip on his shoulder. That is what caused your injury and that is what kept you from entering the pros." She paused and knowingly added, "That and your drug problem."

"Not a drug problem, Saamyah."

Saamyah peered into his eyes and listened for his confutation.

"But an unethical physician who enabled me."

Saamyah broke their gaze. "Patrick, I have a press conference to prepare for. So, I need you-"

The office door opened and Bryan entered. "Good morning, Saamyah," he mindlessly greeted without looking up from his phone.

Paralyzed by fear induced anxiety, Saamyah said nothing. She took a deep breath, held it, and prepared for the altercation ahead.

Recognizing her silence, Bryan looked up from his phone and stopped short of his office door. He looked at Patrick then Saamyah. "Are you fucking kidding me right now?"

"Mr. Barnes is here to provide a witness statement," Saamyah declared.

"Witness statement my ass," Bryan turned toward the exit. "I'm going to Duncan."

"He knows, Bryan," Saamyah lied.

Bryan stopped and faced her. "Knows what exactly?"

Saamyah cleared her throat. "About my interviewing Mr. Barnes."

"Then you won't mind if I sit in on the remainder of it," he snapped, calling her bluff.

"I prefer to continue our conversation in private, Detective Russell," Patrick requested.

"Of course you would. It is the only way to misguide my partner of your ill-doings."

"Bryan-" Saamyah attempted to interject.

Patrick rose and spoke to Saamyah, "I will come back at a later time to comp-"

"So, tell me, do you get off assaulting all women or just Saamyah?" Bryan inquired.

"Bryan!" Saamyah exclaimed.

Patrick scoffed in amusement and taunted, "You aren't much of a detective are you, Detective Russell?" He looked at Saamyah and nodded before exiting the office.

"So, we are lying to each other now?"

Saamyah avoided his gaze and simply answered, "I'm not lying."

"Bull shit!"

Saamyah looked up at him and exhaled. "What do you want from me, Bryan?"

Bryan pondered her question and finally responded, "I want you off this case." He started toward his office, stopped, turned to look at her, and added, "Better yet, I don't want you as my partner." He walked into his office and slammed the door behind him.

Tears ran from Saamyah's eyes as she lay in bed and reflected on the earlier events of the day. Bryan's requests had devastated her. Never in her law enforcement tenure had anyone made such demands. He not only wanted for her a new case, but also a new partner. Because of that, feelings of inadequacy weighed heavily on her chest. So she turned on her side and wept into a deep sleep.

Hours later, Saamyah was startled awake by the sound of breaking glass. Though her heart immediately pounded in her chest, her mind was sluggishly delirious with exhaustion. She slowly sat up and blinked her eyes until they adjusted to the darkness of the room. When she saw a silhouette at her window, Saamyah threw back her bedding and made an attempt to reach the bedroom door.

He grabbed her leg before she could dismount the bed and pulled her close to him. Ignoring the sting of her powerful blows, he wrestled with her limbs to bring her into submission.

"Get off me!"

Saamyah breathlessly panted as her pulse raced.

"Let me go!" She demanded after he successfully pinned both her hands at her ears. "Get off of me!"

She turned her head and strained her neck to bite down on his leather-covered thumb. When he shrieked and released her, Saamyah grabbed the first thing her hand touched on her nightstand and struck him with it.

The intruder rolled off of her in pain, gripping the knot the alarm clock had begun to form on his head. Before Saamyah could strike him again, he shoved her body to the floor.

She winced when her bare shoulder hit the carpeted floor; the weight of her body followed. Discounting the pain, she grabbed her cell phone on the nightstand, yanked it from its charger, and dashed into the master bathroom.

Saamyah quickly locked the door and switched on the lights. Pressing her back against the door, she nervously dialed Bryan's number while trying her best to block out the pounding fists and abusive threats.

"Come on. Come on," she said after the phone started ringing. "Bryan, pick up. Please pick up."

Her body jumped when she felt his body hit the door. She pushed more of her weight against it. The tears dropped from her eyes as she kept praying that the phone would be answered.

"…Hello," a sleepy voice answered.

"Bryan!" She exclaimed crying. "Bryan, you have to help me."

"Hello…"

"Bryan, wake up!" She yelled.

She screamed when the door slightly popped opened, but she forced it back closed. "Please…There is a man in my condo and his going to kill me. Please-"

The door popped open wider the second time forcing her phone out of her hand and onto the tiled floor. When the screen shattered, Saamyah wept and squatted on the floor. She placed both feet against the toilet bowl and used it as leverage to pin the door shut.

His might forced the door off its hinges with a loud *crack* and she scurried into a corner. Her heart now pounded in her throat and breaths hissed from her lungs as he entered the room. Behind his mask, his eyes briefly met hers before he grabbed her arm and yanked her out of the bathroom.

Saamyah's body slammed against the mattress when he threw her down. She quickly rose to her feet but immediately fell back to the bed when he struck her face with an open hand.

"Please," Saamyah whimpered behind the hands that held her sore face. "Let me go."

He pulled her hands from her face and gripped her wrists tightly. A loud knock on the front door distracted him and he did not see her powerful kick before it made contact with his abdomen. He flinched in pain, but did not release her. Instead, he tightened the grip on Saamyah's wrists, yanked her to stand, and swung her into the wall. His hands firmly gripped her throat

"Saamyah!" Bryan exclaimed banging at the door.

Saamyah frantically clawed at the hands at her neck. "Please…just…just tell me…tell me what you want," she cracked.

"Recuse yourself," he simply demanded.

The limited amount of oxygen to her brain made it difficult for Saamyah to decipher his demand. She tried her best to piece it together, but the room began to spin and her lungs began to burn.

"Saamyah, open the door!" Bryan yelled outside.

She fell to the floor after he released her and she gasped frantically for air. Recovering as hastily as she could, she sprinted out of the bedroom to the front door.

"Bryan," Saamyah cried after she unsecured the door and yanked it open.

She fell into his arms, hugged his body tightly, and wept.

"Shhh," he soothed her, holding firmly her trembling body as he stroked her hair. "It's going to be okay."

He released her. "Stay here, okay?"

Saamyah nodded and watched him retrieve the weapon from his back waistband and walk into the unit. Minutes later the police arrived and Bryan emerged from the condo.

"He's gone," he announced.

Saamyah exhaled loudly with relief and wiped her eyes. The officers entered the unit to confirm that the perpetrator had retreated.

"Are you okay?" Bryan asked, walking to the steps where Saamyah stood.

She rubbed her bare folded arms and nodded.

Barefoot and wearing only her blue and white striped, pajama shorts and solid blue camisole, the night air chilled her. Saamyah noticed Bryan had little time to dress also after observing the thin gray cotton t-shirt he wore, matching drawstring pants, and black slippers.

"What happened?"

Saamyah shook her head and shrugged. "I don't know...He was there when I woke up and just attacked me."

"He just attached you?"

She nodded.

"You get a look at him?"

She shook her head. "Completely covered."

Bryan exhaled loudly and watched one of the officers exit the condo and walk towards them.

"Well, I can confirm the coast is clear, Detectives." The officer looked at each of them. "Which of you made the call?"

"It was me," Bryan answered. He folded his arms across his chest and asked, "So, what do you have?"

"Well, it's kind of hard to say." He paused then added, "I have few questions and we can go from there."

Though vexed with his questions, Saamyah knew the importance of answering as best as she could. So, she relived the entire experience and offered as many details as possible. They soon discovered that the details were scarce.

The officer scribbled his final notes in his steno book, cleared his throat, and then explained, "Based on your statement and my observation, the intruder had entered the bedroom by way of cutting the class, then unlocking and lifting the window. The window was then intentionally broken with whatever weapon he had as a method to wake you…There is reason to believe that this person wanted you to know he was there before the attack and had no real intentions to seriously harm you or he would have done so while you were sleeping. It may even be possible that he knows you and has been watching you for some time."

The officer's eyes met Saamyah's and he asked, "Did he say anything to you? Any threats? Anything at all?"

She swallowed hard, dropped her eyes, shook her head, and whispered, "No."

Bryan read the language of her body and discerned that she was lying.

The officer exhaled loudly and said in conclusion, "Well, if you can recall anything, anything at all, you contact me immediately. Better yet, give me your contact information so that I can follow up later today."

"I…I…don't know. I mean I have to replace my cell phone and I won't be staying here. More than likely I will get a room for the night or so until I can fix this place up."

Bryan disagreed. "No, take my information. She'll be with me." He took the steno book and pen from the officer and started writing.

"No, Bryan, that's alright. I will just-"

"No, it's okay. It's no big deal. I'd rather cover your broken window and you stay with me than me be up half the night wondering if you're okay." He extended the steno book back to the officer.

Saamyah searched his eyes.

Bryan wrapped his arm around her shoulder and rubbed it to assure her that she was of no imposition.

She flinched when he touched her injury.

Bryan quickly moved his hand and asked, "Are you okay?"

"Yeah...I, uh, just bruised it when I fell. That's all."

"This is more than a bruise, Saamyah," Bryan remarked after scrutinizing the purple knot under the bright moonlight.

She gently eased him away from her and said, "I'm fine." Looking at the officer, she promised, "I will be in touch."

After the police squad left, Saamyah walked into her unit behind Bryan and locked and chained the door.

"How long do you think it will take for you to pack a bag?"

"Bryan, you don't have to do this."

"Saamyah, I don't want to argue about this. You can't stay here and spending money on a hotel is just stupid, especially since I have a guest bedroom."

Saamyah took a deep breath and pushed back her hair. "Just give me a minute."

Once inside, Saamyah took a seat on his espresso leather sofa and dropped her overnight bag at her foot. She watched Bryan turn on a few of lamps and walk into his kitchen.

"You have a beautiful home," she complimented after noticing the fine art hanging on the walls, flat screen T.V. mounted over the fireplace, matching loveseat and chair on each side of the sofa, marble coffee and side tables, and to the right, a breakfast bar set up behind the cherry wood and glass dining table and chairs.

"Thanks…All compliments of an interior decorator." He added laughing, "I have no interior decorating skills."

Saamyah laughed halfheartedly and replied, "Few men do."

Minutes later, Bryan returned with two mugs in his hands and extended one to her. "Chamomile tea. It will help you sleep."

Saamyah took the mug and sipped the hot beverage. "Thanks."

Bryan sat next to her, sipped his tea, and placed it on a coaster on the table in front of him. He glimpsed at his watch and saw that it was almost three in the morning.

She stared into her cup and broke the silence, "He wants me off the case."

Taken aback by the serendipity, Bryan asked, "He specifically said that?"

Saamyah sat her cup on a coaster and answered, "No, but I do believe that is what he was trying to convey to me."

Bryan drank from his cup and placed it back on the table. "This is so bizarre, Saamyah… Especially, since-"

"You told me the very thing a few short hours ago."

Bryan nodded. "Yes… About that, Saamyah… I'm sor-"

Saamyah shook her head and lied, "It's fine."

A brief silence fell in the room before Bryan asked, "What do you want to do?" She exhaled loudly and pushed her hair back with both her hands and then covered her lips with her fingertips. "…I don't know." She paused and looked at him. "I really don't know."

He gently rubbed her back. "Come on, let's go to bed. We can figure this out later in the morning once we've gotten some rest."

Bryan turned off the lights and led her down the long hall past two rooms and a bath and a half until they reached the master bedroom. She stood at the side of his king size bed and watched as he got comfortable under his bedding. He invitingly patted the spot next to him.

"I'll be good. I promise," he assured, noting her hesitation.

Shaking her head, Saamyah smiled, stepped out her slippers, and lowered herself on the bed and under the sheet and comforter. Her back against him, she moved close to warmth of his body.

Cautious not to touch her bruised shoulder, Bryan wrapped his arm around her waist and held her tightly. He waited until she fell asleep before he closed his own eyes.

*** *** ***

The next morning, Saamyah rolled on her back and woke to an empty bed. As she stretched, she glimpsed at the clock next to her and saw that is was approaching the ten o'clock hour. She slowly rose from the bed, made it, and then stepped into the master bathroom. After splashing a handful of warm water on her face, she inspected her shoulder in the mirror.

"Great," she whispered in disgust with the worsened, dark, purple knot. "Just what I need—another beauty mark."

Walking out the bathroom, she combed her fingers through her hair and followed the scent of bacon that permeated the air.

"...Yeah, I know...Right...Right...Okay."

Bryan acknowledged Saamyah with a wink and a smile as he listened tentatively on the phone. He placed a plate of food and a glass of orange juice in front of her after she took a seat at the breakfast bar.

Bryan watched her lower her head, bless her food, and bite into a forkful of scrambled eggs. He smiled when she gave him two thumbs up.

"Well, look I am going to get back with you on that...Yeah...Yeah...Okay, sure...Okay, then...Yeah, you, too...Alright. Bye." Bryan ended the call on his cordless phone and took a seat next to Saamyah in front of his own plate.

"Morning."

"Morning," she replied after sipping her juice. "You must have thought you were cooking for an army," she added referring to the stack of pancakes, several slices of bacon, and mountain of eggs that covered her plate.

Bryan laughed. "Sorry, I kind of have a heavy hand...Rachel always detested that about me."

Saamyah nodded and took another forkful in her mouth.

"So, how did you sleep?" He asked.

"Good and you?"

Bryan smiled. He cut into his pancake while answering, "Considering it has been a while since I had a nice warm body to sleep next to, I would say my night of sleep was exceptionally good, too."

Saamyah laughed in disbelief. "And how long is a while for you, Bryan. A night? Two?"

Bryan coughed when his food started its way down to his lungs rather than his stomach.

Saamyah snickered. "Less than that, huh?"

He drunk the remainder of his juice and wiped his mouth with his napkin and placed it in his plate. He turned to face her and spoke, "You know you should really stop feeding into all those rumors you hear about me."

"Oh, really. Why is that?"

"Because they aren't true."

She rolled her eyes before saying, "Even the devil won't confess his own guilt."

"Cute."

A brief silence fell in the room before Bryan said, "I spoke with Lieutenant. He knows not to expect us 'til later."

"So, he knows?"

Bryan nodded. "I've actually been up for a while. I gave him a call earlier so that he could know not to expect us for the run. He just returned my call for additional details... He and I, uh," he cleared his throat and watched her sip her juice. "We think you should consider a recusal."

Saamyah slowly lowered her glass on the breakfast bar.

"We?" She asked angrily dismayed.

"Saam-"

"Who's we, Bryan?"

Bryan reached out to her. "I just thought-"

She pushed his hands away and stood to her feet. "That's the problem, Bryan, you're always thinking you know what's best for me." She walked away from him in an attempt to cool her temper.

"Damn it, Bryan. How could you do this to me?"

"Saamyah, I am just concerned about your safety. We don't know-"

"I know that this is what you initially wanted, but I am not doing it. I won't let this case be taken from me."

"You have nothing to prove and so much to lose staying on the case," Bryan reminded her. "...Besides it's not your choice to make."

Saamyah laughed halfheartedly. "We will just have to see about that, now won't we?" She grabbed her belongings and walked out of Bryan's condo, slamming the door behind her.

"Then send me home!" Saamyah demanded in Lieutenant Duncan's office later that day.

"Cambell, please-"

"Please, what?" She interrupted. "I worked this case from the moment it was transferred and I want to see it through...A captain never abandons ship and never forsakes his crew."

"Saamyah-" Bryan attempted to speak to her illogic.

"I don't believe anyone asked your opinion, Detective Russell," Saamyah affirmed.

"Cambell, we are just concerned about your safety. You were physically assaulted in your own home by a man you similarly characterized as our perp," Lieutenant Duncan intervened in an effort to lighten the tension in the room.

"What?...I never said that." She looked at Bryan. "I never said that!"

Bryan tried to interject, "Saamyah, you know that-"

"Bryan, shut up!" She ordered.

Saamyah took a deep breath and tried to let the silence calm her. "Look, all I am asking is the opportunity to make the decision for myself."

"No," Lieutenant Duncan simply answered.

She turned her back to him in frustration. "I can't believe this."

"This man is volatile and losing you is too much of a risk, and clearly not the purpose of your TDY. So, you will be reassigned." Lieutenant Duncan took a seat behind his desk and Bryan took one at the corner of it.

Saamyah turned to face Lieutenant Duncan and argued, "We aren't improving matters by giving him what he wants. He wants me off the case." She pondered more the motives of the perpetrator and added, "He knows that we are honing in on him, and a recusal would only advance his efforts."

"My decision is final, Cambell," Lieutenant Duncan reiterated.

Saamyah laughed feebly and shook her head in disbelief. "This is unbelievable...I am a former special agent. I've dealt with guys bigger, stronger, and more dangerous than him...I know what I am doing, damn it! I know how to handle him!"

Bryan smugly remarked, "Yeah, just like you handle Mr. Patrick Barnes, right?"

Saamyah's abdomen ached where his words struck her. She was deeply wounded by his use of her personal problems she had entrusted him with to weaken her argument. Her eyes met his, but when she felt tears swelling in hers, she hurried to the door.

Bryan stood quickly and grabbed her arm before she could open the door. "Saamyah, I'm sorry."

"Get off of me." She tried to free herself from his unyielding grip, but he only pulled her closer.

"Saamyah, please-"

"Get off me, Bryan!"

"Release her, Russell," Lieutenant Duncan commanded.

Bryan saw the tears drop from her eyes and finally loosed her arm.

Saamyah hurried out of the office before its walls closed in on her. She raced down the hall and sped down the stairs. When her lungs ached, she realized she was depriving her body of oxygen and exhaled the air she held inside.

Turning the corner to the back exit, she collided into the person coming in the opposite direction. His folder fell, but he held her at her lower back to protect her from falling as well.

"Are you okay?" His blue eyes met hers.

Saamyah backed out of his embrace, turned away in embarrassment, and quickly wiped her eyes. "I...I'm so sorry, Drew." She lowered to pick up the scattered papers.

"It's okay." He knelt to help her.

She rose to her feet and handed him what she had collected.

"So, do you want to talk about the crappy day that you are having?" Andrew asked after he took notice of her red, forlorn eyes.

She laughed, looked away, and pushed her hair back. "It's that obvious?"

Andrew shrugged. "We all have them."

The humor left her face and she looked at him. "I've got to go." She walked around him, ran to and pushed opened the double doors.

Outside, the cool breeze hit her face but it did not dry her tears. Furious, the hand that wrapped her waist and the other that pressed against her lips trembled as she paced.

"Saamyah," a voice called out to her.

She looked over her shoulder and saw that it was Bryan walking towards her. Sucking her teeth and dropping her hands, she turned to walk back in the building.

"Saamyah, wait," Bryan protested.

She turned to face him.

"I'm sorry."

She shook her head in opposition. "How could you be? This is what you wanted. Now what is left to determine is whether or not you orchestrated it."

Astonished by her deduction, Bryan could not find the words to respond before she walked away.

"Lieutenant, you have to let her back on the case." Bryan announced after finding him in the one of their several kitchenettes.

Lieutenant Duncan, bewildered, looked at Bryan. "What?"

"You have to let Cambell back on the case."

The lieutenant added sugar to his coffee and sipped it. "Just this morning you convinced me to have her removed."

"Yeah, I know, but it was for very selfish reasons. Lieutenant, this case means a lot to her. For her it has become very personal—a matter of individual achievement...I don't understand it, but I now know that it is important to her," Bryan reasoned.

Lieutenant Duncan sipped his coffee, contemplated for a moment, and then shook his head. "No, my decision is final... In fact, I am going to have her transferred to homicide to ensure my authority is not undermined."

Bryan exhaled loudly. "Come on, Lieutenant. Please?"

Lieutenant Duncan turned to exit, but Bryan quickly blocked his path and beseeched, "Please?"

Lieutenant Duncan searched Bryan's eyes in hopes of determining the thoughts of his mind. When nothing was found but contrition, he exhaled loudly and asked, "Why do I feel like I am about to make the biggest mistake of my life?"

Bryan cracked a smile. "You're not."

"Where is she?"

"She went home. Had to be there for the repairs." Bryan paused. "Sooooo, is that a yes?"

Duncan exhaled loudly again, but this time with worry. "Yes."

"Yes!" Bryan pumped his arms in victory.

"BUT!" Duncan interjected. "But, Russell, you have to keep a close eye on her. It will not look good for this department if we have to send her back to Texas in a body bag. Is that understood?"

"Completely," Bryan assured him and turned to leave.

"Where are you going?"

"To tell her the good news."

*** *** ***

Saamyah stood at his office door with her arms crossed. Bryan sensed her presence and looked up from his reading.

"So, I guess I owe you a thank you?" She inquired then paused. "I just spoke with Duncan and he said that your good word changed his mind about my being on the case."

"I had come by your place yesterday to tell you, but you weren't there; and at this morning's run, you didn't want to be bothered."

She dropped her arms. "Look, I'm sorry. It's just that-"

"Think nothing of it. It was my saying something in the first place that had you snatched off the case."

"Yes it was, and now that you have made things right I forgive you."

"Lucky me," Bryan simply retorted wanting to end the conversation before it escalated to a squabble. He dropped his head to continue reading.

Saamyah saw the FedEx envelope and its contents leafed out on his desk. "Is that the package I gave you a few days ago?" She inquired.

"Yeah, just some things I wanted to look into," he responded without raising his head.

"Care to share?" Saamyah asked assuming the documents were material to their current case. She walked further into his office.

Bryan quickly closed the folder before she had a chance to read over his shoulder. "It's nothing that you would be interested in."

"Really?" She asked, stretching her eyes to read the papers left uncovered. Her heart dropped when she recognized Patrick's name on a few forms. "What the hell are you doing, Bryan?!" She snatched the papers within her reach.

Bryan rose and tried to retrieve the documents from her, but, with her quicker reflexes, she pivoted before he could.

"What is this?" Saamyah inquired.

Bryan avoided her glare and did not answer.

"What the hell is this, Bryan?!"

He finally met her eyes. "It is information on a potential perp."

She shook her head in dismay. "I can't believe you did this." Exasperated, she repeated louder, "I cannot believe you did this!"

"Why?" He asked.

Saamyah scoffed. "Because we are partners. Because you are to have my back. Because I trusted you...Because..."

"Because you left me no choice with all of your damn secrets," he finished.

Saamyah shook her head again in disbelief and shoved the documents in his chest. "You had no right, Bryan...You had no right." She walked out of his office.

"The hell I didn't." Bryan tossed the documents on his desk and followed her out.

In front of her desk, she turned to face him. "How did you get that? His record has been sealed...What you obtained is not public information. So, how did you get it?"

Bryan shoved his hands in the pockets of his navy slacks and shrugged his shoulders. Evading her question, he alternatively responded, "Yeah, it's interesting how the timing of it all worked out in his favor. Then again, he is the brother of a notable slain federal special agent; so, that gives him the sympathy vote...He is also a former semi-pro athlete with a sizeable amount of discretional income due to family wealth and great investments; so, that gives him the power vote."

Saamyah closed her eyes, inhaled deeply through her nostrils, and exhaled slowly through her pursed lips. When she opened her eyes, she asked again, "How did you get the information, Bryan?"

"Due diligence coupled with a few favors," he finally answered and then started towards his office.

"You mean your law enforcement clout?"

He stopped at his threshold, peered at her, and shrugged.

"Why? Why are you doing this?...You have to stop."

"No, I don't. And I am not."

Saamyah paused and thought for a moment. "So, this is why you wanted me off the case? Why you no longer wanted to partner with me?"

"Yes," Bryan simply confessed. He then added, "Your judgment is clouded and, based on whatever history you have with Mr. Barnes, you cannot effectively investigate this case."

Saamyah broke their gaze so that Bryan would not see the sting of his words. She considered all that she had recently discovered and all that he had just declared and calculated her next move carefully.

She met Bryan's eyes. "I know Patrick. He is not a sex offender, and the timing of it all is not in sync."

"Well, let's be thankful that your knowing is not all that we have to bank on despite the lack of synchronization of events."

Saamyah angrily huffed and explained, "Bryan, he was a depressed, local celebrity that abused prescription drugs to cope with the collapse of his career and the demise of his brother...What he needed was treatment—not prison."

"Then he should have appealed the conviction."

"And compromise the judge's agreement to seal the record?!" She hotly inquired of his recommendation.

When he did not respond, Saamyah chuckled halfheartedly and walked behind her desk. "Just stay clear of him, Bryan. You have no idea what you are getting yourself into."

"No, Saamyah, you don't know. And truth be told, I don't think you want to."

Taken aback by his response, Saamyah lowered herself into her chair and stared blankly into a corner of the room. In a brief moment of self-reflection, she considered whether Bryan's assessment of her was accurate. Did she subconsciously avoid the truth because she had no desire to know it? If she did, why? Could the reason be that the truth would unravel the utopia she had created, and then built upon, after each tragedy?

Saamyah met his eyes, "You seriously think Patrick is doing this?"

Bryan broke her gaze, crossed his arms, and with some doubt he responded, "I have my suspicions."

"Mere suspicion is not enough to jeopardize a man's freedom…You need evidence."

"You are wrong, Saamyah. I can get him in here on my suspicion. I will just have to work on the evidence to keep him here."

Defeated, she asked, "Why are you doing this, Bryan?"

"It's my job, Saamyah."

Saamyah sneered. "Your job? This is more than just your job, Bryan, and you know it…You loathe Patrick and will do whatever you can to destroy him." She turned back to stare in her corner. "…I will have nothing to do with it."

"Fine. I will do it on my own. Just stay out of my way."

*** THREE ***

"We have no DNA—no hair, no bodily fluids, no skin…Nothing," Saamyah recounted with Bryan midday Monday at a local soup, sandwich, and salad shop. After their obligatory run Saturday morning, Saamyah made herself scarce and unavailable for work the remainder of the weekend.

Bryan washed down his fries with lemonade before saying, "This perp is meticulous."

"Very." She exhaled loudly. "Unless he falters soon, we don't stand a chance in making an arrest before the attack on his next victim."

Bryan looked down at her half-eaten salad. "Haven't eaten much."

She pushed her plate away. "Not really hungry."

Nothing else was said between as Bryan consumed his turkey wrap.

"There is Drew," Saamyah said, finally breaking the silence after recognizing their colleague when he entered the shop. She called out to him.

Andrew noticed his caller and walked towards her with a smile. "Hey, Saamyah."

"Hey," she said, returning the smile and making room on the cushioned bucket seat next to her.

Once seated, he made brief eye contact with Bryan across the table, nodded to acknowledge him, and simply said, "Russell."

After sipping from his glass, Bryan replied, "Bryce."

Saamyah laughed and shook her head. "Men."

An uncomfortable silence fell at the table and again Saamyah broke it. "So, Drew, you aren't eating lunch?"

"I called in my to-go order. It's not ready yet, but I am working on a double homicide so I can't stay."

"Good," Bryan remarked under his breath.

"Bryan," Saamyah spoke appalled.

"It's okay, Saamyah," Andrew assured. "We all at the office are used to the ass that Russell has come to be."

Bryan looked at him and then out the window they were seated next to. "Weren't you leaving?"

"Anymore of the women you fucked turn victims?" Andrew vehemently rejoined.

Saamyah choked on the water she had just sipped from her glass and instinctively started coughing. Neither men broke his gaze to assist her.

"What?" She asked perplexed after regaining her bearings.

"You're working that Miami Beach case with him, Saamyah. Why don't you ask your partner how many on your whiteboard has he bedded."

Saamyah looked at Bryan. "Bryan, what is he talking about?"

Without looking away from Andrew, Bryan answered, "That's the problem. He doesn't know what he is talking about."

Andrew huffed. "You were always one to deny your evil deeds, even when it pertained to Rachel."

"You son of a-" Bryan growled.

"Your food, Mr. Bryce," the waitress announced.

Andrew took the bag and stood to his feet. He tipped the woman then smiled and said to Saamyah, "Enjoy the remainder of your day."

They both watched him exit the shop and then Saamyah darted her eyes to Bryan.

"You bastard," she said slightly above whisper.

Bryan reached into his pocket and tossed two twenties on the table—enough to cover both their meals and the tip. "Let's go."

Saamyah ignored him. "I thought it was just Kimberly, but all of them, Bryan?"

Bryan stood. "I said, let's go."

"No, you are going to sit down and talk to me before I go to the lieutenant with this."

Bryan sat, but despised the ultimatum. "I have nothing to do with these attacks."

Saamyah leaned back against her seat and slowly shook her head. "Then what he is saying is true...Damn it, Bryan. How could you keep this from me?"

"It's not relevant."

"NOT RELEVANT!" She yelled, getting as far in his face as the table between them would allow.

Several heads turned in their direction and Saamyah lowered her voice. "Not relevant, Bryan? It IS relevant. For weeks we have been trying to find the link that connected these women and it's you...IT'S YOU." She shook her head in dismay. "All along it has been you and you knew it and ignored it because you so badly want to pin this on Patrick."

"He is pinning this on me," Bryan speculated.

"Oh, please. Granted, your promiscuity isn't much of a secret, but why would Patrick go through the trouble of searching for and sexually assaulting the women you screwed?"

"Because with me out the way, he can get as close to you as he wants."

Furious beyond words, Saamyah scoffed. "..I can't believe you kept this from me." She stood to indicate her readiness to leave. "This changes everything, Bryan...You better get a list together, because the women on it have a right to know of their peril."

She walked away, leaving Bryan at the table.

That evening, Bryan opened the door to his office and walked a few steps into Saamyah's. She did not look up from what she was reading.

"So, I had uh, made some calls to some women whose contact information I had saved in an old journal…Just to, uh, inform them of their potential risk."

No response.

"For the most part, all of them had already made changes to their lifestyles because of what they have been reading in the paper or heard on the news."

She flipped the page of the notebook and continued to read while mocking, "Well, let's be thankful that you still had your little black book."

Bryan exhaled loudly with frustration and walked over to her desk. He placed a large envelope that he held in his hand on the corner and set his keys on top of it. "See, this is why I didn't want you to know that I knew these women."

Saamyah looked up for the first time. "Why? It's not like the rumors swarming around here are true, right?"

Bryan lost his bearings with her unexpected blow. When he regained himself, he defended his reputation. "I am not going to be made ashamed for the things that take place in my private life. I am not doing anything different from what other sexually healthy adults do."

"Well, I can't agree," she simply responded. "Your loose behavior may not be viewed as inappropriate or unorthodox in today's society, but in your case, IT IS different."

"Look, Saamyah, I am sorry that I kept this from you. Okay? Damn. Now, can we move on?"

Saamyah dropped her head and started reading again with no thought of giving him an answer. Bryan looked at his watch, snatched his keys, and walked out of her office, slamming the door behind him.

Two hours passed and Saamyah was still sitting where Bryan had left her. Her review of the case from a different perspective was interrupted when the shrilling rings of the phone startled her. She glanced at her watch—the hands read 10:57. Saamyah was astounded at how time had escaped her.

"Detective Cambell," she greeted.

No answer.

"Hello."

Still no answer.

Saamyah hung up and went back to writing.

Minutes later the phone rang again. She looked at it. Initially hesitant to answer, she finally did. "Detective Cambell."

Like the first time, no one replied.

"Listen, if you are not going to say anything then stop calling." She hung up.

The phone immediately rang again.

"WHAT?!"

"Saamyah, it's me."

"Bryan?"

"Yeah, what's wrong with you?"

"Nothing, just someone playing on the phone. What's up?"

"Did I leave an envelope on your desk?"

Saamyah looked around on her desk and spotted it in the corner. She grabbed it. "Yeah, I got it."

"Okay, good. Hey, listen, I'm already on my way home from dinner so can you just bring that to me when you get in?"

"I don't see the harm in doing that. I will be heading out soon," she said, opening the unsealed envelope and removing the binder clipped documents.

"Great, thanks."

"Umm hmm," she simply responded and hung up.

She thumbed through the contents and digested the information that Bryan had collected on Patrick. "Damn you, Bryan," she whispered, flipping pages as she skimmed them.

The phone rang again. Saamyah looked at it and decided against answering it. She gathered her things and left the office with it still ringing.

After walking across the glass enclosed catwalk and taking the elevator down to the level she parked her car, she dug in her tote for her keys. Once found, she pushed the button on her keypad to unlock the door, but before she could lift the handle to open it a gloved hand covered her mouth. She dropped her belongings to clasp the hand and immediately tried to pry it from her mouth.

"Don't scream," he simply warned.

"Fuck!" Bryan exclaimed when Saamyah did not answer his call. He had remembered that he had left his thumb drive in the USB port of his laptop, and hoped that he would reach Saamyah before she had left the office. Because of his misfortune, Bryan made a U-turn at the traffic light and begrudgingly drove in the direction of the police department.

He spun her to face him and pushed her against her vehicle. He flipped open his pocket knife and held it to her throat.

Saamyah tried to capture as much as she could of the man covered in black. "What do you want?" She asked calmly through her panic.

When he did not reply, she shared, "I don't have much cash on me."

Her fingers slowly crept toward her firearm and panic gave way to disappointment when it was not there. She had removed it and placed it in her tote.

"You are a very stubborn woman, Detective Cambell." He pushed the knife deeper into her neck. The pressure of the blade broke the skin and blood slowly dripped to her collarbone.

Saamyah gasped and the tears swelled in her eyes. "I... I can't do what you are asking me."

He placed the point of the knife under her chin and lifted her eyes to meet his. Saamyah noticed that his eye color was milk chocolate and underneath them were streaks of black paint. "You can and you will, Detective." He removed the knife from her head and closed it. "It is not my intent that you get hurt, but casualties may occur if you get in the way...And you're starting to get in the way."

The quiet stillness of the garage was broken when a car slowly entered. The offender looked up to see a silver sedan approaching.

Seizing the opportunity, Saamyah shoved his body away from her and quickly ran in the direction of the approaching car. She looked behind her and saw the man not far behind.

"Help me!" She screamed. "Somebody! Please!"

Saamyah's body hit the trunk of a parked vehicle after a powerful push came from behind. He gripped a handful of hair and yanked her head to whisper in her ear, "Stay out of my way."

She nodded and cried, "Okay."

He shoved her head into the steel of the trunk then absconded in the opposite direction of the approaching car.

Bryan abruptly stopped, placed in parked, and exited his vehicle to assist the battered woman. Rushing to her aid, he caught her falling body just before it hit the cement.

He gently moved her hair from her face and gasped when he recognized the victim. "Saamyah?"

She opened her eyes and touched his face. "Bryan…You came back."

Bryan saw the smeared blood on her neck and covered the cut were it was still seeping from. "…What happen to you?"

She touched her neck. "I'm okay…I'm okay…I…" Saamyah whispered before she slipped into unconsciousness.

Bryan carried her lifeless body to his car, and carefully placed it in the back seat. He burned the rubber of his tires when he sped in the direction of the emergency room.

Saamyah gradually came to in a cold, dimly lit room. Bewildered, she abruptly sat up and asked, "Where am I?"

An entity clicked on the lamp next to her and her eyes struggled to adjust to the light. Bryan then rose out of his chair and walked over to the bed. "You're at the hospital." He sat next to her. "How are you feeling?"

She touched the gauze bandage on her neck and the pulsating knot on her forehead. "I don't know. Fine, I guess."

He gently rubbed the goose bumps on her arm. "That's good."

"What happened to me? What did they do?"

"Nothing. Just bandaged you up…It was just a cut and dehydration." He stroked her hair. "You need more fluids."

"Did you get him?" Saamyah asked without acknowledging the advice that she was certain came from the physician on duty.

"Get who?" Bryan asked.

"The one who attacked me…It was him, Bryan. He came for me again."

Bryan exhaled loudly as many regrets plagued him. "No, he left by the time I got to you." He paused to consider his next words carefully. "Saamyah, you have to stop…You have to stop before there is no next time for you."

Saamyah did not respond to his request.

Bryan took and held her hand. "Please, just work on something else. Maybe something with Bryce."

Saamyah slid her hand out of his. "May I go?"

Disappointed, but not surprised by her resoluteness, Bryan simply nodded. "Yeah, the doctor just wanted me to wait until you woke up."

"Please take me to my car."

*** *** ***

In her leggings and sports bra Saamyah raced up the trail faster than she ever had before. Though her recovery from dehydration made it challenging to keep a wide distance between Bryan, Saamyah pushed through the difficulty to avoid talk of recusal. When she reached their final checkpoint, Saamyah closed her eyes, placed her hands at her waist, and took several deep breaths. She then began to stretch her limbs and roll her neck carefully not to agitate her healing cut. Opening her eyes to start back down, she saw a figure sitting on the rail.

"Patrick?" Saamyah asked baffled. "Patrick, what are you doing here? Have you been following me?" She walked toward him.

"What happened to your neck?" He averted her question after seeing the small adhesive bandage at her neck.

"Freak accident." She looked behind her.

"The hell." He noticed her swollen forehead and commented, "You look like you just lost a fight with a bully."

Saamyah exhaled in frustration. "Look, Patrick, you can't be here. Bryan is not that far behind me."

Patrick laughed at her distress and the allusion that he should care. "This park is open to the public," he smugly reminded her.

The both of them looked in the direction of the footsteps they heard on the gravel. They belonged to unknown joggers.

She turned to him and pleaded, "Please just go. We can talk later, just not now and not here."

The desperate look on her visage compelled him to contemplate her request. "I will if you agree to-"

Footsteps on the gravel swiveled their heads once more. This time they belonged to Bryan.

"Bryan, wait," Saamyah called out when he immediately turned to leave. She knew with certainty that he was en route to discuss the affair with Lieutenant Duncan.

Patrick grabbed Saamyah's wrist to intercept her attempt to stall Bryan.

"Let him go, Saamyah," he urged.

She tried to yank out of his grip. "Let me go, Patrick."

When he realized there was no swaying her, Patrick obliged, timing the release of her wrist just as she pulled forcefully away from him.

Saamyah fell to the ground—her torso then head impacted the gravel. Immediately, the air was knocked from her lungs and drops of blood trickled from her nose.

"You brought that on yourself," Patrick admonished without empathy. He departed with no offer to help her from the ground.

Saamyah groaned her misery as she moved to rise, flinched, and then opted to rest on the terrain until the pain in her back dissipated and the spinning earth stilled.

Once steady to her feet, she wiped the blood from her nose and took several deep breaths. After her strength was renewed, Saamyah started after Bryan.

At the mouth of the trail, she noticed that Bryan was a few yards from Lieutenant Duncan. Saamyah called out to him several times, but he ignored the bellowing of his name.

Bryan exchanged a few words with Lieutenant Duncan and pulled out of his grip when he tried to stop him. He then snatched his towel from the bench and walked to his car.

Saamyah picked up speed and called out to Bryan again. When she reached Lieutenant Duncan, he enveloped her at the waist.

"Whoa, whoa, whoa…Where are you do you think you're goi-" Lieutenant Duncan conducted a quick scan of her brokenness. He wiped her nose and touched her neck. "My God in heaven. What the hell happen to you?"

"BRYAN!" Saamyah yelled.

Bryan got into his car, started his ignition, and drove off.

Saamyah exhaled loudly in disappointment. Her lungs ache and she felt incredibly weak, light-headed, and dizzy. To combat the urge to vomit, she leaned forward to catch her breath and stop her spinning head. She lowered herself to a seated position on the sidewalk and watched Lieutenant Duncan squat down to her.

He touched her face and asked, "Did Russell do this to you?"

She shook her head.

"If he did, Cambell, just say so. Do not lie for him. This type of behavior is unacceptable."

She shook her head again and slowly rose to her feet with his help. "I have to go, Lieutenant…Forget about it, okay? I am fine." She walked away to get her towel, wiped her wet face as well as bloody nose, and departed in her vehicle.

He grabbed her by the elbow and swung her around to face him.

Saamyah gasped. "Geesh, Bryan, you scared the hell out of me," she said, embracing her chest.

Ignoring the few people who walked past them in the catwalk, Bryan burned his eyes into hers and shook a rolled piece of paper in her face. "You told lieutenant that I hit you?!"

"What?...When?" Saamyah asked confused.

Bryan gripped her arm tighter and pulled her body into him. "Don't play fucking games with me, Saamyah. My job is on the line."

"Bryan, you are hurting me," she acknowledged.

"Today, at the park, did you tell Duncan that I hit you?"

She finally broke free of his tight grip. "No, I didn't tell him anything."

He shoved her and her body hit the glass with a loud *thud*. "Well, you better fix this, Saamyah, because if I lose my job over this stupid shit I swear on everything that I love..." His voice trailed off. He threw the paper that he held at her and walked off.

Saamyah swallowed the knot in her throat and picked up the paper that landed at her feet. Once unfolded she saw that it was a suspension without pay for disorderly conduct and aggressive behavior.

*** *** ***

"Aaaaaw. Sshhiiiitt," Bryan moaned his pleasure as he filled the condom that separated their flesh. His arms intertwined hers and his hands pulled down on her shoulders as she continued to move in his lap.

"Fuck," he cursed again, hugging her close enough to bury his face between her taut breasts. He kissed the tan skin between them.

Bryan lowered his hands, gripped each cheek of her firm buttocks, and aided her grind until the last of him spilled into the rubber. He growled with delight, dipped his hot tongue in her cool mouth, and fell back onto his mattress. When Bryan pulled her down to him, they both laughed tired and breathless, but satisfied.

"Thank you," he huskily whispered to her.

She smiled, held the condom at its base, and slowly rose from him. Taking the space next to him, she propped herself up on her side and gently caressed his rippled abdomen.

Bryan watched as disappointment and guilt surmounted the lust and excitement initially evident in her eyes. He had once again made an adulteress of her.

Stroking her long, soft hair, he said in a whisper, "You're a good woman, Allie K." Short for Allie Kat, a nickname he gave her because of the way she purred each time he stroked her. "We all have our flaws and this is just one of the very few that you have."

She hesitantly responded, "This can't go on, Bryan. It would kill him if he knew."

He pulled her close, waited until she rested on his firm chest and continued to stroke her tresses. "I know."

A brief silence fell in the room and she broke it by saying, "He wants to start a family."

Bryan was taken aback by the revelation. He lifted her face so that her eyes would meet his and asked, "When?"

"At the beginning of the year."

"Is that what you want?"

"Bryan, you know that it is," she simply responded.

"But are you happy?"

"I am here right now with you. That says a lot about my happiness with him."

"But you still won't leave him?" He inquired though he already knew the answer.

"He is my heart, Bryan." She paused before saying, "You can't live without your heart."

Bryan rolled his solid body onto hers and stared deep into her amber eyes. They matched the highlights in her brunette hair and both complimented the glow of her tan skin. He wiped the few tears that fell from her eyes and admired the beauty that came close to having his own heart—a woman that rightfully belonged to another man.

The gravity of their situation and the fact that they could never be resonated with her a long time ago. Since that time, she never again contemplated leaving her husband for Bryan. She knew more of him than most, and that made them close. But in knowing more than most women, she knew that being with him was an intense game of Russian Roulette. Bryan was infamously known to be a person committed to no one or nothing but himself.

She played with his soft curls when his head found a resting space between her breasts. "Lo siento, papi," she whispered in her native tongue.

He lifted his head and covered her full lips with his. He loved it when she spoke Spanish to him. "Don't apologize... You have been waiting for this for some time and you deserve it most."

Changing the subject, Bryan's hand traveled down the center of her body and stopped at her warm, swollen femininity. He watched her eyes close as he gently stroked her. In a whisper he asked, "How many?"

She giggled at the question and then lost herself in the soothing caress of his fingertips.

"Tell me," he urged on her lips.

She bit his bottom lip and then turned her head from him. "Why? Why do you always ask me that?"

Bryan used his free hand to turn her face to his. "Open your eyes."

She obliged.

He eased his finger inside her body and folded it toward her pelvic bone. He grinned when she fought to exhibit the pleasure she got from the strokes of her G Spot. "How many?"

She rolled her eyes at his ego and lied, "Two." Telling him the truth about her orgasms would have swollen his head more than it already was.

Bryan knowingly grinned and seductively dipped his tongue in her mouth.

"I have to get going," she panted.

He nodded in acknowledgement and brought his hand to her outer thigh. Bryan kissed her again. "I am going to miss what we have, Allie K, but I am happy for you. I truly am."

More tears formed, but through them she whispered, "I hope you find her, Bryan. I really do." She paused and then begrudgingly admitted, "You are an incredible man and an amazing lover; you would make any woman happy." She stopped and gently tapped his heart. "I just pray that you're able to be faithful to her when you meet."

She gently pushed him off her, rose to dress herself, blew a kiss in his direction, and left.

"So, how is it going with Russell being out of the office?"

Saamyah, standing at the whiteboard, looked up from her folder to see Andrew walking into her office. She shrugged her shoulders answering, "I don't know. It's just the end of day one; ask me again at the end of the week."

"Couldn't get Duncan to budge on the reconsideration, huh?"

She shook her head and walked over to her desk. "No, I guess he figures we need the time apart considering the trail runs and car washing weren't doing the trick."

Andrew took the folder she held after she offered it to him. "It's only a week though. That's not too bad."

"But it's a week without pay and Bryan's suspension goes in his jacket."

"Ouch," he responded.

"Yeah, I know. I feel awful about it."

Andrew dismissed her feelings, "Well, don't. Russell had this coming for sometime now. We all had it with his piss poor attitude around here—Duncan more than anyone else. Trust, it was just his time and it had very little to do with you."

Saamyah nodded. Curious, she asked, "What was he like before Rachel died?"

He laughed and took a seat on the other side of her desk. "Not much different than he is now, I guess. Probably not as bitter and angry when Rachel was still living...She had a calming presence that was very contagious."

Saamyah smiled and sat down at her desk. "Sounds like she was an incredible woman."

Andrew nodded in agreement. "She was." He paused and observed Saamyah's disposition. "Saamyah, underneath the façade, I am sure Russell has the potential to be a great person, but don't burn yourself out trying to change him." Andrew caught her eyes and warned, "He is who he is—a man that possesses an overwhelming desire to conquer by destruction...Honestly, I don't think he is not capable of change. So, please don't get caught in his web."

Saamyah could feel her cheeks flush and she tried to conceal it with laughter. "What are you talking about?"

Stoic, Andrew replied, "I have witnessed him break a lot of hearts, including Rachel's...In my opinion, she stayed with him longer than she should have."

"Very seldom do people want to live out their last days alone." Saamyah absent-mindedly responded, but regretted her words as soon as they left her mouth.

"Be that as it may, it does not warrant infidelity."

"No, it doesn't...I don't know what I was thinking. I shouldn't have said that." Both ashamed and embarrassed, she apologized.

"Just be careful and take heed to what I am saying, Saamyah...It's not difficult to see the chemistry between the two of you."

Saamyah broke their gaze and pushed a lock of hair behind her ears. She contemplated refuting his observation, but opted instead to change the subject altogether. She cleared her throat and asked, "So, now that you have read my summary profile on this case, what is your opinion of it?"

Andrew tossed the folder on her desk and rubbed his weary eyes. Assisting her with this case while Bryan was out was taking a toll on him. He leaned back into the chair before saying, "You already know my opinion, Saamyah."

"I have an inclination, but I don't know for sure." When he did not respond she exhaled loudly and continued, "For some reason you believe that Bryan is connected to this case and that is just about all that I know."

"And you believe that I am wrong for assuming Russell's connection."

She folded her arms across her chest. "Do I think your assumption is unwarranted? Yes, I do. Is your assumption wrong? I can't say for certain."

"Well, what is it that you believe?"

Saamyah shrugged, but did not answer.

"Well, Detective Cambell, you're close, but not quite the hammer on the nail."

She chuckled and rolled her eyes at his wit.

"I think this case is a crime of revenge."

"Revenge," she repeated.

"Hear me out," he pleaded, moving to the edge of his chair. "Someone is attacking women that Bryan is acquainted with to avenge his wayward ways."

Saamyah erupted with laughter. "Are you serious? I mean, come on, Drew, who would seek revenge in such a way?"

Andrew stared blankly at her without answering.

"…What?" Saamyah inquired further. "What would they hope to gain?"

When Andrew provided no response, Saamyah supposed, "Would they hope that he would be prosecuted for the crimes?"

"Jealousy is the rage of man and will not spare in the day of vengeance," Andrew finally offered, breaking his brief moment of silence.

Saamyah was impressed by his Biblical knowledge. "Proverbs?"

Andrew nodded and confirmed, "Proverbs."

She shook her head and dropped her hands in her lap. "I don't know, Drew. It's a bit far-fetched to believe that some heart-broken man, or woman, would go these lengths to see that Bryan gets the electric chair...Wouldn't it be easier to put a bullet in his head?"

"And where is the solace in that? A bullet to the head is too easy...Gratifying revenge is slow, sweet, and served cold."

Saamyah snickered, making light of his innuendo. "Revenge is sounding a lot like my favorite churned ice cream."

She ceased her laughter when Andrew did not crack a smile. She then peered deep into his blue eyes and asked, "You seriously believe this?"

"Would it be a complete waste of tax payers' money to look into it?"

She started stacking folders on her desk preparing to leave. "I don't know, Drew...And I really don't know what is worse: my old partner thinking my ex-fiancé's brother is involved or my new partner thinking that my old partner is involved."

"Wait...Why does Russell believe that your brother-in-law is involved?"

Saamyah shook her head and corrected, "Ex-fiancé's brother." She exhaled loudly and explained, "Just pure speculation based on past and recent events."

"...You want to talk about them."

Her eyes dropped as she answered, "Honestly, I don't."

Andrew noticed the distress in her face and gently spoke, "Well, when you do, I am here for you, Saamyah."

She lifted her head to see the sincerity in his eyes. "Thank you."

He nodded and brought the conversation back to his point, "Now, back to what I was saying-"

Saamyah respired in aggravation, "Drew-"

"Before you totally dismiss the possibility, consider all of Russell's enemies."

"I don't know of any."

"Well, I do," he assured. "And, trust me, the possibility is not that difficult to fathom."

Saamyah massaged her temples with the pad of her fingertips and closed her eyes. "Drew, stop. I can't...I can't deal with your hypotheticals right now."

"You can't or you won't," he pushed.

She opened her eyes and dropped her hands to her desk. "Okay, even if this were true that would mean everyone in this building would be a suspect because all of you have this disdain for him—including you."

"At least now we have an investigation."

They both laughed and when the laughter died, Saamyah inquired, "How long did you know?"

"I'm sorry?"

"About the victims and their common link to Bryan."

Andrew inhaled deeply and exhaled loudly. "The day we met."

Confused, Saamyah inquired further, "The day we met? How?"

"The whiteboard of familiar faces...I mean, I don't know them all and I was never really sure, but I've known Russell long enough to not put it past him. His reputation precedes him."

"...So, it was a mere assumption until Bryan confirmed it the other day at lunch."

Andrew nodded and repeated, "I've known Russell long enough to not put it past him...Sexual conquests are his badges of honor." He paused and finally answered the question he knew Saamyah was struggling to ask, "I couldn't tell you because I wasn't certain. I'm sure you are aware of the Russell rumors swarming this department. I didn't want to add to them despite the bad blood between us."

Saamyah nodded and glanced at her watch—it was approaching the ten o'clock hour. "It's getting late."

"I will walk you out."

Saamyah shook her head, refusing the offer. "You don't have to."

"Yes, I do. There are no secrets among MPD and I am well aware of your recent assaults...Ironically, the police station is not as safe and secure as many perceive."

Saamyah stood and began packing her tote. "It's the price we pay for being in public service within a public service building."

Andrew nodded in agreement as he stood to escort her to her vehicle.

*** *** ***

The following morning, Saamyah stood at and stared out her office window. With her arms folded across chest, her head rested on the pane as her fingertips raced her silver pendant back and forth on the chain around her neck. Her thoughts of last night's conversation with Andrew were interrupted when two people and their laughter entered her office.

"Bryan?" Saamyah asked surprised. "What are you doing here?"

Bryan's smile faded. "I still work here, Saamyah."

She shook her head. "I know you still work here, Bryan. It's just that you aren't supposed to be here," she explained while walking towards him and his female companion.

Slightly raising his voice to convey his annoyance with her, he replied, "I am just here to grab a few things. Is that alright with you?"

Diffusing the tension, Bryan's guest interjected, "Hello, Detective Cambell, I am Tiffany." She extended her manicured hand towards Saamyah.

Saamyah weakly shook the soft hand and admired her splendor. From the black loose hairs that meticulously fell from her bun to the heather grey business suit that accompanied her taupe stilettos, Tiffany was polished perfection. Saamyah released her hand and fought to suppress her growing envy. Tiffany's bright eyes sparkled like the diamond studs in her ears, her makeup accentuated the natural beauty of her glowing face, and her luminescent smile unveiled white teeth.

Realizing that she was ogling, Saamyah turned to Bryan and asked, "So, are you doing some work at home or something?"

"Or something," he responded. "Um, Tiff., can you go into my office and give us a sec.?"

"Sure…It was nice meeting you Detective Cambell."

"Likewise," Saamyah replied, giving her the best smile that she could conjure.

Once his office door closed, Bryan asked, "What's with the questions, Saamyah?...What? It's not enough that you get me suspended, but you now have to dictate the terms of my suspension?"

"She's pretty," Saamyah commented then walked to her desk.

Bryan did not allow himself to be captivated by her strong legs elongated by her navy heels or pencil skirt and collared shirt that fitted her form. Instead, he set his sights on her hair pulled back in a tight ponytail and the pendant she kept racing on her neck

"Yeah, Tiffany is something," he merely agreed, aware that she was baiting him.

Saamyah laughed halfheartedly. "She's more than something, Bryan. She's drop dead gorgeous."

"Okay. I will be sure to tell her that."

She did not respond, but kept racing her pendant.

"Why are you doing that?" He asked her, diverting the conversation.

"Stress habit," she immediately replied, knowing exactly what he was referring to. "I do it most often when I am deep in thought."

"I never noticed you doing that before."

"It is a habit that I am trying to break. As you can tell, I am not succeeding." Reverting to the prior subject, Saamyah asked, "So, is this Tiffany aware of the potential dangers of associating herself with you?"

"Associating?" He contorted his face in offense. "Saamyah, Tiff and I have more than a mere association. We've been-"

The door to his office swung open and Tiffany announced, "Bryan, I have to get back to my office. I just got a call from opposing counsel."

"Oh, okay. I will walk you down," he offered.

"Don't be silly. I've been here thousands of times. I know the way out." She kissed his cheek, said good-bye, and hurried out the office.

"Well, I guess I should head out, too, before anyone else makes a fuss about my being here."

Saamyah grabbed a pen and legal pad from her desk and started walking towards the exit while saying. "Yeah, I have to go down and meet Drew anyway. He's helping me while you are out."

Bryan chuckled. "Oh, yeah? How's that going?...I am sure he is manipulating everything to make me out the culprit—no doubt."

Saamyah did not respond to his comment, but did stop to say, "For what it is worth, Bryan, I am really sorry for all this...You know, your suspension and all."

"Don't sweat it. It was just my time, I guess."

Saamyah nodded and walked out the door.

*** *** ***

Waiting outside of the police department the next morning, Saamyah impatiently tapped her foot and glance at her watch again—9:37.

"Come on, Drew," she whispered to herself and began to pace the sidewalk. The intense morning sun exacerbated her irritation.

Saamyah checked her watch—9:40. She growled in frustration and walked back in the building. After flashing her credentials to the guard, she walked in the direction of Andrew's office.

"I am so sorry, Saamyah," Andrew apologized, rushing towards her.

"For crying out loud, Drew, can't pick up the phone?!" Saamyah asked, glaring at him. She turned on her heel to start back out the building.

"I know, I know. I saw you calling, but couldn't take the call," he stated, walking at her side to the exit. "Had a reporter threaten to go public with one of my other cases."

"Oh no. That's not good," she sympathetically acknowledged.

"Tell me about it." He opened the door for her and allowed her to pass before he followed. "I temporarily parked in one of the visitors' spots." He pointed and led the way.

"So, this therapist," Saamyah started while climbing into his champaign colored Tahoe, "specializes in what?"

Andrew started his truck and drove in reverse to exit the space. "Victimology."

"And why do you think meeting with her will help?"

Speeding towards the interstate he answered, "Well, I figured she could add to our knowledge of sexual victimization."

"In what way?"

"Well, SCD is in its infancy stage and a lot of the detectives in the division are cross-training to become subject matter experts—including myself. I just thought that the therapist would be able to articulate the concerns of potential rape victims so that we can develop the skills needed to speak to those most likely to become one."

Saamyah contemplated his convoluted explanation. "So, we are going to meet a therapist to inquire as to how to do our jobs?"

Andrew hesitated then finally answered, "Not exactly."

"Sorry, but I'm still confused. Exactly, what are you getting at, Drew?"

He exhaled loudly preparing himself for her rejection. "It was mentioned in your summary that Russell called and forewarned a few of his past acquaintances."

"Okay," Saamyah responded in apprehension.

"What if we targeted those women as decoys to the perpetrator?"

Saamyah sat in silence taken aback by his suggestion. After contemplating the possibility, she shook her head in dissent.

Andrew quickly glanced at her reaction and redirected his attention to the traffic. "What?" He asked her.

"Drew, that will never work," she finally spoke.

He quickly caught her eye then looked away. "Why?"

"Why? Because, Drew, one—the information about the journal was unveiled to you in confidence, two—Bryan would never turn it over for official use, three—if he did, knowing Bryan, it would probably be for my eyes only, and four—there is no way that this specialist of victimology could properly train us to convince a group of women to endanger their lives more so than what they already have."

Andrew abruptly slammed on breaks when the car before him did the same. Saamyah's body jolted forward, but she was thrown back by the seatbelt.

"Saamyah, I am so sorry. Are you okay?" Andrew asked after regaining his bearings. He leaned over to stroke her hair back from her face.

"Yeah," she said, pushing back the remaining hairs.

"Are you sure?"

"Yeah, I'm fine."

"Damn," Andrew said returning to his seated position and pushing his glasses on the top of his head. He looked out the side and front windows. "Must have been an accident if traffic is this bad."

"We aren't going to make it are we?"

Andrew shook his head.

"What about next week?"

He shook his head again. "Unless a patient cancels, nothing until the end of July." Andrew pulled his glasses back on his face and muttered again, "Damn."

After he exhaled his frustration aloud, they both sat in silence waiting amongst the bottle-neck traffic.

"Okay," Saamyah whispered, ending the uncomfortable silence.

Andrew looked over to her. "Okay what?"

Her eyes met his gaze and she repeated, "Okay, I will do it…I will talk to Bryan and try to convince him of this plan."

He nodded at her decision. "Okay. Do you want me to be there when you do?"

"No, I am sure the idea will be better received if I went to him alone."

Andrew nodded.

Saamyah turned her head to look out the passenger window. Battling with her commitment to the job and loyalty to her partner, she pondered the thought of legally compelling Bryan to surrender his journal if he failed to do it willingly. Feeling overwhelmed by the guilt, she placed her head on the headrest behind her and closed her eyes.

"No, I'm not doing it." Bryan quickly answered standing before Saamyah while she sat on the edge of his sofa.

Saamyah closed her eyes and rubbed her temples. It had been a long day for her at the office and she did not possess the energy to debate the issue of the journal. Nevertheless, at Andrew's request, Saamyah pushed past the pain of her migraine and met Bryan at his condo.

"Why not, Bryan?" Saamyah asked when she finally opened her eyes. She watched as Bryan began to pace the floor. "It's evident that the way you live your life is no secret…The journal is material to the case."

"Saamyah, I do not care…Case or no case, I am not going to expose myself to the entire goddamn Miami police department!" He yelled.

Determined to remain the calmer of the two of them, Saamyah simply replied, "Well, Bryan you may not have much of choice in the matter."

Bryan stopped in mid-step and examined her. He tried to construe her subliminal message and when he could not, he asked, "Saamyah, what are you talking about?...Why are you doing this to me?"

Saamyah lowered her face in her hands in frustration and answered, "Bryan, I am not doing anything to you." Before continuing she dropped her hands in her lap and looked up at him. "I just think-"

"I would never ask this of you. NEVER."

"You wouldn't have to. Because never would I allow myself to be put in a position like this."

The living room grew silent as they stared at each other. For a moment they communicated with their eyes, conveying nothing but the unwillingness to compromise. Saamyah finally broke the gaze when she glanced at the clock on the wall. It was almost midnight.

She stood preparing to leave. "Bryan, I know that this is difficult for you, maybe even humiliating, but I will go to Duncan if I have to."

Bryan scoffed. "So, this wasn't his bright idea?"

"No, it wasn't."

"So, this is all you? You came up with this all on your own?"

"What difference does it make? None of us are out to get you, Bryan," she assured. "Believe it or not, this is not even about you. This is about the women you reduced to sexual prey that have now become victims to another predator."

"It was Bryce," Bryan revealed after having an instant to contemplate it. He ran his fingers through his hair in anger. "That conniving bastard."

"Good night, Bryan." Saamyah turned to leave, but Bryan moved swiftly to barricade the door.

"Move, Bryan."

"No, you are going to stay here and we are going to talk about this and everything else the two of you have been conspiring upon."

"Bryan, I am hungry and tired with a migraine headache. I cannot do this song and dance with you all night. Unlike you, I have to report for duty in the morning."

Infuriated by the reminder of his suspension, Bryan coaxed, "All the more reason you should feel obligated to stay and chat."

Saamyah exhaled loudly and searched Bryan's eyes in the dim light casted by the television. So many emotions were found behind them that she could not decipher which prevailed at that moment. Saamyah could only assume that it was a combination of distrust and resentment.

"Bryan, just give me the book," she whispered. "No one has to see it but me...I promise no one will know about anyone who does not agree to participate in the undercover operation."

"That's not good enough, Saamyah." He stepped from the door so that she could navigate her way to it and then warned, "You can go to Duncan if you want, but I am telling you now I will fight this until the end. And by the time this gets resolved, it will be too late for a lot of those women."

Saamyah shook her head in dismay and disgust. "I can't believe that you're that damn selfish."

"Putting my best interest first is not selfish—it's self preservation."

"Fine, Bryan, fine," Saamyah conceded. She pushed back the few hairs on her face and then placed her hand on her waist. The game of quid pro quo was a dangerous one to be played, but she was desperate. "What do you want?"

"Give me Patrick," Bryan responded with no need to ponder his response.

Saamyah dropped her hand. "What?"

"I want Patrick brought in and questioned as a suspect in this case and I want you to back me on it."

"I'm not doing that, Bryan."

"Look who is being selfish now."

"We had this discussion before."

He closed the space between them. "And yet here we are again. Only this time I have something you want."

"If you want Patrick, you get him on your own."

"Oh, you had best believe that I am working on it."

Saamyah nudged him to the side the final inches needed to get to the door. "Good night, Bryan. Rest assured you can expect a call from Lieutenant." She walked out leaving the door open for him to close himself.

...The sounds of gunshots rang in her ear like a constant echo. Struggling to breathe, Saamyah lifted a heavy body off her and saw that her clothes were covered in his blood. Overcome with fear and nervousness, she hesitantly rose to turn over the body that was next to her. When she discovered it was Bryan, Saamyah released a penetrating scream that—

Saamyah jolted awake to the racing pounds of her heart. Her body and bedding were wet with perspiration, and she immediately became cool by the chill in the air. After gathering the comforter close to her for warmth, Saamyah turned on her side and glanced at the alarm clock. It was almost noon. She wiped away the small beads of sweat that traveled down her temple and closed her eyes to drift back to sleep.

A loud knock at her door forced her eyes open. She silently prayed that the visitor would retreat as she pulled the bedding over her head. Despite Saamyah's attempts to ignore the sound, the knocks were persistent and grew louder.

Saamyah groaned her disappointment, yanked back her coverings, and stepped out of bed. She snatched her robe from her cushioned chair and slipped it on as she walked down the hallway.

"Coming," she announced to the impatient knock.

After checking the peephole, she swung open the door. "What do you want, Bryan?"

"Good afternoon to you, too."

She rolled her eyes and widened the door so that he could enter. "Thanks," Saamyah murmured.

Bryan noticed the pajama shorts and matching camisole she wore under her gaping robe. "Sleeping in?" He taunted.

"One of those days I guess." Saamyah closed her robe and tied it at her waist. She then folded her arms across her breasts to conceal her harden nipples.

"What brings you here?" Saamyah asked, walking over to her thermostat to switch the cooling system off. When she had returned, Bryan extended to her his journal without answering.

Surprised by his gesture, Saamyah admired the black leather binding and cream-colored pages as she searched for an adequate response. "Nice," was all that she could conjure.

"It was a gift from my mother some time ago...After Rachel's diagnosis."

Saamyah nodded sympathetically. "...I am sure your mother did not intend for it to be used for the purpose that you do."

Bryan rolled his eyes. "It was intended to help me cope...and it did just that."

Saamyah nodded once more.

"Your eyes only, Saamyah, and I mean it. There are some racy things written in there."

"Of course. And, I won't judge you for whatever's written in here."

Bryan huffed. "Doesn't matter. I'm the animal, right?"

Saamyah was not sure how to respond to his regurgitation of her earlier words. So, she simply answered, "Right." Saamyah paused before asking, "What made you have a change of heart?"

"You."

His response astonished her and all that she could reply was, "Thank you."

"You're welcome," he stated and turned to leave.

Saamyah grabbed his forearm to stop him. "Maybe sometime this weekend I can treat you to a movie or something." She dropped her hand. "I mean, I know that this was something extremely difficult to do and I just want to show that I appreciate you doing it."

Bryan smiled. "Are you asking me out on a date?"

Saamyah shook her head. "No, just an invitation to hangout...You do know that partners who have healthy working relationships do hangout, right?"

"I do, but you and I don't have a healthy working relationship."

The truth spoken from his lips stung and Saamyah fought to conceal its impact. "You're right. You and I have had a rocky start...I just figured that an outing would be a great way to start over."

Bryan watched her fidget with the belt of her rope and then the tangles of her hair. After discerning that she was purposefully avoided his eyes, he spared her the torment in waiting for his response. "Okay...But, not today or tomorrow. I'm leaving in a few hours to enjoy my final days of my suspension outside the city."

"Okay, another time then."

Bryan nodded and repeated, "Another time." He opened the door and stepped out.

Saamyah closed and secured the door, then turned and pressed her back against it. She sighed in relief and silently thanked God for the non-contentious meeting. Thoughts of a budding friendship provided feelings of euphoria and, though Saamyah was uncertain of how long the feeling would remain, she was happy for the temporary break from fighting.

*** FOUR ***

The first day of his return to the office, Bryan sat across Saamyah at their frequented soup, sandwich, and salad shop for lunch. Breaking the silence between them, Bryan confessed, "I am feeling a bit slighted."

Saamyah chewed and swallowed a forkful of her steamed vegetables and asked, "And why is that?"

He pushed away his uneaten sandwich, leaned back in his cushioned bucket seat, and answered, "Because, you know all this stuff about me. A lot of personal stuff and I know very little about you."

Saamyah chuckled. "It's not really personal, Bryan, if everyone in the office knows your business."

"Everything in the office is gossip. You, on the other hand, now know what's true… You've seen me naked."

Saamyah rolled her eyes and sipped from her water glass. "Bryan, your journal was shared with me for purposes of the case not as a bargaining mechanism to get dirt on me." She sipped once more from her water glass and then placed it on the table. "Besides it's not office gossip if your book confirms what's being said in the office."

"And what's being said?"

Saamyah huffed and rolled her eyes again. "Don't act as if you don't know."

He sat up to rest his crossed arms on the table and peered into her eyes. Without blinking, he asked, "Well, answer me this, do you believe any of it?"

"I don't entertain unsubstantiated tales," she honestly answered. "But to answer your question, yes, I do think you are a womanizer."

Bryan grinned at her response, not surprised at all by it. He searched her expressionless face and asked, "Is that your polite way of calling me a whore?"

Saamyah pushed away her empty plate and simply replied, "If the shoe fits…"

Bryan scoffed and tossed the napkin that was in his lap onto his plate. "Well, you're right, I have heard it all…But, contrary to popular belief, I haven't done it all."

Saamyah shrugged. "No matter to me, Bryan. I just want this case solved before it slips into an investigatory crevice."

When the silence fell between them a second time Bryan ended it by encouraging her to oblige, "So?"

"So what?"

"So, tell me something about yourself that few people know…Even better if no one knows."

Saamyah chuckled. "You are relentless."

Bryan shrugged.

"Fine…" She thought for a second. "I don't smoke."

"Not good enough."

"Not good enough? What does that even mean?"

"It means dig deeper."

Confused, Saamyah asked, "Dig deep into what?"

Bryan sipped from his glass and set it back on the table. "Your closet." He stared at her with an arched brow and curious eye. "We all have skeletons…Dig deeper."

"Dig deeper…" She pondered the request as she brought her glass to her lips.

"Okay, fine. Just even the playing field…How many men have you bedded?"

Saamyah quickly drank the water she held in her mouth before she choked and placed her glass on the table. Overtaken by feelings of discomfort, she asked, "Digging just a little too deep, don't you think?"

Bryan shook his head. "Hardly...Given the circumstance, I don't think so. It's a fair question."

Her belly tightened with anxiety and Saamyah bit her bottom lip to hide its quiver. She tugged a lock of her hair behind her ear and gave him a sly smile. "A lady never tells," she sheepishly said, hoping to dodge the question.

"Bull shit. Lady or no lady, if I were your man you would tell."

"But you're not," she reminded him.

"Come on, Saamyah. I'm feeling extremely vulnerable here. You know that I fucked more than half of those women in that book; so, even the score. Tell me your number...You can trust me with your secret."

She cringed at his vulgarity, rolled her eyes, and then responded, "I'm not as willing to share my intimate, personal business as you are, Bryan."

Ignoring the sting of her comment, Bryan started, "I just-"

"Will this number somehow unveil your prospects with me?"

His face contorted at the question. "What? No."

Because she believed his response, Saamyah digressed. "Shall we get the check?" Without waiting for his response, she raised her hand until the waitress acknowledged her request from afar.

Feeling marginally defeated and uncomfortably vulnerable, Bryan pleaded, "Please?"

She shook her head and repeated, "No."

Determined to sway her, Bryan bargained, "Okay. How about I guess; so, technically, you won't be telling me."

Saamyah rolled her eyes again, knowing that his tenacity would not permit him to take no for an answer. "Fine," she finally conceded.

Bryan exhaled in relief at her concession; he was close to conceding himself. With excitement, he clapped his hands and rubbed them together preparing for the challenge. "Hmmm," he taunted, examining her with squinted eyes. You are a very classy and respectable woman, so there probably aren't that many."

"Gee, thanks."

"BUT," Bryan continued, "you are beautiful, sexy, and very VERY healthy-"

Saamyah shook her head and laughed lightheartedly feeling her cheeks flush.

"So, I would say that you had your share," Bryan speculated. He paused then asked, "Is it more than a hundred?"

Saamyah's mouth dropped in dismay. She took her crumpled napkin and tossed it at his face. "You can't be serious."

Saamyah laughed off the offense and so did he.

"No, I'm only teasing," Bryan assured. He took the napkin that bounced off his nose and put it in the plate in front of him. "It can't be that easy or else I would have had it by now," he added, alluding to her earlier comment about his prospects.

Saamyah rolled her eyes at his large grin and even larger ego. Her heartbeat increased in anticipation of his series of questions.

"Less than fifty?" He asked.

"Yes."

"Less than forty?"

"Yes."

"Less than thirty?"

"Yes."

"Less than twenty?"

"Yes."

Bryan grew aggravated by his lack of accuracy, but continued, "Less than fifteen?"

Saamyah drank from her glass, placed it back on the table, nodded her head, and said, "Yes."

"Really?" Bryan asked in disbelief.

Saamyah chuckled nervously and repeated, "Yes."

Close to announcing his defeat, he finally asked, "Between fourteen and seven or six and one?"

"Neither," she simply replied and broke their gaze.

"Neither," Bryan repeated to himself, pondering her response.

"Sorry, it took so long," the waitress apologized, placing the check face down on the middle of the table. "Lunch is the busiest time for us."

"It's okay," Saamyah said, quickly grabbing the check before Bryan could. She fumbled in her tote for her wallet, careful to avoid Bryan's gaze. She handed the waitress the receipt back, along with her credit card.

After contemplating Saamyah's answer, Bryan came to his own. He leaned back in his seat and watched her. Though she would not meet his eyes, Bryan knew she felt him gawking. He looked upon her with much admiration and wondered how such a gorgeous specimen of a woman could have gone her whole life untouched by a man.

"The answer is zero, isn't it?" Bryan finally asked for confirmation.

Biting her bottom lip, Saamyah looked at him, but did not answer. She broke their gaze and started racing her pendant on the chain around her neck. She then started to bounce a single leg on the ball of her foot.

Bryan leaned over to meet her distracted eyes. "Well?"

She looked at him and he returned to his original position. "Well," she mocked.

"Am I right? I'm right, aren't I?"

Laughing feebly, Saamyah confessed, "This is so embarrassing."

He shook his head in disagreement. "It shouldn't be…It's actually very commendable."

Saamyah turned her head and chuckled, "How depressing is it to discuss my virginity with a sex-pert."

Bryan shook his head again. "That, I am not. Trust, there is something always new to learn when it comes to sex and women." He paused until he caught her eyes again. With much esteem, he sat up and said, "You are this All American Good Girl. You hardly swear, and when you do, it's laughable. You don't drink, you don't smoke, and you don't have sex. Please believe that all of this is something to be proud of, not depressed about...They just don't make them like you any more."

"Sorry, again," the waitress said returning to their table. After she handed Saamyah two receipts, her card, and a pen, she quickly walked away to tend to an impatient patron.

Saamyah nervously filled in the tip and signed the receipt; the other, along with her card, she stuck in her wallet, closed it, and secured it back in her bag. She felt Bryan's eyes on her as she pulled her hair to rest on one shoulder and placed her tote on the other.

"Ready?" She asked then forcefully smiled.

"So, why the wait?" Bryan inquisitively asked.

"Excuse me?"

"Is it because of your religion and you're waiting for marriage? Haven't met the right man? What?"

Saamyah dropped her tote back on the seat when she realized they were not leaving. "Wow. You really want me to bear my soul today, huh?"

"I told you—naked."

Saamyah exhaled loudly and then answered, "Ideally, yes, marriage is why I am waiting. Chastity is a major religious tenet in my family."

"Raised Catholic?"

Saamyah nodded. "One of the few black families in my community who were. Baptists, as per my father, are too," she used air quotes to emphasize, "'liberal.'"

Bryan chuckled and jested, "Perhaps, but at least we are not so heavenly bound to where we are no earthly good. We enjoy life while here on earth."

Uncertain how to respond to his slight, Saamyah knowingly responded, "I am sure that you do."

Bryan yielded before the conversation went awry. To lighten the air he commended, "I am impressed by your virtue because you do have a body that suggests otherwise."

Saamyah rolled her eyes and grabbed her tote. "Let's go."

Saamyah yawned while asking, "Exactly how old is this book, again?"

Bryan lifted his eyes from his notepad and looked at her. They were sitting in his office working late into the evening. As she read off names from his journal he wrote down favorable contenders, a list of pros and cons as well as additional notes.

"Old," he answered to conceal the truth that she apparently had forgotten. "Many of those women I have lost contact with… It's not at all an inclusive record."

"Okay…Well, should we continue going through this? I mean, technology has made these obsolete."

"No, technology has gotten a lot of men in trouble. Women know to go through a man's cell, tablet, and computer, but very seldom do they remember the written dairy."

"That's because most men don't keep one."

"Exactly."

Saamyah shook her head in disbelief. "Spoken like a true player."

Bryan laughed to himself. "I know many worse than me."

"Of course you do—birds of a feather," Saamyah mumbled under her breath, flipping through pages.

"Come again?"

Saamyah looked up at him and changed the subject. "So, is Miami your home?"

Bryan fought the urge to redirect and simply answered, "Born and raised."

"What about your parents?"

He dropped his eyes to his notepad.

"Home for them, too." Before she could ask the traditional follow-up questions, he offered, "And they are still alive and still married. Thirty-six years."

"Wow…"

"Tell me about it. You won't find love like that anymore."

"I still believe it exists."

"Of course you do," Bryan commented, turning to a blank page to record more notes.

"You don't?"

Without looking up, he shook his head. "I think the realization of it has made me who I am."

Saamyah observed his impassive visage that remained fixed on his handwritten notes. "Who broke your heart?" She finally inquired.

Bryan lifted his head and responded, "Excuse me?"

Saamyah shrugged. "No person becomes a cold-hearted, over-sexed maniac just because. So, who broke your heart?"

He studied the concern in her eyes and pondered if the question was a mere ploy to save him like so many others have miserably attempted in the past.

"My college sweetheart," Bryan answered at last.

"How so?"

After closing and stacking his folders and notepads in the center of his desk, he offered as a cavalier response, "Your typical good guy-bad girl combination."

"Meaning?"

"Meaning I was good to her, but she was better to my best friend."

Saamyah cringed and immediately regretted prying. She was all too familiar with the pain that accompanied past disappointments. "I'm so sorry…Sorry I asked."

"It's fine. I'm fine. I eventually learned to cope…in my own way—of course."

"What about Rachel?"

"What about her?"

"You loved her, so you seemed to have," she used air quotes to emphasize, "'coped' just fine."

Bryan exhaled loudly and leaned back in his chair. "Rachel was God sent. She literally saved me from myself—from the person I was doomed to become on the path that I was on…And still yet, somehow, I could not bring myself to be good to her." He briefly recalled the effervescent smile that met him at the altar and his heart ached. "…I didn't deserve her…"

"But she married you, so obviously she thought the world of you," Saamyah dissented.

Bryan shook his head. "I could never measure up and perhaps that is why I could never bring myself to do right by her."

"Measure up? She was your wife, Bryan. Why would you have to measure up?"

"Because that is what the good Dr. Ernest J. Russell says I must always do."

She contorted her face and confessed, "Sorry, I don't follow."

"My father—a sharpshooter who takes his liquor straight with no chasers." Bryan exhaled loudly to release some of the ever growing tension between his father and him.

"He never passes up the opportunity to remind me of the disappointment that I am—my grades, college admissions, major selection, career choice—you name it. In the eyes of the good doctor, my accomplishments could never rival his." Bryan chuckled at himself and added, "Except the women. That…that—he could never hold a candle to me." He stared blankly into the abyss and whispered, "I make sure of it."

Unsure of how to comfort him, Saamyah cleared her throat and offered, "I have three brothers that endured the same plight. So, an Absalom spirit is not special to you. Every son wants to be greater than his father, even if to his own demise. But what every son must realize is that, until the father dies, he is forever in the shadow of his father's footsteps."

Bryan considered the Biblical reference and the analogy she made between King David's son and him. He met her eyes in confusion and spoke with contempt, "Is that your piss poor attempt to console me?...I mean I feel as if I am going to receive a hefty bill for this dismal therapy session."

Saamyah rolled her eyes. "No, Bryan, it is not my piss poor attempt to console you," she answered truthfully. "But, I am concerned about you. You are living dangerously close to the edge."

"Don't be. I'm always protected."

Saamyah huffed at his smugness. "STIs are not your only worries. Your wayward behavior is either going to have you kill or be killed."

"And that there is exactly why I married Rachel. My mother said those very words to me; so, to appease her I got married." He rubbed his weary eyes and reflected on his history. "And what little good that did me. As per usual, I was a total fuck up...I fucked up and hurt her in the process."

"Bryan, I-"

As fatigued set in, Bryan rambled off his confessions. "I really did put her through a lot of shit—lying, cheating, women calling her phone, appearing at her job."

Taken aback and uncomfortable by the revelation, Saamyah closed the journal and placed it on his desk. She glanced at her wristwatch and saw that it was a few minutes past nine. She was ready to retire for the day.

"Truthfully, if I could do it all over again I would have never made her my wife."

Saamyah looked at his solemn face and asked, "Why is that?"

"Because I wasn't ready and she deserved better."

"It is our nature to be selfish. It is the never-ending conflict between man and himself," Saamyah offered in her best attempt to alleviate his guilt.

"Perhaps, but I was just way too damn selfish...I didn't realize what I had in her until she was gone."

"Do you think you can ever love and marry again?"

The question abruptly heaved him from his fleeting moment of self-pity. He avoided her eyes and shrugged. "I don't know, Saamyah. Old habits tend to die hard."

Saamyah nodded as she raised her hand to cover a yawn.

Bryan smiled and met her gaze. "Ready to call it a night?"

She laughed. "Could I be any more obvious?"

"I will walk you to your car."

*** *** ***

"Oh, good, Saamyah, you're here." Bryan proclaimed the next morning. He walked through her office door and announced, "I want you to meet someone."

Saamyah closed her file draw and walked behind her desk with a manila folder in hand. Without sitting, she watched Bryan and his female companion move toward her.

"This is Samantha Hayes. Samantha this is Detective Saamyah Cambell."

Saamyah dropped the folder on her desk, weakly smiled, and shook the hand of the woman who appeared to have walked out of beauty magazine.

"Pleasure," she said.

"Likewise," Samantha responded.

"I continued our work last night after you left," Bryan began. "Samantha is the best contender…She has agreed to serve as our decoy."

Saamyah took in Samantha's appearance. Not surprisingly, her look paralleled that of the women on the whiteboard. "Is that right?"

"It is," Bryan affirmed.

Saamyah dashed her eyes between the two of them and folded her arms across her breasts. "Have you fully explained to Ms. Hayes the risks of such a task, the invasive measures, lack of freedom, and the minimal compensation?"

"He has," Samantha answered for herself. She flipped her hair off her shoulder and shared, "I'm here to help, Detective Cambell, and I'm glad to do it—all things considered and without compensation."

Saamyah locked eyes with Samantha and held it for several seconds. She then spoke, "Bryan, may I have a moment with you in your office?" Without waiting for a reply, Saamyah moved from behind her desk and walked towards his office.

Bryan murmured something in Samantha's ear then followed Saamyah. He closed his office door and then turned to meet her folded arms and hard glare. "Seriously, Bryan?"

"What?"

"You have got to be kidding me."

"What now, Saamyah?"

"We can't use her. That's what."

Bryan bit his bottom lip to refrain from yelling a host of expletives. He took a deep breath and exhaled his frustration. When had calmed himself, he simply asked, "Why?"

"Outside of the obvious, her intentions are duplicitous."

In confusion, Bryan squint his eyes at her. "What?"

"You are still sleeping with her and she is only doing this to get closer to you," Saamyah clarified.

Bryan did not confirm nor deny Saamyah's accusations. Instead, he walked to sit on the corner of his desk.

Saamyah stood in front of him and asked, "What happens when you grow tired of her, Bryan?"

He shrugged and gripped her folded arms at the elbows. "Nothing lasts forever, right?"

Saamyah shoved his hands away and spat, "You're such a whore."

"And you're such a tease."

Saamyah growled in frustration. "Bryan, if we lose her we will lose everything we have accomplished thus far."

Bryan laughed. "We are at ground level, Saamyah. Trust me, it doesn't get any worse than this."

Ignoring his cynicism, Saamyah asked, "So, should I tell her or you?"

Bryan stood and paced the floor. "I don't get you, Saamyah. You are never satisfied." He paused in his step and met her eyes. "You wanted the truth, I delivered. You wanted the journal, I delivered. You wanted a contender for this whimsical idea of yours, and once again, I delivered."

"Fine, I'll tell her. At least that way you can keep sleeping with her if you'd like." She turned to leave.

"If not her, then who?"

Saamyah released the handle and looked at him. "I don't know, Bryan, but I am sure you have a ram in the bush."

"No, I'm done. You figure it out...Everything has to be done your way anyway."

"Just pick someone else, Bryan."

"You."

"What?"

"If not her, then you."

Her face twisted at the suggestion. "Bryan, that will never work and you know it."

"Well, there goes your plan," he knowingly taunted.

Defeated, Saamyah swung open his office door and stepped out in time to catch the tail of Samantha walking out of hers. She grinned and turned to Bryan and mocked, "And there goes yours."

Bryan rose from his seat to see what she was referring to. He stopped a couple inches from Saamyah's face and watched the door close.

"Looks like you may have to call up another bedmate for tonight," she teased.

"Damn," he whispered to himself.

"So," Saamyah started, interrupting his thoughts of regret, "if I were to participate in this ruse, your lifestyle would have to change."

He looked at her and asked, "How so?"

"Our relationship would be authentic to everyone, but Duncan." She paused to brace herself for his reaction before adding, "Our relationship would be one that is exclusive."

Bryan burst into laughter. "Yeah, that's not happening." He turned to walk back into his office. "I'll try Kimberly. She was second on the list."

"I figured it was too much for you to handle," Saamyah called out after him.

Bryan walked back to meet her stance. After he held her gaze, he gently grabbed her face, and pulled her into a kiss.

"Bryan," Saamyah protested, pushing him away.

"Just like I said," he repeated, "it's not happening...You can't even stand for me to touch you."

Saamyah parted her lips to explain, but stopped when Bryan appeared uninterested. She observed as he walked into his office and shut the door.

Saamyah stepped to the chair behind her desk and slowly lowered herself to the seat. She bit her bottom lip and cracked a smile when his lingering scent gained a familiarity—cherry Jolly Ranger.

A light tap at the door broke her trance.

"Come in."

The door cracked open and Andrew peered in. "Am I interrupting anything?"

"Not at all. Please come in."

Andrew stepped in and then closed the door behind him. He walked to the seat in front of her desk and sat. "I had some time before court so I figured I'd stop by. We haven't talked much since Russell's return."

Saamyah admired his grey, tailored suit and took notice that he was without his glasses. "I know and I'm sorry. It's been busy...How are you?"

Andrew placed the expanding folder of documents in the chair next to him and answered, "The same." He rubbed his tired eyes and added, "We finally made an arrest in that double homicide."

Saamyah beamed a bright smile at him. "I heard. Congratulations—by the way."

He returned her infectious smile. "Thank you... I am sure the media will find a way to put a negative spin on this."

"That, we can be sure of. It's not good enough that we catch the bad guys, we now have to do it at lighting speed."

They both laughed.

When the laughter faded, Andrew scanned her visage. She was as beautiful as the day he met her, but day-by-day her effervescent glow was dwindling.

"How are you, Saamyah?"

She took in a deep breath and exhaled. "I'm tired...Truthfully speaking, I am really tired."

Andrew acknowledged her plight with a sympathetic nod. "...And the case?"

Saamyah groaned in agony.

Andrew chuckled. "That well, huh?"

"You have no idea." She pushed her hair back from her face and released her frustration. "Even with Bryan as a viable link, I still can't manage to build a solid perp profile…"

"Maybe your link is the perp."

Saamyah met his eyes. "Drew, don't joke."

He shrugged. "Saamyah, he is a man of questionable character."

"I just think-"

Bryan's office door swung open and both their heads turned in its direction. "Bryce," Bryan greeted, stopping in mid-step.

Andrew grabbed his folder and stood. "Russell."

"Here to deceive my partner with more of your vicious lies?"

"Bryan, please," Saamyah beseeched.

"Actually, I was stopping by to check in and say hello to a friend. You wouldn't know anything about that since you have so few around here."

"Well, I don't know about you, but I enjoy our small talks. It kind of adds something extra to my day." Bryan paused before adding, "Besides, with honesty like ours, why ruin it with friendship—it's grossly overrated?"

Saamyah exhaled loudly as she looked upon Bryan. She could not decipher if she was more frustrated, angry, or disappointed by his childish banter.

Andrew turned to Saamyah, declining the invitation to spar with her partner. "I'll see you around."

She nodded and replied, "Okay. Thanks for stopping by."

Once Andrew left the room, Saamyah tossed the pen she held in her hand and watched it hit Bryan in his muscular torso.

"You're such an ass," she scolded.

Bryan picked up the pen and placed it on her desk. "Kimberly is a go for the undercover operation."

"What?"

"Yeah, I am a bit surprised myself, but I just spoke with her and she agreed."

"Are you serious?"

"Yes, like everyone else, she just wants this guy caught."

"Well, I guess we can just talk it over with Duncan and see what he thinks of it."

"So, you are okay with her?"

"A former victim would not have been one of my picks, but whatever. If that is all that we've got, that is all that we've got."

Bryan took the seat that Andrew once occupied. "Humor me. What would your pick consist of?"

"I would prefer a woman you had not previously engaged in copulation with."

Bryan snickered. "Copulation?"

Saamyah rolled her eyes at his mockery. "Had sex with," she restated, and then continued, "she should have never been attacked, because it's highly unlikely that the perpetrator will attack the same victim." Saamyah paused and leaned forward into her desk to emphasize her final point. "Most importantly, I need someone strong enough to say no to you, and without regret, fail to give you a second look."

Bryan swallowed the knot in his throat. Afterwards he cleared it and wished, "Good luck finding that woman."

"You and I both know that I won't waste my time searching. You despise rejection so you press until you get what you want."

Looking beyond her weary eyes, Bryan saw a guarded soul. He ignored her observation and inquired, "Why are you so hard?"

"What?" Saamyah asked blind-sided by the question.

"You have this wall that keeps people from getting close to y-"

"Kind of how you use satyriasis to keep women from getting close to you," she interrupted.

Bryan concealed the sting of her comment and continued, "Because if someone managed to get close enough, there is a possibility that that wall would come crumbling down, making you vulnerable and weak in your own eyes."

Saamyah cleared her throat and swallowed. "So, is that what you think? That I am incapable of loving again?"

"Are you?"

"I think the real question is, are you? You're the one loving with your penis instead of your heart. Spreading yourself so thin until there will be nothing left for your next wife—assuming that you allow someone close enough to even wed again."

Bryan smiled and nodded. "Reprimand from the world's oldest virgin."

Saamyah huffed at his insensitive remark. "Which makes me objective, don't you think?"

"Hardly."

She leaned back in her chair and swiveled it from side to side. "What is this really about, Bryan? The kiss earlier?...You really don't handle rejection well."

"It's not rejection when one fights what we both want."

She ceased moving her chair and asked, "Do you always want what you can't have?"

"Don't know. As you have notably stated, I have always had what I wanted."

"Well, you can't have me," she affirmed.

Bryan licked his lips and smiled. "All I have ever needed was time, Saamyah."

Saamyah rolled her eyes and opened the folder on her desk. "Trust me, it will be like moving mountains."

"Then I will start with the smallest one."

Saamyah looked up at him, growing faint with his cocky exchange. In lieu of responding, Saamyah allowed a quiet stillness to settle in the room. She watched him as he watched her, both trying to discern each other's thoughts.

Dropping his eyes, Bryan spoke first. "I, uh, lied to you about Kimberly's response."

"So, she did decline?"

Bryan looked at her. "No...Actually, I didn't bother to contact her."

"Then why tell me that she had agreed?"

"To prove my point."

Rolling her eyes in aggravation, she leaned to open her desk drawer and reached for an elastic band. After she pulled her hair back, Saamyah slammed the drawer shut, and asked, "And what point is that, Bryan?"

"That no matter my pick, you won't be satisfied." He paused. "If we are to seriously pursue this U.C. op, you have to be the target, Saamyah."

She looked down at her watch and flinched at the time. "Bryan, I have to go. I am due in the lab in fifteen minutes."

Bryan moved to the edge of his seat and placed a hand on top of hers. When she met his gaze, he offered, "Think about it. If this person is determined to persecute me then why not come after you—my partner in work and, with good acting, in life."

Saamyah slid her hand from underneath his. "I've played that role before, Bryan, and I am still coping with the outcome." She stood and confessed, "I don't have the best feeling about this. It can all back-fire, especially since I am working the case and the perp knows that I am working the case."

"It's still worth a shot don't you think?"

"No, I don't...But, if you insist, we can run it by Duncan."

Bryan leaned back in the chair and observed her until she left.

"Much luck at the lab?" Bryan called out to her from his office when he heard her return.

Saamyah walked over to lean against the pane of his opened door. She held her legal pad close to her chest and answered, "No...Well, it was discovered that the black fibers collected from a few of the victims' bodies were that of the same perp."

"So, we can now officially confirm that we are dealing with a serial rapist?"

Saamyah nodded. "Yes, but an especially motivated serial rapist."

He pondered her remark and confessed, "Well, if we follow my link to these women, then we can conclude that he is motivated by the desire to avenge whatever wrong-doing I have committed against him."

"And this heinous wrong-doing would be?"

Bryan shrugged his shoulders. "...I don't know."

Saamyah dropped her arms and rolled her eyes. "Of course you don't," she replied turning to walk to her desk. Bryan rose to follow her.

"Do you keep account of all your transgressions?"

"Bryan," she began, dropping her legal pad on her desk.

"Do you?"

"What human being does?"

"My point exactly. And to be clear, we have not officially established that it was anything I've done that would warrant these attacks. I only offered it as hope against the lack of hope."

Saamyah sighed. "...You're right...You're right, and, at this point, everything that we have is pure conjecture. But," she began as a glimmer of hope, "great police work always follows the strongest lead and right now, Bryan, that is you."

Bryan grew faint by the exchange. After a brief moment of reflection, he conceded. "So, what do we do?"

She rubbed her forehead with fingertips and answered, "Honestly, I don't know."

"Have you talked to the lieutenant?"

"Not yet." With apprehension she said, "We have to tell him everything, Bryan. At least that way he can clearly assess this situation and direct us in the way that we should go."

Bryan allowed himself an instant before he responded. He used the time to consider the repercussions of releasing his skeletons, the accusations that would accompany them, and the people that would be injured in the process.

With hesitation, he peered into Saamyah's eyes and asked her, "With all that you know, do you believe that I have any connection with these crimes?"

Saamyah diverted her eyes from his inquisitive stare. "It doesn't matter what I think, Bryan."

Bryan reached across her desk and gently turned her face to meet his. "It does matter...It matters to me."

"Why?"

"Because if my own partner doesn't believe in my innocence then why should anyone else in this department?"

Saamyah moved his hand from her face and took a seat before saying, "Bryan, no, I don't think you are a sadistic sex offender. But now knowing the extent that someone will go to get revenge makes me question your character." She looked up at him. "What could you have possibly done to cause the danger that has consumed these women's lives?"

Bryan took a seat in a chair in front of her desk and pondered her question. After several seconds passed, he finally shrugged his shoulders and answered, "I honestly don't know. I have selfishly double-crossed so many people in my life that who's to say."

"Anyone recently?"

"Probably," he simply answered. "But the point I am making is that if you, the person perceived to be the closest to me, have your doubts, then so will everyone else. That's why we can't go public with this."

"Putting everything on the table will exonerate you."

Bryan laughed halfheartedly. "You haven't worked here long enough to know how we operate around here. A confession is just a mere foreshadow of guilt."

"Then take a polygraph."

"What?"

"Take a polygraph," she repeated with emphasis.

Bryan stood and began pacing the floor. "...No...No, I can't do that. I could be asked anything."

"So, let me get this straight—just so, you know, that it is all clear in my mind. You would rather be convicted of a sex crime to avoid having your lack of sexual inhibition exposed?"

Bryan stopped and looked at her. He thought of how to articulate that the cons, though fewer in number, outweighed the pros. When he could not form an adequate defense, Bryan simply confessed, "I just can't do it."

Saamyah exhaled loudly with disappointment. "Fine, I guess we can discuss with Duncan what you are willing and deal with everything else as it comes."

Bryan nodded in agreement. "Let's go now and get it over with before I lose my nerve...Besides, I have a feeling that Duncan is going to be a very hard sale."

"Kiss me," Bryan huskily whispered on Saamyah's lips after cornering her in the elevator.

"Bryan, please," she repulsively replied, pushing him out of her personal space. "This relationship is merely a charade." She glared at him and repeated Lieutenant Duncan's warning to him, "So, don't get beside yourself."

Bryan gave her an impish grin. "Oh, honey, I am going to milk this for every drop that I can."

Saamyah grimaced and hurriedly descended the elevator when the doors opened. She abruptly stopped and gasped when Bryan's swatted her tantalizing backside.

He laughed at the look of death she gave him as he brushed passed her. "Just playing the role, babe," he assured. "Just playing the role."

*** *** ***

Saamyah's face brightened when she arrived to the office the next morning to a beautiful assortment of lilies on her desk. She walked around her desk and quickly dropped her tote to read the card, "Just because...Bryan."

Saamyah sucked her teeth and respired. She grabbed the flowers, walked to his closed office door, and opened it without knocking.

"Good morn-" Bryan sang, looking up from the email he was in the midst of typing. The loud *thud* from the dropped vase on his desk interrupted him.

"Okay, Casanova, here are the rules: there will be no touching, groping, fondling, feeling, caressing, finessing, popping, spanking, OR gift giving of any kind," she counted off her fingers. "Let me make it EMPHATICALLY clear. For the sake of this case you are ONLY entitled to grandma hugs and dry kisses, meaning without tongues. Comprendéz?"

Bryan grinned. "You're such a kill joy."

"And I'm okay with that," she confessed and turned to leave. "And," she added, turning back to face him, "all the pet names…"

"What of it?" Bryan asked.

"Cut it out!"

Bryan chuckled and thought for a moment. "What about-"

"If you have to ask about it, Bryan, then it's most likely a no as well as anything else I may have forgotten."

Bryan rose from his desk to follow her out.

"In all fairness, Saamyah, you aren't giving a guy much to work with. How believable is the relationship supposed to be if we share no P.D.A.?"

Frustrated, Saamyah stood face-to-face with him and responded, "This relationship ISN'T real, Bryan."

"Yes, I know that, but it's supposed to appear real."

She growled and turned from him to calm the urge to throttle him.

Bryan grabbed her arm, turned her to face him, and pressed his lips firmly against hers. He pulled and held her firmly until the fight left her. When she finally returned the kiss, he loosened his grip.

After a light tap, her office door swung open. "Saamy-"

She broke their kiss and saw Andrew standing at her door.

"Drew," she choked, pushing Bryan away.

Astounded, Andrew cleared his throat and suggested, "Maybe I should come back."

Bryan smiled, licked his lips, and rubbed his brow. It pained him to say nothing, but he knew any comment would make the situation more awkward for Saamyah.

"No, Drew, wait." Saamyah said, stepping in his direction.

"It's okay. Just, uh, I will be in my office." He left closing the door behind him.

Saamyah closed her eyes and dropped her head in her hands. "That was so embarrassing."

Bryan laughed and went to hug her. "Don't worry about it. Bryce is not the type to talk…Which is a bit counterproductive for us though."

"Bryan," Saamyah whined, lightly pounding at his chest. "What am I suppose to tell him?"

Bryan lifted her chin so that their eyes would meet. "Don't tell him anything."

Saamyah exhaled loudly and eased out of his embrace. "Let's just stick to the rules, okay?"

"Well, it's going to be hard to do, now."

"What are you talking about? You just said that Drew would be discreet."

"Well, I kind of got the ball rolling on this sham while I was out with the guys last night."

"What?…Bryan, what did you do?"

Deflecting, Bryan crossed his arms and said, "Well, in my defense, you have been the want of every man employed here since your arrival."

"Bryan?"

"I kind of disabused them of the notion that they had a chance with you and alluded to the fact, albeit bogus, that I was already the lucky man sleeping in your bed."

"Geesh, Bryan. You couldn't wait 24 hours?!"

"The way I figured, the lie could only help us."

"Not by making me out to be your trophy whore, Bryan." She paused before saying, "You're such an ass." She walked out of the office and slammed the door behind her.

Saamyah tapped on the cracked door and poked her head in. "Hey, Drew."

On the phone, Andrew signaled with his hand for her to enter.

Saamyah walked in and nervously smoothed out the gather in her black, high-waisted, midi skirt and took a seat in front of his desk. She admired the neat office and studied his degrees, certificates, and pictures.

"Sorry, about that," Drew said hanging up the phone.

"It's okay."

"So, you and Russell-" he said cutting to the chase.

"Drew, it's not what you think," she interjected.

"It never is, Saamyah." He paused before saying, "Just be careful."

She nodded in deference to him and asked for the reason for his visit.

"You left this in the lab," he said handing her a folder. "The technician said that it belonged to you."

"Thanks."

An uncomfortable silence fell in the room and Saamyah contemplated an exist strategy. She decided with, "Well, I better get going."

"See you around, Saamyah."

She smiled weakly and replied the same.

Saamyah walked into her office to find Bryan at her desk scribbling with the vase of lilies next to him.

"A new message," Bryan said after he completed his text. He extended the card to her.

Saamyah read the card and smiled. "I forgive you." She took the lilies and positioned them on her file cabinet and placed next to it the folder Andrew had given her. She then took a seat on her desk. Bryan sat next to her.

"Seriously, Saamyah, I know that what I did was very immature and I let my ego get the best of me…For a moment I lost sight of the task at hand."

"This is going to be difficult for the both of us and will require a lot of sacrifices…Aside from my tarnished reputation, you may have more to sacrifice and I recognize that now. I apologize for being insensitive about it before."

"Thank you. That means a lot to me."

"You're welcome…Let's just stick to the rules, okay?"

Bryan exhaled in annoyance. "The rules."

"Yes, the rules."

"I can only promise to do whatever it takes to get the job done." He stood and added, "But I will always keep in mind that this is just a ruse."

Though a skeptic, Saamyah apprehensively replied, "What more could a girl ask for."

Bryan glanced at his watch and asked, "How about lunch on the boardwalk?"

"Boardwalk?"

"Miami Beach. There is this amazing fish and chips shop not far from Baskin Robins. So, maybe ice cream afterwards?"

"Ice cream. What woman could resist?" Saamyah laughed with sarcasm.

"You don't like ice cream?"

"I love it actually. I just have other plans. A lunch meeting."

Bryan nodded and warned, "Not with Patrick Barnes."

"No," She simply answered. "How about dinner? I can meet you there."

"Wow, I have been pushed back to dinner. Must be some lunch meeting..." Bryan waited for a response hoping that she would take the bait. When she failed to, he gathered that it was a personal and not professional lunch meeting. "I can do dinner. How about seven?"

"I can do seven," Saamyah confirmed.

"Then it's a date. Well, non-date," he corrected.

Saamyah feebly smiled at his wit. "It's a date, albeit a bogus one, but a date nonetheless," she assured.

Bryan stood as he presented her with a single red rose. He sealed the greeting with a soft, lingering kiss on her lips. Saamyah rolled her eyes, shook her head, and then smiled at his obstinacy. She took the seat that he had pulled out for her.

"Trouble finding the place?" Bryan asked taking his own seat.

"No, your directions were faultless." She admired the wooded patio setting that overlooked the water. "No seating available inside?"

"Why waste a night like this inside?" He leaned forward and stared into her eyes. "Besides, the view is much better out here."

Saamyah bashfully broke their gaze and picked up her menu.

Bryan smirked and then asked, "How was your lunch meeting?"

"As expected," she responded, offering nothing more.

For some time, they both watched as the evening tide came in until the waiter arrived to take their beverage and meal orders. After he left, Bryan asked, "How upset would you be if I brought in Mr. Barnes for questioning?"

Saamyah returned her gaze to the water and answered, "I want no part of it, Bryan, and you know that."

"I do, but I have information that makes you very much a part of it."

She turned her stare to him and inquired, "Bryan, why are you doing this?"

"Doing what? My job?"

"No, making me and my life your job."

"This isn't about you, Saamyah."

They both intensely held the other's eyes deciphering what to convey next. Bryan was the first to turn to watch the evening sun slowly set behind the ocean. Breaking the silence, he disclosed, "I only asked because it's the plan to bring him in for questioning before the end of the week."

Saamyah closed her eyes and took a deep breath. When she felt that she had contained her rage, Saamyah opened her eyes and reminded him, "It's Thursday, Bryan."

"I am telling you as a courtesy in the event that you want to be present."

"Wow," she breathed and then looked at him. "Your first week back and your level of civility has catapulted." She rose from her seat.

"Saamyah, please," Bryan beseeched, rising from his own seat. He extended his hand towards her.

"Don't," she ordered pushing it away. "You made your intent emphatically clear some time ago. Don't do me the favor now by including me." After tossing the rose on the table, she left him to dine alone.

*** *** ***

Patrick turned around at the calling of his full name. He watched as two men approached him in the grocery parking lot. "Detective Russell," he greeted, pushing his sunglasses to the top of his head. "Are you trailing me?"

"I am," Bryan plainly admitted.

Patrick eyed first the professionally dressed companion and then Bryan. "For what purpose?..Another showdown I hope."

Bryan laughed halfheartedly. "Not this time. I was actually hoping that you could explain this." He took a document out of the folder he held and pressed it into Patrick's chest.

Patrick took the paper, glimpsed at it, and gave it back to Bryan. He chuckled before saying, "You can't detain me on weak evidence like this; so, this must be your poor attempt to win Saamyah's affections."

"Not at all. I have actually won that already—multiple times, with the panties as proof." Bryan grinned then added with confidence, "And I must say that the sex is AMAZING…But you wouldn't know anything about that, now would you?"

Patrick's smile faded and he swung his fist. Bryan ducked and, with the aid of the accompanying detective, grabbed Patrick's arm, and twisted it behind his back.

"Weak evidence may not work, but assaulting an officer will," Bryan advised while he handcuffed him. He led Patrick to the unmarked vehicle as the second detective recited to him his Miranda rights.

Saamyah raced down to the interrogation rooms as soon as she learned of Patrick's arrival.

"Saamyah," Bryan called out to her when she turned the corner.

She completed an one-eighty, took a deep breath, and asked, "Where is he, Bryan?"

Bryan nodded in the direction of the first interrogation room then grabbed her arm before she had a chance to step to enter it. "Saamyah, wait."

"Don't touch me," she commanded, pulling from his grip.

Bryan raised his hands as to surrender. "Saamyah, you have to know that I found some very troubling evidence that involves you."

"What? What are you talking about?"

"I just think-"

The door to the room opened and a voice announced, "Russell, we're ready."

Saamyah brushed passed Bryan to enter first. A knot grew in her throat when she saw Patrick sitting at one side of the table. She caught his eyes, but only for a brief moment. He broke their gaze in repugnance.

"Are the cuffs necessary?" Saamyah asked no one in particular.

"Actually, Detective Cambell, they are," an uniformed officer responded. "He has already attempted an assault on Russell."

Saamyah's eyes burned into Bryan as she contemplated a stealth departure. When her curiosity bested her, she backed into a corner rather than step towards the exit. Feelings of unease rose in her as she awaited the start of the exhibition.

"Mr. Barnes, as previously stated you do have the right-" Bryan began.

"I know my rights," Patrick interjected, watching him walk towards the table.

Bryan nodded and took pictures out of the envelope that sat on the table and spread them in front of Patrick.

"Recognize any of these women?"

"What does this have to do with my assault charge?" Patrick asked.

"Just answer the question."

Without looking at the pictures, Patrick answered, "No."

"How could you if you don't bother to look."

Patrick peered at them and said nothing.

"These are some of the women you raped."

Patrick met his eyes and spoke, "You really are a shitty detective."

Snickers enveloped the room, but Bryan ignored them in an attempt to maintain his composure.

"Be that as it may," Bryan stated, "you still have not adequately answered the question."

Keeping his gaze, Patrick answered, "I do not recognize them."

Bryan shoved the photos aside in frustration and retorted, "Fine, let's move on to something you do recognize." He took the chair underneath the table, opposite of Patrick, and turned it so to sit in it backwards. After folding his arms on the back of the chair, he rested his chin on his forearm and requested, "Tell me about your twin brother."

Saamyah started toward Bryan, but an uniformed officer stopped her. "Bryan, what are you doing?" She called out to him.

Bryan ignored her and continued. "His name was David, right?"

"What do you know about my brother?"

"Well, I know that like Detective Cambell, he was an agent for The Federal Bureau of Investigations—a supervisory special agent at that."

"Bryan, stop this," Saamyah demanded.

"Cambell," Lieutenant Duncan called to silence her.

"Are you really going to let Russell carry on with this farce?" She asked in an accusatory tone. "His questions have nothing to do with our investigation."

Lieutenant Duncan gave her a glower that forewarned her removal if her outbursts did not cease.

Bryan continued, "In fact, they partnered at times." He paused. "Partners in work…and also partners in life—if we were to sum it all accurately."

Patrick did not respond.

"And how can we forget his tragic death?" Bryan paused searching Patrick's expressionless face. "…A death so tragic, so sudden…so heinously conspired by you."

"…What?" Saamyah whispered in dismay.

"Detective," an uniformed officer hushed her.

"You can't prove any of this," Patrick confidently stated.

"Actually, Mr. Barnes, I can." Bryan opened the second folder and spread the documents before him.

Patrick kept his glare on Bryan, refusing to lower his eyes to the several sheets of paper.

"It's amazing what time, a badge, and a little due diligence can uncover." Bryan smirked and then teased, "Not bad for a shitty detective, don't you think?"

"Get to the point, Russell," Lieutenant Duncan urged.

Bryan nodded and redirected, "They say blood is thicker than water, but, of course, that was until water was given the name Saamyah Anne Cambell…Two brothers in love with the same woman; do you care to elaborate on the family feud?"

Patrick smiled, but did not respond.

"It is your right not to talk, but why not use this opportunity to proclaim your innocence?"

"My brother was all that I had in this world. I did not kill him," Patrick simply stated.

"Of course you didn't. Someone else lit the match, but you first doused him in gasoline."

Patrick did not entertain the accusation.

"You're a man of few words today, Mr. Barnes. That is unlike you."

Patrick inhaled deeply and exhaled loudly as he rolled his eyes with contempt.

"The proposal—why did you do it? Cambell was already engaged to your brother."

Patrick grinned and knowingly shrugged. "She said no…So, no harm, no foul."

Bryan sneered at his haughty response. "Maybe, then again, maybe not. At the end of the day, David was still a man—a man that did not take too kindly to your action…Didn't he renounce you as his brother afterwards? I believe the exact words of my witness were that you were dead to him." He paused and finally asked, "Is that why you wanted him dead in return?"

Patrick leaned his body into the back of the chair and placed his cuffed hands in his lap. He inhaled deeply and exhaled loudly. "Are you finished?"

"Why did you do it?"

No response.

"I guess there are some things your heaps of money can't buy."

Patrick laughed half-heartedly and finally relented. "It got me here. Right here in front of you." He smirked and confessed, "I knew about you, Detective Bryan Terrell Russell. You, this department, all long before Saamyah accepted the keys to the condo she leased for the summer."

Unmoved by the revelation, Bryan replied, "I believe it. Money and people in high places can afford you quite a bit of information—even while in federal prison."

Patrick shrugged. "Time affords the opportunities to plan and to plot." He leaned forward and peered deep into Bryan's eyes and added, "Even if it's all for immoral and unethical gains."

Bryan stifled his anger at the innuendo, remembering that his superior officer was present in the room. "You mean plan your scour of women and plot to sexually assault them?"

Patrick slouched again in his chair and exhaled loudly in frustration at Bryan's continued false allegation.

"It's quite the parallel to the conspiracy to have your brother murdered."

Patrick snickered and met Bryan's glare with impassion. "As I mentioned earlier, you really are a shitty detective."

Bryan shrugged and responded, "That is merely a matter of opinion, just like the one circulating that there was a renegade among that task force."

He watched Patrick drop his gaze and nonchalantly finger the metal links of his handcuffs. "So, who was your informant?"

Patrick offered no response, so Bryan rephrased, "You could not have planned to murder your brother on your own. So, on the day of the undercover operation, who within that task force helped you?"

Patrick chuckled and finally replied, "All your degrees, training, and evidence and you still can't resolve the conundrum."

Bryan began to collect the pictures and documents and placed them in their respective folders. "Well, the evidence speaks for itself and it's enough to get a conspiracy to murder charge."

Bryan stood, turned the chair around, and pushed it under the table. He leaned forward and whispered in Patrick's ear, "Don't worry about Saamyah. I will gladly keep it tamed while you serve your mandatory minimum."

Patrick abruptly rose from his chair, knocking it over, and grabbed the collar of Bryan's shirt. He growled a slew of obscenities as they grappled with each other. Instinctively, uniformed officers rushed to separate them and Bryan was vigorously yanked from Patrick's grip.

Bryan adjusted his clothing, regained his composure, and taunted, "Enjoy your weekend in lockup," as he watched the uniformed men force Patrick back to his seat.

"You stupid son of a bitch!" Patrick called after Bryan when he turned to exit the room. He sneered then unveiled, "I did not devise the plan to kill my brother, you asshole…My brother and I devised the plan to kill her."

Bryan stopped at the door, released the handle, and turned to face Patrick. The appalling revelation caught his breath and the annoying laughter pierced his eardrums.

The tears that blurred Saamyah's vision finally fell from her eyes. She dabbed them, walked towards Patrick, and inquired, "Why?"

Saamyah stopped at the table that separated them and asked again, "Why?"

Patrick offered nothing but a smile.

"Why, damn it?!"

"…You were the wedge that was driving our family apart," he arrogantly confessed at last.

Saamyah slapped his face with all the pain of her past and misery of her present. "I HATE YOU!" She cried as she repeatedly struck him. "I hate you! I hate you!"

"Saamyah," Bryan spoke, racing to intercede. "Saamyah, stop." He held her from behind, lifted her off the ground, and carried her out of the room.

After Bryan placed her on her feet, she hurried to the nearest exit.

Several hours later, Bryan found Saamyah gazing out her office window. As per usual, she was racing the pendant across the chain around her neck.

Sensing Bryan's presence, Saamyah asked without facing him, "How long did you know about this?"

Bryan closed her door and walked towards her. "I didn't know that it was a ploy to kill you, Saamyah."

She turned to him and repeated, "How long?"

Bryan's heart dropped when he saw her red eyes and wet face. "I don't know. A few weeks maybe."

"And you couldn't tell me?"

"You wanted no part of it, remember?"

"Really? Is that your defense?!"

Bryan repressed his emotions realizing that Saamyah was the victim in her crumbling world and, at that moment, needed a friend and not another foe. He took a deep breath in an effort to calm himself and asked, "Saamyah, would you have believed me?"

She disregarded the question. "You still should have tried."

"I know," he conceded. "And I am so sorry." Bryan moved closer to wrap his arms around her waist. He held her as a new wave of cries overcame her.

"They wanted me dead, Bryan," she spoke, allowing the words to resonate within her.

Bryan gently took her face in his hands and said, "Not they, Saamyah, just Patrick…When you think about it, David couldn't go through with it. That's why he took the bullet…He died for you; he died loving you. Remember that. Always remember that." Returning his arms around her waist, he allowed her to rest on his chest and continue to cry.

Finally exhausted of tears, Saamyah lifted her head and wiped her eyes. She then wiped his shirt in an attempt to rid it of the faint traces of makeup. "I'm sorry about your shirt."

He shook his head. "Don't worry about it….How are you? Are you okay?"

"No, but I will be." She gently moved his arms from around her and walked to her to her desk and lowered herself in her seat. "You can't hold him, Bryan."

"I can until Monday."

"And then what? You pick another fight to drag him back in here on more trumped up charges?" She caught his eyes. "You didn't think O'Brien would tell me?" She asked referring to the fellow detective that accompanied Bryan in the pursuit of Patrick.

Bryan dropped his eyes, feeling convicted of his compromised police work. "We can hold him until word comes back from Texas…He is in violation of parole."

Saamyah huffed. "Don't bother. The conditions of his parole are lax…No charge will stick. He has too many high-powered people in his pocket." She sat in silence for a moment and contemplated just how far into Patrick's pocket was her brother, DeVaughn.

"Who is he, Saamyah?" Bryan inquired breaking the silence and her trance.

Saamyah looked at him, "What?"

"Patrick Barnes, who is he?"

She dropped her eyes, exhaled loudly, and said, "It's not so much who he is as it is who and what he knows."

Ignoring the *who*, Bryan asked, "Then what does he know?"

She shook her head and answered, "Evidently, too much."

After a long silence Bryan asked, "How about we get our minds off this work stuff and cash in on that rain check tonight?"

Saamyah shook her head. "No, I want to be alone."

"Come on," Bryan coaxed. "We can catch a movie or something. You shouldn't be alone after the day you had."

"Thanks, Bryan, but, no thanks." Saamyah met his eyes. "I need this; I need to be alone." She feebly smiled and added, "…Maybe another time."

Bryan nodded in concession and left her to be alone.

"Bryan, what are you doing?" Saamyah asked after she opened the door to her condo that evening.

He smiled brightly and held up the pizza box and bag of groceries. "I brought comfort food."

She exhaled loudly and said, "I thought you understood that I needed to be alone."

"Saamyah, come on. Do you really think that I would let you cope with this on your own?" When he noticed her red, swollen eyes, Bryan offered, "Invite me in and we can cry this out together."

Saamyah laughed off her discomfort and explained, "I am watching *My Girl*; everyone cries at the end of *My Girl*."

Bryan feigned his belief in the impact the classic movie had on her and replied with sarcasm, "That would explain the tears." He stepped past the threshold after she widened the door for him. "Wasn't sure if you were a popcorn or chips type of girl, so I bought both."

Saamyah shook her head and rolled her eyes at his defiance. "I will get the plates."

Over the meal he had purchased for them, Saamyah and Bryan sat on the floor, comfortable in their lounge wear. The muted television continued to display the new movie selection as they shared stories of their childhood.

"Are you serious?!" Saamyah exclaimed before choking on her water.

Bryan laughed and asked, "Are you alright?"

Saamyah nodded and coughed until her lungs were cleared. "My parents would have never let me get away with pouring Kool-Aid packets into the fish tank."

Bryan laughed again. "Well, my father was irate, but my mother interceded on my behalf. Had she not, I probably would have gotten the worst beating of my life." He pressed his back deeper into the seat of the sofa, looked at her, and confessed, "My mother actually faulted him for leaving a mischievous five-year-old boy unattended."

Saamyah shook her head and breathed incredulously, "Unbelievable." After she sipped from her water bottle, she taunted, "You're such a momma's boy."

Bryan reflected on his years as a young boy and admitted, "I can't deny that." He drank from his own bottle and recalled, "My sister loathed that about me."

"I can believe that, and can relate...I think that if I wasn't the youngest and the only girl, my brothers would have hated that about me, too. But, my father raised them to love and protect me." She exhaled and reminisced, "DeVaughn, Christian, and Trévion— my knights in shining armor, always protecting the precious princess."

Bryan snickered at the analogy. "So, you were a daddy's girl?"

Saamyah propped her folded arm on the seat of the sofa and rested her head in her hand. "I was everybody's girl... And everybody was my momma and my daddy."

Bryan nodded and grinned at her Texan accent that crept into the conversation now that she was exhausted by the late hour. "Must have been rough having so many to answer to."

Saamyah covered her yawn and then shrugged. "It had its perks."

"Really? Like what?"

Saamyah smiled and answered, "With three older brothers, the path to adulthood was not arduous for me...I always had a network of watchmen and forerunners that fought me. So, I never really had to fight for myself."

Bryan huffed at the entitlement. "Seems like more of a drawback than a perk to me."

Saamyah shrugged. "Maybe, or maybe it's the universe way of assuaging the pain caused by the loss of my parents. Either way, I never had to confront my own bully until the day I met you."

Bryan laughed. "I'm no bully."

She rolled her eyes and retorted with sarcasm, "Yeah, I know."

After another sip from her water bottle, Saamyah placed it on her coffee table in front of them. Gazing at Bryan, she murmured, "Thank you."

Searching her eyes, Bryan asked, "For what?...Leaving you alone?"

Saamyah chuckled. "Yes, for leaving me alone."

He lowered his eyes and answered, "No problem. It was the least I could do for the support you have given me." Bryan exhaled aloud and acknowledged, "I have you tightly woven into my web of a mess."

Bryan reflected on his crass comments spoken weeks earlier and laughed half-heartedly, "...And to think that I initially thought you needed my protection." He turned to her. "It is you who needs protection from me, or at the very least, I, who needs your protection."

Saamyah shrank the short distance between them and placed a hand on his cheek. "Keep nothing from me and I will do whatever I can to insulate you."

Bryan removed her hand from his cheek and moved it to his lips to kiss. "Thank you."

She lifted his chin with her finger and whispered, "You're welcome," before kissing him.

Bryan returned the kiss, allowing her warm tongue to enter his mouth. Her soft hand gently stroked his face and he instinctively pulled her closer. He heard a soft moan escape her when she moved to straddle his lap. Bryan's heart raced and swelled in his chest as she wrapped her arms around his neck and deepened their kiss. He felt her part their mouths only for air and, even then, she nibbled on his bottom lip to heighten his desire for her.

A cool chill rose in Saamyah's spine when felt Bryan hands drop to her hips and pull her closer to his pulsating member. She planted a trail of tantalizing kisses on his neck and listened as he breathed her name. Her hands slowly moved down his muscular chest and rippled abdomen to fumble with the drawstring of his lounge pants.

Bryan abruptly grabbed each of her wrists before her hands reached past his waistband. "Saamyah," he panted. "Saamyah, we can't do this."

Saamyah ignored his conscience and leaned to kiss him. Her heart sunk when he turned from her lips. "Don't you want me?" She asked searching his eyes for the truth.

"No...I mean yes." Bryan exhaled loudly as he tried to find the words that would accurately convey how he felt. "Not this way, Saamyah." He released her wrists and cupped her face. "I understand that you are hurting, but sex won't heal your heart...Trust me, it will only be a temporary fix." He finally added, "You will regret it and hate me in the morning."

Saamyah scanned his face and considered all that he had said—his summation was precise. In her own selfish desire to alleviate her pain, she was preparing to exploit Bryan for his infamous talent. The revelation of what she was becoming sickened her and incited a heartfelt cry. "I'm so sorry, Bryan."

"Shhhh," he silenced her. "It's okay." He took her in his arms and held her tightly as she rested on his shoulder and cried.

When Saamyah finally regained her bearings, she pushed back her hair and exhaled loudly.

Bryan wiped her eyes gently with the tail of his shirt. "Feel better?"

She smiled and said, "No."

Bryan rubbed her back. "Take your time getting through this, Saamyah. It's not every day that you learn that the man you loved wanted to take your life."

She rose to sit on the sofa and watched Bryan do the same. "How do you get over news like this?"

He stroked her hair and answered, "You redirect your focus from what could have happened to what didn't happen…You are still here, Saamyah, so you are the victor in all of this. And that is what you hold on to in the process of getting through this."

Fresh tears fell from her eyes. "I don't think I can, Bryan."

Bryan reclined into the back cushion and took her with him. After she rested her head on his chest, he kissed her forehead, and then continued to stroke her hair. "Yes, you can, Saamyah, and you will because you are one of the strongest women I know."

Saamyah sobbed until she fell asleep. Shortly after, Bryan drifted to sleep, too.

*** *** ***

Saamyah silently pleaded with her legs to walk her out of the interrogation room before the officer returned with her request. They not only stubbornly defied her, but grew weak beneath her weight forcing her to sit in a chair and await his arrival. She took a long, deep breath through her nostrils and exhaled slowly through her pursed lips. Despite calling upon her inner strength, just as her therapist taught her years ago, the small room closed in on Saamyah. Naturally, her mind stressed, body tensed, temperature rose, and skin flushed. She began to question if the closure she longed for was worth the hassle.

Patrick entered the room and was immediately astonished by Saamyah's presence. He grinned while slowly following the uniformed officer to his chair. He kept his eyes on her with each step.

"To what do I owe the pleasure of this visit?" Patrick mocked.

Saamyah watched him sit across the table from her. She searched his eyes for answers to questions she hesitated to ask. When all that was discovered was emptiness, she finally said, "I feel sorry for you."

"Don't be. I will be out of here sometime this week."

"It's not because you are in here, Patrick, because you belong here."

"And you came here on your Saturday to tell me this?"

She ignored his question and said, "Your malicious behavior tried to take me from your brother, but instead you took him from the both of us. THAT is why I feel sorry for you, Patrick."

Patrick laughed lightheartedly. "You give me far too much credit, Saamyah. You really do." He nonchalantly slouched into his chair. "...Do you really think I was cunning enough to meticulously plan your death? To conspire an entire U.C. op and use it as a ploy for your demise?" He paused to allow her to contemplate his inquiries before saying, "That was all David...He was the older brother, but also the weakest. His heart could handle more the pain of your death than the pain of your life with me."

Saamyah shook her head in disbelief. "You are lying."

"And you are naïve. Always have been and, quite possibly, always will be."

Saamyah dropped her gaze, knowing that his comment was somehow a slight to her idolization of her brother, DeVaughn. She struggled with the knot in her throat before finally swallowing it and spoke, "Okay, that explains his reason. What was yours?"

Rather than offer a simple answer, Patrick allowed a moment of silence to pass before responding, "There is a long time family dynamic, particularly among siblings, that surpasses all understanding. The younger is always trying to validate their worth and loyalty to the elder—even to extent of deceit, bribery, and lawlessness."

He observed her hands as she fidgeted with her fingers in distress then continued, "I'm sure you can relate, because, like you, I, too, idolized my brother…Basketball was what I was good at, but, in everything, David was *great*…He was everything I wanted to be and had everything I wanted to have—including you."

Patrick watched her slowly lift her eyes to meet his. In them, he saw the many nights David's career and/or exhaustion left them to entertain each other. He saw her heartbreak and Saamyah saw his disappointment each time life kept David from keeping several of their engagements. Saamyah was his support, and Patrick was her solace.

"You were the first woman to see me for who I really was. To you, I was more than fame and money," Patrick confessed.

Saamyah dropped her eyes to his hands that reached across the table to rest on hers. As his thumb caressed her fingers, he spoke, "I loved you more than life and eventually you became my life."

Saamyah recalled the evening of their late night dairy fix at a local creamery. She had a strawberry-banana nut, almond milkshake and he had two scoops of vanilla ice cream—always simple and straight to the point. Patrick had kissed her and confessed that he had fallen in love with her.

The memory swelled a chill in Saamyah's spine and she slid her hand from underneath his. "You misconstrued my affections."

"Did I?" Patrick asked, challenging her falsehood.

Saamyah did not answer, but instead reflected on how her affections may have unintentionally warranted the night he proposed to her. It was the same night his serendipitous half-court shot at the buzzer won the final game of the regular season. As per usual, the two of them were forced to celebrate without David. After dinner, but before dessert, Patrick had removed his brother's ring from her finger in hopes that she would wear the one that he had presented. Without answering, Saamyah exited the restaurant and left both requests for marriage on the table.

"David was no fool, Saamyah…You and I had something special and it pained him to know that he could never make you smile the way that I did…Every woman wants to feel like a priority to her man. I gave that to you; David didn't."

Saamyah opened her mouth to contest the assumption, but stopped when Patrick urged, "You were never as happy with him, Saamyah. I knew it; you knew it; he knew it. But before he'd lose you, he'd let me go…And he did just that."

Refusing blame for the demise of their familial relationship, Saamyah retorted, "Your prescription abuse was the wedge between you—not me."

Patrick smiled feebly and confirmed, "Yes, and you were the drug of choice."

Saamyah huffed at his quip then finally admitted, "Yes, I loved you both, but I was in love with David. I wanted a life with him."

"No, it was the life that Dr. Cambell reluctantly approved you to have," Patrick corrected.

"Yes…Yes, it was," she conceded, lacking the energy to disabuse him of his erroneous belief. "My brother knew all too well what a life of fame and money had done to you and he did not want that for me…He did not want a life of sex, drugs, alcohol, and abuse for me."

"Putting the carriage before the horse, aren't you?"

Saamyah squint her eyes in confusion. "What does that even mean?"

"It means that the very thing that the good doctor was trying to keep you from, he was continually perpetuating."

Saamyah huffed again, this time at his convoluted statement. "You so desperately want me to loathe my brother. But my hating him will not make me love you."

Patrick licked his lips and watched her. He pondered heaving the veil from her eyes, but decided against it. She needed time to recover from the current heartache.

He finally answered her initial question, "My brother was everything to me and I would have done anything to get back in his good graces. We had a strong, special bond and you, Saamyah, had weakened it. I wanted it back. I wanted him back…Even if it meant killing the woman I loved."

"…That's not love, Patrick," Saamyah protested. "Love wouldn't have allowed you to go through with it."

At her dismissal of his genuine feelings for her, Patrick nodded, stood, and then said, "Well, I guess in his death my brother proved that he was the one who loved you the most."

He exited the room with the guard following behind him.

*** FIVE ***

At the onset of another work week, Saamyah stood at her office window racing her pendant at her neck. The Sunday drive up the coast had done nothing for her restless mind. She still found herself reliving the conversation she had with Patrick.

"Saamyah," Bryan interrupted after opening his office door. "Can you take a look…" His voice trailed off when he noticed her at the window non-responsive. He dropped the folder on her desk and walked to stand behind her. "Saamyah, what's wrong?"

"I went to go see him," she answered in a whisper without breaking her gaze.

Though he yearned to, Bryan refrained from asking her a series of when's and why's. Instead, he asked, "What happened?

"He told me everything." She dropped her pendant and folded her arms across her breasts. "…And it's true; they both wanted me dead… But it was David who conspired it."

Bryan's heart dropped and ached for her. He wrapped his arms around her waist and held her tight. "Saamyah, I am so sorry."

"…Yeah, me, too…" She dropped her arms and turned to face him. "So, what is it that you want me to take a look at?"

"Don't worry about it. I can figure it out."

Saamyah nodded and then recalled his earlier voice message. "I was off the grid yesterday, but I did get your message last night about Torrie Daniels." She searched his eyes for all that he had omitted in the message.

Bryan exhaled slowly, "Yeah, I was going to catch you up on everything later."

She shrugged. "Tell me now. What's her status?"

"I don't know…Based on the medical report, he really did a number on her."

She dropped her eyes and nodded. That was not the answer she was hoping for. "Is she one of yours?"

Bryan hesitated, but finally answered, "…I do know her, yes."

Saamyah rubbed her forehead in frustration and exhaled aloud. She stepped out of his personal space to walk to the whiteboard. She recorded the new victim's name and commented, "He is escalating."

Bryan walked and stood next to her.

"And HE is not Patrick," Saamyah knowingly remarked.

Bryan conceded, "…I was wrong."

Saamyah looked at him, "You were…and you made a mess of my life in the process." She started toward her desk, but stopped when Bryan grabbed her arm.

"What do you want me to say, Saamyah?...That I'm sorry?"

She twisted out of his grip. "For starters, yes. That would be nice."

"Fine, I'm sorry…I'm sorry for doing my job and that you had to find out the truth about your past while I did it."

Saamyah scoffed at his sarcasm and continued behind her desk. She sat and began typing at the keys of her laptop.

Bryan regretted his smug comment, but refused to apologize for it. Instead, he offered, "Okay. Look, we are obviously getting nowhere. How about we take a moment to allow cooler heads to prevail?"

"We need Kimberly James to talk," Saamyah stated, disregarding his question.

"We've tried that, Saamyah…She is not talking."

Saamyah looked at him. "Then get her to talk."

"And how do you suppose I do that?"

Saamyah shrugged. "I don't know. How do you typically get what you want from women?"

Her words stung and for a moment all that Bryan could reply was, "Wow." He turned to walk out her office, but changed his mind and faced her again. "Okay. Did I say or do something wrong here?"

"Where were you this weekend?" Saamyah simply asked.

"What?"

"Where. Were. You. This. Weekend?" She repeated.

"So, we are back to this now?"

"Just answer the question."

"In The Keys with my family for a belated Father's Day trip...Do you want to speak with my parents and sister to confirm my alibi?"

Saamyah returned her gaze to her laptop and started typing again. "Just get Kimberly to talk."

"Oh, I will." He walked to her desk and leaned forward on his hands. "And just so we are clear, sweetheart, I am going to do *whatever* it takes to get the job done."

They sat in the waiting room in silence awaiting the physician's return. The unexpected call that Torrie Daniels was conscious and willing to make a statement shifted their afternoon plans.

Saamyah smiled at the toddler across the room that was enamored by his mother's animated faces.

"Did you and Rachel want children?"

Bryan looked at her as she continued to look at the child. "We did."

Saamyah nodded and smiled at the child's laughter.

"Do you?" Bryan asked.

Saamyah felt his eyes still on her and she finally turned to meet them. "I do."

"You'd be a great mother."

"Thank you."

The physician returned, granting them permission to see her patient. Saamyah stood first and they both followed her to Torrie's room.

"Please rest, Ms. Daniels," Saamyah encouraged when Torrie attempted to sit-up from her reclined position. She privately winced at Torrie's beautiful bronzed complexion now blemished with orange knots, purple bruises, and red cuts. Despite her best efforts to use her long, brown hair as a veil, Saamyah could still see her swollen jaw, blackened eye, and busted lip.

"Detective," Torrie greeted Saamyah. She then finger combed her hair when she saw Bryan. "Bryan," she acknowledged.

"Hello, Torrie," Bryan said, walking to take a seat on the bed. He leaned over to kiss Torrie on the top of her head. "You're looking as beautiful as the day we met."

Torrie shook her head and rolled her eyes. She looked at Saamyah and said, "He's such a beautiful liar."

Saamyah raised her brows and smiled. "I will keep that in mind." Keeping the gaze that the two of them shared, Saamyah asked, "How are you feeling?"

Torrie shrugged. "A lot better than I look, I guess...Thanks to the morphine..."

Bryan took her hand in his and asked, "What happened to you?"

Torrie dropped her head and tears fell from her eyes as she unhurriedly recounted her experience. The café she owned just off the boardwalk had just closed for the evening. She had urged all her employees to immediately depart to enjoy the final hours of the beach barbeque and bonfire. Torrie recalled that she was in her office tallying the day's sales when she heard a stir in one of the restrooms. Upon entering, she was attacked and awoke later in the hospital.

Bryan gently wiped her tears from her swollen face. Guilt overwhelmed him and he could not help but whisper, "I'm so sorry that this happened to you."

Saamyah cleared her throat in an effort to disrupt their intimate exchange that straddled the fence of ethical professionalism. "Ms. Daniels, I know that this is very difficult for you, but, if you can, can you tell us anything distinguishing about your attacker?"

A pregnant silence grew in the room as Torrie contemplated an answer. The perpetrator had no skin complexion, no hair color, no distinguishing voice, but he did have, "...His cologne..."

"His cologne," Saamyah repeated.

"Yes, his cologne. I still feel it burning in my nostrils from my fight to get free of him."

Saamyah exhaled loudly with relief by the olive branch given to them and she silently thanked God.

Bryan understood Saamyah's respire and encouraged Torrie to elaborate. "Do you happen to know the name or what it smelled like?"

Torrie shook her head. "No, but it's definitely something that I have smelled before." She met his eyes. "It...It was...a very light, fresh, clean scent."

Recalling on her knowledge of how trauma heighten the senses, Saamyah asked, "Would you recognize it if you smelled it again?"

Torrie nodded. "I believe so. Yes."

Saamyah caught Bryan's eye, but he was the first to break the stare. He gently wiped Torrie's eyes with one hand and held her hand with the other. "We're going to need your help with capturing this perp, Torrie. Can we count on you?"

Torrie nodded. "Whatever you need me to do."

Bryan thanked her and kissed her forehead.

"Thank you so much for speaking with us, Ms. Daniels. We'll be in touch."

Bryan rose from the bed and slowly followed Saamyah out of the room.

Inside the elevator, Bryan waited for the doors to close before asking, "So, what do you think?"

Without looking at him, Saamyah responded, "Outside the obvious?"

Bryan looked at her. "Obvious?"

"That you are too close."

"Well, in all fairness, I do closely know these women, Saamyah," Bryan retorted.

Saamyah matched is glare. "Yes, you do and that is becoming more painfully obvious with each new victim."

Bryan turned his face from her in frustration. "...And the not so obvious?"

"You are a man who doesn't date outside the box."

Confused, Bryan looked at her and asked, "What?"

"You exclusively date the supermodel type," she stated another way. "There are women less plastic who are worth your pursuit."

"Women like who? You?"

Saamyah did not answer.

"Take a look around, Saamyah, we are in Miami. Over ninety percent of the female population here are the supermodel type—plastic or not." He wanted to continue, but a group of physicians and their interns stepped into the elevator.

Once they arrived to their floor, Saamyah was the first to step off and she quickly walked to the exit. Outside, Bryan stepped and stopped in front of her, making it impossible for her to walk around.

"Yes, I admit that I am superficial," Bryan began. "I date women of a certain caliber, but it's what I like. And, yes, it may be wrong to some people, but least I am honest with myself." He turned to continue the walk to his unmarked vehicle.

Saamyah hurried to meet his step and pulled him around to face her. "What the hell is that supposed to mean? That you're honest with yourself?"

He pushed her hand off him. "You know what it means, Saamyah."

Saamyah scoffed. "You think I am lying to myself because I am not groveling over you?"

"This isn't about me, Saamyah." He paused to ponder the repercussions of revealing what he learned by observing her interactions with Patrick. Despite the blowback, he opened Pandora's Box. "This is about you and your history of poor choices."

"What are you talking about?"

"I am talking about you choosing David to wed when you knew you would have been happiest spending your life with Patrick. Your heart bled for him, hell, it still bleeds for him. So, the heartaches, betrayals, and bloodshed could have been all avoided had you just chose him…So, if you want to judge, let the judgment start with yourself."

Saamyah stared at Bryan with fiery derision. His assessment of her history fell like a ton of brinks on her recovering ego. At that moment, she realized that she had been throwing stones from the inside of her glass house—a skill she had learned and perfected from her eldest brother.

Bryan closed his eyes with regret no longer able to witness the agonizing impact his words had on her. He felt her body brush against him as she walked around to continue the journey to the car. Rather than have her wait for his arrival, he unlocked the car with the key fob, and watched her climb into the passenger seat.

Once behind the wheel, Bryan put the key in the ignition and started the engine to allow the cool air to circulate out the sweltering heat. Still in park, they both sat inside the vehicle—motionless and silent.

Bryan was the first to speak. "Saamyah-"

"Don't," Saamyah interjected. She looked at him. "Our discord all day has been my fault, so don't apologize for calling me out on it."

Bryan nodded, placed the car in drive, and began maneuvering out of the parking lot into the traffic that led back to the office.

"I think we should start with you," Saamyah announced, breaking another moment of silence that settled in the car.

Frustrated with the afternoon traffic, Bryan placed his elbow on the door and rested his head on his hand. The other hand held the wheel.

"What do you mean?" He asked while slowing to a stop at a red traffic light.

"This perp is no amateur. For whatever reason, he has spent a great deal of time concocting this case against you…If his agenda is to convict you by feigning to be you, then, presumably, he would smell like you."

Bryan lifted his head and dropped his arm from the door. He looked at her and lauded, "You're a genius."

"So I have been told."

Bryan ignored the opportunity for playful banter and, instead, forewarned, "We do have our work cut out for us. I have a rather large collection."

Saamyah shook her head and rolled her eyes. "Please, you don't have that much cologne."

*** *** ***

Saamyah stood when Bryan struggled to enter her office with a banker's box.

"Bryan, what are you doing?" She asked apprehensive of his response.

Bryan kicked her door closed behind him and stumbled to her desk. He dropped the heavy box in front of her.

"Morning to you, too."

Saamyah ignored his greeting and raised the lid off the box. "What the…Please, Bryan, tell me this isn't-"

His nod answered her inquiry before she could complete the question.

Saamyah dropped the lid on the box and lowered into her chair. "I can't believe this...How does one man come to acquire that many bottles of cologne?"

"I told you we had our work cut out."

Saamyah shook her head in dismay. "There are over fifty bottles in there."

Leaning to rest her back in the chair, Saamyah folded her arms across her chest and sat quietly. She felt his eyes on her, but avoided them so as to think her way through their dilemma.

"Which of these do you wear often?" Saamyah asked standing to her feet.

"I rotate them."

Saamyah looked at him, rolled her eyes, and began scanning the box. She lifted and replaced one bottle after the other while reading the labels aloud, "Gucci, CK One, Usher, Sean Jean, Perry Ellis, Burberry, Cartier, Ralph Lauren, Giorgio Ar-"

"That's a favorite."

She set the bottle aside and asked in frustration, "Bryan, who buys this much cologne?"

Bryan shrugged and simply answered, "Women."

Saamyah huffed. "...You and your women."

"Not again. Don't do this, Saamyah. I am not the enemy here."

"No, Bryan, you're not, but you might as well be."

Aggravated, Bryan exhaled and yielded to her unrelenting attack. "It's disappointing to know that you feel that way, but since we going to take it there again why don't you just put everything out on the table."

Though she tailored her temper, Saamyah allowed her eyes to burn into him as she spoke, "I really hope that you've learned from this Bryan because a lot of innocent women are paying the price for your mistake—whatever that mistake may be."

Bryan swallowed the knot in his throat and turned to walk to his office, but thought against it and turned back to face Saamyah. "Contrary to what you may believe, I didn't want this, Saamyah...and if I had known then what I know now, then I would have changed a million things to keep this from ever happening."

Ignoring his contrition, Saamyah looked down at the box and nudged it towards him. "Start pulling out all your favorites."

"I will start with something even better...Come on," Bryan commanded, walking towards her office door.

"Where are we going?"

"To pay Ms. James a visit."

"Kimberly James," Bryan saluted, walking in on her photo-shoot.

Kimberly turned in the direction of the familiar voice. "This is a private set. How did you get past security?"

"With a badge and a gun," Bryan answered with a knowingly smile.

Kimberly looked at Saamyah. "There is a reason why I didn't return any of your calls." She turned to her models and proceeded to take their pictures.

"Kim, don't be that way," Bryan protested. "I came all this way to show Detective Cambell the beauty on the other side of the lens. The very least you can do is show her that we Miami natives are not all plastic—that some of us have bleeding hearts and intellectual minds."

Saamyah glared at Bryan. He shrugged and chuckled. "Just a little late morning humor."

Neither Saamyah nor Kimberly laughed.

"I have nothing more to tell you," Kimberly affirmed.

"Ms. James, please," Saamyah pleaded. "Just give us five minutes of your time."

Kimberly lowered her camera from her eyes in annoyance. "Take five, everyone," she ordered. She looked at Bryan then Saamyah and said, "You've got five minutes."

Kimberly walked towards her office, extending her camera to her assistant en route. Once Bryan and Saamyah were in the room, she closed the door, walked to her glass desk, and lightly rested on the corner. Kimberly offered them no seat so Bryan and Saamyah stood. Bryan stood the closest to her.

Different from the first time they met, Kimberly wore a black, belted shirtdress that Saamyah admired. It fit her form well and the black pumps on her feet complimented the ensemble.

Kimberly flipped her hair over her shoulder and crossed her arms over her breasts. "So, what do you want?"

"Can you recall if the man who attacked you wore a particular fragrance?" Saamyah candidly asked.

Kimberly thought for a moment, shrugged, and then replied, "I don't know. I tried to force that day out of my mind."

"Well, can you try to recall?" Saamyah encouraged.

Exasperated, Kimberly made an effort to recollect anything that would expedite an end to their meeting. "...Yes," she finally admitted. "...Yes, I can recall."

"Can you recall the scent?" Bryan urged.

Kimberly pondered the question and the name of the scent. When the fragrance resonated, she met Bryan's eyes. "...What did you do, Bryan?"

When Bryan offered no response, Kimberly allowed the pieces of the puzzle to forge themselves in her mind. She shook her head in dismay, "I know you—you're no rapist, but you did something...and now I'm a target. Aren't I? We all have been." She looked at Saamyah for confirmation, but received none.

"Ms. James-" Saamyah started.

"DON'T YOU DARE Ms. James, me. I have a right to know! WE ALL have a right to know!" Kimberly breathed deeply to calm herself before she returned her glare to Bryan and answered, "It's the fucking cologne that I bought you."

By her tone, Bryan discerned that her anger derived from a place deeper and darker than her victimization. Kimberly was still disgruntled about their past. She had loved him immensely and he had not reciprocated it at all.

The office fell silent as they awaited a response from Bryan. When none came, Saamyah pleaded, "Could you help us by being more specific?"

Kimberly laughed halfheartedly at the question that suggested Bryan had been gifted several scents. She dropped her arms, caught Bryan's eyes again, and confessed, "You never changing is the one thing I could always count on." She rose from the desk, brushed past Saamyah, and opened the office door to signify that their time had expired. "Good luck with your case."

"Ms. James, plea-" Saamyah beseeched.

"I'll call you if the name comes to mind, Detective," Kimberly interrupted.

With nothing left to say, Saamyah walked out of the office and Bryan followed.

In the vehicle, Saamyah gawked out the window as Bryan took the scenic route back to the police department to avoid traffic.

"I know she is lying," Saamyah confessed, disrupting the silence in the car.

Bryan did not respond.

She looked at him and asked, "Why do you think she is doing this?"

Bryan shrugged. "I don't know, Saamyah. Like you, Kimberly is a very complicated woman."

Saamyah sprayed another bottle of Bryan's favorites and smelled the scent. "Wow, this one is really nice." She placed the bottle on her desk next to the others that she believed did not fit the light, fresh, clean scent description.

Sitting in one of the chairs on the opposite side of her desk, Bryan looked up from the list he was reading. "Wait a minute," Bryan objected, flipping through his notes. "Here it says that Marc Jacobs has a green-woodsy scent. That can constitute as fresh."

Saamyah disagreed. "It's too spicy."

Bryan crossed Marc Jacobs off the list and reached into the box for the next scent. He was more than relieved to find it empty. Bryan removed the box from the desk, placed it on the floor, and commenced to putting the scents of no use to them back in it.

Saamyah deeply inhaled, for the final time, the scent emanating from the coffee beans, then slouched in her chair. "Thank God we are done. I don't think my sinuses could take another sniff of anything."

Bryan concurred. "At least now we have reduced the number down to seventeen scents."

Saamyah exhaled loudly. "Yeah, give or take a margin of error of about seventeen scents."

Bryan looked at his watch. It was a little after five that evening. "Should we head over to the hospital? We still have about two hours before visiting hours end."

Saamyah shook her head. "Tomorrow's another day. Let's try then."

"I wish there was a way that we could track past sales of the local merchants," Bryan thought out loud.

"That's highly unlikely. Especially with today's technology and skyrocketing internet sales, any one of these could have been purchased online."

"…That's true…Maybe future sales. Torrie can narrow this list and then we can request that store managers keep a log of sales and contact us if any of the scents are purchased."

"This is assuming that the perpetrator makes another purchase," Saamyah reasoned, thwarting his desperate logic. "A bottle of cologne can last for some time even with everyday use."

Bryan exhaled in disappointed frustration. He was anxious for an end to this nightmare, but was absent ideas to bring the end to fruition. "Look, I know that that was a shot in the dark, but it beats burning the candle on both ends and achieving nothing."

Saamyah nodded in concession and wrote herself a reminder in her daily record. "I will ask a few of the officers to help with this so that we can cover more ground." She tossed her pen in the book and then surveyed Bryan. "May I ask you something?"

"If I say no, will you ask anyway?"

"Of course."

"Then why ask for permission?"

Saamyah smiled. "To be courteous."

Bryan rolled his eyes and begrudgingly directed, "Ask me."

"The answer to Kimberly's question, do you know it?"

Bryan shook his head, "Nope, but something tells me you already knew that answer."

"Well, I didn't want to assume…You know what they say about those who do."

"So, now answer my question. What are you doing on Thursday?" He inquired without giving her an opportunity to decline being asked a question.

Saamyah shrugged, "The usual—work. Why?"

"I would like you to accompany me to a cookout."

Bewildered, she asked, "A cookout for what?"

The look he gave her was uncanny. "Are you kidding me?...For Independence Day."

Astonished at how time had quickly passed, Saamyah flipped through the pages of her daily record to confirm the upcoming July 4th's date. She laughed at herself and said, "I can't believe I forgot."

"All the more reason you need to come. You are all work and no play."

"Well, in all fairness, Bryan, the purpose of this temporary duty assignment is to work—not play."

"No," he rebutted, "the purpose of the TDY is to expose you to all that MDPD encompasses, including social events that strengthen the fraternal bond between officers."

Saamyah was speechless by the legitimacy of his argument. She could not contest that, since her tour in Miami, she had not made much effort to acquaint herself with the LEOs of the department. She needed to improve on her efforts, but not necessarily then, and certainly not with him.

"Bryan, I really won't feel up to it."

"Today is Tuesday. How do you know how you will feel on Thursday?"

She started to answer, but Bryan interjected, "It's one day and it will do you some good to do something non-work related."

Again, Saamyah opened her mouth to protest, but Bryan added, "You'll enjoy it. My friends host these throughout the year and I always have a great time…Please. I don't want to go to this one alone…Plus, an appearance together can only help our case."

Saamyah rolled her eyes and conceded in a grumble, "Fine."

Bryan smiled and sang, "Thank you."

"You're welcome…Speaking of appearances, tomorrow, I was thinking…"

*** *** ***

"This truly is testing the bounds of my commitment to the job," Saamyah muttered to Bryan as she climbed out the driver's side of her government ride. She walked to the trunk to collect her beach bag. "Whose idea was this again?"

Bryan lowered his lips to her cheek, kissed it, and then whispered in her ear, "Yours, my love."

Saamyah yanked the trunk closed feeling regretful of her plan to serve herself as bait. As she began her stroll toward the sand, Saamyah speculated that Bryan would spare no sexual advance for the sake of their undercover operation.

"It is moments like this that makes my job worthwhile," Bryan breathed after he pulled his shades down to the bridge of his nose to take in the panoramic view of Miami Beach's finest.

Saamyah rolled her eyes and sucked her teeth. "Don't be a pig."

Bryan pushed his shades back up the bridge of his nose. "Sweetheart, you know I only have eyes for you."

"Sure." She stopped in the sand and lowered her items into it. "This seems like a nice spot to set up shop."

Bryan stopped and looked around. "I couldn't agree more."

"Eyes on me, Casanova."

Bryan laughed. "I think I deserve a little eye candy considering."

Saamyah pulled her hair into a ponytail and kicked off her sandals. "Considering what?"

Bryan watched her strip down to her bathing suit. "Considering I have been abstinent since the inception of this ruse."

Saamyah smirked. "And I bet that is just killing you."

Bryan admired the chocolate two-piece on her caramel complexion. "You have no idea."

"Well, for what it's worth, I am proud of you."

Feeling appreciated, Bryan tested the waters by saying, "A kiss would show me just how much."

"Hold your breath on it," she directed. "…I am going in the water for a bit. Please inform security of our arrival and confirm the tower we are near."

Bryan watched her walk and dive into the water. He continued to watch until she swam out of view. He then scrutinized his surroundings, cautious of becoming too paranoid of childish horseplay. After radioing their position, Bryan sat down on a towel, kicked off his sandals, and buried his feet into the warm sand. Committed to the cause, he fought temptation and ignored the flirting women that walked by. In doing so, he chuckled at himself and the respect he recognized he had developed for Saamyah.

Moments later, he removed his sunglasses for a clearer vision of Saamyah emerging from the water. Resembling the supermodel type she despised, Saamyah gracefully adjusted her bathing suit and slowly walked towards Bryan. His heart raced with anxiety and he grew jealous of the stares and whistles she received.

"What's wrong, Bryan?" She asked while grabbing her towel and patting herself dry.

He placed his shades back on his face, shook his head, and lied, "Nothing."

Saamyah laid a second towel in the sand and sat next to him. She tossed him a bottle of water and drank from the one she had for herself. "You should go for a swim. The water is amazing."

Bryan drank from his bottle. "You don't say."

She sensed his aggravation, but did not want to inquire more about what vexed him. Prior years with her brothers had taught Saamyah that, despite their strength, men, too, were emotionally weak. Such learning compelled her to allow Bryan the time he needed to be human.

The penetrative sunrays that heated the flesh of her forearm reminded Saamyah of skin protection. She retrieved sunscreen from her beach bag and proceeded to reapply a generous amount to her body. The oils in the natural product made her skin glisten and the onlookers showed their gratitude with whistles and howls.

Bryan shook his head. "Do they not see me here?"

Saamyah looked at him and laughed. "In this dog-eat-dog world people, are always looking for upgrades. It's called the 21st century, Bryan, welcome to it."

"Pathetic is what it is," he commented before drinking from his bottle.

"Hey, ma," a young male from a walking group called out to Saamyah. "How about you lose the chicken dinner and get with a real winner?"

Saamyah smirked and replied, "I happen to love chicken." She turned Bryan's face to her and kissed him until their audience left. He tried to pull her closer, but she gently pressed him away. "Slow down cowboy, the show's over now."

Bryan bit his bottom lip, tasting the salt from hers. His racing heart slowed and then melted when he peered into her eyes. Unexpectedly, a familiar feeling—not felt since the death of his wife— roused in the pit of his belly. Unsure of what to do with the newfound possession, he turned from her soft eyes and murmured, "I'm going to go for a swim."

"Okay," Saamyah acknowledged.

Bryan stood, removed his sunglasses, and shed the layers that covered his blue, black, and white swim trunks. He walked towards the ocean giving no second looks to the women he passed. Once in the water, he swam until his lungs ached and muscles burned. Despite his heart feeling as if it could not pump anymore blood to his limbs, Bryan propelled himself farther—farther away from her and the emotions she was making him feel…Feeling anything was not a part of his initial plan.

After swimming more than a hundred yards out, Bryan stopped to tread water. He took deep meditative breaths to aid his effort to refocus. When his second wind came, he slowly made his way back to shore.

"Are you okay?" Saamyah asked after he stretched out tiredly on his towel.

"I'm fine." Bryan grumbled.

"For a minute there I thought you were going to swim your way to The Keys."

"If I did, it still wouldn't be far enough," he said under his breath.

Hearing him, Saamyah asked, "Far away from what?"

Bryan did not bother to answer. Instead he closed his eyes and soaked in the Vitamin D of the late afternoon sun.

Saamyah did not press him for a response. Instead, she looked on all that was occurring around her, allowing her mind to drift. Thoughts of David, thoughts of Patrick, and thoughts of DeVaughn took her back to the place that therapy had helped her flee...

David was a special agent scouting his alma mater, University of Texas at San Antonio, for new recruits. He had introduced himself to Saamyah while at the career fair her final year in graduate school. She and David had been in touch up until his death. Patrick, also an UTSA alumnus, opted for a semi-professional athletic career while he steadily recovered from the loss of David's and his father. Saamyah was formally introduced to him at a game to which she had accompanied David. Several games following that introduction, Patrick was injured and his transition into the professional league was postponed indefinitely. Arthroscopic surgery brought him to the office of Dr. DeVaughn R. Cambell. DeVaughn was-

Saamyah immediately took back control of her wandering mind. She was not ready to delve deep into the dark unknowns of her family history. Among them was the truth—quite possibly the criminal truth—and she was not psychologically prepared to confront it.

Saamyah glanced at her watch and was astounded by how quickly an hour had passed. She began to repack her beach bag.

"Where are you going?" Bryan asked opening his eyes.

"I need to go and get some of this salt off my face. I'm starting to feel a little dry." She stood and dressed herself.

He sat up. "Wait. I will come with you."

Saamyah laughed. "I am capable of getting to the restroom and back on my own, Bryan."

"I know. I just want to make sure that you do safely."

Saamyah did not bother arguing with a comment like that. Instead, she watched him towel off and dress himself. As she gawked, Saamyah reveled in God's perfect image of Himself.

"Ready?" She asked in defense when he caught her embarrassingly staring at his fit, muscular body.

He stretched his hand toward the boardwalk. "Lead the way."

In the large restroom, Saamyah dropped her bag under a sink and splashed cool water on her face and neck several times. She then peered at herself in the mirror and loathed what the pressures of the case had done to her youthful appearance. After drenching her face again, she watched each drop of water take with it down the drain a portion of her stress, worries, and fears. For a spell, she felt rejuvenated.

Interrupting her fleeting moment of tranquility, a faint moan escaped a stall and it startled her. Saamyah turned off the rushing water and listened tentatively. She heard the noise again, this time with movement.

"Hello?" Saamyah asked, grabbing several paper towels to pat her face dry. En route to trash them, she checked under the stall doors. They were empty.

"Is someone in here?"

No response.

"Hello?"

A muffled sound sent her quickly shuffling for her firearm in her bag. With her heart pounding in her throat, she walked to the first stall and pushed the door open. Nothing. She walked over to the next and did the same. Still nothing. The muffled groans grew louder as she made her way to the end of the row. At the handicapped stall, Saamyah tried to push it open, but it was locked. She braced herself for what was on the other side of the door, kicked it open, and stepped in.

The naked, teenage culprits jumped at the sight of Saamyah and her weapon.

"Geez, you guys!" Saamyah yelled, covering her eyes, turning her head, and lowering her firearm. "You didn't hear me come in?"

"No, ma'am." They answered in unison trying their best to cover their bare bodies with their hands.

Saamyah looked at their scared, pale faces. "Get dressed and get out of here."

"Yes, ma'am." They stammered as they scrambled for their clothes.

Saamyah walked out of the stall and exhaled loudly. She grabbed her bag, shoved her weapon in it, and walked out to see Bryan waiting for her.

Bryan saw the distressed look on her face. "Saamyah, what's wrong?"

She shook her head, rolled her eyes, and answered, "Teenagers having sex in one of the stalls."

Bryan exploded with laughter.

"It's not funny, Bryan," she contested. "I drew my firearm."

"What?!"

The door swung open and the two scared culprits scurried past them.

Saamyah watched them rush away hand-in-hand and then turned to Bryan. "I heard noises and thought that…"

Bryan smiled and mocked her, "Noises, what noises?"

Saamyah pushed him. "Considering the reason why we are here, I thought she was in danger."

Bryan took her bag, wrapped his arm around her neck and hugged her. He planted a kiss on her temple, walked her towards an ice cream vendor, and jested, "Well, I am sure their parents will thank you for your public service. It will probably be a while before the two of them have sex again."

"Ha ha."

"So, what's your flavor?" Bryan asked.

"Pralines and cream."

"That sounds good." He looked at the adolescent working the station. "We'll have double scoops of that on two cones."

Bryan paid the merchant and waited for his change and then cones. He shoved the money in his cargo shorts and handed Saamyah her cone.

She flashed him a childish grin. "Thank you."

"You're welcome," he replied, before indulging in his sweet treat as they walked away.

"EXCUSE US...EXCUSE US!" Shouted skateboarders that raced up the boardwalk behind Saamyah and Bryan.

"Fuck!" Bryan hollered after he dropped his cone when he was abruptly forced into the sand.

"Are you okay?" Saamyah asked, snickering as she helped him wipe the liquid from his clothes.

"Why aren't those damn kids in school?"

"It's the start of July, Bryan. They are on summer break." She picked up his cone and tossed it in a nearby trash can. "Don't worry though. In two months you will get your peace back. They'll be back in school and I'll be back in Texas," Saamyah joked.

For Bryan, the conversation had gone from lighthearted to serious. He had become so incredibly comfortable with Saamyah's presence, that he had forgotten that it was only temporary.

"Do you want another cone?" She asked.

"No, I'm fine," he simply answered.

"Do you want some of mine?" She teased.

Bryan smiled and shook his head. "It's after six. Do you want to head back to the office?"

She swallowed the crushed pecan she had in her mouth before saying, "Sure. Just let me tell security that we are leaving."

*** *** ***

Bryan regained consciousness and made an attempt to rise to his feet. A powerful kick to his abdomen sent him collapsing back to the floor. The blows that followed quickly reminded him of his capture before he blacked out. When the beating finally ceased, he laid in a fetal position, coughing up blood.

"Get him up," a voice commanded.

Bryan groaned in misery when the men pulled him to his knees. He lifted his head and saw Patrick standing in front of him.

"Welcome to my release party," Patrick greeted with a huge smile on his face.

"How many does this one make it?" Bryan asked also with a grin.

Patrick punched him in the abdomen and watched Bryan hunch in pain. He coughed more blood.

"Bring her out," Patrick ordered.

They awaited Saamyah's stumble into the room, she was wearing pajama pants and a racer-back tank top. Immediately, Bryan grew delirious with anger at the mere sight of her. Saamyah's red eyes and damp face burned him.

"You sick son of a bitch!" Bryan growled at Patrick. "If you touch her, I will kill you! You hear me? I will kill you!"

Patrick laughed. "Please, shut him up."

A hard fist impacted his face and Bryan fell again to the floor.

"Bryan!" Saamyah yelled, attempting to run to his aid, but Patrick stopped her.

"Get him up," Patrick ordered as he wrestled Saamyah down to the cold floor. "I want him to see this."

Once more, Bryan was yanked to his knees. This time, in front of him was Patrick tearing the clothes from Saamyah's body. Infuriated, he struggled to free himself from the men that held him, but he was too weak with pain. He was crushed when she desperately cried out for him as Patrick wrestled with her and finally forced himself inside her body. Bryan cried with her as Patrick violated her with each aggressive thrust. The cuts on his face burned from the salty tears he shed.

Their teary eyes met for a brief moment.

"I'm…I'm sooo sorry, Saamyah," Bryan choked.

When she turned from his gaze, Bryan erupted in a cry that pained his broken ribs.

Bryan jumped in his sleep and winced at his aching muscles. The pain made him immediately regret having swum earlier that day. Taking deep slow breaths, he tried to decrease his elevated heartbeat.

"It was only a dream," he whispered to himself. "It was only a dream."

He wiped the sweat from his brow and slowly turned to glance at his alarm clock—12:34 is what it read. Though it was late, he had to call her just to be certain that she was safe. He had to confirm that what he experienced was indeed just a dream.

Bryan reached for the cordless phone on his nightstand and dialed Saamyah's number. It rang several times before she answered.

"Hello," she huskily greeted.

"Saamyah."

"Bryan?"

"Sorry to wake you."

"What's wrong?" She asked.

"Are you okay?" He asked in return.

"What?…Yeah, I'm fine."

"Then nothing's wrong. Go back to sleep…Good night."

"Good night, Bryan."

Despite his aching body, Bryan slept more soundly after he ended the call.

*** *** ***

"Hey, you," Saamyah cheerfully greeted Bryan the next afternoon as she climbed into his car.

"Hey," he murmured before closing the door for her.

"Want to talk about my late night phone call last night? Or this morning—rather," she asked after he climbed into the driver's seat.

"No, I don't," Bryan simply answered. He secured his seatbelt, started the engine, reversed out of the parking space, and drove in the direction of the July 4th festivities.

Saamyah pleaded, "Well, will you even though you don't want to?"

Bryan exhaled loudly and quickly glanced at her, "I had a dream about you last night and it wasn't good...I just thought I'd call to make sure you were okay."

Taken aback by his concern, she was absent words. All that she could conjure was, "That bad, huh?"

"...You couldn't imagine," he spoke under his breath.

"Well, thanks for checking in on me."

"I wouldn't have it any other way."

Saamyah sat in silence for the hour drive. She took in the melodic tones of his satellite radio and the view that became more scenic the deeper they drove into suburbia. When they finally pulled into a long driveway, a striking, brown-toned woman exited the house to greet them.

"Heeeeeeeeeeey, I am so glad that you could make it," she gleefully sang as she watched them climbed out of Bryan's car.

Saamyah smiled brightly at her enthusiasm and said, "Thank you for the invitation."

Bryan laughed, embraced the host's waist, lifted her from her feet, and spun her around. "It's so good to see you," he expressed after placing her back on her feet. Bryan then placed a lingering kiss at her temple and rested his hands at her waist. "How have you b-"

"Well, well, well, look at what the old cat has dragged to the neighborhood."

Everyone looked in the direction of the deep, male voice.

"You being the old cat I hope," Bryan teased, grabbing the equally fit and muscular man's hand and bringing him into his body for a fraternal embrace. "Good to see you, Maurice." Bryan playfully patted his slightly swollen belly. "I see that life after the police force is starting to catch up with you."

"Whatever, man. I can still out P.T. your ass," Maurice defended.

Everyone laughed.

"You guys, this is Saamyah Cambell, the one I have been speaking about. Saamyah, this is Robyn and Maurice Washington."

The last name rang a bell and Saamyah instantly connected the name to Bryan's former partner. She extended her hand to Robyn and said, "Nice to meet you."

Robyn playfully pushed her hand away and gaily said, "We're family around here," and gave Saamyah a warm, welcoming hug.

Maurice gave Saamyah a hug and then a slow look over. "Not bad," he remarked, grinning at Bryan.

Robyn elbowed her husband hard and ignored his whimper as he rubbed his sore arm. "Please excuse my brute. He doesn't always say the most politically correct things."

Though it did not displace the wave of discomfort she suddenly felt, Saamyah accepted her apology. She smiled weakly and complimented the African goddess on her dreadlocks that were neatly formed into a bun on top of her head.

"Thank you so much," she said, taking Saamyah's hand to lead her out of the driveway into their beautiful home. The men took an alternate route to the backyard.

"I love your outfit," Robyn commented, adoring Saamyah's pink halter top, white linen slacks, silver sandals and wristlet. "Nordstrom?"

"Thanks," Saamyah said. "No, Neiman Marcus."

Robyn winked and nodded. "Great sense of style."

Saamyah thanked her again and complimented her maxi-length yellow and black tube dress and accessories. "Oh, I almost forgot." Saamyah stopped to reach into her large tote and pushed pass her sunscreen and bug repellant to grab the bottle of Merlot. "This is for you."

"You shouldn't have, but thank you." Robyn accepted the bottle and led her into the house.

When they arrived in the sizeable kitchen, Robin took Saamyah's wristlet and tote, consolidated them and then secured it in a hall closet. She then introduced Saamyah as Bryan's 'lady friend' to those sitting in the kitchen and adjoining informal dining and living area. Only a few of the women extended warm welcomes. Those who did not, greeted Saamyah with hard, evaluating glares, ill-mannered body language, and inappropriate grumbles under their breath.

"Don't let them get to you, Saamyah," Robyn encouraged out loud. "They're just jealous because their own pursuit of Bryan failed miserably."

The air erupted with laughter, making the atmosphere more tolerable.

"Do you want something to drink?" Robyn asked Saamyah, diverting the subject.

"Yes, water, please."

Robyn nodded and walked to the stainless steel refrigerator to store the Merlot and retrieve a bottle of Evian.

"Thank you." Saamyah looked around to see the raw, seasoned meat and freshly cut vegetables on the table and counter tops. "Do you need help with anything?"

Robyn shook her head. "No, hun. Everything is done, but you can help me carry some of this stuff outside."

Saamyah tucked her bottle under her arm and grabbed a platter for each hand. When she followed Robyn outside, she was immediately enveloped by the loud party stretched across the large yard. Happy guests were swimming, game playing, running, dancing, and eating. Saamyah hastily stopped in mid-step when a child hurried past her to catch up with his friend.

Robyn threatened him with a reprimand, then looked at Saamyah and offered, "I'm so sorry about that."

Saamyah chuckled. "It's fine." She turned in the direction of Bryan's laughter and found him standing at the grill with Maurice. In his khaki cargo shorts and red Polo shirt, Bryan sipped his beer bottle as he helped Maurice flip burgers on the large gas grill. She blushed when Bryan caught her eyes and winked.

Saamyah broke their gaze and carefully placed the food and her water on the table. She followed Robyn back into the kitchen.

Robyn handed Saamyah a tray of raw meats and gave her a conniving smile. "Will you give these to Bryan to add to the grill?"

Saamyah chuckled nervously in embarrassment. "You saw that didn't you?"

Robyn shrugged and simply said, "It was kind of hard to miss."

Saamyah shook her head and bit her bottom lip. She despised her involuntary affections and immediately suppressed them, remembering the purpose of their ruse.

"He's not a bad catch, you know," Robyn coaxed.

Saamyah recalled the unscrupulous beliefs that governed Bryan's past actions and murmured, "It's not the exterior that I am worried about,"

Robyn smiled knowingly. "Trust me, he cares for you just as much as you do him. You can see it in his eyes…He hasn't been this effervescent since Rachel."

Saamyah hesitated, but finally asked, "Were the two of good friends? You and Rachel?"

Not wanting to reopen a healed wound, Robyn nodded and shared, "The best—she was my sorority sister. I actually introduced her to Bryan years ago at an event like this one." Robyn reflected on the fond memories and smiled lovingly. "She's gone now to a better place and we're blessed to be alive." She grabbed a dish off the counter and added, "So, let's go out there and start living because this moment is the only time promised."

Saamyah pondered Robyn's advice and followed her outside. As she had been asked, Saamyah walked towards Bryan to deliver the meat that was to be added to the grill.

"Hey, there, beautiful," Bryan greeted as he brushed the ribs with barbeque sauce.

"Hey." She stopped at Bryan's side. "I have some more goodies to add to the grill."

Maurice took the tray off her hands and thanked her. "Are you having a good time?"

Saamyah exhaled loudly. "I don't know. I guess it would depend on your definition of a good time."

Bryan looked at her with concern. "What do you mean?"

Saamyah pushed her hair back from her face and scanned the yard for the eyes she felt on her. She then said with sarcasm, "If it means enjoying being scorned by all the Mrs. Russell wannabes then I am having a blast."

Both Bryan and Maurice looked to view what Saamyah had referenced.

Maurice laughed, sipped from his bottle of beer, and advised, "Don't worry about them. They're just jealous."

"Yeah, that's the advice Robyn gave," Saamyah confirmed.

"If you're that uncomfortable then we can leave, Saamyah," Bryan offered, hoping to ease her tension.

Saamyah was taken aback by his concern. Because of his selflessness, she could not help but look at him and say, "No, it's okay. I'll be okay."

"Are you sure?" Bryan asked, searching her eyes for an honest answer.

She nodded. "Yes."

"Come here." He touched her waist, motioned her body into him, and kissed her.

Maurice exhaled loudly and commanded, "Get a room."

Bryan's laughter broke their kiss. He turned to Maurice and said, "You should worry less about our room and more about that Spades ass whoppin' later."

Maurice shook his head and laughed. He gave Saamyah a look over and smugly remarked, "Pretty typically can't play."

Saamyah's jaw dropped at his chauvinism. She then snickered and warned, "Don't let pretty fool you."

Maurice met her eyes, sipped from his beer bottle, and said, "We'll see."

Though the sun had crept behind the horizon and the crowd slowly dispersed, the four of them sat at the patio table and continued their card game.

Maurice played his card then looked to his left. "So, Saamyah…what's your story?"

Saamyah played her card then asked, "What do you mean?"

"You must be some catch if our Bryan here has thought enough of you to bring you to hang out with us common folks."

Robyn laughed and elaborated, "What my husband means is that we don't see much of Bryan's companions." She looked at Bryan, reached to touch his cheek with her palm, and confessed, "We hear of them, but don't see them." She lowered her hand to rest on his and then turned to wink at Saamyah. "So, you must be someone special."

Maurice collected the book that he and his wife had won. He played another card and joked, "Either that or she really knows how to put it down."

Maurice was the only one to laugh at his quip, but his laughter was cut short when Robyn delivered an evil glare.

"Saamyah and I are taking things slowly," Bryan defended. "So, rest assured that she is very special to me." He played his card then collected the book that he and Saamyah had won. He threw out another card, caught Saamyah's eyes, and winked.

Saamyah smiled and looked away. "So, Mr. Washington, what is your story?" Playing her card, she asked, "Why did you leave the police force?"

Maurice collected his winning book. "You work with Russell; I'm sure you are aware of the bastard he can be." He played his card and added, "And I was with him since we were beat cops."

All at the table, but Saamyah, laughed. She did not feel comfortable making light of a relationship she had little knowledge of. Adding to the concern, Saamyah was not certain of what they knew of Bryan's working relationship with her.

Maurice cleared his throat and clarified, "But seriously, my wife and I are trying to start a family. So, we thought it best that I choose a less demanding career." He played his card. "I teach now at Miami U. while I complete my criminal justice Ph.D."

Saamyah nodded and lauded, "Impressive."

Bryan collected their winning book. "Your ass, man," he challenged Maurice. "You got out not long after the commissioner mandated a special crimes division." Bryan played his card. "You knew that shit was going to be dropped in our laps."

Maurice chuckled. "Damn right I did. Best career decision I ever made...I've been watching the news; you have your hands full." He played his card and then added, "My hands are needed elsewhere."

Bryan huffed and shook his head. "...So, how is everything going in the baby making department?"

Maurice shrugged and took a sip from his fresh beer. "Just letting nature run its course."

"Actually-" Robyn started. The table fell silent and all eyes centered on her. She placed her cards face down on the table and looked at her husband. Her nervousness grew as she continued, "I was going to wait to tell you at the marina—right before the fireworks, but now is as good of a time as any."

"We're pregnant!" Maurice anxiously interrupted.

Tears fell from Robyn's eyes as she nodded. "Almost five weeks."

Maurice tossed his cards on the table and rushed to his wife. He lifted her from her seat and spun her. After he planted her on her feet, he kissed her long and deep.

Bryan stood and jested, "Get a room." He then pried them apart to firmly embrace and kiss Robyn. After he whispered a brief message in her ear, he spoke audibly, "Congratulations, love...You are going to be a great mother."

Robyn smiled, wiped her eyes dry, and replied, "Thank you, Bryan."

Bryan released her, turned to Maurice, grabbed his hand, and brought him into his body for a firm, congratulatory hug.

"Nice job, bro.," Bryan told him.

Maurice laughed. "Thanks, man."

After Saamyah congratulated them, Robyn turned to Bryan and took each of his hands into each of hers. "Bryan, I know we made this pact when Rachel was with us, but Maurice and I would still love to have you be the godfather of our child."

Bryan peered adoringly into her eyes and smiled. "I'd be honored."

Robyn wrapped her arms around his neck and Bryan wrapped his around her waist. They held each other in a warm embrace as if to provide comfort for a loss that still pained them both.

Maurice interrupted the moment of awkwardness by insisting, "You must come to the marina and celebrate with us."

Bryan released Robyn and looked at Saamyah for confirmation, but she only offered a shrug. He hesitantly said, "I don't know. It's getting late."

"Aaaw, come on," Robyn chimed in, beaming her eyes at Bryan then Saamyah. "It's only after eight. The fireworks start at 10:30 and we can leave right after."

Not able to disappoint her angelic face, Saamyah felt compelled to accept the invitation. "Okay."

"Great," Maurice interjected, "it's a date, now let's finish this game."

"Not a chance," Bryan spoke. "We have to get going if we are going to meet you before the fireworks."

"Scared you're going to lose, huh?" Maurice asked.

Bryan laughed and reminded, "Pretty and I are up a hundred points; you're not coming back."

Maurice snickered as his own words were force fed to him. He nodded in concession. "See you at the marina."

Bryan parked his car, removed the key from the ignition, and held the set in his hand.

"You don't have to go to the marina if you aren't up to it, Saamyah." He turned to her and added, "I know Robyn can be a bit uh-"

"Cunningly forceful," Saamyah finished.

Bryan grinned. "Yeah, and I also know that spending time with my friends and me is not what you would consider the best use of your holiday."

She smiled and admitted, "It wasn't so bad. I actually had fun."

"Really?"

She nodded.

"...Well, nonetheless, you don't have to come to the marina. I will just think of something to tell Robyn on the way...You have not only fulfilled your duties as a friend, but also those of a law enforcement officer. So, consider yourself freed of the obligation."

Saamyah laughed after realizing that in those few weeks, he had come to know her so well. She opened the car door and before she proceeded to climb out, she beamed at him and said, "I'll be ready in an hour."

Standing in her large walk-in closet, Saamyah carefully slipped into her satin cream colored, asymmetrical dress. After zipping it at the side, she adjusted the spaghetti straps, then lightly fingered the cowl drop that exposed modest cleavage. Methodically, she stepped into her single-strap stiletto sandals, and tightened the buckle at her ankles.

She walked out of her closet, into her master bathroom and she gazed at her reflection in the vanity mirror. She applied an additional coat of mascara to her eyelashes and added more gloss to her pout. When Saamyah heard the loud knock on her front door, she quickly reaffixed the bobby pins that held her hair up and gently brushed her long bang that she had swept across her left eye. She nervously secured her diamond studs in her ears, drop necklace around her neck, and tennis bracelet on wrist before walking out of her bathroom and down the hall to her front door.

Saamyah opened the door to greet Bryan. Straight away, her breath was seized by her attraction to him. He wore a tailored light brown suit and cream shirt.

"Hi," Bryan stammered after he took in her full ensemble. He forced his eyes away from the bottom of her dress that stopped mid thigh on one leg and just below the knee on the other. "You look...amazing."

Saamyah could feel herself blushing under her flawlessly applied makeup. "Thank you. You aren't too shabby yourself." She stepped to the side and opened the door wider. "Come on in. I am almost ready."

Bryan walked in and closed the door behind him. "These are for you." He presented her with a bouquet of red roses.

She took the flowers, kissed his cheek, and said, "Thank you, Bryan."

Bryan shoved his empty hands in his pants' pockets and said, "You're welcome."

The room fell silent for a brief moment as they stood before each other like high school crushes.

"...I...I am just going to put these in water and grab my clutch."

Bryan nodded and went to take a seat.

Saamyah hurried through her final tasks and arrived back with her clutch in her hand. "I'm ready."

Bryan rose from the sofa and gawked at her.

She touched her hair, searching for a flaw. "What?...What's wrong?"

Bryan shook his head and smiled. "Nothing. You just look..." Not able to find the right words, he repeated, "amazing."

"Stop with all the flattery...You're embarrassing me."

Bryan laughed. "I'm sorry...Let's go see some fireworks."

Bryan pulled out Saamyah's chair and waited for her to be seated before he sat next to her.

"Couldn't find a table closer to the water?...I mean, any closer and we'd be celebrating with the fish." Bryan joked to Maurice and Robyn.

Robyn laughed and shrugged. "We'll get a better view of the fireworks from here."

Bryan humorously rolled his eyes at her and scanned the large pier that stretched out into the Atlantic Ocean. He observed several patrons opted to dine outside the high-end restaurant to view the demonstration. Glimpsing at his watch, Bryan saw that it would be another twenty minutes before the first firecracker burst in the sky. He reached for the bottle of wine in the center of the table and poured himself a glass.

Saamyah could hear the tide coming in underneath them, but it did not eclipse the music coming from the live jazz band. She lost several minutes in her admiration of the instrumentalists and the fervor with which they played. It reminded her of the many years she had played the violin. Her lingering thoughts were interrupted by a suited waiter who arrived to their table with a pre-ordered chocolate dessert.

Robyn grinned when Saamyah looked at her with hesitation. "Just a little something to help us celebrate," Robyn explained.

Saamyah feebly smiled, took her fork, and forced a small bite between her lips. She prayed that morsel would find space in her already compact stomach. To her relief, the cake melted in her mouth and slid down her throat with ease. When it settled nicely in her belly, Saamyah reached for another forkful.

Maurice watched Saamyah as she took a second bite. "Almost as good as sex, isn't it?" He mocked.

Saamyah sipped from her water glass then said, "I'm a virgin so I wouldn't know."

When the table fell silent, Saamyah could not help but laugh.

Bewildered at the unexpected confession, Maurice and Robyn looked at Bryan who only shrugged his shoulders and sipped his wine. After returning his glass to the linen covered table, he took Saamyah's hand and asked her to dance.

Saamyah and Bryan laughed in unison once they stepped onto the dance floor.

"I don't think Maurice will be mocking you for the remainder of the night," Bryan predicted.

"Good," Saamyah said as she swayed to the quick tempo, "that was the idea in mind when I made the comment."

The music later slowed to a soft ballad and Bryan gently pulled her into him. One hand held hers and the other found a place in the small of her back. He led her in small circles on the wooden deck.

"I never would have guessed you to be a dancer," Saamyah confessed.

Bryan smirked. "Just one of my many hidden talents."

"Really? Tell me more."

He shook his head. "Not a chance. I've got to save something for my next wife, right?"

She smiled. "Touché."

Their dancing ceased when the music stopped and the countdown to the fireworks began. After the last second, the sky exploded with bright colors and the band proceeded with patriotic anthems.

Saamyah looked above her head in astonishment. She was amused by the explosion of color in the sky and captivated by the lights reflected in the ocean.

Drawn by the twinkle in her eyes, Bryan lowered his lips to hers. She did not immediately break their kiss, so he wrapped his arms around her waist and intensified it. The deeper he kissed her the more he could smell the sweetness of her gloss and taste the richness of the cocoa. His eyes slowly closed and a faint sigh escaped him as he felt the ice that encased his heart chip away.

"Bryan," Saamyah finally whispered while tenderly nudging him away. She felt the heightened passion behind his kiss and discerned that they were no longer role playing. She searched his eyes in hopes that they would not confirm her suspicion.

"I...I'm so sorry, Saamyah...I just got caught up in the moment with the fireworks and music and..." Bryan rambled until his voice trailed off.

Saamyah's heart raced and breath shortened when the truth surfaced. She shook her head in dismay as she acknowledged, "I felt it, Bryan."

Bryan huffed in denial, "What are you talking about?"

With her face shadowed with solemn seriousness, she said, "You know, Bryan."

He exhaled slowly and turned from her, regretting having kissed her.

Saamyah grabbed and tugged at his suit jacket, forcing him to face her and the truth. She was weary of their potential plight, but had to substantiate what was now obvious. "You've fallen in love with me, haven't you?"

Bryan held her gaze and said nothing.

Saamyah respired as she released his jacket. His eyes had confirmed her suspicion and tears swelled in hers. "Why, Bryan?"

Bryan lowered his head in grief at the sight of her tears. When he lifted his eyes to meet hers, he answered, "Trust me, Saamyah, it was not something I planned."

Despite the noise rupturing above her head and music ringing in her ear, Saamyah could still hear the pounding of her heart. Pondering the how's, why's, and what if's of their new dilemma, Saamyah's head began to spin and legs grew weak beneath her. She needed space from the crowd, from the pressure...from him.

"Please take me home."

Bryan parked his vehicle, removed the key from the ignition, and sat motionless in his seat. The drive home from the marina was uncomfortably long and quiet despite his best efforts to ease Saamyah's discontentment.

Exhausted by the silence, Bryan cleared his throat and declared, "I'm not sorry about the way I feel about you, Saamyah, because what I feel is real—I want you, I want to be with you…But I do regret that knowledge of my feelings have ruined your evening."

As with his previous attempts to engage her in conversation, Saamyah did not respond.

He exhaled loudly in defeat and ultimately assured, "Look, just forget it. Forget it and nothing has to change."

Saamyah found his face with the aid of the lamppost's dim light and searched his eyes. She toiled with his decision to give his love to her—a woman with a reproachable history passing through his life.

Struggling with the knowledge that his love guaranteed changes for both their lives and, with her record, not for the better, Saamyah finally spoke, "Bryan, our working relationship won't ever be the same…We can't return to work feigning to be in a romantic relationship. I can't—I won't put you through that."

Bryan turned from her eyes and nodded. He glanced at the hands of his watch and saw that it was almost midnight.

"Want to come up for a drink?" He asked, desperate to make light of their dilemma."

Saamyah shook her head. "I don't think that is a good idea, Bryan. Let's just say good night here-"

"Please," he beseeched. "I don't want the night to end like this. It will have us feeling uncomfortable around each other at the office and that is the last thing I want." He paused and then added, "I at least owe you a nightcap for the stellar way you handled Maurice."

Saamyah burst into an unexpected laughter. "…Yeah, he was a bit of a jerk."

Bryan grinned. "Yes, he was." He placed a hand on top of hers and gently squeezed it. "So, is that a yes?"

Saamyah exhaled loudly and nodded. "Sure, why not?...This moment is the only time promised."

Bryan rolled his eyes and chuckled as he opened his door. "I see that Robyn has made quite an impression on you."

He descended the driver seat, closed the door behind him, and walked to open the passenger door. After assisting Saamyah's exit, Bryan closed the door behind her, secured it, and then led her to the stairs, allowing her to step up before him.

After she ascended the last step, Saamyah waited for Bryan to unlock the door and open it. She crossed the threshold first then waited and watched Bryan shut, lock, and chain the door behind him. He illuminated the room with the light switch.

Saamyah squinted her eyes as they adjusted to the soft lights of the table lamps. Once they adjusted, she noticed the cluttered sofa. "Someone has been bringing their work home," she acknowledged.

"As of late, I feel like I am in an unwinnable race against time," Bryan explained. "Sorry about the mess though…Let me move some of this stuff out of your way."

Bryan removed his jacket and tossed it in a nearby chair. He then hurried around her and began moving documents, folders, notebooks, and writing utensils from one end of the sofa to the other. Saamyah placed her clutch on the end table and aided him in his efforts.

"I'm sorry," he apologized when his forearm brushed her breast.

Saamyah sensed his nervousness and tried to ease it by smiling and saying, "It's okay."

After completing their task, they stood facing each other. Bryan looked on and admired the woman he involuntarily loved. He felt as if he had dived into deep waters knowing that he could not swim. Feeling extraordinarily vulnerable, Bryan searched her captivating eyes for reciprocity. His heart ached when the search returned empty.

Bryan dropped his eyes in disappointment, cleared his throat, and said, "I'm going to get that nightcap I promised you. Tea, okay?"

"Bryan, wait." She stepped in his path before he had a chance to walk past her. "…You and I have had a rough start. In the beginning, we were two different people with two different lifestyles and at times working together seemed almost impossible. But, somehow you and I managed to make it work…day in and day out; and, in each one of those days, I have had the opportunity to learn you for myself…I have come to realize that you aren't such a bad guy and that there is so much more to you than the tough male exterior that you present to the world…" She struggled with her emotions, but finally confessed, "You are very special to me and I wouldn't have wanted to work with anyone else during this TDY."

Bryan smiled feebly, grateful for what she offered, though it was not what he hoped for. He kissed her forehead and said, "Thank you."

Again, she blocked his attempt to walk past her and softly gripped his face with her hands. Saamyah brought him closer to her and kissed his lips. "You're welcome…And thank you for a wonderful evening. You were right; I did enjoy it."

Bryan lifted her long bang away from her eye and returned the kiss. "You're welcome and thank you for accompanying me." He gently stroked her face and confessed, "For me, it was more than a ruse."

She nodded in response. When his fingertips traveled down her face again, she closed her eyes and smiled. "Kiss me again," she whispered.

Bryan held her face close to his and obliged without hesitation. Pecking her lips to indulge in the sweetness of her lip gloss, he lowered his hands to wrap her in a warm embrace. When she opened her mouth, he used his tongue to taste it.

Saamyah felt a chill move up her spine as their kiss deepened and his firm hands gently caressed her back. Her body surrendered to his masterful touch and a soft moan escaped her as his mouth placed slow, sensual kisses on her neck. Gripping his soft curls, Saamyah pulled him closer.

Bryan deeply inhaled her intoxicating fragrance as he backed her trembling body into the front door. When Saamyah's misty eyes opened and met his, he expected a request to end the exchange. But, none came. Keeping the gaze with the windows of her soul, Bryan dropped a hand to each of her thighs and grazed them with his fingertips. He moved without hurry, awaiting her objection. But, again, none came. So, he eased his hands under her dress.

Saamyah closed her eyes and whispered Bryan's name as his exploring fingers found their way into her lacey thong. She bit down on her bottom lip as they gently stroked the swollen, sensitive flesh that made her a woman.

"Bryan," she moaned as the fervent suckles on her neck moved down to the fullest part of her breasts. Saamyah shifted her weight when Bryan methodically lifted her leg and held it at his waist. Her hands moved to his shoulder and held them tightly as he slipped a finger inside her body and folded it forward to stroke her G-spot.

Before she collapsed with pleasure, Saamyah pushed his finger from her body and hand from her underwear. She dropped her leg, requesting, "Bryan, please stop."

Bryan rested his weight against her, pressing her further into the door. Between his own breathless pants, he kissed her forehead and whispered, "Okay."

"I'm sorry...I'm just-"

"Saamyah, it's okay," he reassured, ignoring the throbbing pain in his groin. Bryan locked their gaze and repeated, "Really, it's okay."

"I'm just so nervous," she admitted, breaking his stare.

Understanding her plight, Bryan lifted her head until their eyes met. "We don't have to have sex, Saamyah."

"But I want to," she confessed.

Taken aback by her confession, Bryan searched her eyes for responses to all that he could not bring himself to ask. Recalling what she was ultimately offering him, he inquired, "Are you sure you're ready?"

Saamyah swallowed the knot swelling in her throat and nodded. "...Make love to me."

Bryan grievously contemplated her request. From the moment they met, her body was all that he yearned. Now, several weeks later, he desired more—much more...He wanted her heart.

"Saamyah, I can't," he finally rebuffed as he lifted his weight off her preparing to provide the distance they both needed to calm themselves.

Saamyah gripped his arm, held him close, and challenged the rejection, "You love me, then show me. She pulled him into her, kissed him, and then whispered, "Make love to me, Bryan."

Bryan lowered his head as he attempted to slow the rapid pounding of his heart and think beyond his confusion. He had never wanted a woman as badly as he wanted Saamyah, but myriad reservations stifled his desire.

Anxious of his doubts, Saamyah lifted his chin and whispered, "Please."

"Are you sure about this, Saamyah?"

She smiled and confirmed, "I've never been more sure about anything in my life."

Bryan nodded, closed his eyes, and kissed her. He rested his forehead on hers and, in a murmur, spoke, "I'll be right back."

"Where are you going?"

He kissed her again before saying, "To make this night special for you."

Saamyah watched him walk away until he disappeared into the darkness of the hall. After she adjusted her dress, she took a seat on the sofa, slipped off her stiletto sandals, and sunk deeper into the cushion. As seconds turned into minutes, she felt her eyelids grow increasingly heavy until she could no longer keep them open.

Moments later, Bryan returned to find Saamyah sleeping on the sofa. Suppressing his disappointment, he grabbed the crocheted afghan from inside the ottoman and gently covered her with it. He then carefully lifted her legs and slowly swung them on to the seated cushion so to transition her body to lie down. Waiting for her to stop stirring in her sleep, Bryan adjusted the afghan to cover her feet.

"Hey," she whispered, blinking her eyes open to see him covering her feet.

Bryan looked up and smiled in response. "Hey."

"I'm sorry that I fell asleep on you."

Bryan stroked her tresses from her face. "It's okay; it's been a long day. You're welcome to rest here."

Saamyah shook her head is dissent as she sat up with the aid of her hands. Taking notice of the colored pattern that covered her, she fingered the texture and murmured, "This is beautiful."

"Thank you; a handmade gift from my mother," he told her, taking her hand and helping her to her feet. "Give me a minute and I will walk you downstairs."

"I'd rather you walk me to your bedroom," she contested.

Bryan smiled at the innuendo, turned off the lights, and led Saamyah by the hand down the dark hallway. When he opened the bedroom door she immediately took in the lit candles, the bed turned down to fresh satin sheets, the scent of diffused lavender and jasmine oils, and soft jazz playing from the speakers.

Saamyah walked further into the room as Bryan closed the door. She turned to face him and began to remove the pins from her hair and placed them on his dresser. After tousling her hair, she unzipped her dress and pushed the straps off her shoulders. The dress fell to the floor and she stepped out of it. Deeply inhaling the scents of the oils to calm her nerves, Saamyah watched as Bryan moved closer to her.

Bryan traced her bare shoulders with his fingertips, trailing kisses behind them. Wanting more her gratification than his own, he curbed the urge to quickly ravish her body. He stroked her skin down to her breasts and his hand fingered her nipples through the black lace fabric of her strapless bra.

Saamyah sighed at the chill that crept up her spine and slowly unbuttoned his shirt. She pushed it off him, lifted his t-shirt over his head, and let them both drop to the floor. Taking in the familiar sight of his god-like body, she caressed the firmness of his chest and the ripples of his abdomen. She then followed the faint hairs on his lower belly down to his belt buckle.

Bryan watched her loosen his belt, then pants, and tugged at them until they fell to his ankles. He stepped out of them and grabbed her waist to pull her into him. He kissed her, seductively dipping his tongue into her mouth as his hands stroked her hair. Panting his pleasure, he broke their kiss and groaned when Saamyah's hand moved down to touch his pulsating manhood.

"Saamyah," he whispered, tenderly pulling her hair.

Bryan nibbled at her neck as he unfastened her bra. He tossed it to the floor then lifted her off her feet. His arms held her hips close as she wrapped her arms and legs around him. He carried her to the bed.

Saamyah kept their fervent gaze as he laid her on the cool sheets. Her back arched when his warm mouth covered her nipple—licking and sucking one then the other. She felt his hands stroke her thighs until one found its way inside underwear. Saamyah sighed, squeezing her eyes shut as he stroked her sensitivity. She inhaled deeply and exhaled slowly as he made a trail of soft kisses down the center of her body. When he stopped at her navel, dipped his tongue in it, and added a lingering kiss. Saamyah reveled each suckle and every kiss as Bryan continued his journey down her body.

Bryan watched her watch him when he separately lifted each of her legs for a trail of kisses. His hands caressed their way back up her body and stopped at the waistband of her thong. After she raised her hips, he slowly removed the wet garment.

Saamyah bit her bottom lip as she observed Bryan remove the lace from one leg then the other. He kissed the sole of her foot and slowly worked his kisses back up her center using his tongue to heighten her pleasure. He stopped at the warmth between her thighs and placed a leg on each of his shoulders.

Gripping her thighs, Bryan pulled her body closer to his mouth and began to drink from her fountain. He watched as her eyes closed and hands gripped the sheets. Her sighs gratified him immensely and the calling of his name propelled him to continue to move his tongue masterfully on her swollen member.

Saamyah felt a hot flash overwhelm her body as her orgasm grew closer. Beads of sweat rolled down her face as Bryan's tongue continuously flickered against the most sensitive part of her body. She released her tight grip of the sheets and lowered her hands to hold Bryan's head as he rocked her body in rhythm to his quick vibrating tongue.

"Bryan," she repeatedly panted between moans.

The racing of her beating heart accompanied the continual build of a strong release. "Bryan," she whined while gripping his hair, "Bryan, I'm cumming."

A chill enveloped her body and she exploded like a crashing wave. Her loud cry sang over the soft melody of the saxophone as she trembled and tightly held Bryan's shoulders.

Saamyah released Bryan when her moment of ecstasy subsided. She opened her eyes and looked on as Bryan kissed his way up to her lips. Desiring more, Saamyah moaned when his warm mouth kissed her cool one. She lowered her hands to remove his boxer briefs, but Bryan intercepted her.

He held her hand and kissed it. Ignoring the throbbing pain of his groin, he admonished, "Don't rush this decision, Saamyah. We can't undo it once it's done."

"I don't want to stop," she assured him.

Nodding, Bryan kissed her hand and said, "Okay."

Bryan worked his way out of his underwear and reached for the gold package on his nightstand. After opening it with ease, he secured the Magnum on himself, and covered their bare bodies with the sheet and comforter. His heart pounding in his chest, he leaned forward and kissed her—his forehead resting on hers.

"I'm so nervous, Saamyah," he confessed in a whisper. It had been a long while since he made love to a woman.

Saamyah smiled and gently stroked his hair. "Don't be. It's like riding a bike, right?"

Bryan laughed. "Yeah, but, I've never ridden a motorcycle...I don't want to disappoint you."

"Well, I've never ridden at all so there is no one to compare you to." She caught his eye and added, "You won't be disappointing me."

"I don't want to hurt you, Saam-"

She touched his lips with her fingers. "Sshhh," she interrupted. "Don't over think it, Bryan...Just make love to me."

Bryan pressed her fingers into his lips and kissed them. After quietly exhaling, he slowly penetrated her body.

Clenching his back, Saamyah squeezed her eyes shut and gasped at the pain.

Bryan stopped. He kissed her lips and asked, "Are you okay?"

Without opening her eyes, Saamyah pressed her lips together and nodded.

"Do you want me to keep going?"

When she nodded, Bryan gently eased a few more inches into her body and clinched his jaw when her nails clawed at his back. His heart ached when she buried her face in his chest and cried out in pain. After waiting for her to regain her bearings, Bryan made the final thrust.

Saamyah arched her back and cried out in misery. Her eyes quickly watered and the tears rolled back into her hair. She slowly breathed through the pain.

Bryan wiped her eyes and kissed her forehead. "Do you want me to stop?"

She shook her head and whispered, "No."

Bryan planted his lips on hers and began to unhurriedly move in and out of her firm, warm body. With each of his motions, her thighs tightened on each side of him and her nails pinched the flesh on his back.

"Try to relax," he spoke softly. He placed small kisses on her neck in an attempt to relieve her stress.

Saamyah released the air she held in her lungs and focused on relaxing her body. When Bryan kissed her lips, she returned it with a more passionate one. She allowed him to remove her hands from his back and hold each of them in his against the pillow her head rested on. Trying to endure the pain that enveloped her as he lovingly opened her body, Saamyah intertwined their fingers and gripped Bryan's hands firmly.

Bryan rose and fell in sync with the harmonious tone that filled the room and groaned at the bliss her body gave him. He was deeply entangled in her sensual web and found it impossible to resist driving further inside her. When he felt her body tense more beneath him, Bryan encouraged her to relax. He switched to moving in small circles while repeatedly whispering her name in her ear and telling her how much he loved her.

Saamyah concentrated on his coaching, fighting the urge to tense her body in response to the insurmountable pain. In an effort to release more tension, she wrapped her legs around Bryan's lower back and gradually began to move with him. The tears continued to fall as she inhaled and exhaled slowly through her discomfort.

He wiped her eyes and then lowered his mouth to kiss her forehead, the bridge of her nose, and then her lips. Bryan followed his kisses with the covering of her taunt swollen nipples—suckling one then the other. He then released her hands to grip her thighs so that he could push himself deeper into her warmth.

Saamyah jumped and gasped at the pain that jolted through her body. She bit down hard on her bottom lip and nodded when Bryan stopped his movement and apologized. She appreciated his wait for her to relax her body before he began moving inside her again. Saamyah breathed slowly and rested her back. More feelings of love and affection enclosed Saamyah when Bryan tenderly wiped her eyes and stroked her hair. She received his passionate kiss and nodded when he asked, "Do you want me to keep going?"

Gripping the sheets and arching her back, Saamyah secretly hid her discomfort when the long, firm strokes in and out of her body began again. Fresh tears rolled back into her hairline despite her focus on his moans and the soft calling of her name. Though she felt the love he possessed for her in each of his thrusts, the pain was far more than what she could continue to bear. Seconds from pleading for him to stop, Bryan announced the advent of his orgasm. Saamyah was never more grateful and relieved. Holding her breath, she braced her body.

Bryan whined with pleasure as his climax grew closer. His heart raced in his chest and lungs burned with fire. The final strokes brought him to his end and he loudly groaned as his seed burst into the latex. Holding her close, he rode the end of his wave and lowered himself onto her. His body trembled from the intensity of his orgasm—he had loved her with everything he had.

Saamyah exhaled gradually and slowly released the sheets. Her body quaked in pain, but she managed to return the kiss he had given her.

"Are you okay?" He asked, regaining his bearings between breaths.

She hesitated sharing the truth, so she simply responded, "Yes."

Though grateful for the generous lie, Bryan's heart ached for the pain he caused her. "I'm so sorry that I hurt you." He gently wiped the tears from her eyes.

She nodded and responded, "It's okay…I'm okay."

After kissing her soft lips, Bryan gently grabbed the base of the condom and unhurriedly slid out of her body. He felt her raise her lower back in pain and he apologized. Bryan then dismounted Saamyah and gathered her in his arms. Stroking her hair, he decided to wait until she fell asleep before removing the condom, blowing out the candles, and turning off the music.

Saamyah found comfort in Bryan's embrace despite the lingering discomfort she felt between her thighs. She rested her head on Bryan's chest, moved closer into his arms, and smiled when he kissed her forehead. Saamyah later fell asleep to soft jazz and Bryan whispering how much he loved her.

*** *** ***

Bryan softly stroked her hair as she peacefully slept, careful not to wake her. He laughed at himself in realization that the woman lying next to him had captivated his heart. He laughed more at the remembrance that she was supposed to be a mere conquest. Instead, she had inadvertently conquered him—a man habitually known to be love's assassin.

Saamyah stirred in her sleep and backed closer into Bryan's warmth. Not ready to wake, she ignored the gaze she felt on her face and commanded her body back to sleep.

Bryan grinned at her lethargy and traced her temple with his index finger. He placed a kiss on the pulse in her head and then glanced at the clock on the nightstand.

"Saamyah," Bryan whispered.

She moaned in response.

"You have to get up."

She covered her head with the comforter and asked, "Why?"

Bryan laughed and nudged her hips. "Because you have Kimberly James waiting."

Saamyah tore the covering off of her head and abruptly sat up. "Oh no. I completely forgot."

She held the sheet close to her breasts and pushed back her tangled hair. Her heart raced as she tried to collect her thoughts.

Bryan smoothed her hair and said, "Relax. She called and rescheduled for noon."

Saamyah exhaled with relief and fell back into the pillows. She silently thanked God for the save and closed her eyes. She opened them again when she felt Bryan's warm lips on hers.

"How did you sleep?" Bryan asked after their lips parted.

"Well."

Bryan smiled. "That's good to hear." He paused, searched her eyes, and asked, "How do you feel?"

"I'm sore," she admitted, "but okay."

Bryan nodded. "Can you stay for breakfast?"

"No, I probably should get going… Are you going into the office?"

"I didn't plan on it," he answered, giving way for her to exit the bed. "Do you need me to?" He asked as she walked to the master bathroom.

She looked over her shoulder, smiled, and answered, "No."

Standing under the nozzle, the hot water rained on her head. As therapy for her skin, she allowed it drench her entire body and pound away her stress. After lathering soap into the cloth she took from the linen closet, she massaged Bryan's scent off her and then rinsed away the suds as well as the blood that trickled down her inner thigh. At the end of her shower, Saamyah dried and wrapped her body in Bryan's oversized bath robe and her hair in a towel. With the spare toothbrush she found in the medicine cabinet, she brushed her teeth and then placed her brush in the cup next to his. She smiled at what the gesture symbolized and then exited the bathroom.

"Wow. You move quick," Saamyah said in reference to the changed bedding.

Bryan lowered the newspaper he read onto the pajama pants he wore and smiled at her. "The blood was beginning to set."

Mortified, Saamyah covered her face with her hands. "Bryan, I'm so sorry."

Bryan moved to kneel at the opposite end of the bed, grabbed her by the belt of the bath rope, and pulled her closer. "Don't worry about it."

"I'll pay for them if the blood doesn't come out."

He shook his head. "I won't allow it. Those sheets do not compare in value to what we shared. In fact, you can't even put a price on what we shared."

Saamyah grinned and kissed him. "Thank you."

Bryan wrapped his arms around her waist and affirmed, "No, thank you."

She ran her fingers through his soft curls. "You're welcome." She kissed him again before asking, "Want coffee?"

He shook his head and smiled on her lips. "Tea sounds better."

Saamyah laughed at the subliminal message after remembering that they never partook in their nightcap. "Okay, I will have it made by the time you get out of the shower."

"Thank you." He tried kissing her again, but she dodged his lips and giggled.

Saamyah walked out of the room in the direction of the kitchen, closing the bedroom door behind her. Finding her way around his meticulously organized kitchen, she filled his kettle with water and placed it on the fire of the gas stove. She then placed green tea bags in each of their mugs and made her way to the refrigerator. Her trip was cut short by a knock on the front door. Saamyah walked to the entrance and absentmindedly opened the door after she unsecured it.

He was equally dumbfounded to see her on the other side of the door as she was him. For an instant, they looked at each other allowing their eyes to converse.

Finally, Saamyah spoke, "Bryan isn't available, Patrick. You'll have to come back later." She attempted to close the door, but Patrick overpowered her strength and the door swung open.

"I was actually in search for you. You weren't home, so I came to inquire about your whereabouts," Patrick admitted, inviting himself in. He pushed the door shut, huffed, and then added, "I definitely did not expect to find you here."

"Patrick, Bryan is in the other room," she warned as she backed out of his personal space.

Patrick ignored her admonition, grabbed her by the robe, and yanked her close to him. "Especially not in *his* bathrobe."

When he searched her eyes for confirmation of what he suspected, Saamyah forced him off of her and said nothing to authenticate his suspicion. Instead, she suggested, "I think you should leave, Patrick."

His glare burned into her causing Saamyah to drop her bashful eyes.

Devastated by what her coy mannerism conveyed, Patrick struck her face with the back of his hand and watched her tumbled to the floor.

Saamyah looked up at him, holding her warm cheek with one hand and pushing the falling towel off of her head with the other. Using her legs, she kicked away from him as he moved closer to her asking, "Why?...Why him?"

Feeling no obligation to dignify his inquiries with responses, Saamyah turned on her knees to crawl in the direction of the master bedroom. Her attempt was cut short when Patrick grabbed a leg and yanked her towards him. Saamyah winced when the hardwood floor burned like flames on her skin.

Patrick dropped on his knees between her thighs when she turned on her back to face him. He gripped her hair, ignoring her commands, and attempted several body blows.

"Get off me, Patrick," she demanded once more, finally snatching her head free. She blocked the hits that followed and then powerfully struck his face.

Patrick relented, succumbing to the pain. He shoved her head into the floor and rose to his feet. Covering his nose and mouth, Patrick watched her trembling hand grip the back of her head as she groaned her misery.

"Patrick, please-" Saamyah began, exhausted by their fight. She unhurriedly sat up and concealed her nakedness by closing the gaping robe. "Please. This has to stop." She looked up at him and confirmed, "It just has to."

He wiped the blood from his nose, yanked her to her feet, and pushed her into the wall.

Saamyah's head ached and spun from the collision that dented the drywall behind her. She cried aloud, but the whistling of the kettle suffocated it.

Bryan's eyes shot open when he heard a loud *thud*. He turned off the sprinkling water to hear the whistling of the kettle and a faint calling of his name. Bryan abruptly jumped out of the shower and yanked his pajama pants over his wet body. After retrieving his firearm from the nightstand, he hurried out of the room without a subsequent thought.

"Patrick…please," Saamyah whimpered, clawing at the hands that strangled her. She gasped at the faintest of air as she stared into his eyes—they were filled with both grief and rage.

"Let her go," Bryan commanded with his firearm pointed at Patrick.

Patrick released Saamyah's neck and backed away from her.

Saamyah collapsed to the floor and coughed profusely.

Bryan slowly lowered next to her keeping his eyes and aim on Patrick. "Are you okay?"

Saamyah nodded through her cries.

Bryan stood and lowered his weapon. "Get out."

"...We will finish this when I return, Saamyah," Patrick assured prior to his departure.

Bryan secured the door, then took a seat next to Saamyah. He gathered her in his arms and kissed her forehead. Knowing that she would not communicate the truth, Bryan did not bother to ask what transpired. Instead, he just held her tightly against his damp body and rocked her as she cried.

"No, Bryan, I'm fine. Really, I am. Like I mentioned earlier, it was just a misunderstanding between Patrick and me," Saamyah confirmed on the phone as she quickly checked her reflection in her vehicle's sun visor mirror. After placing more powder foundation on her bruised cheek, she lowered her sunglasses to her face, tossed her compact back into her black leather clutch, and lifted the sun visor shut.

"Of course, I understand your concerns...Look, I've got to go. I'm already late...How about I stop by later?...Yes...Okay...See you soon." She ended the call on her cell phone, climbed out of her car, and walked toward the establishment.

"I'm so sorry that I'm late. I had some trouble getting here," Saamyah said after she walked into the oceanfront lounge and hopped upon a stool beside Kimberly. She pushed her sunglasses on the top of her head and placed her black clutch on the bar table.

"That's alright," Kimberly said drinking her cranberry juice. "I was being entertained by the bartender."

Saamyah looked at him and smiled. "Water with no lemon, please," she ordered.

Adoring Kimberly's khaki belted tube dress and matching peep toed pumps, Saamyah said, "You look amazing," to break the ice.

Kimberly looked at her knowingly, sipped her drink, and said, "Thanks."

Saamyah received her water and thanked the bartender. After flipping her hair off her bare shoulders, she drank from her glass. "I really appreciate you meeting me, Ms. James."

"Please, call me Kimberly."

"Okay, Kimberly. Thank you for meeting with me today."

Kimberly shrugged. "Not like I had much of a choice. Meeting you was the only way I could get you to stop calling."

Saamyah laughed, but stopped when Kimberly did not do the same. She cleared her throat and explained, "Yeah, I have a hard time taking no for an answer."

"So I see," Kimberly confirmed. She admired Saamyah's black and white printed tube top and black slacks that she wore; but, she would never tell her. While playing with the straw in her drink, she offered, "The fragrance you're looking for is *L'Homme De Tes Rêves*. I bought it from a French boutique downtown for Bryan's birthday."

"Are you sure?"

Kimberly sipped her drink then said, "It's a unique scent. I'd recognize it on any man a mile away."

A pregnant silence grew between them as they both sipped their drinks and watched the other patrons.

The first to break the silence, Kimberly asked, "So, you and Bryan, how long has that been going on?"

"Excuse me?"

Kimberly smiled. "That long, huh? I see he's getting better. You took no time at all."

Saamyah ran her tongue across her teeth in an effort to refrain from saying what she really wanted to say. "What Bryan and I are doing isn't really your business."

Kimberly laughed halfheartedly. "Of course it isn't...I usually don't concern myself with the competition anyway." She smiled knowingly then met Saamyah's eyes, adding, "Bryan and I have an arrangement. I can have him anytime I want."

Saamyah grinned and responded, "Well, I usually don't have to compete for what's already mine. And, as for your arrangement," she added, "it has been nullified."

Kimberly sipped from her glass and smirked. "You're so cute. Just as Rachel was…So cute, so smart, and so damn naïve."

Saamyah shook her head and looked at her in dismay. "Kimberly, why are you doing this?"

She sipped her drink again and then answered, "Bryan is a wandering stray dog that is willing to drop his seed in any available bitch." She met Saamyah's gaze. "And this season, you just happen to be that bitch."

Saamyah went into her clutch for cash to place on the bar table for their drinks and tip. Afterwards, she stood to leave. Before doing so, Saamyah spoke, "Thank you for your time, Ms. James. I hope that you enjoy the rest of your day."

Bryan swung open his front door hoping to see Saamyah on the other side. His smile faded when it was Kimberly.

She chuckled and invited herself in. "Hello, to you, too."

Bryan closed the door and asked, "What are you doing here, Kim?"

She turned to face him. "We do have quite a history. Would it kill you to express a warm welcome?"

Bryan exhaled with frustration. "You can't stay, Kimberly. Please leave."

"Expecting someone?" Kimberly asked.

"Yes," he simply answered.

"Not Detective Cambell, I hope."

He recalled their earlier meeting and asked, "What did you say to her?"

Kimberly laughed and then answered, "Nothing she didn't already know."

He walked towards her. "If you said anything to compromise what she and I are building, I swear to you I will-"

"You…will…what?" She taunted.

Bryan did not answer. Instead he stepped from her personal space and said, "Just leave, please."

Kimberly saw the softness in his eyes and her heart ached at the newfound revelation. "Wow," she breathed in astonishment. "You're in love with her."

Bryan turned from her glare.

She laughed lightheartedly to conceal her jealously. "All this time I thought she was the fool, but she isn't...You are, Bryan." She paused then venomously asked, "Do you really think that that caliber of a woman would seriously build anything with you—a liar and a cheat."

"I've changed, Kimberly."

"Since when? This morning? Bryan, you're the same man that betrayed Rachel and you'll do it to Saamyah. All it ever took was a time of distress, a bottle of liquor, and a willing participant." She moved closer to stroke his cheek with the back of her hand. "You are incapable of change, Bryan Terrell Russell."

He pushed her hand away spewing more her resentment.

"She's prim and proper and you, Bryan, are a heartless womanizer. She's too good for you and you know it. Just as Rachel was...You're better off staying among your own."

"Like you?" He asked with sarcasm, alluding to her string of high-profile romances.

"We're two of a kind, Bryan. Both with blemished pasts and tainted histories." She unbuckled the large belt in front of her dress and tugged at the zipper in the back. After the dress fell to the floor, she stepped out of it.

Bryan struggled with the bulge in his throat as he turned from her remarkably sexy body in pink lingerie.

"Don't fight it, Bryan. Don't fight what you really are." She caressed his torso and added, "You'll only be lying to yourself if you do."

Bryan grabbed both her wrists and squeezed them tight. "Get dressed and get the hell out of my condo before I throw you out on your ass."

Kimberly yanked out of his grip and raised her voice, speaking, "She doesn't love you, Bryan. I loved you, a part of me still loves you...So, don't let her beauty and good sex fool you. Just as the ride is good for you, it is for her; but, when she gets off, and, believe you me she will, don't think you can return to me…Not this time, not anymore."

"Are you done?" Bryan calmly asked.

"Yes."

"Good." He picked up her dress and tossed it at her. "Now get the fuck out of my house."

Bryan started down the hall towards his bedroom, but a knock at the door stopped him. He looked at Kimberly with repugnance. She crossed her arms and gave him a calculatingly stare. There was another knock.

Bryan walked to the door, looked through the peephole, and saw that it was Saamyah. He silently cursed and then quietly commanded Kimberly to remain silent. He despised the smirk she gave him in return.

He slightly opened the door and was in immediate aw of her splendor.

"Hey, you." Saamyah cheerfully greeted. She kissed him, but stepped back when he gently pushed her away. "What's wrong, Bryan?"

Bryan saw the worry on her face. He contemplated telling her the truth, but thought against it after considering everything that Kimberly had said.

"I'm not feeling well…I was lying down before you came."

"I'm so sorry. Do you need anything?"

Bryan rubbed his forehead. "No, I'm just going to take some aspirin and lie down for a little while longer."

"Bryan, honey," a soft voice cooed in the unit. Kimberly walked up to Bryan and nibbled then dipped her tongue in his ear. "Our bath water is ready."

Bryan was instantly paralyzed with fear, anger, and embarrassment. He exhaled loudly, dropped his head, and shook it.

Saamyah's heart sunk into her belly and nausea overcame her.

"Hello, Detective Cambell." Kimberly said while widening the door so that Saamyah could get a better view of her close-to-bare physique.

Saamyah's tear-filled eyes glared at Bryan. "That's some aspirin, Bryan. I hope you feel better." She turned to leave.

"Saamyah, wait!" Bryan yelled.

Kimberly grabbed his arm and commanded, "Let her go."

Bryan gave her a glare that threatened her life. "Get the hell off of me," he growled.

Kimberly released him and gasped when he shoved her into the door.

Bryan raced down the stairs behind Saamyah. "Saamyah, please, let me explain."

He almost tripped down the final steps trying to catch her. Grabbing her arm and turning her to face him, he was taken aback by the vicious slap across his face. Bryan ignored the pain as well as the taste of blood and pulled her into him.

"Let me go, Bryan."

She tenaciously twisted in his embrace, hoping to free herself before he could see her cry.

"Saamyah, I am so sorry. I'm sorry you had to see her like that."

She victoriously pushed him away and released the somber cry she could no longer hold back.

Saamyah's red, tearful eyes met his dreary, regretful ones. "Why, Bryan?" She asked. "How could you do this to me—to us?...I believed you. I believed everything you told me...I...I gave myself to you."

The pieces of his heart crumbled further as he listened to her cries. Fighting to suppress his own tears, he choked, "Saamyah, I swear to you on everything that I love, nothing happened."

"Don't you fucking lie to me! I know what I saw, damn it."

Bryan looked around at the crowd that was enveloping them and then asked her, "Can we talk about this inside?"

Astounded by his audacity, Saamyah assured, "Trust me, you don't want to be around me without witnesses."

He halted his step toward her when she stepped back and gave him a look of repulsion. "I'm not lying, Saamyah. I didn't touch her."

"So, she invited herself over and took off her clothes?"

"As crazy as it sounds, yes."

Saamyah wiped her eyes and chuckled to keep from striking him again. "You must take me for a fool."

"No, Saamyah, I don't, but you have to believe me. I'm not-"

"I should have never given you the benefit of the doubt. Everything she has said about you is true."

Deeply wounded by her comment, Bryan asked, "How are you going to believe a complete stranger over me?"

"It's not that hard when you're a stranger to me yourself." She turned and walked towards her condo. Bryan followed and then barricaded the door before she had a chance to unlock it.

"Move, Bryan."

"Saamyah, please, can we talk about this?"

"Move!" Saamyah exclaimed. She pushed him into the door when he failed to comply. She did it a second time in frustration and added a punch to his chest in anger.

"I HATE YOU!" She screamed as fresh tears rolled down her face.

Saamyah contemplated the many ways that she wanted to hurt him, but, ultimately, she turned and walked away. She knew that the best thing for her to do was to put distance between them, so she climbed into her vehicle, and left.

*** SIX ***

Bryan's eyes lit up when Saamyah walked into the conference room Monday afternoon. Having not seen her all weekend or that morning, he thought she was going to miss their meeting. She entered just as the chief started his briefing.

Saamyah scurried to take the closest seat she could find without drawing too much attention to herself. She quickly surveyed the room to see who was all in attendance. When Bryan caught her eye on the opposite end of the long conference table, she quickly turned to face the projector screen in front of her. The entire first half of the meeting she felt Bryan's eyes burning into the back of her head.

"Okay, everyone, let's break here and report back in fifteen minutes," the chief advised.

Saamyah rose from her chair, as many others did, and smoothed out her short sleeve, lavender shirt and heather grey, pencil skirt. She checked her watch to see if there was time to return to her office to make a quick call.

Bryan quickly maneuvered through the congested room to get to Saamyah as she collected her supplies from the table.

"Saamyah," Bryan greeted, blocking her way to the exit.

"Bryan," she saluted without meeting his eyes. Saamyah attempted to walk around him, but his side step impeded her.

"Bryan, please, not here and not now," she beseeched under her breath.

"Then when?" He asked, matching her tone. "You haven't returned any of my calls."

She exhaled loudly and finally met his eyes. "I'd like to keep my personal and professional life separate if you don't mind. I don't want this past weekend's blur to affect my working relationship with you."

Bryan was pained by the puffiness of her red eyes. She had been crying and, like him, did not get much sleep. "Is that what you are reducing it to? A blur?"

Saamyah did not answer him. Instead, she quickly walked around him and out of the room. She headed in the direction of the stairs that would take her to her office.

Once at the top of the stairs, Bryan grabbed her arm and turned her to face him. "Can we please just talk about this?"

Saamyah yanked out of his grip. "You want to talk? Fine. Let's start with WHY she was NAKED in your house."

The eyes around centered themselves on their commotion.

Close to a murmur, Bryan asked, "Can we please take this in the office?"

Saamyah turned on her heel and walked in the office. Bryan followed and closed the door behind him.

She dropped her supplies on her desk and folded her arm across her chest and said, "You've got 60 seconds."

He exhaled loudly and walked towards her. "Saamyah, I love you too much to hurt you the way you think I did."

She held up her hand to stop him. "Don't do that, Bryan. Don't talk about how much you love me while trying to justify your wayward ways."

"Saamyah, Kimberly and I slept together plenty of times, but Friday was not one of them."

Saamyah shook her head and huffed. "You really expect me to believe that she invited herself over, took off all her clothes, and threw herself at you."

"Yes, but not because I want you to, but because it is the truth."

She dropped her arms and simply said, "Well, I don't believe you."

"I know you don't and I understand why…My reputation precedes me and now I can't even get you to believe me even when I am telling the truth."

Bryan paused to try to read her expressionless face. When he could not, he knew that it was too soon to fight for reconciliation. Temporarily conceding, Bryan stated, "If losing you is my karma…then…then I guess I will just have to learn to live with that. Just know that what I feel for you is real, Saamyah, and disclosing my affections was not a ploy to get you in my bed regardless of what Kimberly has told you."

He pivoted and walked in the direction of his office door.

"Bryan," Saamyah called out to him.

Sensing a glimmer of hope, he turned to face her.

"Please take your flowers with you," She told him referring to the beautiful arrangement of red roses he had placed on her desk. Without looking at him, she collected her supplies again and headed back down stairs for the second half of their meeting.

After the conclusion of the meeting, Saamyah tiredly walked through her office door, dropped her supplies on her desk, and fell into her chair. Noticing the flowers still on her desk, she rolled her eyes at Bryan's defiance. With his door ajar she could see him sitting at his desk facing the wall to his right. He repeatedly clicked the pen in his hand.

"What happen to you at the second half of the meeting?" Saamyah asked rising from her chair to gently push his door open. She rested her weight on the door pane and folded her arms across her chest.

Bryan stopped clicking the pen, but did not turn from staring at the wall.

"I had an important phone call that needed to be returned right away…I figured I wouldn't have been missed or wouldn't miss much."

"Well, you did miss the talking points for tomorrow's press conference."

Bryan only shrugged, allowing the room to fall silent.

Despite not wanting to care, Saamyah sensed that something was not right and, as his partner, she felt compelled to inquire.

She dropped her hands, exhaled loudly, and asked, "Bryan, what's wrong?"

No response.

She walked further into his office and stood in front of his desk. "Bryan?"

Still glaring at the wall Bryan finally answered, "She's pregnant, Saamyah."

"What? Who?"

"…Kimberly."

When his reply struck her like a blow to her lower abdomen that forced air from her body, Saamyah lowered herself in the chair across from him. Though the walls began to enclose her, she still noticed Bryan face her but carefully avoid her eyes.

Bryan watched Saamyah sit stoic and silent. She stared blankly into the atmosphere and inhaled deeply and exhaled gradually.

Despite the success in maintaining her composure, tears fell from Saamyah's eyes. She closed then opened them and asked, "How far along is she?"

Bryan looked away and shrugged. "About eight weeks."

Although she was confident of the anticipated answer, Saamyah still asked, "Is it yours?"

Bryan faced her to see the hurt in her eyes when his red, tired ones finally met them. Though he knew the truth would disappoint her, he could not bring himself to pain her again with another lie.

"The possibility is pretty strong."

Saamyah lowered her lids over her eyes and tried her best to hide her despair. When she opened them again Bryan eyes were still on her. She asked, "What is she going to do?"

Bryan dropped his eyes and said, "I don't know."

"Is she keeping it?"

"I don't know."

Her voice slightly elevated with irritation. "What do you mean you don't know? Do you want her to keep it?"

Bryan looked at her equally vexed. "I don't know, Saamyah."

She dabbed her wet face with the back of her hand, allowing herself the time needed to calm her many emotions. "Well, Bryan, what do you know?"

"That I wish it were you instead of her."

Though his confession pained her more, Saamyah was determined not to shed another tear. Acknowledging her defeat, she swallowed the knot in her throat and said, "Well, it's not and I guess that makes her the victor."

"This is not about winning or losing, Saamyah. This is about my life."

Saamyah shook her head in dissent and corrected, "No, Bryan, it isn't. It's about the life that you created with her." She stood and began to walk to the door. Bryan immediately jumped from his chair and grabbed her forearm before she reached the threshold.

She yanked out of his grip and yelled, "Don't touch me!...Just...Just don't..." Her voice trailed off.

Bryan gave her a moment to compose herself before starting, "Saamyah-"

"How could you do this to me, Bryan?" She interrupted.

Perplexed, he responded, "What? Saamyah, I didn't plan this."

"I know. You never plan anything, you just *do*." Saamyah paused and breathed deeply to avoid an explosive tirade. Realizing that Bryan was and will forever be at Kimberly's disposal, she conveyed, "I don't want to be a part of this debacle; so, please, keep me out of it, Bryan. It was hard enough having to deal with everything she said to me Friday only to have it all come to fruition today."

She proceeded to exit his office, but yielded when he proclaimed, "Saamyah, I need you."

Saamyah stopped to face him and responded, "How dare you be so damn selfish?"

"Because I don't want to go through this alone and, more importantly, I don't want to lose you."

Refusing to allow his words to penetrate her soul, Saamyah shook her head and shared, "You never had me, Bryan," she corrected him, "at least not my heart."

Bryan's heart ached and it was reflected in his misty eyes. His voice cracked as he refuted, "I don't believe you and if you were truly honest with yourself you wouldn't believe you either, Saamyah…You may not love me, but you do feel something."

Saamyah blinked back the water than began to fill her eyes and cleared her throat. "I have to go, Bryan. I'm, uh, meeting Drew…Congratulations on your baby." She left his office closing the door behind her.

Later that evening, Saamyah stepped out of her car and secured it by the button on the door handle. When she felt the vibration of her cell phone at the bottom of her tote, she struggled to find it in the dimness as she slowly walked in direction of her condo.

"Saamyah," he spoke, rising from and stepping down the final steps.

Saamyah jumped back in fear clutching her phone to her chest. "Geez, Bryan. You scared the hell out of me…What are you doing out here?"

"Waiting for you."

"In the dark?"

"It wasn't dark when I initially started to wait."

Saamyah exhaled loudly and rolled her eyes. "What do you want, Bryan?"

"Just to talk."

Annoyed, she asked, "Haven't we done enough of that today?"

"No, actually, we haven't and it doesn't help that you keep dismissing the issue, walking away, and ignoring my calls."

"You made your decision, Bryan, now live with it." She stepped to walk away, but Bryan seized her arm.

"I wanted you, Saamyah, not this. This decision was decided for me."

She twisted out of his firm grip and commented, "Like you didn't have a hand in making it," before walking to her door.

"Yeah, walk away, Saamyah…That's real mature. I hope that you don't handle all your problems this way."

Saamyah turned around and walked back towards him saying, "For some odd reason you seem to think that somehow this is my problem, but it's not. It's yours, Bryan; and, if you didn't want to deal with it, then perhaps you should have handled yourself differently eight weeks ago."

Bryan nodded. "You're absolutely right… and I can't change what is, but I don't see why it has to change us."

Saamyah shook her head in disbelief. "There is no us, Bryan…Yes, we shared something intimate." She caught his eyes and spoke sarcastically, "Thank you for being that man to make it special for me."

Bryan searched her eyes trying to read the genuine emotions behind her facade. "Saamyah, why are you doing this?"

Vexed she asked, "Doing what, Bryan?"

"Dismissing what you gave me as yesterday's news."

"Because, Bryan, I don't want to keep crying over spilt milk. More importantly, I don't' want to keep crying over you—this…I don't want to be the second Rachel in your life."

"What is that supposed to mean?"

Saamyah simply answered, "I can't trust you, Bryan… And, if I can't trust you there can be no 'us'." Her phone vibrated in her hand and she quickly silenced it. "Look, I have some phone calls to return before it gets too late. So, I'll see you in the morning, okay?…Have a good night, Bryan."

"Yeah, you, too," he muttered feeling like he had just lost that battle. He watched as each footstep took her further away from him. After she made it safely into her unit, he walked to his car and entered it. He dialed Kimberly's number as he slowly backed out of the parking space.

"Hey," he greeted. "Yeah, I am on my way over...No, don't. I'm not staying long; I'm just coming to talk..." Bryan abruptly stopped his car. "Really? Is that your final decision?...Okay then. I guess there isn't much left to discuss...Alright. I'll be there...Yeah, you, too." Bryan ended the call and tossed his phone in the passenger seat next to him. Trying to wrap his mind around the idea of fathering a child with Kimberly, he proceeded to the nearest bar.

Saamyah deleted her final voice message and decided to call DeVaughn back first. She fell back into her sofa preparing herself for the long conversation.

"Look who has finally found the time for the little people in her life," DeVaughn quipped.

Saamyah rolled her eyes and shook her head. "Hey to you, too, big brother."

"Hey, babe sis. How are you?"

"You know, the usual: husband's gratified, kids are satisfied, so, I am content."

DeVaughn laughed loudly at the familiar banter shared amongst their family. "That bad, huh?"

Saamyah huffed. "You can't even imagine, but I am hanging in there."

"That's the spirit of the strong woman that I've raised you to be," he encouraged.

Saamyah feebly smiled. "So, how's Simoane?" She asked in an attempt to divert the topic.

He exhaled loudly. "Honestly, some days are better than others. She wants to be induced, but her physician is trying to get her to carry as close to full term as possible."

Saamyah's heart went out to her sister-in-law. "Is she in a lot of pain?"

"No, just discomfort. The twins don't allow her to sleep much at night. So, her days are spent napping."

Saamyah sighed in despair for her. "Please tell her I said to hang in there."

"I will...Maybe you can call her? I know she gets stir crazy in the house all day by herself. She'll be happy to hear from you."

"Yeah," Saamyah simply responded, her mind now traveling to other thoughts.

"How is Bryan?" DeVaughn inquired in an effort to draw her back into the conversation.

"He's fine."

"Are you working better together?"

"We're managing."

DeVaughn could discern that something was amiss, but rather than press the issue, he decided to table his concern for another time.

"Saamyah, I called because of an ominous phone message."

"Really?..From who? About what?"

He exhaled. "I don't know, and nothing I want you to be concerned with." DeVaughn paused and then asked, "Are you okay? You aren't in any danger, are you?"

Saamyah chuckled and responded with sarcasm, "I'm a detective, DeVaughn. I am always in danger."

DeVaughn was not amused by her jest. "I'm serious, Saamyah Anne."

At the call of her full name Saamyah's smile faded. In an instant, she again became the seven-year-old he raised since their parents' fatal car crash.

"Sorry, I didn't know that you were being serious."

He forgave her and asked, "Any peculiar communications?"

"No. DeVaughn, what's this all about? Where is all of this coming from?" She paused to brace herself for the worst before asking, "Did something happen?"

"No, but there seems to be some looming ghosts and, until I can confirm the source, I need everyone to be watchful...The less you know, the better."

Saamyah vehemently despised his go-to phrase: the less you know, the better. She felt it not only perpetuated the belief that ignorance shielded her, but also that she was too weak to cope with the truth. Despite her many petitions, DeVaughn never shared much concerning the family's welfare. All she ever knew was that they never lacked shelter (the home in which each of them was born and raised), food, or clothing; and, none of them were ever asked to sacrifice anything more but their time to keep the family bond strong. Thus, activities and hobbies remained status quo unless used as mediums for punishment—a tactic Saamyah was all too familiar with.

Saamyah rolled her eyes and huffed. "Looming ghosts? What does that even mean?"

DeVaughn ignored her question.

"Has Patrick Barnes contact you?" He instead asked.

Frustrated with his lack of obligation to answer her question, she rhetorically asked, "Isn't he still in prison?"

"No, he was paroled a couple of months ago." DeVaughn breathed deeply then shared, "In exchange for my favorable recommendation at his parole hearing, he has agreed to refrain from contacting any member of this family, specifically you."

Saamyah squeezed closed her water filled eyes, but tears still fell from them. She held her breath hoping that DeVaughn would not hear her cry.

"Are you crying?"

Saamyah wiped her face, sniffled, and lied, "No."

DeVaughn exhaled in frustration and disappointment. "Babe sis, I know you had strong ties to that family and you loved them, but you did not need those adverse connections...Not with all that we—YOU—have been through and the progress that you were making."

"Adverse connections? DeVaughn, they were going to be my family," She corrected, hoping that he would finally acknowledge and accept her reality.

"And thank God they are not now...I'm sorry about David. Saamyah, you know that I am, but that family was never truly what I wanted for you."

"Why? Because of the celebrity lifestyle that would have finally taken me from under your thumb?"

"What?! No."

"Then it must have been the drug addictions that you perpetuated and clandestinely kept from me," she boldly snuck in.

DeVaughn was blindsided by her accusation and immediately caught his tongue before he released an abusive rant.

After sitting a moment in silence to cool his fiery flame, DeVaughn finally announced, "We are revisiting the issue of therapy when you return."

Saamyah did not have the courage to strike again the hot iron. She had already pushed the bounds of parental respect DeVaughn always commanded from his younger siblings. He felt it was the least that was owed to him after reconstructing his medical school and residency plans to keep the family together.

"Good night, Saamyah." DeVaughn hung up the phone without waiting for a response.

Saamyah burst into a heartfelt cry as several family demons resurfaced. She loathed her brother for forcing her to recall things she had labored tirelessly to forget—things that therapy repeatedly failed to console.

*** *** ***

"What is this?" Saamyah asked after walking into Bryan's office.

Bryan's gaze left his laptop as he placed his coffee on his desk. He squinted at the yellow post-it note that she pinched between her fingertips. "Oh, that's information that I received from *Parfum Français*, the exclusive seller of *L'Homme De Tes Rêves*. There was a cologne purchase and I need you to check it out."

"And why can't you do it?"

"I have a conflict."

She shook her head and rolled her eyes. "A conflict? Really?...Is this a lead even worth following? We can't feasibly track fragrance sales. As I mentioned before, the internet makes that impossible."

Bryan shrugged. "Maybe, maybe not. But it's a lead." He leaned back into his chair, folded his hands behind his head, and confirmed, "We have to follow it."

"Then you follow it." She stuck the note on his desk and walked out of his office.

Bryan exhaled loudly and wiped his face of the agitation. He glanced at his watch, stood, and followed her out. "Saamyah, I can't." Bryan hesitated and finally confessed, "Kimberly has an appointment with an OB/GYN later this morning...I gave her my word that I will be there."

Despondent by the revelation, Saamyah slowly lowered herself to her seat behind her desk. She said nothing as the news defined their plight and solidified her position.

"...Good for you...You're doing the right thing, Bryan."

Bryan caught her eyes and spoke, "I am hoping the right thing will count for something."

Saamyah turned from his gaze. "If you give me back the post-it, I will go find out what I can."

She collected the items needed for the trip, awaited Bryan's return with the note, and departed without another word.

Saamyah bit her bottom lip as she inspected the tomatoes she needed for her Greek salad. Once two were selected, she maneuvered to the fresh greens, and picked through them in search of the greenest leaves.

"Detective Cambell."

Saamyah looked up to greet the familiar pair of brown eyes.

"Ms. James." Saamyah placed her pick into a produce bag, tossed them into her cart and met her eyes. "A pleasure to see you fully clothed."

Kimberly grinned. "Just in the neighborhood. My new OB/GYN is not too far from here."

Saamyah flashed her a bogus smile. "So, I've heard. Congratulations."

"Thanks. We really appreciate it."

"We?"

"Bryan and I."

Saamyah laughed halfheartedly. "Please, he doesn't want this baby, Kimberly, and you know it." She tried to get to the cucumbers, but Kimberly barred her access.

"I have no doubt that he'll come around. He loves children and was devastated when Rachel miscarried theirs."

Saamyah swallowed the news hard as she was taken aback by Bryan's omission. It was now apparent that Bryan and Kimberly were a lot closer than what he led her to believe.

"Well, in support of your new family, I'll be sure to stay out of the way."

"Thank you," Kimberly smugly appreciated. She then smiled knowingly and walked away with her hand basket.

Saamyah eyes vehemently burned into the back of Kimberly's head until she disappeared down the aisle. Saamyah desperately wanted to loathe her, but she knew better. Her hatred had to be channeled toward the person who had brought the turmoil into her life.

Bryan swung open the door and hastily walked out of his office. He stopped abruptly to avoid tripping over the several bags on the floor. "Planning an all-nighter?"

Saamyah stopped racing the pendant around her neck and looked away from the window. She answered, "They're groceries I bought during lunch after my interview."

"Well, do you mind moving them from the middle of the floor?"

She did not answer. Instead, she shared, "The fragrance purchase was made by a 47 year old Asian female. It's a gift to her husband in celebration of their twenty-first wedding anniversary."

Bryan nodded. "Okay."

Saamyah looked him over several times before she asked, "So, how did it go?"

"It went," Bryan simply answered not wanting to go into details about Kimberly's pregnancy with her.

"Kimberly's comfortable with the new doctor?"

"Isn't that all that matters?"

"Not entirely."

Bryan exhaled loudly and finally confessed, "Honestly, I am going to have difficulty finding any comfort with this pregnancy until I find out for sure that this child is mine."

Saamyah huffed and returned her gaze to the window, "I am sure it's yours. Kimberly doesn't seem like the type of woman who would lie about something like this."

"You would be surprised to know the lengths women would go to get the man they desire."

Saamyah looked at him and disagreed, "No, I wouldn't. I have three brothers, remember?... Nothing surprises me anymore." She walked to her desk, grabbed her steno book, and stretched her arm to him. "But I still like to think that Ms. James is more emotionally stable than that."

Bryan took the notebook and flipped through her pages of notes. "Of course you would, because it is contrary to what I think."

"...I saw her today."

"Good for you." He tossed the pad on her desk and started his way out for a late lunch.

"She told me about Rachel's baby," Saamyah called out to him.

Bryan stopped in his tracks and looked at her. His head shook in disgust. "Why would she tell you that?"

"Maybe because she knew you hadn't. Or maybe because she wanted me to know that the two of you are closer than what you seem to be conveying to me."

"Saamyah, a lot of what Kimberly and I had was all in her mind."

"Yeah, I am sure it was, Bryan."

Bryan squint his eyes with confusion and walked back to her desk. "Why are you doing this?"

"Because I would like to know the man that I have bedded."

"Yeah, well, I'd like to know the woman, but that's not going to happen with all your damn secrets, now is it?"

The room fell silent and Bryan was the first to break it. He inhaled deeply and exhaled slowly then said, "I didn't know that Rachel was pregnant. We had planned to eventually start trying, but neither of us knew she was until she miscarried." He paused before continuing, "Kim knows all of this because she has always been a constant in my life; always available and always willing."

"Then why not marry her?"

"Because I can't trust her."

Saamyah laughed with cynicism. "Now that's a song that I've sung before…I guess you really are two peas from the same pod."

Bryan did not bother dignifying her comment with a response. Instead, he told her good-bye and walked out of the office.

*** *** ***

"Beautiful, aren't they?"

Startled, Saamyah jumped at the deep voice behind her and turned to face her unexpected companion. She felt her heart palpitate at the sight of the handsome man.

"Yes, they are," she managed to speak through her captivation of his dark, smooth skin. His linen attire and loafers gave the impression that he was en route to a paradise adventure.

He smiled at her, revealing his perfect white teeth. "I'm Tyson," he said, extending his hand.

Saamyah took it, shook it, and said, "Saamyah." She released his hand and asked, "Are you typically out here watching the horses?"

"Most days…But, today, something else caught my eye."

Saamyah blushed and dropped her head. Tyson grinned at her coyness and inquired, "So, do you ride?"

Saamyah turned to face the horses. Tyson moved to her side, propped a foot on a wooden bar, and rested his weight on the white fence.

"Not since my youth," she responded.

Tyson nodded. "Maybe you should today. We have the perfect weather for it."

Saamyah shook her head. "I don't think so. I just came out here to break up the monotony of my work day." She tried her best to refrain from staring at the man that appeared to have stepped out of the men's fashion and style magazine. "Besides, I don't think the owner will allow it."

Tyson nodded a second time. "Perhaps, but I think you should ask him anyway. I hear he is a pretty nice guy…Very handsome, too."

Saamyah looked at him after contemplating the comment that revealed his identity. "You're the owner, aren't you?"

He chuckled and nodded. "Guilty as charged."

She laughed and then took in all that he had owned. "Wow…You must live the most amazing life."

Tyson shrugged. "It depends on the part you are referring to—the life in which I am working eighty hours a week at my firm or the life in which I am constantly stealing moments to be with my son and horses."

Saamyah smiled with admiration. "Either way, it seems to me that you are a very accomplished man, Mr. Tyson."

His soft eyes captured hers. "Accomplished, but not complete."

She blushed again, but this time held his gaze. "You're quite the charmer."

"Not in the least." He looked at the racing horses. "So, what do you say? Want to go for a quick ride?"

Saamyah shook her head. "My lunch hour is over."

"Well, maybe next time."

"Yeah, maybe...It was great meeting you, Tyson."

"Likewise."

Saamyah started across the grass towards her car and felt Tyson's eyes on her until she was out of view.

That evening, Bryan tossed a white envelope on her desk.

"What is that?" Saamyah asked after she quickly glanced over her shoulder. Her fingers moved in haste over the keyboard.

Bryan took a bite into his apple before saying, "Open it."

Saamyah huffed, ceased typing, and retrieved the envelope. After she tore it open, she tugged at the folded invitation and two tickets fell into her lap.

She gathered the tickets and scrutinized them. "What are these?"

Bryan bit his apple and between chews answered, "The committee is late getting them out this year, but they're tickets to the annual gala."

"Oh okay. Are you going?"

"Wouldn't miss it for the world."

"Who will be your guest?" Saamyah asked.

"Why?"

Saamyah shrugged. "I don't know. Just making conversation."

"It won't be Kimberly if that's what you're thinking."

She nodded. "I wasn't, but okay."

"What about you?"

"Patrick."

Bryan stopped in mid bite of his fruit.

Saamyah erupted with laughter. "You should see your face right now—priceless."

"So, you're kidding?"

"Of course I am."

Bryan exhaled with relief. "What's going on with Mr. Barnes anyway?"

Saamyah shrugged as she placed everything back into the envelope. "...I don't know."

Bryan was not convinced of her answer, but thought it too soon to relive their recent encounter with Patrick. "Well, if you happen to come up short, I will be more than happy to accompany you."

Saamyah grinned at his ego. "Thanks, Detective Russell, but I won't need your services... I have someone in mind.

Bryan noticed the glow on her face and he grew jealous. "Oh really? Who?"

"No one you know, I hope."

After taking another bite, Bryan commented between chews, "I guess we will see in three weeks."

"Yeah, I guess."

A brief silence fell among them as Saamyah considered her next statement. She had experienced an unusual encounter with a fellow officer earlier that morning and initially did not think it necessary to disclose the matter. But, because the incident still troubled her, Saamyah finally voiced, "I was accosted by Officer Jenkins in one of the break rooms this morning."

Bryan took a moment to put the name to a face. When it resonated, he asked, "Really? Concerning what?"

"You," she simply answered.

Befuddled, Bryan repeated, "Me?"

"Yes, you. Apparently, there is a question as to how serious our relationship is considering you always get the girl, but never manage to keep her."

Bryan's jaw clenched in anger as he swallowed the last of his apple. He folded the core in the napkin and gestured for permission to place it in her wastebasket. When Saamyah nodded, he tossed the core in it.

"What did you tell him?"

Saamyah folded her arms across her breasts. "I don't think that is the focal point here, Bryan... But, so that you are aware, I told him that my personal business is none of his business."

"Do you want me to talk to him?"

"No, I don't want you to talk to him. I want you to talk to me…What the hell is going on around here, Bryan?"

"Saamyah, I don't entertain office gossip and neither should you."

Saamyah knew better to dismiss her concern as mere office gossip. "What have you done to develop such a poor rapport in this department?"

Bryan did not answer.

"Should we be investigating our fellow LEOs?"

Bryan's face contorted at the suggestion. "What?!... No, of course not."

Saamyah dropped her arms and exhaled loudly. She massaged her temple and revealed, "I don't believe you…I don't believe you and I don't trust you. Something has happened here and I am now in the middle of it."

"Look," Bryan started, "I've done my dirt just as anyone else in this department. Hell, even this city. But, jealousy is what is shining light on my transgressions."

"Not jealousy, Bryan—vengeance," Saamyah corrected then peered at the whiteboard. "Were any of the victims married or dating at the time of your pursuit of them?"

Bryan looked at the board and scanned their faces. "Not married, but maybe dating."

Saamyah pondered his response. It was becoming painfully clear that the investigation was on the brink of becoming a cold case. They could not continue to squander tax dollars to chase false leads and stage romantic ruses.

Bryan took notice of her distress and grew weary. He took a seat in front of her desk and then asked, "What are you thinking?"

Saamyah closed her eyes and rubbed her forehead. When she opened them again, she looked at Bryan and regrettably whispered, "That someone is going to die before we solve this case."

*** *** ***

"So, how about that ride?"

Saamyah smiled and turned to greet the owner of the familiar voice. She watched him walk to her.

"Hey, you," she saluted while accepting the assortment of flowers he presented her. "How did you know that I was here?"

"I didn't. I requested that my staff contact me if and when you were."

She shook her head in disbelief and noticed his suit. "Off to somewhere important?"

"Just a couple of contract meetings."

Saamyah nodded. "Well, I won't keep you. Thanks for the flowers. They're beautiful." She stepped in the direction of her car, but Tyson extended his arm and enveloped her waist before she walked past him.

"Have dinner with me?"

Saamyah looked in his eyes. "I don't even know your last name."

"Troy."

"Of Troy-"

"Smith and White," he finished for her. "Yes, that's me."

"Your firm did the pro bono work on that new youth center not far from here."

Tyson smiled. "You watch the news."

"Someone has to...Are you married, Tyson Troy?"

"Divorced with a four-year-old son. You?"

"Never been and no children."

His lips stretched into a smile and he asked again, "Please, have dinner with me?"

"Twenty minutes, Mr. Troy," a suited driver announced after approaching them.

"Thanks, Ron. I'm on my way," he assured without breaking eye contact with the woman he held close to him.

The driver nodded and stepped back towards the car.

"Please?"

"Yes."

"Thank you...Call me whenever the time is convenient for you, Detective Cambell."

Perplexed, she asked, "How did you-"

"I know people," he answered before she could finish. He released her. "Will you call?"

"Yes."

"Promise?"

Saamyah chuckled. "I promise."

Tyson nodded, bid her farewell, and hurried in the direction of the luxury sedan that waited for him.

Saamyah was mesmerized by his confident stride. Her mystical thoughts of him were interrupted with the realization that she did not retrieve his contact information.

"Wait!" She called after him.

Tyson turned in her direction.

"I don't have your number!"

"Read the card!" He climbed into the back of the car and his driver rolled away.

Saamyah gently plucked the envelope that stood in the middle of the arrangement. She then removed the card and silently read, "To the new Black Beauty in my life. Tyson 305-555-1516." She smiled and held the card close to her heart.

"Nice flowers."

Saamyah quickly minimized Tyson's biography on her laptop.

"Thanks," she told Bryan hoping that he would not take notice of the vase. She had used the one he had given her.

"Who are they from?" He asked snatching the envelope from the flowers.

"Bryan," Saamyah protested, standing to her feet as she tried to reclaim the item.

Bryan laughed and moved out of her reach before she had a chance to pry the card from his fingers. He quickly read the note.

"Who is Tyson?" Bryan asked giving back the envelope and card.

"Don't worry about it," she said while meticulously placing the card back in the envelope and then back in its place among the flowers.

"I'm not worried, but I would still like to know."

Defensively, she reminded, "My personal business is none of your business."

Bryan concealed the sting of her comment by changing the subject. "We received a call from parents of a statutory rape victim. I believe it to be a Romeo and Juliet matter, but the father insists that we take his daughter's statement...I will be out front waiting in my g-ride."

Saamyah sunk deeper into her bed and pulled the comforter to her chin. She pressed the phone firmly against her ear as her heart raced with anticipation. Looking at the clock on the nightstand, she realized that calling a quarter before midnight was not only rude, but inconsiderate. On the verge of hanging up, a voice stopped her.

"Hello," he tiredly greeted.

Saamyah immediately recognized his voice. "Hi, Tyson. It's Saamyah. How are you?"

He grinned despite his exhaustion. "...Better now that I am talking to you."

"I'm sorry to call so late. I wanted to keep my word to you."

Tyson stifled a yawn and offered, "Think nothing of it. I actually was waiting up for you."

A smile stretched across Saamyah's face. She appreciated the generous lie.

"Detective Saamyah Anne Cambell, tell me about yourself," he huskily requested.

Saamyah chuckled. "What? You mean you haven't had your staff research all there is to know about me?"

"And take away the pleasure of getting to know you for myself? Absolutely not...Besides, I'm no betting man. I could not gamble the chance of anyone wanting you for themselves."

"You are a man of great faith, Mr. Tyson."

"That I am, but how did you come to that conclusion?"

"You assume that I am available to you."

"You strike me as a woman who would have told me otherwise."

She smiled at his accurate summation. "That—I would have."

"Now, stop stalling...I want to know as much as you are willing to share in the time you allot for this call.

His chivalry made her blush and she silently prayed that he could not detect it through the phone. "I am originally from San Antonio, Texas. Born and raised," she began.

Tyson listened intently as she spoke of her Native-American and Creole roots; deceased parents (who were abruptly taken from her by a sleeping truck driver); three elder brothers; a few passions; some hobbies; and brief career as a federal special agent.

"Why the brief stint with The Bureau?" He inquired after allowing her to talk without interruption.

Saamyah hesitated to respond and Tyson sensed her uneasiness. "I'm sorry, Saamyah. You don't have to answer that. I apologize for prying."

"No, no. It's fine...It's just difficult to relive sometimes." She cleared her throat and finally answered, "My fiancé was also an agent—a supervisor actually. He was killed in the line of duty."

Struggling with the appropriate words to comfort her, Tyson finally breathed the words, "I'm sorry."

"Thank you," she replied in a whisper.

Saamyah glanced at her clock and noticed that she dominated the half hour of their conversation. "I have completely monopolized our time."

"As you should," he offered.

Saamyah blushed. "You're spoiling me."

"As I should," he assured.

Saamyah lightly bit the tip of her tongue to confirm she was not dreaming. When the pressure of her teeth proved her consciousness, she loaned him the conversation. "Your turn. Tell me about you."

"What do you want to know?" Tyson asked.

"I don't know—anything…Why did your marriage fail?"

Tyson exhaled loudly as he searched for an adequate answer. "The short answer, I lost sight of what was most important in my quest to build my empire."

His vagueness intrigued Saamyah. "And the long answer?" She asked encouraging him to continue.

"My ex-wife and I married really young. Right out of college to be exact. With her as an accountant and me as an architect, we had dreams of building my firm together. But, somewhere along the way, the money and becoming one of America's prominent businesses didn't matter as much to her as it did me." He paused then continued, "I later learned that the company was never her dream; she just wanted and supported it for me because she loved me."

"And you couldn't work it out?"

"Kellie tried, but it's tough to make a marriage work alone. I never made myself available to her or my son…And, in my eyes, we weren't in need of fixing because we weren't broken. So, I never entertained the suggestion for counseling." Tyson yawned and then concluded, "When Kellie discerned that I loved her, but was *in* love with my career, she served me with divorce papers."

Saamyah's heart went out to him. "Tyson, I'm so sorry."

"Don't be," he advised. "I have always been a man who learned best the hard way. But, after much growth and maturity, I learned that the things of greatest value are the things we can't place a value."

Saamyah smiled and lauded, "Spoken like a true changed man."

Tyson laughed and then, at her request, shared details about his son and his retired parents in North Carolina. As the only grandchild to their only child, Tyson's parents anxiously awaited every summer to enjoy six weeks of energetic fun.

"Malachi is my greatest blessing. But, if I can be completely honest, I am thrilled for the break."

They both laughed.

"That in no way makes you a bad parent. Parenting is challenging—at least that is what my eldest brother tells me."

"Kellie says the same as she, too, looks forward to the annual break."

"Well, there you have it; even the strongest of co-parents need to be reprieved. Saamyah glanced at her clock and noticed that it was after one in the morning. "I hate to end this call, but I need to get some rest."

"I understand...Are you available for dinner tonight?"

Saamyah contemplated the question and responded, "...I don't know, Tyson. I have another long day ahead of me. I would hate to make plans and then have to cancel them later."

"Then let's meet for dessert. We can eat ice cream and watch the horses."

Saamyah chuckled. "A bit anxious, aren't we?"

Tyson laughed at himself and confessed, "I just want to see you again."

She conceded. "Okay, tonight. I will meet you at the stables at eight."

"I'll be there."

"Good night, Tyson."

"Sweet dreams, Saamyah."

*** *** ***

Saamyah nervously paced the outside grounds of the police department's secured back entrance. When her bravery finally set in, she dialed DeVaughn's home phone number and anxiously awaited an answer. The phone rang several times in her ear.

"Hello," Simoane finally greeted.

"Hey, it's me."

"Oh, hey, babe sis. How are you?"

"I'm okay," Saamyah partly lied. "All things considered, I guess. How are you? Last I heard you weren't doing so well."

Simoane groaned. "Some days are better than others, but your niece and nephew give me no rest."

"I'm so sorry to hear of it."

Simoane chuckled lightheartedly. "Me, too. But at least I have Trévion's wedding to keep my mind off the discomfort...The plans are going well."

Saamyah nodded in remembrance of her brother's late fall wedding and made a mental note to contact him concerning her bridesmaid's dress.

Grieved, Saamyah stopped pacing, and finally spoke after a brief pause in the conversation. "...Is...is he around?"

Simoane sighed with despair. "He is, but he isn't accepting your calls right now... I'm so sorry, babe sis."

Saamyah's heart dropped at the rejection and the tears fell from her eyes. "No, don't be...I completely understand..." She paused and added, "I just thought that..."

Simoane waited for her to complete her thought, but when Saamyah was slow with her delivery, she offered, "I can pass a message. You know I hate being in the middle of your sibling squabbles, but, for you, I will do it."

Saamyah so desperately wanted to tell the brother who took on the role as her father, "Thank you, I'm sorry, I love you," but she could not bring her mouth to utter it. Even after reflecting on the sacrifice of DeVaughn's plans, dreams, and life, Saamyah still could not speak.

"Babe sis," Simoane encouraged.

Saamyah noticed Bryan climbing out of his parked vehicle and walking toward the secured entrance. She quickly wiped her face and cleared her throat. "No...No message."

"Are you sure?"

"No message." With that Saamyah ended the call.

"What's up?" Bryan asked after realizing Saamyah's presence.

Saamyah avoided his stare so that he would not notice that she had been crying. "Nothing, just making some personal calls."

Bryan pushed his sunglasses to the top of his head. His assumption was correct, she had been crying. "Are you okay?"

Saamyah looked at him and smiled feebly. "I will be."

He returned his sunglasses to his eyes to protect them from the afternoon sun. "Did you get my message about evidence review?"

"Yeah, I did... Sorry that I have not had the chance to respond."

"Sure...I spoke to Lieutenant and he wants-"

"I can't do it today, Bryan," Saamyah interjected.

"Saamyah, this is not up for negotiation."

She respired in frustration, walked to the glass door, and waved her secure card in front of the black box. Once inside, she displayed her credentials to the duty officer. Bryan did the same.

"I have a conflict," Saamyah confessed as she briskly walked and climbed the steps to their office. Bryan followed closely her heel.

"What time? I can push back the review." Bryan closed the door behind him after entering the room behind her.

"You just can't push it back, Bryan. Change the day. Change it to another day. Hell, change it to tomorrow."

Bryan observed her body and knew that something was amiss. "Why?"

"Why what?"

"Why not today? Why a different day?

Saamyah shrugged and finally confessed, "I have a date."

"A date?" Bryan inquired with disbelief and jealousy. "No...You don't get to pass up evidence review for a date."

Saamyah walked behind her desk and took her seat. She looked up to Bryan and professed, "I want a life outside of this work...outside of you. You yourself have said that I need to explore all that Miami has to offer."

Bryan stifled the burn he felt in his chest. Holding his composure, he commanded, "Cancel the date...If I am to be here on a Friday night, then so will you." He walked into his office and slammed the door.

Saamyah closed her eyes and inhaled a deep breath. She took a moment to decompress from both her conversation with Simoane and exchange with Bryan. When she felt that she had re-centered herself, Saamyah unlocked the screen on her cell phone, dialed Tyson's number, and informed him of the disappointing news.

In the file storage room late that evening, Bryan brushed past Saamyah to get to a shelf. He took a lid off its box and rummaged through its contents.

"So, this cancelled date of yours, was it with Tyson?"

Saamyah huffed in astonishment while exploring her own box. "You remembered his name." She smiled to herself and added, "I'm impressed.

Bryan despised her iridescence at the mention of his name. He placed the top back on his box and shoved it back into the shelf. He turned to face her and hotly inquired, "Are you sleeping with him?"

Disheveled by the unexpected question, Saamyah looked at him and breathed, "What?"

"You heard me," he retorted, closing the space between them and shoving the box she held ajar back into the shelf.

"I'm not you, Bryan," she reminded him. "I don't sleep with people I just met."

"You did with me. Or was I just the exception?"

Saamyah swallowed the knot in her throat. "...I am not having this conversation with you." She again pulled out her box, shoved a file in it, and then pushed it back into the shelf.

"Do you plan to?"

She looked at him and stated, "That's none of your business, Bryan."

Bryan nodded and responded with regret, "You do. I can see it your eyes."

Saamyah made an attempt to walk past him, but Bryan barricaded the walkway. "Saamyah, why are you doing this to me?"

"Doing what?" She asked in frustration, avoiding his gaze.

"Tormenting me this way when you know how I feel about you."

She met his eyes. "I don't know how you feel, Bryan. I really don't...I mean I know what you say and I know what you do; but, honestly, I don't know what you feel."

"What I feel-" Bryan began.

"Was the need to cheat on me," Saamyah reminded him.

His heart dropped and ached at the accusation. "I never cheated on you, Saamyah," he defended. "...But if you want to use that as an excuse to fuck Tyson, then by all means, enjoy the ride." Bryan nudged her aside and attempted to move past her.

Saamyah grabbed his arm and turned him to face her. "I may take a lot of crap from you, Bryan, but I will NOT tolerate your disrespect."

He yanked out of her grip. "I never give anything I don't receive."

Saamyah shook her head in incredulity. "You've changed, Bryan."

"Yeah, Saamyah, so have you." With that he walked off.

*** *** ***

Saamyah hastily fumbled through her walk-in closet searching for an ensemble fit for her evening with Tyson. When each scan of her limited wardrobe returned with nothing, her frustration grew and she instantly regretted not adequately packing for occasions outside the office.

Before feelings of defeat set in, Saamyah noticed a clear garment bag tucked in the rear of the closet. She retrieved it and immediately noticed the familiar satin, cream colored, asymmetrical dress, and recalled the intimate memories of Bryan. His passion. His tenderness. His—Saamyah forced the thoughts out of her head and yanked the dry cleaner receipt from the plastic. She made the decision to wear the dress in hopes of creating new memories.

Outside, Bryan jogged down the final steps just as a vehicle pulled into the available space between his and Saamyah's cars. Slowly walking toward his Lexus, he watched the suited man descend out of his silver Mercedes. When they caught each other's glance, they acknowledged each other with a mere nod and brief hello. Tyson then walked to Saamyah's door and entered when she opened it.

Bryan stood at his car overwhelmed with many emotions, unsure of how to manage them. The beast in him wanted to kick down Saamyah's door and take back what he believed to be his, but the man in him desired her to be happy even if it was not with him. Yielding to the beast, Bryan shoved his keys in his pocket and turned in the direction of Saamyah's unit. He was stopped short by a fast approaching stranger who struck his face. Bryan fell to the ground and other blows followed.

"Did you have any trouble finding the place?" Saamyah asked Tyson as she placed her second diamond drop earring in her opposite ear.

Tyson lowered himself onto her sofa after the invitation to sit and shook his head. "Not at all."

She grew nervous by his stare and smoothed out her dress. "What?"

"Nothing," Tyson responded turning his gaze, realizing it was making her uncomfortable.

"You don't like it, do you?"

Tyson looked at her and smiled. "To the contrary...Actually," he rose to his feet and stepped to her, "you look radiant." He lifted her chin and planted a lingering kiss on her lips.

Saamyah felt a chill rise in her spine and she nervously turned away. She then walked to her breakfast bar to complete the transfer of items into her clutch. "So, ummm, this art show, do you know any of the artists?"

Tyson ran his tongue across his teeth as he tried to discern what he did wrong. When nothing readily came to mind, he finally answered, "I do. Many are actually locals."

Facing him, she avoided his eyes and nodded. "That's wonderful. I can't wait to meet them."

"Ready?"

Saamyah met his gaze and answered, "Yes."

After Saamyah secured her front door, Tyson walked her to the passenger side of his car and opened the door for her.

Saamyah smiled and thanked him before climbing in. As she watched him walk to the driver's side, she noticed a battered silhouette sluggishly crawling up the stairs.

Tyson closed his door and push-started his engine.

"Wait," Saamyah requested, grabbing his arm. "There's someone hurt on the stairs."

She unlocked the door, hurried out of the car, and raced to the stairs. "Bryan! ...Bryan, is that you?!" Her heart raced with panic as she climbed the final steps to get to the wounded body. She gently rolled the body over to confirm her suspicion.

"Oh, Lord, please, no," she whispered in prayer. "Bryan...Bryan. Are you okay? Who did this to you?" Her eyes swelled with tears and she could not stop them from falling.

Bryan coughed blood and gurgled, "I don't know."

Tyson made it to her side and was taken aback by his recognition of the injured person—he had just greeted him moments earlier.

"Come on, Bryan. Let's get you to the hospital."

Bryan shoved her arm away. "No, I am fine...Just leave me here. I'll be okay."

"Bryan, you're crazy to think I am going to leave you here."

Tyson concurred, "We should probably get him to the hospital right away. He could be seriously injured."

Saamyah nodded. "Can you help me get him to my car?"

"Of course."

Bryan groaned his pain as he was brought to his feet.

"Sorry," Saamyah muttered as they made it to her vehicle.

Once Bryan was secured in the back seat, Tyson looked at her and said, "I'll follow you."

Saamyah nodded and thanked him.

Saamyah's nerves were aflame as they were forced to remain in the waiting room. At Tyson's request, she stopped pacing the floor only to take a seat next to him and rock and pray. She felt his soothing, warm hand stroke her back and a new wave of tears fell from her eyes.

"I don't understand what's taking them so long," Saamyah whimpered. "...We have been waiting for almost two hours. Someone should come and tell us something."

"Hey," Tyson whispered, turning her face to his. "He is going to be fine... They're probably just crossing all their t's and dotting all their i's."

Saamyah nodded. "Thanks for being here."

Tyson pulled her into him. "There is no place I would rather be than here with you." He wiped her wet face and tried to kiss her, but she dropped her head. He lifted her chin until their eyes met. "What is it, Saamyah? What am I doing wrong?"

She gently moved his hand from her face. "I just can't right now, Tyson." She turned away from him and added, "...There is a lot going on in my life right now and a lot you don't know."

He took her hand and held it. "Well, I want you to share these things with me because I am not going anywhere."

Saamyah looked at and adored him through her blurred vision. She allowed him to wipe away her tears and cover her lips with his full ones.

"Ms. Cambell," the physician greeted, walking into the room.

Saamyah abruptly stood and Tyson followed suit.

"Dr. Hasan," he introduced himself, extending his right hand to each of them.

"How is he?" Saamyah asked, cutting to the chase.

"Well, he does have a few badly bruised ribs and a mild concussion, but he'll be fine."

Saamyah exhaled loudly with relief. "Thank God."

Tyson rubbed her back to comfort her and asked the physician, "May we see him?"

"Yes, but only briefly. Visiting hours are over and he needs to rest."

Saamyah nodded and thanked him as she followed him to Bryan's room.

"Hey, you," Saamyah softly spoke.

Bryan opened his eyes and saw both Saamyah and the man he presumed to be Tyson, stained with his blood, at his side. "Hey," he managed to say.

Saamyah fought hard the tears that swelled in her eyes, but they fell anyway. She quickly brushed them away and asked, "How are you feeling?"

"Like a new man."

Tyson grinned. "Must be the morphine."

Bryan loathed the suited man's presence and turned his head from him after repeating, "Yeah, morphine."

Tyson sensed that he was not welcome and pardoned himself. "Saamyah, I am going to head home."

She looked at him with disappointment. "So soon?"

Tyson nodded. "Yes, that way the two of you can have time alone before you are forced to leave." He kissed her temple and urged, "Call me."

"I will."

Tyson looked at Bryan and wished, "Get well soon."

Bryan said nothing in return.

Saamyah touched the icepack taped to his ribs then gently stroke his swollen face. "Bryan, who did this to you?"

He shrugged. "I don't know."

"Did you get a look at him?"

"No—I don't know."

"Did he say anything?"

Bryan thought back on the threats hurled at him and exclaimed, "Saamyah, please!" He groaned his pain the excitement caused and calmly stated, "I don't feel like being interrogated."

"You're right...I'm sorry." She pulled up a chair to sit close to him and held his hand in both of hers. "I am so sorry that this has happened to you."

"Me too." He paused then asked, "So, that is the infamous Tyson?"

She released his hand. "Bryan, please don't do this. Not now."

Disregarding her petition, he faced her and questioned, "What does he have that I don't?"

Saamyah looked upon him in abhorrence. "You really want to have this conversation now? In your condition?"

"I can't go anywhere. So, no better time, right?"

Despite her lingering feelings of sympathy, Saamyah found it impossible to suppress the new feelings of hurt, disgust, and anger. She could not fathom why Bryan could not be content with her presence. His selfishness not only disappointed her, but prompted her response, "...He has me."

He turned away from her and looked at the ceiling. "So, is that why you are wearing that dress? To blatantly showcase that you are with him?"

"No, Bryan. I wore the dress because I had nothing else to wear."

"Bull shit," he retorted then coughed. He winced at his discomfort.

Saamyah jumped to his aid, but he pushed her back. "Just leave, Saamyah...I don't want you here either."

Too exhausted to contest his request, she nodded. "...Okay, but I'll be back tomorrow to check on you."

He shook his head. "No. Don't come see about me."

"...Alright, if that's what you want."

"Yes."

She sadly nodded and leaned to kiss his forehead. Her heart dropped when he turned his face, dismissing her. She then resorted to kissing her fingertips and gently touching his bare bicep. "Good night, Bryan. I hope you feel better."

He said nothing in return.

Saamyah hurried to her car. Once in it, she locked the doors and wept profusely.

*** *** ***

Tyson waved his hand in her view to interrupt her blank stare. "Are you still with me?"

Saamyah immediately returned to their Sunday brunch on the boardwalk. She then realized that she had been subconsciously picking over her fruit.

"I'm so sorry, Tyson... I really am somewhere else right now."

"Yeah, I can tell." He looked at her solemn face. "Maybe we should have waited a day or two to do this?"

Saamyah did not answer instead she said, "I just don't understand why Bryan doesn't want me to go see him...I don't understand how he can be so selfish."

Tyson placed his fork in his plate, retrieved the linen napkin from his lap to wipe his mouth and placed it on the table. "I didn't plan on sharing you and my Sunday afternoon with him, but if that's what it takes to have you here, then I am all ears."

Saamyah looked up from her dish. She touched his arm and apologized, "Tyson, I'm so sorry...You know what? I am done talking about him—I promise...I am here with you now and you deserve all of me."

Tyson accepted her apology, but knew better than to accept her promise of commitment. With all that had happened, it was unreasonable to expect her to be totally devoted to him at that very moment.

"You should go see him," he encouraged.

"You think so?"

Tyson nodded. "Absolutely. You're his partner and it only makes sense. Regardless of what he has said, he wants you at his side."

Saamyah pondered his statement. "You're right." She thought for a moment more and added, "I am going to go now."

Tyson choked on his juice. Once his cough cleared his lungs, he asked, "As in now, now?"

"Yes, while it's still early...That's...That's if you don't mind."

Tyson remained composed through his discontentment. "No, not at all."

Saamyah grabbed her handbag and stood. "Thanks so much for understanding, Tyson. You're the best." She leaned to kiss his cheek and said, "I'll call you later," before leaving him to dine alone.

Saamyah stealthy entered Bryan's room to see a woman lying next to him in the bed. It was Tiffany. When they spotted her, Saamyah knew it was too late to turn around.

Tiffany raised her head from the pillow and spoke first, "It's so good to see you again, Detective Cambell."

Saamyah conjured the best smile she could and walked further into the room. "Thanks, same here." She placed the flowers on the table next to the others that Bryan had received.

She looked at Bryan and said, "I know you don't want me here, but I just came by to make sure that you are okay...I'll leave now."

"Nonsense," Tiffany said, interrupting her departure. "I was on my way out to get something to eat anyway. You can stay here and watch *Martin* reruns with him until I return."

Saamyah looked at Bryan for approval, but he refused to return her gaze.

Tiffany slipped on her heels and grabbed her tote. "Please stay. I will be back in an hour."

Saamyah nodded. "Okay."

Tiffany left closing the door behind her, and Saamyah took the same chair she had the night before and sat next to him.

"So, how are you feeling?"

Staring at the television, Bryan simply said, "Fine."

"Are you in a lot of pain?"

"Saamyah," he snapped, annoyed with her questions.

"I'm sorry." An uncomfortable silence fell in the room and for a while they both stoically watched the television—neither of them was moved by the humor of the show.

When bravery settled within her, Saamyah took a deep breath and broke the silence. "Bryan, I never wanted us to end up like this—angry and hostile and unable to talk to each other...If I could, I would go back and uncross the line that we should have never crossed."

Because he felt differently, Bryan did not respond.

"I just don't know how to fix this," she confessed.

"Your happiness and enjoyment of a life outside of work and me is all that matters to you, Saamyah. So, you do just that."

"Must you be so indignant?...For the record, you did this to us, Bryan—not me. You were the one that repeated that you loved me, wanted to be with me, and then pissed it all away the very first chance you got."

Bryan turned up the volume on the television.

"Yeah, that's real mature, Bryan!" Saamyah said, raising her voice over the sitcom's laughter. She rose to leave.

Bryan muted the television and called after her before she reached the door, "I did love and wanted to be with you, Saamyah...I really did and I still do...And no matter what others may have told you, it was never my intention to hurt you the same way that I did Rachel." He turned his head in her direction. "I wanted to beat the odds and make us work."

She turned to face him. "Tyson's a really nice man, Bryan. And even though nothing may come of it, I'm in a good place right now." She stopped to regain control of her emotions. "Just let me go, Bryan."

"...I can't and I won't. Not feeling the way I do about you, and not when I know I haven't wronged you...I'll find a way to make this right—that's my word."

Saamyah shook her head. "Don't...I won't jeopardize my heart."

Bryan closed his eyes to hide his agony. When he opened them again, he assured, "I'm not letting you go, Saamyah. I'm not, especially when the only thing I am guilty of is conceiving a child before I met you."

"That's not all you're guilty of, Bryan. You lied to me also."

Feeling ashamed, he turned his head toward the window. "I wish I could-"

There was soft knock on the door and then it crept opened.

Saamyah was greeted with Kimberly's glowing face. For a brief moment, their eyes locked, exchanging no words until Kimberly finally said, "Hey."

"Hey," Saamyah merely returned.

"I..I can come back. I just wanted to drop this off to him," Kimberly confessed, holding a Get Well bear and balloons.

"No, go right ahead. I was just leaving," Saamyah insisted. "Bryan, be sure to tell Tiffany that I had to go." She brushed past Kimberly and left.

*** SEVEN ***

They walked in the park and appreciated the midday reprieve from Florida's sweltering heat and humidity. As he attentively listened to her perceptions of crime and public policy, Tyson held Saamyah's hand and, on occasion, chimed in with his opinion on the subject matter.

After laughing off their different views on the death penalty, they finally agreed to disagree on gun control. When the humor left them, Tyson felt it appropriate to ask at last, "So, what's the story with you and Bryan? I mean, I know the two of you work together at MPD, but something tells me that there is more to it than that…Am I right?"

Saamyah huffed at his would be loaded question if his assumption was not accurate. "…And now our honeymoon phase ends," Saamyah spoke then stalled, knowing that her response could adversely affect whatever the two of them were building. She suspected the issue would come to light and be impossible to avoid, but she thought to have more time.

"Not necessarily…I just need to know what I am getting into before this goes any further."

Saamyah halted her steps and so did he. When he turned to face her, she said, "I think that 'this' is the more important topic to discuss. What exactly is 'this'? It's only been a couple days shy of a week, but are we really trying to build something here?"

"Saam-" Tyson attempted to answer.

"Because if we are then we really need to consider the fact that Florida is not my home and it probably will never be…Tyson, I am here on a TDY and when my assignment is over at the end of August, I go back to Texas."

Slightly taken aback by the revelation, Tyson quickly recovered and said, "First, take a breath and calm down. I feel that you are growing anxious for no reason at all."

Saamyah realized his point and took a moment to breathe and calm herself.

"Second, your TDY is definitely unexpected news to me, but we will cross that bridge when we come to it. Right now, I am just concerned about the bridge you keep going back to…with him."

Saamyah dropped her eyes and exhaled slowly. Despite the advice of several wise elders, she did not feel as if the truth would set her free. To the contrary, she believed the truth would forever shackle her to the man she was trying to break from.

Recalling how Bryan's lies painfully shattered her, Saamyah looked up at Tyson and finally confessed, "…Bryan and I allowed our emotions to cloud our judgment while employed in a ruse to entrap a perpetrator."

Tyson burst into laughter at her ambiguity. "What does that even mean?"

Saamyah covered her face with her hands in embarrassment. When she dropped them she simply answered, "It means we had sex."

"Okay," he said, nodding.

"It was only one time and-"

Tyson gently touched her lips with his fingertips. "Details I don't want to know, but what I *need* to know is should I be concerned about a second time?" He dropped his hands to her waist and pulled her into his body. Searching her eyes for the truth, he asked, "Is it over?"

"Yes," she answered without hesitation.

"Are you sure? Because I think there is something here and I want to see it through. So, I am willing to commit to this and I would like you to do the same."

A wide smile stretched across Saamyah face. "Yes, I am sure."

"Thank you." Tyson lowered his mouth onto hers and kissed her until she broke it for air. They both laughed and he took her hand to continue their walk.

"Any news on Russell?" Andrew asked Saamyah in his office after lunch. He watched her stuff D.A.R.E. folders across from him.

She shook her head. "I had other lunch plans today, so I couldn't make it to the hospital...Besides, he has made it clear that he doesn't want me around, so I am not going out of my way to visit anymore." She paused then added, "He seemed better when I saw him yesterday though."

By Saamyah's rambling, Andrew concluded that something went sour between her and Bryan. Pushing aside the folders he was assembling, he gave her his full attention and asked, "What happened, Saamyah?"

Saamyah shook her head, and, as she kept working with her packets, she simply answered, "You were right... I mean, I can't confirm or deny his infidelity, but he is definitely one who can't be trusted." She quickly wiped the tears from her eyes and breathed deeply. She looked at him and laughed at herself. "I can't believe I am fretting like this."

Andrew reached across his desk to cover her hand with his. "It's only natural to feel the way you do, Saamyah. He has hurt you and it burns; so, don't rush yourself trying to heal from it...I am so sorry Russell did this to you...and, for the record, I didn't want to be right."

Saamyah smiled. "Thanks, Drew."

He nodded and released her hand. He looked at his watch. It was almost two o'clock. "We should probably head to the school. The program starts in forty-five minutes."

*** *** ***

"Are you sure about this, Saamyah?" Andrew questioned the next morning after lowering the window of his government vehicle. The heat immediately enveloped him.

Saamyah dabbed her perspiring forehead with the back of her hand and then shielded her eyes from the morning sun. "I'm positive," she simply responded. Saamyah was desperate to end the conversation and enter the café. She felt every degree of the 96 Fahrenheit as she stood outside his SUV.

"I still think it's best that I come in with you. I can get my own seat at the bar and she will never know that I accompanied you."

Saamyah shook her head in opposition. "I gave her my word, Drew. You being in the vicinity is already a stretch of the truth…It's 11 A.M. I will be fine." With that she turned and walked to the entrance of the café.

When she swung open the glass door, bells chimed. A waitress pouring a patron's coffee immediately greeted and instructed her to sit anywhere. Saamyah smiled and then searched the establishment for a description of the woman who requested the meeting. After Saamyah spotted her near the window, she hurried to the table.

"Michelle?"

She turned her gaze from the window to the calling of her name. "Yes?"

"I'm Detective Cambell." Saamyah extended her hand, but Michelle did not receive it.

"You said you would come alone."

Saamyah took notice of Andrew's vehicle outside the window. She lowered herself to the seat in front of her and lied, "I did. He was just asking for money."

Unconvinced, Michelle asked, "What did you tell him?"

"I told him that I didn't have any and that maybe the owner of the café will allow him to bus tables for a few dollars."

Michelle struggled to believe Saamyah, but found her too quick with her responses to further press the issue.

"Let's talk out back in the event he is watching us."

Saamyah opened her mouth to contest, but Michelle started toward the exit and left her no choice but to follow.

A right turn at the first corner led them down the cobblestone alley that separated the café and bakery next to it. Before the second right turn to take them to the rear of the café could be made, a pair of hands grabbed Saamyah by the lapel of her cropped jacket and swung her into the side of the dumpster behind the building.

Saamyah fought the urge to faint when the air in her lungs was violently forced from her body. She panted until she caught her breath and then met the eyes of her attacker. They were green.

"Don't look at me," he growled. He struck her lower abdomen with his fist and moved to watch her bellow in pain and drop to her knees.

Michelle stood stiff in fear despite meeting his eyes and his commands for her to leave. She shook her head in defiance and moved forward to aid Saamyah, but halted her step when he drew his firearm.

"Please," Michelle beseeched, raising her surrendering hands. "...Please just-"

"I said GO!" He yelled. Michelle took off in the direction from which they came.

The twinge that shot through Saamyah's kneecaps paled in comparison to what she felt at her core. Before she could recover from either, he pulled her to her feet and pressed her against the dumpster.

"Is this case really worth your life or that of your family's?" He asked holding the barrel of his gun at her temple.

Saamyah did not answer. Instead, she silently took in his physical profile.

He pressed the barrel deeper into her temple and demanded, "Answer me!"

Saamyah shook her head. She then swallowed the knot behind her tongue, cleared her throat, and whispered, "No."

"Then act like it." He struck her abdomen with his fist a second time and then inconspicuously left the scene.

Saamyah fell again to the hot cobblestone. Though disoriented by the pain and heat, she could indistinctly hear the calling of her name.

"What the hell, Saamyah? Are you okay?" Andrew asked when he finally reached her. He helped her to her feet.

"I'm fine," Saamyah whispered. She held her abdomen as she leaned to take rest against the dumpster.

Andrew gave her a moment to regain her bearings. "What were you thinking, Saamyah?...Leaving the café like that?"

Saamyah rolled her eyes at his inquisition. "I was thinking of creating the ideal interview space for the victim." She paused to breathe slowly through the pain and then added, "She suspected that you were an officer," before she pushed past him to begin the agonizing limp back to her unmarked vehicle.

Andrew knocked on and widened Saamyah's partly opened office door. He immediately apologized and quickly looked away as she, in haste, pushed down and affixed her shirt. She had been scrutinizing her bruised abdomen.

"What is it, Drew?" Saamyah asked inviting him in while she took a seat at her desk. She tried her best to mask her discomfort.

Andrew crossed the threshold, closed the door, and walked further into the room. "Are you sure you don't want that looked at?"

Saamyah shook her head. "I've experienced worse."

After he had stopped and stood behind the chairs in front of her desk, he folded his arms across his chest and looked down at her. Andrew knew she was intentionally avoiding his stare.

"What happened this morning, Saamyah?"

"Drew-"

"No, Saamyah. You don't get to Drew me." He paused to rein his anger and frustration. "Just tell me why you broke protocol? Why did you leave the café?"

She finally met his eyes and confessed. "She didn't trust me...She didn't believe that I was alone, so I obliged in an effort to get her to talk."

Enraged, Drew shook his head and asked. "What happened?"

Saamyah shrugged. "Someone for-hire knocked me around a bit."

"The café's cameras captured that much...What did he say? What did he want?"

She exhaled loudly and hesitated with her answer.

"Saamyah...what...did...he...want?"

"Me off this case."

"Why?"

"I don't know why, Drew. Maybe the perp believes I am zeroing in on him. Maybe I'm in the way of his plan...I don't know."

Andrew dropped his arms and huffed at her evasive response. He then pushed his glasses on the top of his head and rubbed his weary eyes.

After inhaling deeply and exhaling loudly, Andrew clarified, "The question was referring to your continued work on this case. Why are you still working this case?"

Saamyah offered no response.

Andrew pulled back a chair and lowered himself in it. He hoped that the gesture would allow his words to fully resonate with her.

"This is the third time he has sent someone to caution you, Saamyah. What next? Your life?" He leaned forward to place his hand on top of hers. "Is this case really worth your life?"

Saamyah grinned at his final question. She placed her free hand on top of his and replied, "That seems to be the million dollar question as of late."

Andrew sat back in the chair sliding his hand from underneath hers. Her cavalier disposition made him uncomfortable. In his twelve years on the police force, Andrew had never buried a fellow officer and he did not want Saamyah to be the first.

"Look, if your lieutenant is the problem then I can have mine talk with him."

Saamyah shook her head. "Lieutenant Duncan is not the problem. He will not hesitate to suspend my work on this case. He has done it before."

"So, let me clarify this in my mind…You are making a concerted effort to subject yourself to danger?"

"Don't we all when we report to work every day?"

"Saamyah, this is different and you know it," Andrew rebuffed.

"Drew…"

"Let's just call it a night." He stood deeply aggravated. "I will walk you to your car."

"You don't have to."

"I do," he insisted. "No one dies on my watch."

Saamyah's humor made Tyson laugh and he did so until she flinched and stifled hers. He watched her hold her abdomen and slowly sit up on the red, gingham blanket.

"Are you okay?" He asked sipping from his wine glass.

Saamyah looked at him. "Of course." She looked out at the ocean and then inquired, "Why do you ask?"

"Because I can sense your pain and discomfort."

"Just a minor incident at work today, that's all."

Tyson moved to the side the picnic basket that separated them and moved closer to her.

"Want to talk about it?"

Saamyah met his eyes and confessed, "Not particularly…I prefer to leave it at the office."

He nodded, finished his wine, and conceded, "Fair enough."

Tyson placed his glass in the basket and moved so that Saamyah sat between his bent knees. He then slowly pulled her to rest in the fold of his arm, gently rested his hand on her abdomen, and sweetly kissed her temple.

As they watched in silence, the sun set behind the horizon and the tide came ashore. Tyson kissed Saamyah's temple again and murmured, "Thank you."

Saamyah closed her eyes and inhaled the cool ocean breeze. "For what?"

"For accompanying me…I had an inclination that you were going to cancel, but I appreciate that you didn't."

Saamyah smiled. "You're welcome… And, thank you. This picnic was quite the surprise."

"In your line of work, I figured you would appreciate something remote, quiet, and still."

Saamyah caressed with her fingertips his forearm that rested on her belly. "Not even a full month in and you've got me pegged…You are an astute learner, Mr. Tyson."

Tyson chuckled and agreed, "That I am."

From the rays of the orange sky, he watched her rest in his security and enjoyed the ephemeral moment of serenity. He stroked the stray hairs from her face and whispered, "Tell me your greatest fear, Saamyah."

Her eyes flickered open and they searched his. She could not recall ever being asked that question from anyone without a Ph.D. "…I have so many," she despondently whispered back.

"Well, if I had the power to eliminate one, which would it be?"

"Death of a loved one," Saamyah answered without hesitation. She had experience so much loss in her lifetime that she would be willing to sacrifice anything including her very well-being, to avoid further losses.

She turned her eyes to the shore and added. "...If I could just live a life free of worry of my family's safety, that would actually eradicate a whole host of my fears."

Tyson took her hand, held it, and assured, "I truly believe that by your faith, your family is covered by the blood of Christ."

Saamyah appreciated his comforting words and allowed them to resonate before she asked, "...So, what is your greatest fear?"

He kissed the back of her hand and then pressed it against his muscular chest. "The heartbeat is an excellent telltale of a person's emotions. Joy, anger, nervousness, disappointment, envy, and love can all be felt in each systolic and diastolic pulse...My greatest fear is that my heart will cease to beat with the same affection that I have for you right now."

Confused by his ambiguity, Saamyah confessed, "I'm not sure I know what that means."

Tyson clarified, "It means that every time I hear your voice, your name, or even have thoughts of you, my heart races just like this." He pressed her hand deeper in his chest. "Whenever I see you or am near you, it races. That's the affect you have on me, Saamyah. I am truly smitten by you."

Saamyah was taken aback by his admission. She parted her lips to respond, but was stopped by Tyson's index finger on her lips.

"Don't respond. I did not confess that for you to respond...Just carry it with you all day, every day."

Saamyah nodded.

Tyson smiled and then leaned over to kiss her. When he broke it, he requested, "Spend the night with me tomorrow."

Saamyah squint her eyes at him. "What?"

Tyson shook his head and laughed. "That did not come out right. Tomorrow, I have tickets to the symphony followed by an elite wine tasting. I would like you to accompany me."

Saamyah covered her face in humiliation and laughed at what she had thought he was asking. Tyson laughed, too.

"I see where your mind is," he mocked.

Saamyah dropped her hands. "It's not. I promise you, it's not." She laughed at herself and then replied, "But, yes, I will spend the night with you tomorrow."

"Oh really?" He asked, pulling her in for another kiss.

In amusement, she playfully held him away trying to keep his lips from meeting hers. Worry overcame her when a look of seriousness replaced his elation.

"What's wrong?"

"You do know that I want more from you, right? That it's not about sex with me?"

Saamyah turned from his gaze not certain how to answer. In her youth, she was taught by her brothers that all men come in search for something. However, time had not yet given her the opportunity to discern what Tyson had come in search for.

She attempted to sit up from his embrace, but his tightened grip inhibited her. Once Saamyah breathed through the pain her in abdomen, she looked at him and asked, "If not sex, then what?"

He used his index finger to gently tap the space between her breasts. "Your heart...Everything else will come in time, and I will follow your lead."

A beautiful flower arrangement and long gift box greeted her when Saamyah walked into her office the next morning. She carefully plucked the card from the bouquet and read, "Looking forward to tonight, Tyson."

Filled with glee, Saamyah dropped the card on the desk and anxiously untied the ribbon on her box. She shuffled through the tissue paper to reveal a black, sleeveless evening gown. In their separate compartments were stiletto sandals and a sheer scarf.

Saamyah fingered the smooth fabric of the dress and beaded sequins of the bust. After meticulously removing it from the box, she held it to her figure and was impressed with the fit.

"Nice dress."

Saamyah jumped at the voice and turned to face her spectator. "Bryan?...What...What are you doing here?"

"I do work here, Saamyah." He closed the door behind him and walked towards her.

"I know that, but I thought you'd still be at the hospital."

"I was released yesterday. Turns out, I am going to live."

She chuckled, but stopped when he did not join her.

"A gift from Tyson?"

"Yes," she answered then turned her back to him to fold the dress and place it back in the box. "I'm returning it though."

"Why? It's a beautiful dress."

Saamyah nodded. "It is. It's also a very expensive dress."

"A man like Tyson can afford to have expensive taste...Even in his women."

She exhaled loudly while thinking of ways to divert the conversation. "So," she began while looking at him, "have you been given clearance to return to work?"

"Not exactly, but until I am, there are some light-weight things I can take care of."

She nodded again. "Anything I can help you with?"

"No, but thanks. I am going to take it home....See you around, Saamyah." He walked into his office and closed the door.

"Bye," she whispered.

After closing the box and retying the ribbon, Saamyah took a seat at her desk to dial Tyson's office number.

"Tyson Troy."

"Good morning, Mr. Troy."

The familiar voice sang in his ear and his heartbeat gained speed. "Saamyah, hey. Hold for a moment, please...That's all for now, Rebecca. Thanks. Can you please close my door on the way out and hold all my calls? Thank you so much...I'm sorry about that."

Saamyah smiled. "That's okay."

"So, how are you doing, sweetheart? Have you received my gifts? I was told they made it through security without a hitch."

"I'm fine, thanks. Yes, I have and they're beautiful. Thank you."

"No need to thank me," Tyson assured. "Seeing you wear the gown tonight will be my reward."

"Actually, Tyson," she started and then exhaled loudly, "I can't accept the gift. Well, at least not the attire."

"Why? Are the sizes off?"

"No, they look to be accurate... It's just that..."

"You really don't like the dress, do you?"

"No, it's not that, Tyson... I just can't accept such an expensive gift from you."

He chuckled and responded, "Saamyah, that ensemble was something I wanted you to have regardless of the cost. Besides, you're worth more than the price I paid for it."

"Tyson-"

"To give it back would be an insult."

"...Okay," Saamyah yielded.

"Is eight tonight okay for you?"

"Eight is perfect."

"See you then."

"Bye."

Tyson lost his breath when she opened her front door. He was truly enamored by her appearance. Although the gown did her beauty no justice, it complimented her body well. The material embraced her curves with much sophistication that both her elegance and sex appeal were accentuated.

"Hi," he managed to choke.

"Trévion, hold on just a second." Saamyah dropped the phone from her ear. "Hey, you," she greeted Tyson with a smile. "Come on in."

Tyson stepped inside and gently pressed his lips on her hers. "You look beautiful," he whispered on them.

"Thank you," she whispered back. "You look handsome yourself," she added, winking at his black tuxedo.

Tyson smiled. "I aim to please."

Saamyah giggled. "I'm going to finish up with my brother and I will be ready."

Tyson nodded. "Don't rush, we have time…I would like to beat the rain though."

Saamyah nodded in return and proceeded with her phone conversation to bring it to an end. As Tyson took a seat on her sofa, there was a light knock on the door.

After covering the phone's mouth piece, Saamyah asked, "Can you get that? I'm going to go get my shoes and bag from the back."

"Sure," Tyson obliged.

"Thank you," Saamyah whispered as she listened to her brother and walked towards her bedroom.

Tyson unsecured the door and opened it. It was Bryan.

"Hey," Bryan simply greeted.

"Hey."

"Saamyah around?"

Tyson widened the door, making way for him to step in from the raindrops that began to fall. He closed the door and answered, "She's in the back getting ready."

Bryan nodded.

A brief silence fell among them and Tyson was the first to break it. "You're looking well."

"Thanks."

"So, how much longer before you can return to-"

"Who was at the door, Tyson?" Saamyah asked rushing down the hallway prepared to be on their way. "Bryan," she said with surprise when she finally entered the living space. "What are you doing here?"

For several seconds, words escaped Bryan and all that he could do was gawk with admiration.

Saamyah nervously touched her pinned hair. She felt that Bryan could see right to her soul. "What?"

Bryan shook his head and cleared his throat. "Nothing…You look really nice. The dress turned out to look really good on you."

"Thank you." She looked at Tyson and elucidated, "Bryan was in the office when I received your gift."

Tyson nodded. "Are you ready?"

266   *LAKEISHA LAKAY*

"Yes, I am." She looked at Bryan and asked, "Bryan, was there something you needed?"

Freeing himself from his daze, Bryan handed her the folder he temporarily forgot that he held. "Take a quick look at this for me."

Saamyah looked at Tyson and then Bryan. "Can it wait?"

"It will only take a second," he urged.

Saamyah exhaled loudly, took the folder, and thumped through its contents. She looked at Bryan in disbelief. "How did you get this?"

"Does it matter?" He closed the wide gap between them. As he flipped the pages, he clandestinely inhaled her sweet fragrance. "I believe this is the silver lining we have been waiting for," he pointed out.

Saamyah ignored the feeling that the information was obtained unlawfully long enough to revel in the potential break in the case. They chatted between each other until Tyson cleared his throat.

Saamyah looked up to meet Tyson's impatient eyes. "I'm so sorry, Tyson." She closed the folder and gave it back to Bryan. "Can we pick this up tomorrow?"

"Sure," Bryan hesitantly agreed. "I'm just going to head over to the lab and see what the technicians can make of this, and see if there is anything more that they may need."

"Again, tonight?"

"Yes, we've lost enough time."

"Bryan, you were just released from the hospital. I don't think it's wise for you to overdo it—particularly since you haven't been cleared to return to work."

Bryan shook his head. "I'll be fine. You two go and enjoy your evening." He turned to leave, but Saamyah touched his forearm.

"Bryan, wait." She exhaled loudly and looked at Tyson. "May I talk to you for a minute?"

Without giving her an answer Tyson followed her to her bedroom.

"Saamyah, what are you doing?" Tyson asked with a voice

filled with frustration. Saamyah closed the door behind them.

"Tyson, I can't let him go to the office by himself in his condition."

Tyson inhaled and exhaled deeply as he watched her nervously fidget with the beads of her bodice. "Why not?"

Saamyah was taken aback by the hostility of his insensitive question. She gave him a disproving look and answered, "He's my partner, Tyson."

"At work. NOT in life," he vehemently retorted.

Saamyah was overwhelmed by the new man who had entered the conversation. Tyson's emotions unveiled a side of him that she had not yet been introduced to, and she was unsure of how to usher his exit.

"You're right, Tyson," she calmly confirmed, "but that doesn't change the fact that I still have an assignment to complete. That is ultimately why I am here."

Tyson huffed as he attempted to wipe the frustration from his face. "Yeah, I know." He turned to walk out the room.

"Tyson, wait." Saamyah reached for the bottom of his jacket to stop him. She gazed into his eyes and said, "I'm so sorry. Whatever the tickets cost I'll return it to you."

He slowly shook his head in disappointment and gently removed her hand from his jacket. "It's not about the money, Saamyah…When will you ever comprehend what this is truly about?" He turned from her gaze, opened the door, and walked out of the bedroom.

Avoiding Bryan's eyes, Tyson walked out the front door and into the rain. Saamyah followed, repeatedly calling his name. She closed the door behind her and rushed to catch up with him.

Saamyah pushed closed the car door Tyson had opened, slid between it and him, and asked, "Then what is it about?"

Tyson stepped out of her personal space. "What?"

Saamyah pushed her wet hair out of her face and repeated, "If it's not about the money, and it's not about sex, then what is this about?"

Tyson laughed halfheartedly with frustration. "You're kidding me, right?"

She did not answer.

Tyson bit his lip in anger and shook his head. If he could, he would hate her, but his heart would not allow it. "I'm not him, Saamyah." He nodded in the direction of her condo. "I don't need work, trickery, or ruses to get next to you. So, if sex and money are all that you have to offer, then let's end this now. I'd rather have nothing."

"Tyson, I-"

"And for the record, just so that I am emphatically clear for the final time, this is about me wanting to give you what I feel you deserve, about me wanting to add to your happiness, and make you a part of my world while I show you the world...It's about sharing everything I am and everything I have with you." He paused, took a deep breath, and finally concluded, "It's about allowing me the chance to love you, Saamyah."

Absent the adequate words to reply, Saamyah stood in silence pressed against the car door. The heavy rain pounded on her face and what her hair and dress did not soak in fell to the puddle beneath her. She jumped at the lightening that lit the sky and the thunder that followed.

"It's too dangerous for you to travel the roads right now. Why don't you come back inside and wait it out?" Saamyah beseeched.

Tyson shook his head, disheartened by her lack of reaction to his confession. "I've lived here all my life. I'll be fine." He paused then added, "You should go though."

Saamyah moved further from the door after he nudged her to the side. She watched him climb into the car, start the ignition, and lower the window.

"These are for you," Tyson simply stated as he extended out the window a bouquet of red roses. Once she collected them in her hands, Tyson raised his window and reversed out of the parking space.

The walk back to the unit was exceedingly long. The weight of the wet gown slowed her steps and her drenched, tangled hair impeded her vision. Frustrated with her slippery feet, she peeled off the stiletto sandals and continued her journey barefoot.

Once inside, Bryan arose to assist her, but Saamyah held up her hands in protest.

"Just give me a minute, Bryan."

He returned to his seat on the sofa and watched her walk to her bedroom leaving a trail of water on the carpet behind her.

Saamyah closed her bedroom door and dropped the shoes and the roses to the floor. Inside her bathroom, she stepped into her tub and shed the wet dress. After wringing as much of the water she could, she hung the dress over the shower rod. Saamyah then removed her undergarments and indulged in a hot shower

In grey cotton lounge pants and a Dallas Cowboy fitted t-shirt, Saamyah slowly made her way down the hall. She cringed every time she stepped into a damp spot in the carpet.

Bryan watched her place her Dallas Cowboy cap on her head and pull her long, thick ponytail through the back opening.

"Are you okay?" Bryan asked after she pulled her cap down further to conceal her red eyes.

"I'm fine," she simply answered as she shoved her feet in her white sneakers at the door. "Ready?"

Bryan stood. "Yes."

With her umbrella, Saamyah walked Bryan to the passenger side of her car. Once secured in the driver seat, she started the vehicle, and drove silently to the police department.

*** *** ***

Saamyah nervously stood outside waiting for him to answer the door. She rung the bell a second time and quickly flipped her hair off her bare shoulder. Her arms struggled with the heavy picnic basket and flowers, but she was determined to conceal it.

"Coming," she heard him announce. The door swung open and his face was without emotion when he saw her.

"Hi," she forced out.

LAKEISHA LAKAY

"What are you doing here, Saamyah?" Tyson inquired.

"Uuumm. The stable guy gave me directions. He told me your house is the one right off the road. Then I realized that yours is the only house period." She laughed, but Tyson did not join her.

"I didn't ask *how* you got here. I asked *what* you are doing here." Tyson clarified, folding his arm across his chest.

"I...I just wanted to apologize, Tyson." Saamyah extended flowers towards him, but slowly brought them back into her when he only stared at, but did not receive them. She placed them on the basket.

Saamyah switched the basket to her other arm and nervously forced her hair behind her ear. "I know you're upset, Tyson, and I'm really sorry about last night...I really am."

He dropped his arms and said, "A phone call would have saved you the trip." He started to close the door, but Saamyah stopped him by placing a hand on the door.

"Okay, I get it—you're pissed and you have every right to be. I am deserving of this treatment, but I am here to make it up to you. So, let me make it up to you...Please?"

Unmoved by her petition, Tyson simply responded, "I'm no longer available to you."

Saamyah exhaled loudly and dropped her hand. "Tyson, please?...Just lunch and...and, if you still want me gone, I'll leave...Please? I took a half-day just to be here."

He shook his head and shrugged his shoulders. "I'm sorry, Saamyah, but I-"

"Ooooo, calla lilies," interrupted a beautifully aged, African-American woman that widened the door. "I thought I heard the door bell ring."

Saamyah's heart dropped and Tyson saw it in her face.

"I'll take those," the woman said retrieving the flowers. She swatted Tyson in his abdomen. "Shame on you, Ty. You have this poor woman standing in the door like this. Come on in, Ms...."

"Saamyah," Saamyah answered, looking at her then Tyson for permission. When he said nothing, she stepped through the threshold and followed the woman into the foyer.

Annoyed, Tyson slammed the door behind them, but neither of them noticed.

"Saamyah—what a beautiful name. I'm Jada, Ty's financial advisor. So nice to meet you." She extended her hand and Saamyah took it.

"Well, I'm not trying to impose. If you are busy, I can leave," Saamyah offered.

"Nonsense. It's not often that Ty has female guests and it would be a shame to run off a future prospect."

"Okay, Jada, I think Ms. Cambell has gotten an earful from you today. Be a doll and leave us be."

Jada rolled her eyes. "He's such a bully. Don't let him be one to you, honey." She looked at Tyson, "I'll have your statements couriered to you on Monday, but for the most part, your numbers are looking good."

"That's what I like to hear and it's the only thing I pay you for," Tyson reminded her.

She chuckled at his insinuation. "I love you too, babe." Jada took the basket from Saamyah. "I can take this off your hands and put it in the kitchen for you."

Relieved, Saamyah thanked her.

"No problem, sweets. It was a pleasure meeting you."

"Likewise." Saamyah smiled while secretly wishing she would not leave her alone with the disgruntled Tyson.

Tyson led her into the sitting room and motioned for her to sit. He opted to stand.

"You have a beautiful home," Saamyah said, breaking the silence.

He walked to the window and stared out it. "My apologies for Jada. She can be forceful at times."

"It's okay. I have three older brothers. So, I am accustomed to forceful. She actually wasn't that bad. I like her," Saamyah rambled.

Tyson looked at her and said, "You've come to apologize, but if you're sticking around for forgiveness, I'm afraid I can't offer you that right now."

Saamyah nodded. "I understand."

"Do you really? Because I don't think you do."

She did not respond.

"How I felt last night is the equivalent to your feelings when you first laid eyes on Jada."

Saamyah dropped her eyes, embarrassed by the fact that Tyson had read her so well. When she lifted her eyes again, she told him, "I don't know what to say other than I'm sorry."

Tyson nodded. "Well, thanks for stopping by. Show yourself out." He proceeded to walk out the room.

Saamyah jumped to her feet and rushed to grab his arm. "Damn it, Tyson!...I'm sorry, okay?...I...I executed poor judgment last night and it wasn't the first and it probably won't be the last time. But, I do regret that I hurt you...Please don't do this to us. It's too soon to throw in the towel."

"Excuse me, Mr. Tyson," a woman of Spanish descent interrupted, "Ms. Jada has left a basket in the kitchen. Would you like me to prepare lunch before I leave for the day?"

Tyson directed his attention to his long time home-keeper. "No, thank you, Maria. Thank you for everything today. Have a great day."

She nodded, smiled, and waved. "You, too, Mr. Tyson. See you next week."

"I see why you're no longer available," Saamyah jested. "You have enough women in your life to fulfill every need."

Tyson could not help but to close his eyes and chuckle at her quip. When he opened them, he looked at her and bit his bottom lip. "Come here," he whispered.

Saamyah walked into his arms and kissed him. "I'm so sorry, Tyson," she whispered on his lips.

"I know and I forgave you last night for it."

She opened her eyes and looked into his. "Then why take me through all that?"

"I had to make sure that I wasn't the only one who wanted this...If this is what you want, too, then I need you to meet me halfway, Saamyah."

Saamyah nodded and simply replied, "Okay," before returning his kiss, opening her mouth to taste his.

Their deep kisses led them to the sofa.

"Is this okay?" Tyson asked.

Saamyah nodded and then whispered, "Yes." Maneuvering to lie on her back, she brought Tyson down to rest on her.

"Saamyah," he moaned between kisses, "don't do this to me. I don't want to rush this…I'm fighting hard to wait."

"You don't have to wait anymore," she assured him.

Tyson opened his eyes and searched hers. "Are you sure?"

She nodded and smiled. "Yes, I'm sure." She paused before adding, "But, know that I am no expert at this."

Confused, Tyson squinted his eyes and asked, "At what?"

"I've only done this one time," she clarified.

Tyson slowly rose off her and sat on the opposite end of the sofa.

Saamyah sat up as well and questioned, "What's wrong?"

He ran his tongue across his teeth and then looked at her. "So, your first time was with him."

Saamyah did not answer.

"With Bryan?"

Saamyah nodded.

Tyson exhaled loudly and shook his head. "It all makes sense now."

"It was while ago, Tyson, and doesn't mean anything now."

"You know that's not true, Saamyah." He huffed and turned away from her.

Saamyah used her hand to gently turn his face back toward her. "I don't want to fight about him, Tyson. He and I are over."

He removed her hand and broke their gaze. "I'm not so sure that it is, and I don't think you do either."

Vexed, Saamyah retorted, "You have a wife. How is that situation any different?"

"My EX-wife," he corrected, "has never interfered with what we are trying to build and she never will because I won't allow it."

"Well, in all fairness your EX-wife is not your business partner."

He looked at her and coldly snapped, "Well, I guess that makes me the better judge on who I sleep with." The look on her face made him close his eyes and regret the slight as soon as it left his lips.

"Saamyah, I'm so sorry. That didn't come out right."

Saamyah rose to leave. "Yes, it did. It was an honest response reflective of your honest feelings. At least now I know how you truly feel." She walked toward the room's exit.

Tyson stood and grabbed her arm. She snatched it from him. "You know what, I think it's best we both cool off before anything else is said that we will both regret."

"Saamyah-"

Without looking at him, she said, "Enjoy the rest of your day," and walked out with Tyson on her heels.

"Saamyah, wait," he called after her. He jogged to catch up with her brisk walk to the car. "Saamyah, please."

She opened her car door only for him to close it back.

He turned her to face him and he pressed her against the car. After pushing the hair back from her face, he cupped it with his hands and whispered on her lips, "I'm so sorry. Please forgive me."

Saamyah moved his hands from her face. "I've got to go, Tyson."

"Go where, Saamyah? I thought we were to have lunch."

"From here and not anymore." She cautiously reached for her handle, thinking he would stop her a second time. When he failed to do so, she opened the door and lowered herself to the driver seat. Through the wound glass she heard him say, "Then I would like to go with you."

Saamyah started her engine and switched the gear in reverse.

"Please," he insisted as she slowly rolled back.

Saamyah stopped the car, closed her eyes, and exhaled loudly. After lowering the window, she invited him by saying, "Get in."

Tyson smiled, walked around to the passenger side, and climbed in the car. "Where are we going?"

Saamyah retrieved her sunglasses from the compartment above her head, placed them on her face, and grinned. "You'll see."

"Can you swim?" Saamyah asked while parking her car.

"I would hope that everyone in Miami would know how to swim," Tyson answered.

"Good." She devilishly smiled, removed her sunglasses, and turned off ignition.

"Where are we?"

"Just a secluded spot I discovered a while back during one of my unhappier times here in Miami." She saw the concern in his eyes and avoided their probing inquiry by saying, "Come. I have something to show you."

Tyson followed her deep into the wooded area. The further away from the car they walked, the clearer was the sound of rushing water. His jaw dropped when they finally reached the waterfall that cascaded into the body of water beneath it.

Saamyah smiled at his reaction, slipped out of her sandals, and slowly pulled her tube-top over her head.

"What are you doing?" he asked, taking a brief notice of the light colored bruise on her belly.

"You said that you can swim, right? Then let's go for a swim."

"Saa-"

"Don't worry, I won't tell your business partners." She laughed, unzipped her skinny jeans, and stripped her herself down to her cheeky boy shorts that matched her strapless bra.

Apprehensive, Tyson watched her gleefully take off towards the high rocks and climb them. Once at the top, she dived into the water and swam to him.

"Are you coming?" Saamyah asked, treading water.

He shook his head. "No, I think I will just enjoy the pleasure of watching you."

"Okay," she sang, pushing herself away from the edge of the rock and floated on her back, "but, you're really missing out."

"Not from where I am standing," he dissented with an impish grin. He watched her submerge and then later grew worried—several minutes had passed and she had not surfaced.

"Saamyah."

No response.

"Saamyah!"

When she did not respond, Tyson hurriedly yanked off his shoes, removed socks, and dove into the water fully clothed. He propelled himself several feet under water in search for her until the burn in his chest forced him to swim back to the surface for air.

"SAAMYAH!" Tyson exclaimed despite the difficulty he experienced breathing. In an exacerbated panic, he submerged a second time confident that a lifeless body could not have floated far.

As he swam toward the direction of the cascading waters, Tyson grabbed an object that he presumed to be limb. He tossed it aside when he realized it was a tree branch. His blazing lungs forced him to the surface once more.

"SAAMYAH!" He coughed to clear his throat of the heartbeat he felt pulsating in it. "SAAMYAH!"

"...I'm over here," a voice echoed as if from within a cave.

Tyson turned in the direction of her call and swam below the surface and behind the waterfall.

Saamyah jumped against the rock when he emerged from the water and screamed, "ARE YOU CRAZY!"

"What?...What did I do?"

"You didn't hear me calling you?!" His voiced bounced off the rocks and reverberated.

Saamyah shook her head and, when she noticed he was fully clothed, she asked, "Why did you get in the water with all your clothes?"

He glared at her and answered, "Because I thought something had happened to you."

Her heart dropped and she reached out to him. "Tyson, I'm so sor-"

Tyson pushed her hands away. "Don't touch me." He watched her back into the rock. "I'm ready to go."

"But we just got here."

"All the more reason we should leave now…Don't want to give you another opportunity to give me a heart attack." With that, he swam in the direction from which he had come. Saamyah waited for the distance to grow between them before she did the same.

Down to his boxer briefs, Tyson wrung out the water from his clothes. He stopped briefly to help Saamyah out of the water and then dressed in his wet garments. His anger allowed him to pay no mind to Saamyah pressing the water out of her hair and dressing her wet body. Instead, he only cared enough for the moment she slipped into her sandals so that she could lead the way to the car.

The drive back to his home was long, quiet, and wet. Tyson increasing grew aggravated by his clothes that stuck to the leather seat and the humidity in the air that intensified his discomfort. Thoughtlessly, he growled his frustration.

"I can close the sunroof and run the air if you want," Saamyah offered, breaking the silence.

"I'm fine," he lied.

She tightly gripped the steering wheel and said, "Look, Tyson, I am really sorry about earlier. I didn't mean to scare you like that…I guess I am just so use to swimming alone—going and coming as I please."

"Forget about it," he coldly responded.

"Okay," she whispered.

Tyson looked at her somber face and his heart softened. He took a deep breath and exhaled before saying, "I'm sorry, too, Saamyah. I shouldn't have yelled at you. You just really scared me." He paused before adding, "I thought I had lost you."

Saamyah parked her car in front of his door and turned off the ignition. She stared at the steering wheel and said slightly above a whisper, "I know, and I am really sorry."

Tyson leaned forward and kissed her cheek. "Come in and have lunch with me."

Saamyah shook her head. "I can't. I have to go home and shower."

"You can shower here."

Saamyah searched her mind for an excuse, but when none could be found, she obliged.

Following him into the house and up the stairs to the master bathroom, Saamyah grew more in aw of his home's splendor. Her intense gaze was broken when Tyson handed her shower accessories and a bathrobe.

"My son has eczema so I have all these moisturizing soaps and lotions. I hope that's okay."

Saamyah smiled. "That's fine. Thanks so much."

"You're welcome. I'll step out until you are in the shower and then return to get your clothes so that I can wash them for you."

She chuckled. "You don't have to do that."

"It's no trouble."

"Okay…Thanks," she sheepishly added.

After her shower, Saamyah found Tyson in fresh lounge wear at the poolside under an umbrella shade. He was reading a business journal. "You have the most amazing home," she interrupted as she tightened the belt of the bathrobe.

Tyson looked up from the publication, closed it, and set it on the stand next to him. "Thank you. Perhaps later I can give a formal tour."

Saamyah sat in the lounge chair next to him and said, "Perhaps."

"Are you ready to eat?"

She leaned back in the chair to stretch out and shook her head. "I want to stay out here a little longer."

Tyson nodded. "Come here," he insisted, reaching out his hand. Saamyah took it and settled into his chair. With her back against his chest, her head found a resting place in the swell of his bicep.

Holding her tightly in his arms, Tyson placed a gentle kiss on her temple and watched her close her eyes. He then closed his own and they both slept by the water.

Saamyah woke up in a dimly lit room. Confused, she fought hard to remember where she was. She eventually concluded that the king sized bed that she had slept in belonged to Tyson. Sitting up, she saw her clean clothes neatly laying at the foot of the bed. After throwing back the comforter and sheet, Saamyah descended the bed to remove the bathrobe and dress herself. She then made the bed, placed the bathrobe at the foot of it, and made her way down the stairs.

"Hey," she greeted, finding Tyson in his living room watching sports on the flat screen television mounted above the fireplace.

He muted the volume and said, "Hey, babe." He patted the seat next to him on the leather sofa inviting her to sit next to him. She did and quickly found comfort in his arms. He kissed her forehead and asked, "How did you sleep?"

"Like a baby."

"That's good. You needed it…Are you hungry?"

She shook her head and asked instead, "What time it is?"

Tyson glanced at his wristwatch and answered, "A quarter 'til eight."

"Oh wow," Saamyah said sitting up. "I didn't mean to sleep that long."

Tyson smiled and pushed her loose hairs back towards her thick ponytail. "It's okay. I understand."

She took his hand from her head, kissed the back of it, and held it. "I've got to head out."

He gently pulled her into him. "No, you don't. You can stay here."

Saamyah laughed. "The drive will be horrible in the morning traffic. Plus, I have to start early tomorrow since I took a half-day today."

"Please," he begged while pecking her lips with short, soft kisses.

She groaned. "Tyson, don't do this to me."

"Then stay." He dipped his tongue in her mouth and pulled her to lie on him.

Saamyah tenderly pulled away. "Tyson, I can't do this. I mean, I thought I wanted to earlier, but I'm just not ready. I'm so sorr-"

"Shhhh," he quieted her, pressing his index finger against her lips. "It's okay. You don't have to explain anything to me. I am willing to wait for you as long as you want...As long as you're with me."

Saamyah dropped her eyes.

Tyson used a hand to lift her face until her eyes met his again. "Are you?"

"Am I what?"

"Are you with me?"

Saamyah gently moved his hand from her face and said, "I've got to go," as she rose to leave.

Tyson rose from the sofa as well. "You can tell me the truth, Saamyah. I would understand if you still love him...I just need to know the truth."

"I don't love him," she simply said. She then turned and walked to exit the room.

"Then love me," he protested.

Saamyah stopped in her tracks and turned to face him. "What?"

Tyson walked to her and took her hands in each one of his. "I get this feeling that something is holding you back from me."

"Tyson, we haven't known each other for that long. How much do you want from me in less than a month?"

"Saamyah, please, I don't want to argue," he yielded after he noticed a slight aggravation in her tone. "Just know that it's okay to give your heart to me. I won't hurt you."

Reflecting on what Bryan had professed to her weeks earlier, Saamyah shared, "Life does not guarantee us a happy ending."

Tyson gathered that a life of loss, disappointment, and pain attributed to her cynicism. But, he still held hope that something promising could come from their acquaintance.

"But it does not preclude us from pursuing our happily ever after," Tyson offered, refusing to be jaded.

Though her heart was warmed by his optimism, Saamyah did not respond. Instead, she leaned forward, kissed his lips, and announced, "I've got to go."

She walked out into the foyer with Tyson on her heels and she stopped at the front door. With her back still to him, Saamyah spoke, "I live a very complicated life, Tyson. One that you couldn't possibly imagine." She turned to look at him as the tears rolled down her face. "People have been hurt and I don't want you to be one of them."

"Let me decide that for myself, Saamyah. Please, don't make the decision for me."

She laughed halfheartedly and shook her head in dismay. After wiping her eyes she told him, "You're crazy. You know that?"

Tyson laughed with her. Again, he walked to her and cupped her face with his hands. "I do." He kissed her several times and added, "I'm crazy about you."

Saamyah's heart raced as she returned his fervent kisses. When their lips parted, their eyes gazed into each other's to convey emotions and thoughts that were difficult to articulate. Somewhere between—I'm afraid: I won't hurt you; I'm confused: I'll guide you; I'm vulnerable: I'll protect you; I'm falling: I'll catch you; I—: Just let me love you—did Saamyah develop the courage to whisper, "I've got to go."

Tyson exhaled his disappointment and released her— physically. Emotionally, he still held on to the hope that their relationship would blossom into something more. He was ready for love, ready for a commitment, and he wanted them both with her.

Recognizing that he was putting himself at risk of becoming love's biggest fool, Tyson silently prayed that she would forget about her past hurts and take a chance at loving him. He kissed Saamyah's lips gently to confirm his commitment, then took her hand and walked her to her vehicle.

*** *** ***

"I got your message," Andrew announced walking through her opened office door the next day. "I am confused by it though... Has Russell returned to work?"

Saamyah completed the task of twisting her hair in a tight knot on top of her head and pinned it. Now that her status meeting with Lieutenant Duncan was over, she no longer felt the need to look polished beyond the black pencil skirt and white blouse she wore.

"No, he hasn't, but he managed to get his hands on this," she answered, extending to him a folder.

Andrew received the folder, opened it, and flipped through the pages. He lowered himself in a seat and asked, "How did he come to obtain this information?"

Saamyah shrugged. "He won't say, but the gynecologist that performed the exam was a colleague of Rachel's."

"Rachel? Bryan's wife?"

Saamyah nodded. "From what she was willing to offer, the patient started experiencing pressure and pain a few days after an assault that she never reported, and still does not want to report."

"So, the condom has been inside her since the rape?"

Saamyah nodded. "It was lodged near her cervix and caused an infection."

Andrew closed the folder and returned it to Saamyah. "What did the lab determine?"

"Nothing other than the brand of the condom."

"So, either the perp didn't finish or finished inside her."

"I believe it to be the former."

"Why? There is no rape kit," Andrew confirmed.

"True, but she's one of Bryan's, and the operating method in that case has never been sexual gratification."

Andrew rested his back in the chair and placed the ankle of his right leg on top of the knee of his left. He rubbed his forehead as he thought. "I don't know, Saamyah. Perceived sloppiness like this in homicide typically means that the perp has grown tired of toying with us and he wants to be captured." Andrew reflected on past cases and offered, "It's as if he is exasperated by the police department's inability to piece together his meticulously crafted clues. So, he begins to intentionally leave behind evidence."

Saamyah pondered his offerings and then asked, "Intentionally left behind for who? For what?"

Ignoring her questions, Andrew blatantly inquired, "What do you know about the brand of the condom?"

Saamyah dropped her eyes when she discovered Andrew's angle. Feelings of awkwardness followed when the allusion that Saamyah was knowledgeable of Bryan's condom preference lingered.

She finally cleared her throat and met Andrew's stare. "I suppose that when you bed a suspected rapist, your private life cease to be private."

Immediately, guilt overcame Andrew. "Saamyah, I-"

Saamyah shook her head. "It's fine, Drew...But, to answer you, I don't know much. I can find out more if this is really something you want to pursue."

"We can leave the gynecologist out of it, for now, as I am sure the HIPAA violation would destroy her career. However, Russell needs to be interrogated and possibly searched."

"Drew?" Saamyah gasped, questioning the suggestion.

"We do it or I'm done," Andrew warned. "I can't keep chasing our tails, Saamyah...I am knee deep in murders and don't have time to waste on sexual assaults if we do not pursue every lead."

Saamyah shook her head. "I'm sorry. I can't back you on this. Not this time...I don't believe Bryan is the perp nor do I believe he is at fault."

Disappointed, but not surprised by her response, Andrew shared a classic riddle, "A man locks a woman in a cage with a lion. When she is mauled, who is at fault? The man or the lion?"

Saamyah considered the question, but did not respond.

Andrew rose from his seat and stated, "I will have my lieutenant talk with yours and have them get you a new set of hands." He then walked toward the exit.

"Andrew," Saamyah called out.

He turned to her.

"Thank you."

"Be careful, Saamyah." With that he walked out the room.

That night, Saamyah slid between the cool sheets of her bed and lowered her head to the pillow. After turning on her side, she pulled a second pillow into her body and held it tight. Though exhausted from the day, Saamyah struggled with sleep. The conversation with Andrew was too difficult to put out of her mind.

Tears fell from her eyes until they graduated into a heartfelt cry. Saamyah was fatigued by stress and confused by competing demands—all she had not felt since her days as a special agent. She eventually fell asleep to Andrew's warning to be cautious.

"…Saamyah!" David yelled as he ran toward her.

Gunshots fired and David's body collided into Saamyah's after she turned to face him. Hitting the ground hard, she groaned her pain, and struggled to lift David's heavy body off her.

Ignoring the revving engines and squealing wheels, Saamyah shook David. "…David…David get up. Babe, I can't breathe."

Laying her head back in the dirt, she rested for a moment, and then used all her might to roll David to her side. She sat up and saw the blood that covered her shirt.

"David!"

David slowly opened his eyes and coughed out the blood that rose in throat. "Saamyah."

"Shhh, don't talk."

"How bad is it?" He whispered.

Saamyah touch the wound in his chest and added pressure to attempt to slow the bleeding. David screamed in pain.

"You're going to be okay."

"…I don't think so, Saamyah."

Crying she argued, "Don't say that. Don't you dare say that…I am going to call for help. Just hang in there."

Saamyah rushed to their unmarked car and made her call. When she had returned David had his eyes closed. He groaned when she shook him.

"Saamyah," he whispered.

"Help is on the way, but, baby, you have to keep your eyes open." Her tears dropped on his face and she gently wiped them away. "You have to stay awake. Okay?"

"I'm so sorry, Saamyah." He touch her face with is trembling fingers and smiled weakly when she kissed and then held them close to her cheek. "I…I love you so much, Saamyah."

He coughed up more blood. "It's getting harder to breathe." The tears rolled down his face. "…Say it, Saamyah…"

"No," She cried slowly shaking her head.

"Please…I…" He coughed and grimaced his pain. "Saamyah, I don't have much time." He started to close his eyes, but opened them when she nudged him.

"Don't you dare die on me, David Barnes!" She screamed. "We've got to get married and have babies," she added in a whisper.

He smiled weakly. "How many?"

"A boy and a girl."

"And a girl," he reaffirmed.

Saamyah laughed through her tears. David loved little girls. "Okay, two girls." When she heard sirens in a distance she said, "They're coming. Just hang in there."

"Please…Say it, Saamyah." He coughed. "Just this once."

Saamyah looked into his eyes as she gently stroked his face. "On our wedding day."

David felt himself fading and eyelids grow heavy. "I love you s-s-so much, Saamyah…Remember that. Always r-remember that." He finally closed his eyes.

Saamyah erupted in a solemn cry when David failed to respond to the calling of his name or the shaking of his body. Fulfilling his last wish, she lowered her lips to his ear and whispered, "I-

Saamyah jolted to a seated position in her bed when the telephone shrilled throughout the bedroom. She pushed back her hair and reached for the headpiece on her nightstand.

"Hello," she murmured.

"Babe sis."

"Tré?" Saamyah glanced at her clock. It was a little after eight in the morning.

"I'm calling with wedding updates."

Saamyah fell back into her pillows. "At eight o'clock on a Saturday morning, Tré? Call Christian."

"No, I am not going to call Chris. I called you."

"But-"

"Just hush up and listen."

She pulled her bedding over head and listened to her brother's rant for over an hour. On occasion, the calling of her name pulled her back into conversation when she drifted to sleep. Talks of tuxedos and dresses reminded Saamyah that her evening gown awaited pick-up at the dry cleaners.

"You look incredibly beautiful," Tyson whispered in her ear.

A bashful grin stretched across her face before Saamyah mouthed, "Thank you."

Tyson sipped from his champagne glass and then added, "I'm grateful that you decided to give the dress another chance."

"I figured it, you, and I deserved a second chance."

Tyson chuckled and tipped his glass to her. "I will toast to that." His intended long sip was cut short by a familiar voice that called his name.

"Surprising to see you here," the man confessed after stopping in front of him.

"And why is that, Mr. Banks?" Tyson asked his Caucasian, male counterpart whose hazel eyes leveled with his brown ones.

He shrugged his strong, broad shoulders and replied, "I figured you would be out celebrating your new contract."

"I am. That's why I am here." Tyson tipped his glass to him and drank from it.

"You must tell me how you managed to outbid me a second time. That's two contracts this quarter."

Tyson swallowed the last of his beverage and placed the glass on the tray that the passing attendant held. "Come on, Dick, we are in the presence of a lady. How about we forego the ugly talk of business tonight?"

He took notice of Saamyah standing to the left of Tyson. He made no effort to suppress his attraction to her. "Please forgive me," he beseeched extending his hand. "Richard Banks, but I prefer Dick."

Saamyah took his hand and greeted, "Saamyah Cambell."

Richard peered deep into her eyes, "It's indeed a pleasure, Ms. Cambell." He turned her hand, lowered his lips, and placed a lingering kiss on the back of it.

Feelings of discomfort overwhelmed Saamyah and she prayed that Tyson did not take notice of her ill-ease. She slightly tugged on her hand and watched Richard rise with a mischievous smirk. As he held her eyes with his shameless gaze, he wished, "I hope you have a night that is as beautiful as you are."

Saamyah broke his stare and simply said, "Thank you."

Richard's smile turned into one of cockiness after he successfully upset Saamyah's sense of security—just as Tyson had done to his business. He turned to Tyson, ignoring the glower he gave him, "Mr. Troy."

Tyson simply nodded and said, "Mr. Banks." He watched him walk away then turned to Saamyah, "Are you okay?"

Saamyah nodded, avoiding his eyes.

"I am so sorry about that."

She shook her head. "It's fine. I'm fine."

"I can't-" he was interrupted by the announcement inviting guests into the theatre.

Saamyah began to move with the crowd, but was held back by Tyson. He turned her to face him and she could not avoid his fixated eyes any longer.

Tyson searched her face for the truth and offered, "We can go."

Saamyah smiled and assured, "If I allowed every 'Dick' I encounter to unnerve me, I would never enjoy life. "

Tyson laughed at the jest and then placed his lips on hers in a gentle kiss. "You're amazing, you know that?"

"I've been told a time or two."

He held her gaze a moment longer to take in the incredible woman that he was infatuated with. "…That settles it."

"That settles what?"

"I'm to leave for Chicago in a few days for the contract I just procured, but my partner can go instead."

Saamyah contested, "Please don't alter your plans on my account."

Tyson took her hand and slowly led her to the double doors. "I can and I will. I'd rather stay here and enjoy what little time we have left."

Her face flushed and she was grateful when the darkness of their box-seats hid the color growing in her face. He took her hand and held it through the entire play, releasing it only for intermission.

*** *** ***

"Keep your eyes closed," Tyson coaxed the following afternoon.

"They are," Saamyah assured, squeezing her eyes shut tighter behind the blindfold, "but it's difficult to match your stride without sight."

Tyson took noticed of his speed and slowed his step. "I apologize…We are almost there though."

Saamyah felt the terrain under her strapped sandals change from soft grass to warm rocks and gritty sand. "Tyson, where are you taking me?" She asked, widening the space between him as far as his clinched hand would allow.

He laughed as he gripped her hand tighter so that she would not break away and would keep pace. "It wouldn't be a surprise if I told you...Now, keep the blindfold on until I say otherwise. Trust me, I am not going to let anything happen to you."

"This has nothing to do with trust, Tyson. I just don't like not knowing where I am going or where I am."

Tyson finally stopped, released her hand, and said nothing as he silently moved about.

Saamyah dropped her hands to her side and stood motionless. "Are we here?"

He did not respond.

"Tyson?"

He smiled, but remained silent.

"Tyson?" A slight panic rose in her when she only heard faint movements that she tried to follow and turn her body towards. "Tyson?...Tyson, this isn't funny...Okay, I am done. I'm done playing this game," she announced as she struggled with the tight knot of the blindfold. In frustration, she finally yanked it over her head, "Ty-"

"Just couldn't wait, could you?" He asked, not surprised at her haste.

Her eyes adjusted on the two black mustangs in front of her. "What is this?" She asked Tyson as he properly affixed the saddles on the horse's back.

"This stallion," he began as he walked over to the second horse "is my pride and joy; my favorite of all my horses." Tyson took the reins and guided the stallion closer to Saamyah. He placed the leather in her hands. "I'm entrusting him to you."

Saamyah chuckled in confusion. "I'm not dressed for a ride, Tyson. I have on sandals and shorts."

Tyson disagreed, "You'll be fine." He patted the horse and added, "I already gave Beast the talk and he knows to take it slow with you."

"Beast?"

"Yes, and that mare," he pointed to the other horse, "is Belle."

Saamyah laughed. "You've got to be kidding me, Beauty and the Beast?"

Tyson smiled. "Belle is a bit temperamental; so, no one typically rides her but me."

"I don't know, Tyson, it's been years since I have ridden."

"I know and that's why we will stay on the trail and trot at most."

Saamyah opened her mouth to protest, but stopped when Tyson interjected with this request, "Thirty minutes."

"Thirty minutes?"

"Just thirty minutes…unless you decide to stay on longer."

Saamyah initially shook her head at the thought, but ultimately conceded. Tyson offered his hand in assistance, but she brushed past it as she dropped the reins. She placed one foot in the stirrup, gripped the saddle to hoist herself, and swung the other foot to the opposite side of the horse. Once comfortably seated, Saamyah again took hold of the reins.

"Looks like she still got it," Tyson knowingly muttered to himself, though making sure Saamyah could hear. He stroked the neck of his horse and reminded him, "That's my heart up there, Beast; be good to her."

Saamyah blushed and tried her best to hide the warmth growing in her cheeks. "Wait," she called out to him after he mounted Belle and signaled for her to turn around toward the trail.

Tyson watched as she moved into his space. She leaned into him to place a short, but sweet kiss on his lips and then whispered, "Thank you."

His eyes met hers when their lips parted and he tugged at her shirt to bring her close for another. To his disappointment, Tyson was forced to settle for what she initially offered because the horses grew increasingly agitated by their close proximity to each other. "You're welcome," he simply said while concealing his disappointment.

Preparing for an adventurous chase, Saamyah tightened her grip on the reins and gently kicked Beast at his side.

Filled with glee, Saamyah shared, "I haven't ridden like that since I was 15!"

"Yeah?" Tyson inquired as he opened the door to his home and allowed her to enter first.

"Yeah…Well, I became really onerous in my adolescent years. So, my brother resigned my lessons. Without them I was no longer able to compete."

Tyson closed and secured the door. He then closed the space between them as they stood in the foyer. With a tender stroke, he pushed a lock of hair from her eye. "Well, it's never too late to start again. Beast is yours whenever you need him."

"Really?" Saamyah asked in disbelief. "Your pride and joy?"

"Anything for my heart," he assured, closing his eyes and grazing her lips. A chill rose in his spine when Saamyah pressed her lips firm into his. When her hands found their way to his neck, his found their way to her waist.

Their fervent kisses lead them through the common areas of his home and up the winding stairs to the master bedroom. Once at the foot of his bed, Tyson lifted her to settle on top of the luxurious down comforter.

He tormented her with the unhurried time he took to unbutton her top. His fingertips danced over satin fabric of her bra and the smoothness of her skin until it met the cold button of her shorts. He pushed the button through its hole and peeled down the zipper. When she raised her hips above the clouds of the bed, Tyson pushed her shorts down past her feet, taking her sandals off with them. He then moved his body between her thighs.

Saamyah slipped her hands under his two shirts and lifted them over his head. After releasing them to fall to the floor, she caressed his muscular chest and rippled abdomen. She felt Tyson's hungry eyes on her as she worked loose his belt and then fastened shorts. When he did not stop her, she eased her hand into the opening and followed the warmth to his loins.

Tyson stifled the groan that grew deep in his larynx when she touched him. Their gazes met, communicating the mutual need for unbridled passion. Desiring more love than sex, he gingerly moved her hand from him and intertwined both her hands in his and leaned forward to rest on her.

Saamyah closed her eyes and inhaled deeply, exhaling slowly as he pinned her hands above her head and worked kisses down the side of her face, earlobe, and neck. She wrapped her legs around his solid waist and held him close to the wet fabric of her underwear. She was tortured by his throbbing member that he purposely ignored as his mouth explored her breasts.

"Tyson, please," she beseeched, signaling her desire through her tightened clinch of his hands. "Please…"

Tyson secretly grinned at her pleas and released her hands to travel down her body, stopping at her panties. He felt the release of her legs around his waist and the slight rise in her hips in anticipation. Her hips dropped in disappointment when the phone pierced the calmness of the room.

"Don't answer it," she pleaded.

Tyson looked into her eyes and smiled. "I won't."

Saamyah returned the smile and pulled him close for a kiss, dipping her tongue in his mouth in motivation. She tenderly bit his bottom lip when his fingers traveled up her inner thigh and found their way to her moist, swollen folds. A soft moan escaped her and she gripped the cool fabric of the comforter.

"Daddy, it's me Malachi!" The speaker exclaimed after the tone. "Daddy, are you there?…Daddy?!"

Both Saamyah and Tyson sulked in disappointment. He face fell into the curve of her neck as he loudly exhaled his sexual tension. "Why does the universe hate me?!" He lifted his face and met her eyes. He pushed her damp hair back from her forehead and regrettably said, "I have to get that."

"Daddy," Malachi began to cry. "Daddy, I want to come home…"

Saamyah nodded, suppressing her own frustration. "I know."

"I'm so sorry," he breathed on her lips, kissed them, and rose off her to get the phone that sat on the nightstand near his bed.

"Hey, son, daddy's here," Tyson greeted.

Saamyah sat up to quietly adjust her bra and button her shirt. After slipping back into her shorts and sandals, she tip-toed out of the bedroom.

"You are still here?" Tyson asked, finding Saamyah seated at his kitchen island thumbing through his men's health and fitness magazine. He fought his way through the arm of his tank top and shoved it down his muscular torso.

She closed the subscription and looked up at him. "I am. I didn't want to leave without saying good-bye.

He leaned in and kissed her. "Thank you."

She smiled and simply said, "You're welcome."

Tyson searched her eyes for the disappointment that dwelt there moments earlier. Though none was found, he still felt the need to apologize. "Saamyah, I am so sorry about the interruption. My son has these moments where-"

"Ssshhh," Saamyah hushed him while pressing her index finger to his lips. "No need to apologize for being a great father."

He smiled beneath her finger, took his hand and pressed it further to his lips for a kiss, and then moved it to kiss her. "I will walk you to your car."

*** EIGHT ***

Bryan extended Saamyah a white business envelope and taunted, "For my other supervisor," when she looked up at him in confusion.

Saamyah rolled her eyes, accepted the envelope, and proceeded to open it. She pulled apart the tri-folded document and saw that it was a work release form completed by his physician. Bryan was at liberty to return to work with duty restrictions.

"Congratulations," Saamyah simply remarked. She re-folded the document, shoved it back in the envelope, and extended it back to Bryan.

Bryan took it and tossed it in her wastebasket. He placed his hands on her desk and leaned forward. "Do you really mean it?"

Saamyah shook her head and huffed. "I did until now." She stood to file a manila folder in her file cabinet. Bryan followed her.

"So, what have I missed?"

"Well," Saamyah started, "as I foretold, there is no real repercussions for Mr. Barnes's parole violation—nothing more than a fine that is a drop in the bucket for him and meager community service hours. All of which I believe is a ploy to deter future run-ins with the law rather than future violations of his lax parole agreement."

"And, you know this because?"

Saamyah closed the drawer and simply responded, "Because I know people." She walked back to her desk and took her seat. Diverting the topic, Saamyah disclosed, "The Miami Beach case is no longer something Drew is willing to work on."

Bryan gave her a look of bewilderment. "Why?"

She watched him lower himself to a seat in front of her desk and answered, "He believes that my judgment is clouded by my intimate relationship with you...And, I...I believe he is right."

Bryan shrugged. "What does that even mean?"

"It means that I am going to Duncan to propose a department-wide investigation. I believe the perp is in-house...Drew believes that it is you."

Taken aback by the revelation, Bryan inquired, "Have you both lost your fucking minds?"

Saamyah did not dignify his question with a response.

"You are about to wage a full-fledge, blue-on-blue war," he warned.

Again, Saamyah said nothing in response.

Bryan peered at the empty space in the corner by the window. He contemplated the words that could possibly sway Saamyah's decision. When he conjured none, he beseeched, "Please don't do this, Saamyah."

"Bryan-"

He turned his glare to her. "I still have to work with these people when you leave."

"We have a job to do, Bryan, and the City of Miami expects us to do it."

Bryan reclined in the seat and pondered all that she said. When he realized that she was steadfast in her decision, he offered, "Then wait for evidence...Our prints and DNA are in the system. So, you'll get your man when you get your evidence and you won't destroy the entire department in the process."

Saamyah swiveled her chair with the movement of her feet. "Fine. Contingent upon Duncan's thoughts, I will wait for the evidence."

Bryan shook his head. "No...You can't go to Duncan. Not yet."

Saamyah ceased the movement of her chair. She felt something was amiss and asked, "Why not?"

"Because he would be obliged to consult the other superior officers...I know him."

"He didn't with our romantic ruse."

"Trust me, that was different. This is different. He will talk."

Saamyah closed her eyes and took in a deep breath and exhaled slowly. When she opened them, she whispered, "I pray that you're right, Bryan."

"I'm going to break early for lunch. I'm meeting Maurice." He stood and asked, "You want anything while I am out?"

Saamyah glanced at her wristwatch. It was half past eleven. "No, thank you."

He nodded. "I will see you in a bit."

Bryan exited the back entrance of the building and immediately noticed Andrew several feet ahead of him. "Bryce," he called out, jogging to close the distance between them. "Bryce!"

Andrew stopped between two government vehicles in the parking lot and turned in the direction of the voice. He huffed in aggravation when he discovered that the voice belonged to Bryan.

"Welcome back," Andrew cavalierly spoke when Bryan reached him.

"What's this bullshit I hear about you initiating a department-wide investigation?"

Andrew grinned. "Not department-wide—just you."

"Well, any investigation that is launched would include you, you sick fuck...And your shit better come back clean," Bryan warned.

Andrew chuckled at the threat. He then lifted his sunglasses to the top of his head so that his eyes could peer deep into Bryan's. "I am more than content with my wife...Trust me, it will."

Bryan suppressed the anger ignited in him by Andrew's allusion to his infidelity. If it was possible to regret anything more than his unfaithfulness, it would be Andrew's knowledge of it.

"Cómo está la señora sexy?" Bryan smugly asked in Andrew's wife's native tongue.

With no thought of the consequences, Andrew punched him in his lower abdomen and watched him hunch in pain. "STAY THE FUCK AWAY FROM MY WIFE!"

Bryan ignored the pain in his body and tackled Andrew into the vehicle behind him…

"Detective Cambell," Saamyah greeted the caller on the other end of her office phone.

"Detective Cambell, it's Maurice Washington."

Saamyah recalled the crass host of the Fourth of July barbeque and smiled. "Hello, sir. How are you?"

"I'm well, thanks. How are you?"

"The same…Bryan just left to meet you for lunch."

"Oh, I'm not calling for that chump."

Saamyah snickered. "Okay. So, what do I owe the pleasure of this call?"

"I'm seeking guest speakers for my Crime and Justice course. Robyn thought that you would be an excellent choice as a former special agent."

"Did she now?" She asked with skepticism.

"Okay, you got me," Maurice confessed. "It was I who thought that you would, but believed it to be a better sell if I mentioned Robyn considering-"

"Considering you were an ass when we first met?" Saamyah finished for him.

They both laughed.

"Yes," he admitted. "My sincerest apologies, by the way."

Saamyah shook her head and smiled. "It's fine…What day and ti-"

"Cambell, quick!" An uniformed officer beseeched rushing into her office. "Russell and Bryce are in the parking lot fighting."

Saamyah rose to her feet. "Maurice, I have to go. I will get your information from Bryan and will call you back for the details." She hung up before he could respond and hurried out behind the officer.

"Stop it! STOP IT!" The police captain commanded as law enforcement officers struggled to pull and keep them apart.

Captain Brown looked at Andrew and then stared at Bryan when they were finally separated. Her anguish grew and was exacerbated by the UV rays that burned into her chocolate skin. Shaking her head at Bryan, she finally confessed, "I'm so sick of your shit. All of it!"

Bryan broke free of the hands that held him and shoved the officer way from him. He adjusted his clothes, wiped the sweat from his brow, and dabbed the blood at his lip. Now that the adrenaline rush had passed, his exhaustion compounded his pain.

Captain Brown felt every eye in the parking lot on her. Since her transition into the male-dominated, leadership role three years ago, her ability to guide was often challenged and all decisions heavily scrutinized. Because of this double standard, she carefully calculated how to respond to every incident—this one being no different.

After sweeping her long bangs off her face, Captain Brown pulled her glasses off her face and took in the two detectives before her—both major assets to her force. One worked well and gave her no trouble; the other worked better and was nothing but trouble.

"Go home," she finally spoke, breaking the silence. She turned on her heels and then turned back to them. "Matter of fact, take the week. The both of you."

Andrew parted his lips to contest, but she raised her hand to stop him. "Go home, cool off, and don't bring this shit to my gala on Saturday."

Captain Brown walked away from them and through the crowd that had gathered. She caught Saamyah's eyes en route to the building, but before she could mouth a few words to her, an officer called for her attention.

The crowd walked back to the building as Saamyah walked away from it. She stood in front of Bryan as he sat on the hood of a patrol car holding his ribs. Andrew had left as commanded before Saamyah could console him.

"I think I reinjured my ribs," Bryan whimpered.

Saamyah glared down at him with no sympathy. "You just couldn't help yourself, could you? Everything has to be a challenge. Your first day back and you had to lock fists with someone. Drew of all people."

Bryan looked up at her. His eyes squinted because of the sun. "He threw the first punch, Saamyah."

"What did you say to him?"

Bryan dropped his head and winced at the pain. "…What?"

"What. Did. You. Say. To. Him?" She repeated.

"It doesn't matter. He still threw the first punch."

"Go home, Bryan," she reiterated before walking away.

*** *** ***

"I'm so glad that you decided to come to the gala after all," Saamyah shared, greeting Andrew with a warm embrace. "And you look incredibly handsome." She released him and brushed off the metaphoric dust on his shoulders as she admired his black tux.

Andrew blushed and thanked her. "You look incredible yourself—no surprise, of course."

Saamyah beamed. "You are far too kind." She took hold of Tyson's left hand and introduced them. "This handsome man is my date. Tyson Troy, meet Andrew Bryce, a fellow detective in homicide."

Andrew extended his right hand and shook Tyson's. "It's a pleasure." He turned to the beautiful Hispanic woman next to him and introduced her as his wife, Karmen Bryce.

Saamyah took in her glowing, honey complexion and matching highlights. The loose bun on the top of her head exposed her narrow, but strong bone structure that was accentuated by perfectly applied makeup.

After her full lips spread into a bright smile that exposed her perfect teeth, Karmen said, "It's so nice to finally put a face to a name. I have heard so many wonderful things about you, Saamyah." Karmen wrapped an arm around Saamyah in a firm embrace and then added, "You are gorgeous."

"Thank you," Saamyah responded, dropping her arm as Karmen did the same. Saamyah then smoothed out her corseted, sleeveless evening gown that paled in comparison to the rich red one Karmen wore. Though Karmen's dress was conservative throughout the body, it fell off her right shoulder to provide just enough sex appeal. Saamyah secretly wished that she had not played it safe with her champagne colored dress.

Saamyah realized she was staring when Tyson tugged at her hand. "Oh my go-, I'm so sorry…I'm being rude. I-"

Karmen smiled and gently rubbed Saamyah's bare arm. "It's okay. I'm not offended."

"Thank you," Saamyah breathed in relief, holding her free hand to her chest. The four of them laughed.

"And now the real awkwardness begins," Andrew commented after he spotted Bryan enter the ballroom with Tiffany on his arm.

Karmen nudged her husband, "Be nice, babe. Tonight's a night of celebration not calamity."

"Yeah," Andrew retorted. "Make sure he knows that."

"Looks like this shindig can finally begin now that the whole gang is here," Bryan announced. He released Tiffany and greeted Karmen with a hug and quick kiss on her cheek; then Andrew and Tyson with strong handshakes. Finally, he slipped his hand around Saamyah's lower back to firmly grip her waist and planted a tender kiss at her temple. "You look amazing," he whispered low enough for only her to hear.

"Thank you, Bryan," she bashfully murmured.

Andrew caught Tyson's eyes and shook his head. He witnessed the anger igniting in Tyson and wanted to make strides to extinguish it. In a good faith effort to diffuse the tension, Andrew confessed, "It's always a treat to see the district's attorney. How are you?"

"You're far too kind, Drew," Tiffany acknowledged, taking the bait. "I'm well. How are you?"

"Living the dream, perhaps more so than others once I get a drink." He took Karmen's hand and bid a good evening to the group before walking towards the bar and then their table.

"I think it's best we do the same," Saamyah suggested to Tyson. When he nodded in agreement, she turned back to Bryan and Tiffany and wished, "Enjoy the night," before she walked away with Tyson at her side.

Tiffany chuckled. "What did you say to her?"

"Nothing—just that she looked amazing."

"Suuure," Tiffany responded in disbelief as she herself walked towards another bar in the opposite direction.

"I swear that's all I said."

Tiffany shook her head and smirked. "But, how did you say it?"

Bryan laughed.

"See—that's why you have so few friends in the P.D.," Tiffany reminded him as they waited to place their drink orders.

Though her words stung, Bryan quickly recovered and assured, "I have you, and, trust, that is more than enough." He placed a kiss on her cheek.

She rolled her eyes. "Ummm hmmmm...Bryan, I see the way you always look at her. We all saw the way you just looked at her." She paused to peer deep into his eyes. "You are only lying to yourself."

Bryan opened his mouth to speak, but the knot in his throat blocked his voice. He swallowed multiple times, but to no avail.

Tiffany grinned at his speechlessness. "Get our drinks. I am going to look for our table."

After the cocktail hour and plated dinner, Tyson excused their brief departure and lead Saamyah from the table.

"Thank you so much for the save," Saamyah breathed, grateful for the intermission. The retired police chief's wife spoke of everything from her remembrance of the police academy to home-baked goods. If she had not been trying to engage Tyson in conversation and avoid Bryan's incessant stares that came from the table angled to hers, Saamyah would have enjoyed more the dinner-long talk. But, the balancing act was exhausting her.

"Yeah, I could tell you needed a reprieve. The Madame was not letting up."

Saamyah laughed at Tyson's humor and continued to laugh as he led her to the dance floor. He began to lead her in small circles in rhythm with the soothing jazz ballad.

"So, what do you think about us skipping out on champagne and dessert? I am not much of a sweets guy anyway."

"Is that right?" Saamyah inquired catching his eyes to see if he would repeat the lie to her face.

He sheepishly grinned. "No, not really."

"I thought not," she replied, recounting the number of shared desserts they had. But, in consideration of his time and patience she asked, "Are you ready to leave?"

Tyson kissed her forehead and responded, "Only if you are."

"Honors are being awarded during the champagne toast, but we can leave right after."

Tyson nodded. "I can stomach that…On the condition that I eat my own dessert—no sharing mine after you devour yours."

Saamyah laughed out loud. "I have a better one."

"Oh really?" He spun her out and then back into his body. "Please tell."

She gathered again her arms around his neck and negotiated, "If you make it through dessert and champagne, then I will make the rest of your evening."

Tyson was held by the passion in her eyes. He lowered his hands to the small of her back and pulled her closer into him. "You've got yourself a deal, Detective Cambell." He placed a gentle kiss on her lower lip, careful not to disturb her perfectly applied lip color.

Saamyah lowered her hand to his lips and wiped away the wine-berry hue from his lips. "Well, at least as much of a deal that Malachi will allow."

They both laughed.

"Oh, trust me, Malachi is getting the do not disturb alert tonight."

She smiled at the innuendo, then lowered her head to his shoulder. The soft caress of her bare shoulders and corseted back eased her eyes closed. She was enveloped by genuine safety—a feeling she had not experienced in a long while.

Tyson kissed her temple and then her cheek before whispering in her ear, "What have you done to me, Saamyah?...I have fallen far too hard, way too fast for you."

"It's a scary thing, isn't it?"

"Indeed it is," he concurred. "Indeed it is."

Tyson closed his own eyes and rested his head on hers. As he continued to hold her close, he inhaled the sweet scent that emanated from her pores as he moved her in slow circles to the tempo.

"May I cut in?"

Saamyah and Tyson simultaneously opened their eyes and lifted their heads. Each of them turned in the direction of a familiar voice.

"Bryan," Saamyah simply responded.

"May I cut in?" Bryan asked again, extending his hand to Saamyah.

Tyson looked at her, indicating that the decision was ultimately hers to make, and inquired, "Saamyah?"

She nodded in approval.

"Are you sure?" Tyson asked, noticing slight apprehension.

Saamyah forced a smile and answered while taking Bryan's hand, "Yes…I'll be fine."

"Okay," he obliged, kissing her temple another time before releasing her to Bryan. He looked at him and confirmed, "One dance."

Bryan lifted his free hand as if to surrender and said, "That's all I am asking."

Saamyah exhaled in nervousness and placed her hands on Bryan's shoulders. A feeling of unease enveloped her when his hand found rest in the small of her back.

Bryan pulled her closer into him to inhale her intoxicating fragrance and whispered in her ear, "You look beautiful tonight."

Saamyah rolled her eyes at his comment and simply said, "As does Tiffany."

Bryan snickered then agreed, "Yes, she does, but," he lifted her chin, "that compliment was intended for you, Saamyah, not her."

Saamyah smiled and shook her head at his matter-of-fact demeanor. "Well, thank you, Bryan….I will be sure to let Tyson know of his fortune."

Bryan scoffed with jealously, "Fortune, huh? And just how fortunate is he, Saamyah?"

She rolled her eyes again and shook her head at his insinuation. Without responding to the question, she asked him, "You only have until the song ends, Bryan. Do you really want to waste this dance talking about Tyson?"

"No, I don't actually," he immediately replied. Pressing her body more firmly into his, he confessed, "I'd much rather use it to convince you of something else."

"Convince me of what, Bryan?" Saamyah asked with aggravation. "What could you possibly want from me now?"

"Leave with me tonight," Bryan boldly proposed.

"What?"

"Tonight—come home with me instead of Tyson."

Saamyah ceased moving her feet to the cadence of the music and removed his hands from her back. As she stepped out of his embrace, she said, "Have a good night, Bryan," before she turned to walk away.

Bryan grabbed her hand and confessed, "I'm serious, Saamyah."

She peeled his fingers from her hand and told him, "Yes, I know…But what I don't know is whether I am more upset at your implication that I am a whore or at your revelation of how selfish you are."

Ignoring the former part of her concern, Bryan questioned the latter. "Selfish? How the hell am I selfish, Saamyah?"

"Because all you care about is your damn self and what it is you want and what it is you need." She paused to let her anger subside. "In conjuring your proposition, did you forget that we are both here with dates or does that not matter to you?"

"Tiffany is a big girl. I'm sure she will be just fine without me tonight."

Saamyah shook her head in dismay and laughed halfheartedly. "Yeah, well, I'm a big girl, too, Bryan, and I sure as hell will be just as equally fine without you tonight."

Saamyah felt a warm hand wrap around her waist and soft lips touch the side of her head. "Is everything okay?" Tyson asked returning at the tail end of their conversation. Though he could not hear their words over the loud music, he noticed their confrontation from afar.

"Yeah, we're fine," Bryan quickly answered. "Can you give us a few more minutes? Saamyah and I were just-"

"No, we're done," Saamyah interjected. "Have a good night, Bryan."

Bryan grabbed her hand before she parted with his nemesis and confessed, "I'm selfish because I love you, Saamyah."

Tyson placed his hand on Bryan's chest to encourage space between them. "She said good night, Bryan, now let her go."

Bryan pushed Tyson's hand off him and warned, "Don't put your damn hands on me…Now, I had asked you to give us a minute-"

"Bryan, please," Saamyah implored after noticing the attention they were garnering.

"Saamyah-" Bryan started in desperation.

Saamyah held up at chest level her hand that Bryan still held firmly. "This isn't love, Bryan." She then dropped her hand and began to peel his fingers off her while adding, "And if it is, then I don't want it." With Tyson at her side, she pivoted in the direction of their table and stepped away.

"Saamyah-" Bryan called, making an attempt to go after her. He was stopped by several male colleagues who immediately enclosed him.

"Russell, just let her go," one advised.

"She's not worth it, man," another chimed.

Bryan yanked away from the hands that held him and ran his fingers through his hair in frustration. Looking around the ballroom, he realized multiple pairs of eyes were on him that he had not noticed before. After affixing his own eyes on Saamyah, he decided not to heed the advice given to him and pushed passed his colleagues to follow her.

"So, what is it?" Bryan asked, following her the final steps to her table.

"What is what, Bryan?" Saamyah asked, avoiding his eyes as she collected her clutch and shawl to leave.

"Love. If it's not what I have for you, then what is it?"

Saamyah stopped and finally met his gaze. "If I have to answer that, then you are more clueless than I thought." She turned to Tyson and announced, "I'm ready." She walked around Bryan expecting him to stop her, but, to her surprise and relief, he did not.

"So, what? It's not love unless I take a bullet and die for you?" Bryan venomously retorted.

Saamyah halted her step and slowly faced him. It took little time for the tears to swell in her eyes and run down her face. "Why…Why would you say that to me, Bryan?"

"For the same reason why you would say that I don't love you…Doesn't feel too good, does it?"

Tyson noticed the affect Bryan's response had on Saamyah. It was if the words had pierced her core to cause the insurmountable pain that Bryan had intended. In his attempt to diffuse the situation, Tyson gently caressed her back to ease her tension. He kissed her cheek and whispered, "He's not worth your tears, Saamyah."

Saamyah inhaled deeply and exhaled slowly. She stared into Bryan's eyes as she replied to Tyson, "You're right, he's not…Let's go home."

Bryan suppressed the heartache caused by the subliminal message conveyed in the words she had just spoken. He shook his head, laughed half-heartedly in dismay, and inquired, "Really, Saamyah? That's how this is going play out?"

Saamyah turned on her heel to exit, and Tyson did the same.

"You would rather be his whore than my queen," Bryan boisterously surmised. Embarrassment froze Saamyah and kept her from preventing Tyson's fist from colliding with Bryan's face. She pivoted in time to see Bryan fall back onto a table. He rose with the aid of those around him and then wiped the blood from his mouth. With no hesitation, Bryan retaliated with a tackle that knocked over several tables and chairs, and scattered the guests seated at them.

Saamyah was repeatedly motioned out of the way by men attempting to intervene. Overwhelmed with astonishment and guilt, she excused herself from the chaos. Saamyah ran towards the double doors, into the grand hotel's lobby, and exited into the night air—all while ignoring the female voice that called her name.

"TAXI!" Saamyah hailed in the middle of the busy street. "TAXI!"

"SAAMYAH!" The voice yelled, ignoring the dangers of the traffic as she, too, stepped into the street.

"TAXI!"

"SAAMYAH!"

Saamyah finally turned in the direction of the voice and saw it belonged to Tiffany.

"SAAMYAH!...Are you crazy?!...What are you doing?" Tiffany ignored the honking horns of the vehicles she ran in front of and dodged between to pull Saamyah out of the street. "You are going to get yourself killed out here...Where are you trying to go? I can take you."

Saamyah stared at the beautiful woman before her and shook her head. "No...You go back and enjoy what's left of you evening with Bryan." She turned to the traffic and hailed, "TAXI!"

Tiffany yanked Saamyah's raised hand from the sky. "Saamyah, this is insane. Just let me take you home."

"Why? So you can feel better about sleeping with Bryan tonight?"

"What? No!" She paused when the taxicab slowly approached them. "Why would you say that, Saamyah?"

Saamyah knowingly huffed. "Because it doesn't seem to matter if I am with Bryan or not. Women like you always seem to find your way back into his bed."

Saamyah opened the door to the vehicle and climbed into the backseat, but was stopped from closing it when Tiffany held the door.

"Is that the reason why you have this disdain for me? Because you think I want to bed Bryan?"

Saamyah did not answer.

Tiffany scoffed in disbelief. "Saamyah, Bryan is my little brother."

Saamyah did not respond to the revelation because she did not know how to. Her conjecture had prompted the mischaracterization of Tiffany and Bryan's relationship.

In lieu of a reply, Saamyah yanked the cab door from Tiffany's grip and slammed it closed. She gave the driver instructions to take her to Miami Beach.

"I knew I'd find you here," Bryan confessed, walking towards her as she stood motionless toward the waters.

Saamyah closed her eyes, prayed, and then slowly opened them again. She had implored God that Bryan's presence was a mere figment of her imagination. Unfortunately, to her disappointment, the warmth of his body next to her confirmed that it was not.

"You are becoming very predictable, Saamyah."

Without breaking the gaze that was fixed on the water, Saamyah asked, "What do you want, Bryan?" When he did not respond, she turned her head to face him. "Haven't you caused enough problems for one night?"

"Hardly...Although you seem to have taken an issue with Tiffany and that definitely was not caused by me."

Saamyah shifted the rest of her body toward him. "Yes, it was, Bryan. You led me to believe that she was something more than your sister."

Bryan chuckled and corrected, "No, Saamyah, your perception of me led you to believe that Tiffany was something more than my sister."

"Okay, Bryan," Saamyah conceded, exhausted and not willing to engage in a confrontation with him. "Good night." She side-stepped to walk around him, but Bryan did the same to stop her. Saamyah flinched when Bryan's hand gently stroked her face. Unmoved by the desire in his eyes, she turned from his lips when he leaned to kiss her.

Pained by the rebuff, Bryan dropped his hand from her face and asked defensively, "How much?"

Perplexed, Saamyah asked, "How much for what?

"The night." He reached into his pocket and pulled out his wallet. "Whatever Tyson has paid you for the night, I'll double it." He grabbed several large bills, folded and tucked them between her breasts. "That's all I have on me, but you know I am good for the rest."

Saamyah slapped him with every emotion she had burning in her, removed the money from her breasts, and threw it in his face. She then pushed past him.

Bryan grabbed Saamyah's arm and pulled her into him. He held her close and kissed her until she gave up her fight and kissed him back. His trail of kisses on her neck preceded the firm groping of her breasts. Her soft moan stiffened his manhood and he began to anticipate the feel of her body on him. With very little effort, his hands found their way underneath the smooth fabric of her dress and stroked the softness that made her a woman.

Tears fell from Saamyah's eyes. She loathed Bryan's familiar touch and the way her body responded to the pleasure she derived from it. Everything in her told her to leave, but everything in her made her stay. She wrapped her arms tight around his neck and returned the deep kisses as he lifted her onto him.

Overwhelmed with ecstasy, Bryan sighed loudly at the joy Saamyah's warm, firm body gave him. As his strong arms rhythmically moved her with each of his thrusts, he buried his faced in her neck fighting the urge to explode inside her too soon.

He kissed her cool mouth to muffle moans that were driving him closer to the edge.

Saamyah gripped his hair with one hand and held it tight as the burn within her deepened with each stroke of her G-spot. Her breath quickened and she panted Bryan's name over...and over... and over until she felt a tremble in her lower abdomen. She whined his name in a whisper when the shiver enveloped her entire body.

Kissing her through the end of her climatic release, Bryan lowered them to the sand one knee at a time. Her legs still wrapped tightly around him, he moved methodically on top of her until he found the spot that made her beseech him to continue. He suckled her neck, occasionally biting down to suppress the excitement her soft moans gave him.

Despite the solemn tears that fell from her eyes, Saamyah was ecstatic by the ravishing of her body. She could feel every thrust that tenderly rocked her body, the many soft nibbles at her collar bone, and then his wet tongue that teased her swollen nipples. And, when his hands gripped her thighs to plunge deeper into her world, she felt another orgasm build in the pit of her abdomen.

"Bryan," she moaned in gratifying exhaustion. "Bryan."

Bryan covered her mouth with soft kisses. "Wait for me."

Saamyah held him tightly against her. "Bryan...Bryan, I can't." With that, she cried out into the night as a second wave crashed within her. She arched her back at the intensity and pulled at his shirt to invite him deeper into her body.

Though it ached him to do so, Bryan ceased moving in and out of her warmth. Saamyah's body trembled immensely from the strength of her second organism and each additional thrust was torment for her. Consequently, Bryan found satisfaction in the pleasure he had given her and subsided rather than exhausting her further for his own release.

When Saamyah finally opened her eyes, she saw Bryan gazing down lovingly at her. She closed them again when Bryan gently kissed her forehead, the tip of her nose, and then her bottom lip. She opened her eyes again to look into his. They both tried to decipher the meaning of their passionate encounter. Saamyah's heart ached at the thought of it being only a favor he had paid for.

Bryan gently wiped away Saamyah's tears that rolled back towards her hair. He made an attempt to kiss her, but she turned from his lips. When he tried to use his fingertips to turn her face back to look at him, she pushed his hand away and continued to cry. Bryan then knew that the encounter was nothing more than a thrill that she now regretted. With disappointment, hurt, and fury, he kissed her cheek and then whispered in her ear, "Thank you. You were worth every cent." He then rose to walk away, leaving her crying in the sand.

*** *** ***

"Saamyah," Tyson called out again.

She finally faced his direction and watched him take the final steps towards her. Like her, he was still in his clothes from the night before. "What are you doing here, Tyson?"

"Looking for you," he replied while pushing back her disheveled hair. Even in disarray, she still appeared alluring to him. "Are you okay? I've been calling you and waiting at your house all night."

Saamyah dropped her eyes. After taking his hand from her head, she kissed it on the swollen knuckle caused by his brawl with Bryan and held it. "I'm fine...I just needed to be alone."

By their closeness, Tyson could smell Bryan's cologne seeping from Saamyah's pores. He also noticed the purple marks on her body—the same ones he once left on his former wife's in the heat of passion. Nervously, he used their intertwined hands to lift her face until their eyes met and then asked, "But you weren't alone, were you?"

Saamyah dropped her head and her eyes swelled with tears. The knot in her throat kept her from answering. So, she simply held his hand close to her heart.

Tyson closed his eyes as his own heart dropped and began to race at the speed of hers. When he opened them, the tears she cried confirmed the suspicion he was hoping against. He gently removed his hand from her breast and shoved it in his pants pocket. No longer able to look at her, he looked out at the ocean as the early morning tide came in.

Tyson cleared his throat before saying, "I'm, uh, going to go ahead and go to that conference in Chicago I was telling you about." He paused to allow his anger and pain subside before clearing his throat and continuing, "I truly believe that time has the power to put distance between us and the circumstances that cause our suffering. My presence there will not only give me the time, but also the space I need to get over you...Prayerfully, when I get back, you will no longer be here."

He turned in the direction from which he came and huskily stated, "...Take care of yourself, Saamyah." Tyson then began the walk to his car and out of her life.

Saamyah abruptly woke from her sleep as the pounding on her door ricocheted throughout her unit. With her weak arms she slowly lifted herself off her abdomen and then the sofa. After pressing her dress down, she sluggishly moved to the door. She wiped her wet face dry before she opened it.

"I thought you were dead in there," Bryan greeted.

Saamyah avoided his eyes. "I'm fine. Thanks for checking." She attempted to close the door, but Bryan stopped her. Their eyes met.

"You look like hell," Bryan told her.

She rolled her eyes at him and shook her head. "In one weekend, Bryan, you have managed to ruin a perfect event, a perfect relationship, and-"

"Your perfect image," he interjected. "Nothing happened last night, Saamyah, that you didn't want to happen."

Saamyah bit her lower lip and nodded. "You're absolutely right. So, I guess that proves that I am no different from you. Thanks for bringing that to light." She attempted to close the door a second time, but Bryan stopped her again.

"Saamyah, I didn't come here to pick a fight with you."

"Oh, really? Then why are you here, Bryan? To extend another offer?"

"What? No...I...I just wanted to apologize for some of the things I said to you last night. They were crass and I didn't mean any of it." He paused to carefully contemplate his next words. "...I just feel as if I am losing control; that I have no control...With work, with the baby, with you—I'm losing it. I'm losing it and don't know to gain it back, so I'm just lashing out."

"You need help," Saamyah offered.

"Then help me," he pleaded.

"Professional help," she clarified.

Bryan did not respond to the suggestion. Instead, he assured, "... If you want, Tyson never has to know about last night."

Saamyah huffed. "Do you really think I can live with a secret like that? To continue on as if nothing ever happened?...I'm not you, Bryan, I can't live with that kind of guilt."

"I know you're not me, Saamyah. I was just trying to help make things right."

"Well, you can't because it's too late." She wiped the tears that rolled down her face and added, "He already knows."

"You told him?"

Before answering, she wiped her eyes again and folded her arms across her chest. "No, not technically, but then again I wasn't that difficult to read...It's over. Tyson has ended us and we're through."

Bryan's heart went out to her. "Saamyah, I'm so sorry."

Saamyah incredulously chuckled and tried to no avail to blink back the flood of fresh tears. "No, you're not. This is what you wanted. Probably was praying for it."

He shrugged. "Well, perhaps wanted, but definitely not praying…In any event, I didn't want you at your threshold crying in misery…Honestly, I didn't."

Saamyah nodded and whispered, "Thanks." She pushed back her tangled hair and added, "I need to get out of this dress and into the shower…Thanks for stopping by, Bryan."

Bryan nodded and finally allowed her to shut the door.

*** NINE ***

"Hey," Bryan greeted in a low voice late Monday morning.

Saamyah broke her blank stare into space and acknowledged his entry. "Hey."

After gently closing the door, he walked to her desk. "I, uh, just received word from Duncan that you will be working homicide with Bryce for the duration of your TDY."

Saamyah nodded. "Yeah, I was informed earlier this morning."

Not sure of what to say next he asked, "Do you need help with your move?"

She shook her head. "There really isn't much more to move, so I will manage what's left. Thanks though."

Bryan watched her sit motionlessly in her seat and yearned to know what she was thinking. "Saamyah, I am so sorry for this. Well, for everything actually...I really am."

Saamyah met his eyes and gave him a weak smile. "I know and I am, too."

Befuddled, he inquired, "Come again?"

She inhaled deeply and exhaled loudly before responding, "Bryan, you are a man accustomed to receiving everything you want and, against the sound advice of others and my own better judgment, I did just that—gave you what you wanted."

Bryan held his silence, uncertain of how to respond.

"I've committed an incredible disservice to you, Bryan, and, for that, I truly apologize."

He held his silence a moment longer, contemplating all that she had said. When Bryan finally spoke, he diverted the conversation by asking, "Has Tyson returned any of your calls?"

Saamyah lowered her head and answered, "No."

"Maybe you should try again."

She shook her head. "He's not answering, Bryan, and he probably never will. Honestly, I don't blame him. I hurt him deeply." She took a deep breath before continuing, "He leaves for Chicago this afternoon. His only request is that I am gone when he returns...After what I've put him through, I figure it is the least I can do for him."

"You don't have to leave, Saamyah."

She chuckled, stood, and placed the items on her desk in the empty box. "Yes, I do. I have done more damage to myself in a couple of months than I have the last twenty-seven years. It's obvious that Miami is no place for me."

"What about us?" Bryan asked with desperation.

"What about us?" Saamyah repeated, looking at him. "You called me a whore in front of all our colleagues, Bryan. Then you offered me an exorbitant amount of money for sex as if I were a top dollar strumpet." She wiped the tears that fell from her eyes and assured him, "There's no coming back from that, Bryan."

"I know," Bryan stated, taking steps toward her to comfort her. He abruptly stopped when she held out her hand in protest. "I'm sorry, Saamyah...I really am...I'm really sorry," his voice quivered in contrite desperation. "If I could take it all back I would because I didn't mean it and I damn sure don't want to lose you over it."

Saamyah's heart ached. She closed her eyes and wiped them with the back of her hand, but, when she opened them again, new tears fell. "I forgive you, Bryan, but your apology is still too late and...it's not enough. It can't fix us."

"Then how?"

"How what?"

"How do I fix us? Tell me, Saamyah, and I will do it."

Saamyah calmed her distressed heart with a few deep breaths and offered, "You're about to bring a child into a broken relationship, Bryan. Work on fixing that."

"I can be a father to my child without being with its mother."

"Yeah? Then do it without me, too."

"Saa-"

There was a knock on the door and it crept opened.

"Didn't mean to interrupt. I just wanted to come and grab whatever boxes you have left to move downstairs," Andrew announced at the threshold.

"No problem," Saamyah assured. "Just give me a sec."

Andrew nodded. "Russell," he greeted before departing the doorway.

Saamyah grabbed the box off of her desk and began towards the door. Bryan blocked her path to stop her.

He looked deep into her glistening, red eyes and promised, "I am going to fix us. And when I do, neither Kimberly, Tyson, nor anyone else will ever come between us again. I will make sure of it."

Saamyah feebly smiled at his obstinate confidence. "Goodbye, Bryan." She kissed his cheek and walked out of the office.

Saamyah was close to ending her call late that evening when he finally answered his cell phone.

"Tyson?" Saamyah asked in astonishment.

Tyson took a deep breath and exhaled. He hated how hearing her voice still raced his heart. "Hello, Saamyah."

Lost for words, all she could do was weep and say, "I'm so sorry, Tyson...I really am... I swear...I never meant to hurt you."

Tyson closed his eyes and said, "I know...and, I'm sorry, too."

Confused, she inquired, "Why?"

He lowered himself onto the sofa of his hotel penthouse suite and answered, "Because I selfishly pursued you when I knew your heart was with another man." He exhaled loudly and continued, "I don't know—I guess, in many ways I thought you would give your heart to me if I were patient…Somehow my better judgment was clouded by your passion, your drive, your energy."

"Tyson-" she breathed between sobs. Even in his pain, disappointment, and anger, he still found the strength to speak well of her.

He stopped her saying, "I knew that you would eventually find your way back to him, but, still yet, I foolishly wanted you for myself. You captivated me and it had been so long since I had felt that way. With you, it was easy to move dangerously fast and fall incredibly hard…" Though it pained him immensely to admit it, Tyson choked, "I should have spared you the pain and humiliation and just allowed you to go and be with him…The truth of the matter, Saamyah, is that he is with whom you belong."

"No, Tyson-"

"Saamyah, I only answered in hopes that this conversation would give you the closure you need. Know that I forgive you and I pray that one day you will forgive me, too…Please don't call anymore." With that, Tyson ended the call.

Saamyah closed her eyes as her heart sunk into her belly. The phone slowly slipped from her fingers and onto her bed. With the dial tone still echoing in her ear, she rested her head on her pillow and cried herself to sleep.

*** *** ***

"When, Bryan?" Saamyah heard a female voice in Bryan's office ask when she walked into her old one. The door was closed, so she could not immediately put a face to the voice.

"Are you ever going to tell them?" She asked.

No response.

Between her sobs, the voice reminded him, "In less than seven months we are going to have a baby and no one in your family knows."

"Kimberly, I am working," Bryan finally responded. "I can't talk about this right now."

"You never can talk about this, Bryan," Kimberly retorted.

"And coming to my job is going to make me talk?"

"It's the only recourse I have!" She protested in frustration.

Bryan's office fell silent, and Saamyah considered leaving to give him and Kimberly privacy. She thought against her departure when she heard a loud *slam* that made her flinch.

"Damn it, Bryan. Talk to me!"

Bryan snatched his hands back before they were caught in the closing filing drawer that Kimberly pushed shut. He looked at her and yelled, "What do you want from me?!" He paused to regain his bearings so that he would not speak out of anger. "…You wanted this, Kimberly. Not me—you. I have no say-so in the matter, remember?" He paused once more and then asked again, "So, what the fuck do you want from me?"

Kimberly looked deep into the eyes of the man she once deeply loved. "You really don't want this baby, do you?"

Bryan broke their gaze. "Kimberly, my answer to that is no secret between us."

He was right, but hearing the truth again still ached—particularly since she was relying on his love for children to change his heart. Kimberly closed her eyes and took a deep breath and exhaled. When she opened her eyes again, she told him, "You have until the end of the week to break the news to your family or I will."

"No, you won't," Bryan challenged her.

"I will and your bastard child won't be the only thing I talk about."

"Considering the paternity of your child is still yet to be determined, I am sure you will have plenty of other things to talk about."

Kimberly struck Bryan's face with an open hand and all the anger and frustration that was tucked away and hidden deep inside her for some time. "You will not treat me like your whores, Bryan…I am the mother of your child. YOUR child, Bryan."

With that, Kimberly swung his office door opened and ignored the loud *thud* it made when it bounced off the wall. She briefly caught Saamyah's eyes and quickly brushed past her to exit without saying a word.

Saamyah peered into Bryan's office and asked, "Are you okay?"

"Yeah, sorry you had to hear all of that."

She walked into his office and said, "I know that this is probably none of my business, but she's right, Bryan. You can't treat her that way, whether or not you are the father of her child." She paused then added, "And, you have to tell your family. It is wrong for them to find out from anyone else other than you."

Bryan looked at her and responded. "You're right. This is none of your business."

"I'm only trying to help."

"If you want to help, then stop talking about it. I am sick of talking about it."

Saamyah nodded and simply said, "Okay."

Bryan exhaled loudly and sat at the edge of his desk. "I'm sorry, Saamyah. I know you are only trying to help…I am not angry at you. I am just frustrated with this situation. This and so many other things could have gone differently in my life had I just conducted myself differently."

Saamyah went to give him a hug. "You are going to get through this, Bryan." She consoled. "This pregnancy or the case will not defeat you. You are much stronger."

Bryan appreciated her comfort and held her waist in return. He then buried his face in her neck and thanked her.

When minutes passed, Saamyah broke their embrace and asked, "So, why haven't you told your family?"

Bryan stood and went to sit in his chair behind his desk. "Telling them is not as easy as it seems, Saamyah." He paused then added, "My family is very traditional when it comes to marriage and children."

Saamyah nodded. It now made sense why Kimberly referenced the baby as a bastard. "Bryan, we are living in a different time now. People's perspectives have changed."

"We have become more tolerant, but the perspectives have not changed," he corrected. "My parents are devout Christians."

Saamyah snickered and mocked, "You are the seed of devout Christians?"

Bryan rolled his eyes at her wit and retorted, "We all fall short, Saamyah."

She stifled her laughter and humbly dropped her gaze.

"My parents tolerated a lot from me, but I know that there are some things they still hold sacred."

Saamyah moved to sit in front of him on the desk. "Bryan, you can't try to live your life according to your parents' expectations. If you do, you will never really enjoy it for yourself." She contemplated then asked, "Is that the true reason why you won't tell your family? I feel like there is something more to this."

Bryan looked at Saamyah. He really did not want to tell her everything. He felt that she already knew too much. Anything more would surely obliterate the possibility of their reconciliation.

"No, not much more."

Saamyah cocked her head to the side and pressed, "Are you sure?"

Bryan leaned back in his chair and exhaled loudly at the way she twisted his arm for the truth. He finally conceded. "My family knows Kimberly. They have actually known her for quite some time now even when Rachel was alive. She was often my guest at several functions that Rachel would cancel on or couldn't attend because of work. My mother always told me that we were getting too close for comfort and all the hanging out we were doing wasn't right. My father would say that she was trouble—that her heart was good, but her intentions were bad."

He met Saamyah's eyes and confessed, "My first indiscretion was with Kimberly."

Saamyah inhaled with astonishment and exhaled with disappointment. "...Bryan..."

He turned from her stare and then continued, "The moment after it happened my parents knew. It's almost like they felt it. Of course I denied it, but they knew. It was a downward spiral after that and my indiscretions became many and with several women...I know that I've created this bed that I am in, but my family believes that Kimberly helped made it." He looked at Saamyah again before saying, "She's not welcome in my family's home."

Saamyah sighed with sadness. "I'm so sorry, Bryan."

Bryan shook his head. "Don't be. I did this to myself."

"Maybe the baby will change things."

Bryan shook his head again. "It's not so much that I am having a baby out of wedlock, but that I am having a baby with Kimberly—the woman that wrecked my home, the woman that wrecked me."

"What are you going to do?"

He shrugged. "I don't know."

"Well, you don't have much time. You have to do something and soon. I believe her when she said she will talk to them."

"Yeah, me, too," he truthfully confessed. "Me, too."

The office fell silent and Bryan was the first to break it by asking "What are you doing this evening? Want to do dinner?"

Saamyah shook her head and teased, "The last time I went on a date with you I woke up the next morning no longer a virgin. I think I will pass before I wake up pregnant, too." She winked at him, rose from the desk, and walked out of his office.

Bryan smiled at her playful banter and silently thanked her for lifting his spirits. He retrieved the phone on this desk and dialed Kimberly's cell phone number. After several rings, the call was routed to voicemail. He opted to leave a message saying, "Hey, it's me. I know you're probably still upset, but whenever you are calm, we really do need to sit down and seriously talk about our situation. Hopefully, we can do that without all the yelling, screaming, and hitting. The sooner the better...How about tonight after you teach your photography class? I can meet you at your place afterwards. Maybe at nine? Call me back to confirm. Thanks. Bye." He ended the call and blankly gazed at the phone until a knock on his door broke his stare.

"Hey, Russell," Andrew cordially greeted.

"Bryce," Bryan returned with annoyance in his voice.

Andrew ignored the invitation to squabble with Bryan and asked, "Have you seen Saamyah?"

"Not in the last five minutes. Why?"

Andrew shook his head. "Nothing urgent. I was just told she was seen headed this way and I wanted to ask her something before I left for lunch...Thanks though." With that Andrew quickly left his threshold.

Kimberly walked into her large, two story house and locked the door behind her. She flipped the switch that brightened the lights in her open foyer, dropped her keys in the dish that sat on a mahogany table at the door, and tossed her briefcase in the coat closet. Prior to her pregnancy, a long, chaotic day would have been topped off with a glass of red wine, but motherhood forced her to settle for a hot shower. En route to her winding staircase, she slipped out of her stilettos and held a shoe in each hand as she slowly ascended the steps. At the top, the huge wall clock read that she had forty-five minutes to unwind before Bryan's arrival.

In her master bedroom, she turned on lights as she walked to her double-door walk-in closet. She placed the shoes back in their place on the shelf and then walked to her bathroom to start the water in her stand-in shower. While drying her hands, she glanced at her reflection in the mirror and hated what the stress of day had done to her eyes. They were tired, red, and puffy. Feeling inspired to cover them with her hair, she took out the clip that pinned it and began to tousle it with her hand as she turned to walk out of the bathroom. She was stopped by an intruder dressed in black.

Kimberly gasped and backed further into the bathroom. "What do you want?"

He did not respond.

"Please, just take whatever it is you want and leave."

As he followed her deeper into the bathroom, he adjusted the black leather gloves he wore and contemplated the best way to exterminate her.

Weary of his intentions, Kimberly attempted to push past him to exit the door. He stopped her with his strong arm that wrapped her waist and swung her body on to the counter. Several bottles of expensive lotions, creams, and perfumes fell over on the counter and many others crashed to the floor. Kimberly struggled to free herself from the hands that throttled her, but his might was greater than hers. The steam from the hot shower thickened the humidity and worsened her plight, but Kimberly managed to move as much as her sheath dress would allow her to knee him in the groin.

He bellowed at the unexpected blow to his body and released her neck. Hunched over in the sink, he saw, through his periphery, the large vase filled with potpourri thrown in his direction. He stood in time to intercept its direction, smashing the vase into the mirror. The vase cracked the mirror and then shattered to pieces.

Kimberly descended the counter and stepped in glass. The pain brought her to her knees and she was forced to crawl out of the bathroom. When she was safely hidden by her large bed, she removed the glass pieces from her feet and watched as he limped out of the room. Once he turned down the hallway, Kimberly dashed towards the stairs.

The intruder immediately doubled back and chased her down the stairs. He lunged forward before she reached the bottom step and they both tumbled down into the foyer. Both groaning in agony, they rested and waited for the pain to subside prior to attempting to move. Kimberly was the first to stagger to her feet.

Wiping the blood from her nose, she hobbled to the kitchen for a knife and to call for help.

"Nine-one-one, what's your emergency?"

"There is an intruder in my house who is trying to kill me," Kimberly panted. "I'm at forty-three, fif-"

He yanked the phone from the wall and wrapped the cord around her neck.

Kimberly dropped the knife and fought to keep the cord from stifling her oxygen. Her powerful kick at the marble topped island with breakfast bar in front of her forced him into the counter behind him. Along with a crack of his back, Kimberly heard several containers that stored baking ingredients roll off the counter and fall to the floor.

A sharp pain zipped through his spine and he growled in misery. He released the cord around Kimberly's neck and heard her gasp in relief of the air that filled her lungs. He anticipated the advent of her escape so he mightily shoved her into the island.

Though several pieces of the decorative place settings fell to the floor, Kimberly's bawl rang louder than the sound of breaking ceramic. She felt an enormous amount of pain in her lower abdomen and something warm ran down her inner thighs. Kimberly slowly sunk to her knees as she fretted about the well-being of her baby. She cried tears of pain and fear as she slid through the sugar and flour on the floor.

"Please," she implored while she sought to put distance between herself and the assailant as he walked towards her.

The combination of pain and exhaustion ceased the fight in her. She only had his mercy to rely on. "Please...Please don't...I'm pregnant."

He wrapped his hands around her neck and applied pressure until the life in her had ended.

Bryan knocked on her door and waited for a response. When there was none, he knocked a second time and added a ring of the doorbell.

"Come on, Kimberly," he impatiently rushed. He looked at his watch and saw that it was a few minutes after nine. He rang the door bell a couple more times and knocked harder at her door.

After a brief moment passed, Bryan remembered the key hider and used it to open the door.

Inside, he saw Kimberly's keys in the dish and they confirmed her presence at home. Bryan knew her well enough to know that she would not have left home without them.

"Kimberly," Bryan called out as he walked further into the house. He noticed a trail of blood from the stairs to the kitchen and followed it. "Kimberly?"

"What the..." His voice trailed off when Bryan saw the massive mess in the kitchen.

"Kimberly?" Walking further into the kitchen, he saw a body on the floor and raced to it.

"Kimberly, Kimberly," he called to her while he shook her lifeless body and checked for a pulse. When he felt none, he began CPR.

"Come on, Kimberly. Come on." Tears fell from his eyes as he pressed on her chest. "Please, God. Please, not her....Come on, Kimberly." He breathed in her mouth several times and then returned to compressing her chest. He repeatedly begged her to respond. When she never did, he gathered her lifeless body in his arms and sobbed.

"Bryan!" Saamyah yelled, running through the open door of the house. "Bry-"

"Sorry, ma'am. This is a secured area and you can't be here," a police officer spoke, halting her further entrance.

Saamyah perused the foyer, took her badge from her waist, shoved it in his chest, and walked away.

"Bryan!"

Bryan rose from the sofa and pushed through the circle of law enforcement officers that surrounded him. "Saamyah."

Saamyah turned in the direction of his voice. "Bryan." She ran into his arms and held him tightly. When she broke their embrace, she looked into his eyes and said, "I couldn't make out your message. Are you okay? What happened?"

Tears fell from his eyes as he opened his mouth to speak, but the words would not flow.

"Bryan, you're scaring me," she told him as her own tears swelled in her eyes. In the short time she had known him, Saamyah has never seen Bryan this distraught.

He brought her in close and gently pressed his forehead on hers. "It's Kimberly…"

She raised her head to meet his eyes in an effort to see what he was trying to convey. "What about her?"

Bryan closed his eyes in sadness and answered, "…She's dead."

Shaking her head, she tried to back out his embrace, but his grip held her close. "No…no," Saamyah responded in denial.

"Saamy-"

She erupted in a loud cry and her knees weakened beneath her. Saamyah felt herself lowering to the ground until Bryan tightened his hold and brought her back to her feet. She buried her face in his chest and soaked his shirt with her tears. She wept so hard that her body trembled. Many regrets and thoughts plagued her mind as her heart was overwhelmed with guilt and sorrow.

"Detective Russell," an uniformed officer interrupted.

Bryan held up his hand to keep the officer from barraging him with a series of questions. "Please give us a minute."

The officer nodded and walked away.

Saamyah found comfort in the warmth of Bryan's warm embrace and gentle caress on her back. She took deep breaths to calm her cries and wiped her eyes with the back of her hands. When she was able to speak, she told Bryan, "I want to see her."

He shook his head in response. "Forensics has the body."

She looked into his eyes. "What happened?...Did you guys have a fight?"

Confused, Bryan searched Saamyah's eyes. "What?…What are you talking about?"

"…You said that you would fix this…that you would see to it that Kimberly would never come between us again…What did you do, Bryan?"

Bryan shook his head in dismay. "Saamyah, you think I did this? That I killed her?"

Saamyah did not answer.

Bryan broke their gaze and released her. He wiped his eyes and said, "We had our issues, but none of them warrant me killing her," before he walked away.

Saamyah watched as several officers escorted Bryan outside to the car that would transport him to the station.

"How is he holding up?" Saamyah asked after she walked into the room and stood next to an officer that intently watched Bryan through the window.

She broke her gaze and responded, "I don't know...I guess no different from anyone else interrogated for murder."

Saamyah nodded and asked her, "Is he under arrest?"

"No."

"Then why is he still here? Are you going to place him under arrest?"

The officer exhaled loudly and again turned to look through the window at Bryan. "I don't know. All the evidence points to him, but his alibi has not changed."

"That's because he didn't do it. He did not kill her."

The officer looked at her once more and said, "I suppose he would say the same thing about you if the roles were reversed, Detective Cambell." With that, she walked away, leaving Saamyah to find someone else to harass.

Saamyah searched the dimly lit room until she spotted a familiar face. She hurried to the other end of the room while calling out, "Captain."

The woman looked up from her file and turned in the direction of the voice. When she noticed Saamyah, she responded, "Detective Campbell."

"May I speak with you for a minute?"

"Sure." She closed her file, lifted her reading glasses to the top of her head, and asked, "How may I help you?"

"I need to speak with him," Saamyah announced.

"Absolutely not," she replied with no hesitation.

"Please, Captain. He has cooperated thus far. So, there is no reason why I can't—especially since he is not under arrest."

She pulled her glasses back down to her nose and responded, "Conflict of interest," before walking away.

"What?" Saamyah inquired, following her to a private corner of the room.

"There is a conflict of interest, Detective Cambell," she repeated.

Baffled, Saamyah inquired, "How so?"

Captain Brown opened her file and read off her notes, "Kimberly James was once a victim in a case that you and Detective Russell were investigating—but you are no longer on. She has now become the victim in a case I am closely overseeing and Detective Russell is the prime suspect." She paused to turn the paper in the folder then continued, "Detective Russell admits to having a cyclic, and often volatile, romantic relationship with Ms. James and to top it off," she closed the file, looked and Saamyah, and concluded, "she was pregnant—about two months. Once the autopsy is completed and there is a DNA match between him and the fetus, I will have a possible motive."

Saamyah shook her head in disagreement. "You know him, Captain. Bryan is not a killer…He did not kill her."

"I know you believe so, Detective Cambell. That is why, as his former partner, I can't allow you to corroborate his version of the facts. It would be detrimental to this case and his."

Saamyah disregarded all that she said and asked, "Ten minutes, Captain, please?"

Captain Brown exhaled loudly and led Saamyah out the room and into the hallway. She waited for the uniformed officers to pass them before saying, "Saamyah, what you are doing? After the gala I was sure that the two of you were finished. You should not be here." Moving closer, she touched Saamyah's forearm to laud and warn, "You are a remarkable young woman with a bright future ahead of you. Don't throw it away by becoming involved in some mess."

Saamyah touched the more seasoned woman's hand that touched hers. In her short stint in Miami, she had come to value her leadership, friendship, and, most importantly, sisterhood. Saamyah knew that she was stretching the bounds of their personal relationship, but still entreated, "Tamala, please, ten minutes."

Captain Brown inhaled deeply and exhaled loudly. Undoubtedly, her waiver of policy would be scrutinized as nepotism, but she felt compelled to oblige. Dropping her hand, she responded, "Five."

"Okay, but no audio and no officers."

She raised her glasses to the top of her head. "Saamyah…" She exhaled as she pondered the over-reaching request.

"Thank you so much, Tam," Saamyah offered before her request could be rejected.

Captain Brown nodded and gave a faint grin before she watched Saamyah take off into the room in which Bryan was held.

Saamyah walked into the room and immediately asked the officers for privacy per the Captain's authorization. Once they exited the room and closed the door behind them, she slowly walked towards Bryan, who had his head resting in his folded arms on the table. She gently ran her fingers through his hair and whispered his name.

Bryan slowly raised his head to see her through his red, tired eyes. "Saamyah?"

She sat in the chair across from him and responded. "Hey."

"Hey."

"…How are you doing?"

He shrugged and answered, "I don't know. Tired, I guess."

"You know that you can leave and go home if you want."

"What for? The evidence is stacked against me, might as well save them the trip for an arrest."

"Bry-"

"Saamyah, I know what I am up against. Please don't try to give me any hope." He dropped his eyes and whispered, "I made this bed, now I must lie in it."

Witnessing his hopelessness watered her eyes. "No, Bryan, someone is trying to destroy you and no matter what you've done, you don't deserve this. These women don't deserve this," she paused then assured, "your baby did not deserve this."

Bryan looked at her and turned away before the tears fell from his eyes. He tried to stifle his cry, but could not fight the urge. Bryan released his agony, anger, and fears in a heartfelt cry that shook his entire body. He felt Saamyah move to sit on the table beside him and rested his head in her lap. As she stroked the soft curls of his head, he held her hips tightly.

When the room finally fell silent, Saamyah wiped her eyes with her hands and then lifted Bryan's head to wipe his. She then kissed his forehead, his nose, and lips. "Don't worry. Everything is going to be okay."

The room door opened after a light knock and Captain Brown stepped in. "Time, Cambell."

Saamyah looked up and nodded. She lowered her lips to Bryan's in a kiss and then whispered once again, "Everything is going to be okay." Saamyah then dismounted the table and walked out of the room.

Saamyah walked into the autopsy room to find a lone medical examiner sitting at a table, intently writing. She looked at her watch and saw that it was quickly approaching midnight.

"Didn't expect to see you here this late," she commented.

He looked up from his notes, closed his folder, and swiveled his stool in her direction to say, "You know crime never stops here in Miami, Detective Cambell. There are dead bodies waiting to be found and gutted all around us, all the time."

Saamyah stood in front of him and chuckled. "So, whose shift did you trade with?"

"Michael's, and it's a good thing I did, too, because his crush on you makes him liable to fold under pressure." He stood to go cover Kimberly's corpse with a white sheet. "I've been given specific instructions not to speak to you about a certain case."

She exhaled with discontentment. "Who gave the order?"

He snickered and responded, "Who always gives the orders?"

"Please, Nathan," she begged, "I won't disclose anything you tell me."

"You're impossible, and no." Nathan walked back to the table and grabbed his folder, recorder, and pens. He made an attempt to head to his office, but Saamyah barricaded his path.

"How about lunch?"

"How about no?" He retorted and walked around her.

"Dinner?"

He stopped and turned to face her. "Your bribery is not going to work this time, Saamyah. I can get into some serious trouble disclosing any information to you."

"I know and I wouldn't ask if I weren't desperate." She closed the gap between them and looked up into his hazel eyes. "Bryan is in a lot of trouble and I am the only one who can help him."

Nathan rolled his eyes and exhaled loudly. "I want lunch, Saamyah."

She grinned and said, "Okay."

"And dinner."

"That's fine, too."

He nudged past her to walk to the table to set down his supplies and added, "And if I lose my job over this, I am coming to live with you...in Texas."

Saamyah chuckled and said, "Okay."

Nathan looked at her, shook his head, and laughed halfheartedly in disbelief. He retrieved a fresh pair of disposable gloves, walked over to the body, and pulled back the sheet.

"Kimberly James, thirty-one year old fema-" he began.

"I kind of know her, Nathan," Saamyah interrupted, meeting him on the opposite side of the table. "So, you can skip the demographics. Just walk me through what happened to her."

"Okay." Nathan pulled on the rubber gloves and walked down to Kimberly's feet. "She has cuts at the bottom of her feet. Glass particles were found in the wounds, indicative of her stepping onto something that was broken." He lifted a foot to show

Saamyah and then added, "It may have happened while she was trying to abscond from her attacker."

Saamyah nodded.

"The victim was pregnant, a little over eight weeks to be more precise," He told her while stepping beside Kimberly's abdomen. "When the DNA results come back we will be able to establish paternity and-"

"It's his," Saamyah interrupted. She looked up at Nathan and clarified, "I mean the baby was Detective Russell's."

Nathan nodded. "I see... Well, that may or may not establish motive."

Saamyah sighed in disappointment. "You think so?"

"Well, I am no criminal psychologist, but it is highly probably that it will...There is, however, a loop hole in that argument. Look here." He drew an invisible circle with his index finger around the bruise on her abdomen. "If, by chance, Detective Russell wanted to terminate the victim's pregnancy, a blow from a man like him would possibly come from a direct hit with his fist a lot closer to the womb, which would have made some sort of round mark...This mark here is horizontal, and it's on her lower abdominal muscles."

Saamyah slowly shook her head trying hard to comprehend what he was attempting to convey. "What does that mean?"

"It means that she was pushed into something, like a high table or counter, with enough force to induce her miscarriage...It is quite possible, and only speculative, that Detective Russell did not intend for her to miscarry, or the real perpetrator didn't know she was pregnant."

He paused for a moment to let Saamyah absorb that information and then continued by pointing out marks on the body, "There are multiple bruises on her arms, legs, and back."

"From what?"

"A fall. Probably from a long flight of stairs...But that is not how she died."

"Then how did she?"

He moved to her neck and highlighted the hand-like mark around it. "Asphyxiation—she was strangled to death."

Saamyah took a moment to regain her bearings after her heart dropped.

"Are you okay?" Nathan asked after noticing the affect his news had on her.

Saamyah swallowed the knot in her throat and nodded. "…Yeah…I'm fine." She looked up at him and asked, "Any prints?"

He shook his head. "But with the type of gloves he wore, I was able to detect a ring."

"A ring?"

Nathan held up his left hand and rubbed his wedding band through the latex. "A ring." Nathan moved Kimberly's head to the side to show proof of his conclusion and then reenacted the strangulation.

"So, the perp is married?"

Nathan moved to cover Kimberly's body with the sheet and responded, "I don't know. People wear all sorts of rings on their ring fingers these days. So, it could have been a class ring, an athletic ring, a cosmetic ring."

"Cosmetic? You think the perpetrator is a woman?"

"I doubt it because of the size of the hands around her neck, but you never know. In Miami, men take shots to be women and women take shots to be men." He walked over to the table to sit on his stool. After her removed the rubber gloves, he tossed them in the nearby wastebasket and opened his file to scribble notes.

Saamyah followed and stood beside him. "So, what is your professional prognosis?"

Nathan ceased writing to take a deep breath, think, and respond. "If Detective Russell killed her, he sure did pick one hell of a time to do it, especially since she was also a victim in the case you were working together…But knowing and working with him for as long as I have, I don't believe he did it. Even if he didn't want her to have his child, he didn't have to kill her."

"Why do you say that?"

"Because the child died before she did; she had already miscarried."

Saamyah thought for a moment and tried to put together all the circumstantial evidence in her head. She looked over at his notes and read some of which he had just shared with her. "Can I get a-"

"Don't even think about it, Saamyah." Nathan closed his file. "You can't afford me to gain this type of information and we never had this conversation." He stood while collecting his things and added, "I will walk you out to your car."

*** *** ***

Andrew watched Saamyah pick over her pasta for a moment before he finally asked, "Saamyah, what's wrong?"

She looked at him and shook her head, "Nothing."

"No, it's something...You want to talk about it."

Saamyah dropped her fork in her plate and then pushed it away. After leaning back in her bucket seat, she responded, "Not particularly."

"Is it about Russell?"

Saamyah looked at him and then out the window. She did not respond.

"Look, Saamyah, if the evidence suggests that Russell is not guilty, he will be exonerated."

"He didn't do this, Drew," Saamyah assured him.

"And how can you be so sure?"

Saamyah turned to meet his cerulean eyes. "Because-" she stopped short of telling him all that the medical examiner had told her the night before. She exhaled in frustration and simply said, "Because I just know." She turned to look back out the window. When it started to rain again, her eyes followed the raindrops that traveled down the window.

"Saamyah, I no more believe Russell is capable of murder than the next person. But, our mere beliefs cannot stand a trial."

She looked at him once more. "Trial?...Bryan has been arrested and charged?"

Bryce shrugged. "I don't know, Saamyah, but I am sure he will be if the evidence is in the state's favor."

Saamyah thought for a moment and then confessed her plan, "I have got to go to the house."

"What?"

"The scene of the crime. I have to go back there."

Andrew shook his head in disagreement. "Saamyah, that is a very bad idea. You were strictly admonished by the Captain to stay away from this case."

Saamyah nervously pushed her hair back and then rested her forearms on the table. "I know, but I can't sit back and watch this happen to him."

"Saamyah, you do this and you will be in world of trouble. We're talking the end of your law enforcement career," Andrew warned.

"...I've got to take the chance."

Andrew scoffed in disbelief as he searched her eyes for her sanity. When none was found, he said, "You are crazy."

Saamyah lowered her head and agreed, "I know."

A moment of silence fell between them and it gave them both an opportunity to ponder Saamyah's plan. Thinking of the lurking dangers, Andrew finally said, "I've never been much of a snitch, Saamyah, but if you do this I will expose you."

Saamyah went into her bag and then her wallet to obtain two twenty dollar bills. After placing them on the table, she looked at Andrew and said, "I understand."

"Saamyah," Andrew said as she stood and walked from their table. "Saamyah, wait," he called out to her again as she continued to walk to the exit. "Saamyah!" His voice drew attention, but she walked outside the shop and into the rain anyway.

There was a light knock at her door just as Saamyah tied the lace on her second combat boot.

"Who is it?" She inquired while rising from her couch.

"Saamyah, it's me," the familiar voice responded.

"Bryan?!" Saamyah rushed to unsecure the door. Once opened, she threw herself into his arms.

Despite being tired from sleep deprivation, weak from hunger, and exhausted from interrogation, Bryan tightly held her close.

"Are you okay?" She asked dropping her arms.

Bryan released her and nodded. "May I come in?"

"Of course," she permitted, realizing they were still standing outside. "Do you want something to eat or drink?"

He shook his head. "No, I'm fine—thanks. I just wanted to come by for a moment to-" Bryan stopped after evaluating her attire. "Are you on your way out?"

Saamyah looked down at her all black attire and knew that even the best of lies could not convince Bryan that her intentions were not unethical or unlawful.

"I, uh, I was just going to…"

"To what, Saamyah?"

Saamyah exhaled loudly and looked away from his inquisitive stare. "If I told you, you would become an accomplice."

Bryan pondered her statement and, when her intentions became clear, he immediately objected. "Saamyah, you cannot go back to that house. You would be accused of upsetting a crime scene or tampering with evidence." He paused to turn her face to him and added, "Not to mention you would be compromising your career because you are prohibited from any involvement in this case."

She moved his hand from her face. "I know what the risks are."

"Then know that I can't let you do this. Not even for me…We have to trust that the system will work this out."

Saamyah laughed halfheartedly. "Bryan, we work for the system. Your life will be equally gambled, if not more, as any other perp's."

"Even if that is true, I can't let you gamble yours."

She felt slightly defeated, but in one last effort to obtain his support she reminded him, "Bryan, you could die…If convicted, you could be sentenced to death."

He nodded, "I know, but I still can't let you do this…I just can't."

Saamyah burst into a soft sob and fought the urge to pull away from his comforting embrace. Her heart ached not only from defeat, but also from Bryan's impending fate. It was evidently clear that Bryan's nemesis sought more than vengeance. He or she wanted death.

After her cries slowed to sniffles, Bryan stepped out of their embrace and said, "I really need to get a shower and some sleep."

Saamyah wiped her eyes and nodded.

"Promise me that this," he waved her appearance, "is over."

"But, I can-"

"No, Saamyah, I mean it. This has to be over. I cannot add your safety to my litany of worries." He locked his weary, red eyes with her forlorn, red ones. "Please, promise me."

Saamyah closed her eyes and exhaled loudly. When she opened them again, she said, "I promise."

Bryan sighed with relief when she did not respond with the long and arduous fight that he expected. "Thank you," he whispered before he closed the space between them and touch her supple lips with his. "Thank you," he said again before leaving for his condo.

*** *** ***

"I'm coming, I'm coming," Bryan announced as he struggled with the white tank top en route to his front door. After pulling the thin, ribbed fabric over his torso, he unlocked the door and swung it opened.

Saamyah dropped her hand in mid-knock. "Hey," she simply said, taking in his slightly disheveled look.

Bryan exhaled loudly, rubbed his tired eyes, and leaned against the door pane. "Hey, Saamyah, good morning."

"It's after two in the afternoon."

"I'm sorry." He yawned and then corrected himself, "Good afternoon."

"May I come in?"

Bryan released the door handle and pushed the door open wider.

"Thank you."

"Sure," he groggily whispered, giving no second look at her curvaceous silhouette in the racer-backed maxi dress she wore.

Saamyah looked around his living and dining area to see the photos, files, and papers spread across the tables. "You've been busy."

Bryan closed and locked the door. Rubbing his red eyes he explained, "Just trying to tie some loose ends."

"I see..." She whispered, dropping her eyes to his plaid pajama pants to avoid his eyes. Saamyah took a moment to muster the courage to reveal the purpose of her visit. "Bryan, I want..." She cleared her throat and corrected, "I would like you to take a polygraph."

Bryan rolled his eyes and exhaled loudly. "Not this again." He started toward his bedroom. "I'm going back to bed."

"Bryan, wait," Saamyah beseeched, grabbing his forearm. "Just hear me out."

"No, Saamyah. I'm tired and I can't even think clearly right now."

She released his arm and said, "Then I'll wait."

"Wait for what?"

"Wait for when you can think clearly because this is only your life that I am concerned about."

Bryan exhaled in frustration then conceded. "Let me get some coffee. Do you want some?...Wait. You don't drink coffee. Tea? Do you want some tea?"

Saamyah shook her head and watched him walk into the kitchen as she took a seat at the breakfast bar. She placed her tote in the seat next to her and began with the statement, "I think a polygraph will exonerate you."

"Of course you do, despite the fact they are inadmissible in court." Bryan bypassed his luxurious espresso machine and lazily placed a mug of water in the microwave. Once the time expired, he dumped two spoons of instant coffee in the boiling water, and stirred with care.

Aggravated by his cavalier attitude, Saamyah pushed her loose hairs from her face towards her ponytail. "Bryan, you have far too many cards stacked against you to concern yourself with admissibility. I need you to start thinking about the possibility that you may not be able to convince twelve jurors of your innocence...Your alibi cannot stand on its own."

He cautiously sipped the strong beverage, swallowed, and asked, "Why do I get this feeling that I am being tasked with convincing you, and not twelve jurors?'

"Bryan-"

"No, Saamyah," he interjected, placing the mug on the counter. "Let's finally embrace the truth here. My word has never been good enough for you. You have this unwavering propensity to believe everything and everyone but me."

"Well, you do make it easy when you lie to me."

"And you, me, with your lies of omission."

Flustered by his partly true accusation, she grabbed her tote and stood to leave. "I didn't come here for this." Before turning on her heel, she caught his eye and said, "What hurts more than being lied to is the realization that you didn't trust me enough with the truth...For the record, I would have believed you, Bryan. If only you would have given me the chance."

Bryan considered all that she had said and yielded. "Fine, Saamyah...You win."

"This is not a game to win, Bryan. This is your life."

He shrugged his shoulders. "Either way, I'll do it. I will take the polygraph if that is what it is going to take to gain your trust."

"Don't make this about me."

"How can I not? If you cannot be convinced, then I have a snowball's chance in hell with twelve other people who know nothing about me."

Saamyah broke his gaze unsure of how to respond.

When Saamyah offered no response, Bryan offered his terms. "I will make the arrangements under two conditions."

She looked up at him.

"You have to be there."

"That's not the best idea."

"If you want this done, then you will be there. And following the proctor's formal questions, I want you to ask the informal ones."

Saamyah squinted her eyes in confusion. "What informal questions?"

Bryan walked out of the kitchen and towards her. "Whatever it is that you want to know. Use the opportunity to ask anything. Have I ever cheated on my taxes; how many sexual partners have I had; did I actually sleep with Kimberly while with you?" He paused and peered deep into her eyes. "Do I really love you?"

Saamyah looked away. "Bryan, I don't care to know any of those things." She turned back to his gaze. "I just want to make sure you're not electrocuted for a crime you didn't commit."

Bryan turned to walk away, stating, "We Floridians typically opt for lethal injection."

"Damn it, Bryan!" She grabbed his arm and turned him to face her. "This isn't funny. Can't you take this seriously?!"

He twisted out of her grip. "I am being serious."

"Fine. I'll be there. Okay?...I'll do it." She inhaled deeply and exhaled loudly. "Just provide the date and time."

Bryan smiled within, trying his best to hide his satisfaction with the progress he was making.

Bracing herself for his answer, Saamyah asked, "What's the second condition?"

"When the polygraph confirms the truth and my innocence, I want you and me to start over."

Saamyah shook her head. "Bryan, too much has happened for us to start over."

Bryan secretly hoped, almost to the point of expectation, that Saamyah would agree. By her heightened level of concern and care that she had shown as of late, he was convinced that their relationship was on the mend. Confused and disappointed, he solemnly nodded, and then turned to walk away.

"But," she continued, turning him back towards her, "we can start again."

Bryan smiled. "Really?"

She nodded and confirmed, "Yes."

Bryan pulled her into his torso and planted short, soft kisses on her lips between her laughter. "You have no idea how happy you've just made me."

"Yeah, we will see just how happy you are when you hear my conditions."

"I have no doubt that I will be jumping through hoops," he touched her lips with his, "but you are more than worth it."

Hopeful, but not completely convinced, Saamyah simply smiled knowing that time would only tell. "I probably should get going...I have some errands to run."

He reluctantly released her. "Dinner later?"

"Uuuuuuh. I don't know if that is such a good idea."

"It's just dinner, Saamyah."

She slowly shook her head in dissent. "It's never just anything with you."

Bryan cupped her face with both of his hands and assured, "It's just dinner."

"Just dinner?"

"Just dinner."

She exhaled loudly and asked, "What time?"

"I'll pick you up at 8, if that works for you."

"Okay."

Bryan took her hand and led her to the door. After unlocking and opening it, he kissed her a last time and watched her walk out, descend the steps, and safely enter and drive off her in vehicle.

*** 𝕋𝔼ℕ ***

"Detective Russell, I know that it is your preference that we wait for Detective Cambell, but I'm afraid that if we wait any longer, we will have to postpone," the proctor of the polygraph warned after entering the room for the third time. He took a quick glance at his watch then a seat at the opposite side of the table.

Though his faith wavered, Bryan assured, "She gave her word that she will be here. So, she will be here…Just give her ten more minutes.

The proctor shook his head in opposition. "Let us just begin with a few preliminary questions and then we will go from there."

Bryan begrudgingly agreed.

"Is your full name Bryan Terrell Russell?"

"Yes."

"Is your birth month and day May 17th?"

"Yes."

"Is your current address…"

Saamyah quietly slipped into the viewing room ignoring the impatient eyes that glared at her. She spotted Lieutenant Duncan and crept to his side.

"How is he doing?" She inquired.

"They just started. Russell stalled as long as the proctor would allow. Any longer and it would have been postponed."

Guilt overwhelmed her. She looked at him and gave a heartfelt apology.

Lieutenant Duncan shrugged. "Life happens." He winked at her in an effort to ease her discomfort.

Saamyah smiled and then quickly scanned the room. She recognized Tiffany among the many suits in the room. When their eyes met, Saamyah feebly smiled, then bashfully turned her gaze. "Who are all these people?" Saamyah whispered to Lieutenant Duncan.

"Legal counsel, Internal Affairs, Homicide—you name it."

"Why are they here?"

"Killing multiple birds," Lieutenant Duncan simply answered.

Later, the proctor entered the room and delivered the results. "He answered truthfully," he announced without delay.

Saamyah sighed with relief and silently thanked God. Though the room erupted in conversation and movement, she managed to make eye contact with the proctor. He gave her a nod and Saamyah clandestinely exited the room.

After lightly tapping on the door, Saamyah entered the interrogation room. Bryan suppressed his excitement and simply stated, "I didn't think you showed."

She took a seat in the proctor's chair. "Honestly, I almost didn't." Before the silence lingered too long, Saamyah confessed, "I was afraid...Afraid to know the truth."

"What changed your mind?"

"You...I figured if you had the courage to endure this, then I could at least have the courage to keep my word."

Bryan nodded. "Thank you for being a woman of your word."

Saamyah nodded. "...You're, ugh, actually free to go. You passed without issue."

"There was no doubt that I wouldn't." He paused then continued, "But, of course those were the easiest of the questions."

"I don't have any questions, Bryan," Saamyah stated, declining his unspoken invitation.

"Yes, you do, Saamyah."

"Well, I don't want to ask them...I don't want to do this."

"We had an agreement."

"Yes, we did and I am here. As for-"

"Please, just do it," Bryan interjected. "I need you to."

"Why?"

"Because I feel that if you don't you will always have lingering doubts and those doubts will inevitably destroy us."

Saamyah held her silence.

"Ask me anything." He paused, took her hand into his, and then assured. "It's just you and me now."

"And the proctor, when he returns from his break," she corrected while slipping her hand out of his. She then continued off topic, "In light of your exam results, the state will temporarily cease building a case against you."

Bryan nodded.

Before the room became uncomfortably quiet, Saamyah stood to leave while saying, "As I said, you are free to go."

Bryan grabbed her hand. "Saamyah, please..."

Saamyah inhaled deeply and exhaled loudly. After taking her seat, she pushed her hair behind her ear, and she covered her mouth with her free hand. She made every effort to avoid his eyes.

"Saamyah..."

She dropped her hand and looked at him at the call of her name. "Okay," Saamyah conceded. "What's your favorite color?"

Bryan huffed. "Are you serious? You can ask me anything and you're asking-"

"What's your favorite color?" She repeated forcefully.

"Grey."

"Own any pets?"

"No."

"Are you afraid of heights?"

"No."

"How many sexual partners have you had?"

"I don't know."

"More than 25?"

"Yes."

"More than 50?"

"Probably."

Slightly taken aback by his response, Saamyah allowed the room to fall silent as she cleared her throat. After she regained her bearings, she asked, "Do you like chocolate?"

"Only dark."

"Do you love me?"

"Yes."

"Are you in love with me?"

"Yes."

She glanced at the needle to gauge any change in his heart rate. When nothing was detected, she peered into his eyes and asked, "Since consummating our relationship, have you engaged in any sexual activity with any woman other than me?"

"No."

"Not even Kimberly?" She pushed, keeping their gaze.

"Not even Kimberly," he affirmed without breaking eye contact.

Once again, she glanced at the needle to gauge any change in his heart rate. When nothing was detected, she finally asked, "Are you capable of being in a monogamous relationship?"

When Bryan hesitated to answer, they both directed their attention to the rapid movement of the needle.

"Honestly, Saamyah," he started while catching her eyes, "I don't know how to answer that."

Saamyah nodded toward the needle. "You just did."

"Why don't you just ask me what you really want to know, Saamyah?"

"What is that, Bryan?"

"If I am capable of being in a monogamous relationship with you."

"I believe we're done." She rose to leave.

Bryan rose, too. "Why are you so afraid of the answer?"

Aggravated, Saamyah finally admitted, "Because I don't want to know if my heart is anchored to something that I need to walk away from."

Bryan was astonished by her emotional revelation to the point of speechlessness, but managed to plea, "Just ask the question."

"How about you just show me rather than have some machine tell me?"

Bryan response was interrupted when the proctor entered the room and ended their spirited exchange.

"I hope I am not walking in on anything too personal."

"No, we were just finishing up," Saamyah responded. Both she and Bryan stood in silence as the proctor reviewed the report.

"Looks good. Detective Russell consistently answered honestly; however, a little inconclusive at the end."

Saamyah looked at Bryan and ineffectually smiled. "Congratulations," she lauded before exiting the room.

Bryan swung open his front door to find a familiar floral arrangement, hand written card, and Saamyah holding both. Nervous from her presence and impending reaction to his gesture, he simply spoke, "Hey."

"I got your flowers."

"…And the note—I see."

Saamyah smiled and it eased Bryan's discomfort. He rested against his door pane.

"And the note," she affirmed. "Although I'm confused by the one-word message 'Yes.'"

Bryan grinned at his vagueness. "I thought you deserved an answer."

Saamyah shook her head and laughed at his tenacity. "What am I going to do with you?"

"I can think of a few things." He pulled her in for a kiss and then led her into his condo.

Later that evening, Saamyah turned in his arms to face him as they both laid close on his leather sofa. "Hey, you," she greeted, tapping his nose. She knew he had fallen asleep by the rhythmic change in his breathing.

"Hmm," Bryan responded.

"You are the worst person to watch a movie with."

"What? I'm awake...I'm watching it," Bryan protested without opening his eyes. He tightened his hold around her waist and pulled her closer to him.

Saamyah chuckled. "The movie is over now, sleepy head."

With his eyes still closed, he kissed her forehead and knowingly replied, "I know. It was the neighbor the whole time."

Saamyah playfully punched his chest. "Lucky guess."

"Luck has nothing to do with, my love. It's the curse of being a great detective."

Saamyah laughed. "Whatever." She checked the hands on her watch that now glowed because of the dark. It read 11:37. "It's almost midnight. I have to get going."

Bryan shook his head and held her even closer. He nuzzled his face in her neck and muffled, "Uh un. Stay with me. Stay the night."

His breath on her neck tickled, forcing her to flinch and smile. She gently pushed him away and said, "I can't. I have that interview in the morning."

Bryan released her, rolled on his back, and exhaled loudly. "I don't know, Saamyah. Something doesn't seem right about this interview. I haven't felt comfortable since you first told me about it."

Saamyah sat up, swung her legs over the edge of the sofa, and placed her feet on the floor. "Bryan, we have been through this already."

"I don't understand why I can't accompany you. You are not even on the case anymore."

"I know that, Bryan, but I was, and sometimes rape victims find it easier to talk to female officers as opposed to male officers. That is why she requested that she only speak with me...Besides, it's probably best considering you've bedded her."

Bryan sat up, turned to switch on the table lamp, and rested his back in the corner of the sofa. "That's the thing, Saamyah. I don't recall an Olivia Bartlett."

Saamyah looked over her shoulder and teased, "Well, that is not incredibly surprising...How many others have you forgotten?"

"Ha ha." He dug his index finger in her waist, causing her to twitch and giggle.

She regained her bearings and reached for her sandals. Saamyah slipped them on lazily, pulling the straps over her heels so that she would not have to unbuckle them. She then turned her body to face him. "Look, I wouldn't be going if I didn't feel safe. I will arrive at the port at 7 A.M. and that should give us enough time to talk before she goes to work...It will be bright; there will be people; I will be safe."

Not ready to concede, Bryan pushed, "Let me ride along...I will stay in the car."

Saamyah recalled the interview incident that Andrew had accompanied. Worse than her injury, the interview never occurred. "No, Bryan. If she sees you, the whole interview will be compromised."

Bryan sat in silence as he fixed his eyes on her.

"I'll call you," she offered. "She has a sailboat and we will just talk there. So, once I arrive, I will call you. And when I leave, I will call again."

Bryan exhaled in worry and disappointment knowing that she could not be persuaded. "Promise me you will be careful, Saamyah."

She leaned forward and pressed her lips on his. "I promise."

*** *** ***

"Hey, Bryan, it's me. Just wanted to let you know I made it to the marina safely. I'm actually a little early. So, I guess that would make me on time, because to be on time would be late." She chuckled at the tutelage of her eldest brother that she could not seem to escape. "Anyway, I'm just rambling on your voice mail to kill time. I will give you a call once I wrap things up here and am on my way to the station. I will talk to you later. Bye."

Saamyah ended the call and dropped her phone in her tote. On the dock, she walked alongside the boat described by the woman she was meeting. "Hello," Saamyah called out.

No response.

"Hello. Good morning."

She heard movement below deck. "It's Detective Cambell. Permission to come aboard, please?"

"Permission granted," Saamyah heard a faint voice call out to her.

Saamyah methodically stepped onto the boat, careful to shift her weight properly so that she did not fall into the water. Once on deck, she spoke, "I know I am early. I can just stay above deck until you're ready."

No response.

Saamyah walked to the bow, took in the morning sun, and inhaled the salt water air. Several minutes passed before she glanced at her watch and saw that it was 7 A.M. Just as she decided to give Olivia more time, Saamyah felt a wet cloth cover her nose and mouth. Against her fighting will, her eyes closed and her body collapsed into the arms of the person standing behind her.

The sound of crashing waves beneath her head woke her from a deep sleep and Saamyah laid still in the unknown bed, trying to account for the lost time. Footsteps nearing the door warned her of an approaching intruder and it gave her a moment to prepare for their entrance into the room. Her heart raced, as the knob turned and the door slowly crept open.

"You're awake," he announced in surprise.

"Patrick?" She slowly sat up and pushed her body into the corner as his steps closed the space between them.

"I guess I over did it with the chloroform," he confessed, stopping at the side of the bed. He stared down at her and added, "You were unconscious longer than I had anticipated."

"Patrick, what are you doing here?" She asked, before realizing she herself did not know what she was doing there. Saamyah rephrased the question. "What am I doing here?" She paused realizing she first had no clue as to where she was. "Where am I?"

"So many questions," he taunted, taking a seat on the bed. "And, I will answer them all in time, but, first, you need to eat something. How about you get washed up and I will make lunch?"

Saamyah did not respond. Instead, she watched him rise from the bed and walk out of the room. Once he closed the door behind him, she stood on the bed and yanked back the shade that covered the window. To her disbelief, all there was to see for miles was the Atlantic Ocean. Saamyah lost her breath in a panic when she deduced that she was aboard a boat sailing away from the Miami marina.

Due to the lunch hour, Saamyah assumed that they had been at sea for several hours. She descended the bed and exited the room in search of Patrick. She found him in the kitchen preparing sandwiches.

"You sick son-of-a-bitch!" Saamyah exclaimed.

Patrick looked up at her, smiled, and then continued as he was while stating, "Have a seat. Lunch is almost ready."

She shook her head in dismay as the pieces of the puzzle forged together in her mind. "There was no victim interview, was there? It was all you, wasn't it?"

He did not answer, so Saamyah did so for him, "It was all a fucking hoax just so you could drug and abduct me to sail the goddamned world with you!" She scrutinized her immediate surroundings for an object to throw.

Patrick ducked before the glass and plate he had set on the table made contact with his head. Before she could launch the second set, he rushed her body into the wall behind her.

"Stop it or the next thing that will get thrown will be you—overboard," he admonished.

Overwhelmed with feelings of defeat, fear, and sorrow, Saamyah wept. "Why, Patrick?...When does this ever end?"

"On a remote island," he answered as an introduction to his plan. He lowered his lips to hers in a gentle kiss and continued, "Where we will wed and," he pressed his groin into her thigh and concluded, "start our family."

She cringed at the thought and assured, "Any children I'd bear will be rape babies and I will treat them as such."

Patrick cavalierly shrugged. "And subject them to the same mental anguish and emotional ruin—so be it."

Saamyah was not certain if he spoke of her plight or his own. In any event, she knew that, truthfully, she could never beget pain with pain, particularly to a life that would come through her. Conquered in that argument, she finally retorted, "I want off this boat!"

Vexed by the request, Patrick released her and started his way to complete their lunch preparations. "There is only one way off this boat for you, Saamyah," he declared.

While his back was turned, Saamyah quickly grabbed a knife off the table and lunged at Patrick. She gasped at the unexpected reversal that spun her into the opposite wall with her hand pinned behind her back.

With one hand holding her throat and the other on the knife's handle behind her back, he commanded, "Let it go."

Saamyah released the knife and the air she held in her lungs when he dropped his hand from her neck. She watched and grimaced as Patrick moved the blade down the center of his palm. He repeatedly clenched his fist to expedite the bleeding.

Ignoring her groans of disgust, Patrick wiped his bloody hand over her face and neck. He then pulled opened her shirt, disregarding the buttons sent in different directions, and ran his bloody hand over her chest and breasts.

Gripping both her wrists with each of his hands, he obliged, "Now, let's get you off this boat."

Despite her tenacious fight, Patrick managed to drag Saamyah across the kitchen floor and past the dining area. As she ferociously kicked and continually screamed, he pulled her up the steps to the upper deck and yanked her to the stern. Exhausted from the unexpected use of exerted energy, Patrick paused to catch his breath. Unmoved by her dejected pleas and melancholic cries, he lifted her into his arms and released her over the pushpit.

Patrick waited a moment for her to break the surface of the water before walking to slow the boat to a stop and dropping the anchor. When he returned, he folded his arms across his chest and watched her swim towards him.

"How's the water?" He called out to her a moment later.

Saamyah panted in exhaustion and began to tread water. "ARE YOU CRAZY?! YOU COULD HAVE KILLED ME?!"

Patrick chuckled. "I doubt it. You've always been a strong swimmer."

"Let down the ladder, Patrick."

"You wanted off the boat, you're off the boat... Now swim back to shore." He held his wounded hand over the rail and clenched his fist until several drops of blood dripped into the calm water. "Good luck with the sharks," Patrick added before turning to walk away.

"PATRICK!" Saamyah screamed in desperation. "PATRICK, PLEASE!"

Saamyah's muscles tired and her body ached, but she fought to keep from completely submerging under water. Fear added to her physical distress when she took a panoramic view of the waters that stretched around her. They were isolated for miles.

"PATRICK!" She screamed in a panic. "Patrick, please... PLEASE."

Saamyah sobbed. No longer solely terrified by physical exhaustion, she feared the sharks that would soon encircle her.

"...Okay..." She muttered, coughing between cries. "I SAID OKAY!...Patrick, please...I'm sorry, okay?...I SAID I'M SORRY!"

Satisfied with her concession, Patrick walked to the port and released the ladder. He waited for Saamyah to swim to it and watched her climb out of the water. Patrick then took her in his arms, aided her over the railing, and purposely dropped her to the deck.

Saamyah winced in pain and tried her best to conceal her discomfort when Patrick crouched next to her. He cupped her jaw and firmly squeezed it. Bringing her eyes to meet his, Patrick vehemently spoke, "As you have just experienced, there is only one way off this boat for you, Saamyah. Remember that the next time you think of leaving."

Patrick released her face with a light shove, stood, and commanded, "Now, shower and change for lunch." He moved past her to; first, raise the ladder; then, raise the anchor; and, finally, increase the boat's speed.

Saamyah entered the dining area to find Patrick at the table waiting for her. He had a spread of sandwiches and fresh cut vegetables on each of their plates. She quietly lowered herself onto the cushioned bucket seat that curved into a C. Now across from him, she avoided his eyes.

Patrick did not find the wet bun she wore twisted on top of her head or the long maxi dress she wore too flattering. "I thought you would be more put together with all the accompaniments I purchased you."

Saamyah nervously avoided his stare and pushed back her loose hairs. "I, ugh, I am not feeling well...I'm still recovering from my unexpected drop into the water."

He took a bite from his sandwich, chewed, then swallowed. "Eat. It will aid in your recovery."

"I don't have much of an appetite."

Growing increasingly vexed, Patrick sipped his iced tea and retorted, "That's fine. You can have it for dinner tonight or breakfast tomorrow." He paused and thought for a moment before adding knowingly, "Although it may not be as appetizing as the bread will be soggy and the vegetables wilted."

Saamyah lifted her eyes to meet his and looked upon him with derision. "You can't break me."

Patrick broke their gaze and drank from his glass before responding, "I don't have to. Your obstinacy will eventually give way to your need to survive." He met her gaze again and added, "For which you will be heavily dependent on me."

Saamyah pondered the truthfulness of his statement and began to contemplate whether no life at all would be more fulfilling than a life with him. The mere thought of having to choose between the two options brought tears to her eyes.

"Excuse me," she stated, rising from the table in a hurry so not to give him the satisfaction of seeing her cry. Before she could start her way to her bedroom, Patrick grabbed her wrist with his bandaged hand.

Unmoved by the tears that ran down her face, Patrick stated, "Dinner will be at 7. Please put a greater effort in looking more appealing."

Saamyah simply nodded. Once he released her, she started toward the room. After closing the door behind her, she released a heartfelt cry. When she finally calmed herself, she crawled into bed and fell asleep to thoughts of her life in Texas—the life she initially thought she had to escape from.

"You look stunning," Patrick complimented Saamyah after she walked into the kitchen promptly at 7. She opted to wear a long sleeved, multicolored wrap dress that rested above her knees in the front and fell to her bare feet in back.

"Thank you," she whispered praying that the makeup she applied hid well her misery so that she looked more appealing.

Patrick walked to her, touched her lips with his, and stated, "Of course. It's a compliment well deserved for your noticeable efforts." He admired and stroked the hair that she had opted to straighten, bump to life, and wear down her back.

"I did not set this table," Patrick began as he dropped his hand to collect one of hers and led her to sit on the cushioned bucket seat. "I figured we could dine above deck this evening and watch the sun set—if you are up to it."

Saamyah evaded his eyes as he stood before her awaiting her response. "I prefer not to if you are truly affording me the option to decline."

"That's fine and I am." Patrick walked to the stove and stirred their meal in the cast iron wok. "We will dine in the formal dining area and take in the view from the bay windows."

Saamyah sulked and began to dread more the second option. The thought of suffocating in a room with him was far less appealing than inhaling the breeze of the ocean that widened the gap between home and the unknown. Based on her knowledge of Patrick's nature, Saamyah knew the first option was no longer available.

"I don't have much of an appetite, Patrick," she professed in an effort to pardon herself.

"Then be good company," he retorted in aggravation. "...I'm confident in your ability considering your training as a debutante."

Saamyah watched him spoon his serving into a plate and pour himself a glass of wine. He did not bother to prepare a plate for her.

"Let's go," he commanded, walking towards her. He waited for her to rise to her feet before leading her to the rear of the boat.

Though Saamyah suppressed her awe of the room's splendor, she could not avoid taking in the lavish bar and barstools; flat screen television mounted before the leather sectional; and, finally, an expandable dining set in front of the large bay windows.

Patrick grinned at the adoration that she poorly concealed. "When you are ready, I can provide you the tour of your namesake."

"No, thank you," Saamyah murmured as she took her seat. She paid no attention as Patrick did the same and lowered his head to bless his food.

After he placed a morsel of food in his mouth, chewed, and swallowed, Patrick advised, "Saamyah, this boat is far too large for you to remain stricken to a single room."

Saamyah turned to face him and confessed, "It's all the same prison to me."

Patrick chuckled and sipped from his wine glass. "DeVaughn really did a number on you."

Saamyah returned her gaze to the window. "Not too good of a number if I still managed to get entangled with the likes of you."

He placed his glass on the table and reminded her, "Like it or not, this is your fate, Saamyah...You, me, and paradise. The sooner you make peace with this, the less discontent you will be."

Saamyah closed her eyes and wished away the tears that she felt forming behind her eyelids. If it were not for her fear of being stranded in the Atlantic Ocean, her response to him would have been an abusive tirade.

"So, am I never to see my family again?"

"I am your family," Patrick responded.

Saamyah opened her eyes and turned to face him. "My broth-"

"Your brother is a medical board-certified drug dealer," Patrick antagonized.

Saamyah shook her head in disgust. "You and your defamations...When will you ever learn that making me hate my brother will not make me love you?"

Patrick ignored her question and offered, "If we are to spend a lifetime together, there should be no secrets between us." He paused for a forkful of food. After chewing and swallowing, he continued, "Your beloved brother, Dr. Cambell, received an exorbitant amount of monetary kickbacks and other favors in exchange for his medical corroboration."

Saamyah allowed the revelation to register after it painstakingly traveled from her ears to her brain. "...You're lying."

"Am I?" He drank from his glass and returned it to the table. "How do you think the life you were accustomed to was sustained?"

Saamyah contemplated the question, but did not answer.

"Don't be naïve, Saamyah...Your parents' insurance policies could no more adequately provide for a medical student let alone his three younger siblings...Believe you me, that income was grossly supplemented by the patients who paid the hefty costs."

"I'm not listening to this," Saamyah announced as she stood to leave.

"Sit down!"

Saamyah flinched at the command, but defiantly remained standing.

Patrick inhaled deeply and exhaled loudly. "Saamyah Anne Cambell, sit your ass in that chair now."

Deeply grieved, Saamyah closed her eyes and lowered herself in the chair. When she opened her eyes again, Patrick's hard glare pierced them.

He ignored the tears that ran down her face and continued. "Your brother and his cohort were under investigation...Far too many accidental overdoses and opioid related deaths linked to medical practitioners of the same practice. Fortunately, for your brother, his conscience compelled him to get out long before the take down...Unfortunately, for your brother, he had a patient who not only abused and sold his prescriptions but had familial ties with the special agent who was investigating him."

"Whaaat?" Saamyah inquired in a low voice. "No...no..." She shook her head in disbelief, but felt in her heart that what he spoke was the truth.

Saamyah burst into a heartfelt cry. The truth, now fully unveiled, was more than she would have ever predicted and could possibly shoulder. She felt misled, betrayed, and confused. Consequently, every gift, opportunity, and relationship was called into question. DeVaughn had not only lied, but made her a victim of his lies.

Patrick enjoyed the rest of his meal as she sat across the table and sobbed. Though he took no pleasure in her suffering, he felt vindicated of his many years as a villain. Accepting a plea bargain in lieu of immunity for his testimony had proven to be the worst mistake of his life, especially since his arrest came shortly after his brother's demise. Patrick detested mourning his twin's death in prison, but hated more that his mother had had to mourn alone. She had "lost" both her sons within a month.

After calming herself and wiping her face dry, Saamyah looked up at him and asked, "Why?"

Without breaking his gaze out the window, Patrick sipped from his glass and asked, "Why what?"

"Why take the plea? You could have testified naming your suppliers and been released into rehab…Why take the plea?"

Patrick finished the last of his wine and placed the glass on the table. "Love."

"Love?" Saamyah inquired in incredulity.

"You already had so much taken away from you. I could not bear the thought of your brother being taken from you, too." He turned to look at her. "I just never thought my decision would result in you being taken from me."

"I was never yours, Patrick."

Patrick dropped his gaze and huffed. "So I painfully came to learn when you left me in prison to rot." He rose with the glass and plate in hand while stating, "We will have brunch above deck at 11. Enjoy your evening, Saamyah." With that, he left her to watch alone the sun make its final descent behind the horizon.

*** *** ***

As Patrick waited for her to come on deck, he sat near the bow on a cushioned seat and sipped his mimosa. He contemplated the life that he and Saamyah would soon embark on together—a life that he would spend loving her, caring for her, and spending every moment making her happy. He would work each day a little harder until she returned the same to him and the children she would bear for him. Patrick knew that the start of their union would be unconventional, but he had hoped that their past love would revive itself. Until it did, he was willing to force it—force it until she succumbed willingly.

Saamyah found him sitting at the bow sipping from his champagne glass. She stretched her lips into a polite, but bogus smile when his face lit up at the sight of her.

"Good morning," he greeted, handing her a glass of ice water and motioning for her to sit beside him.

"Good morning," Saamyah spoke. She accepted the glass, gathered the chiffon material of her long halter dress, and sat next to him.

Mesmerized by her beauty, Patrick watched as she purposely avoided his eyes and sipped from her glass. He gently stroked her hair that she had let hang past her shoulders, paying little attention to how she tensed her body as he touched her.

"How did you sleep?"

"Not well," she confessed.

"That's unfortunate." He ceased stroking her hair to refill his glass. "Perhaps you should try sleeping in my bed tonight."

Saamyah did not answer. Instead, she looked out to the endless waters and said, "By this time, there is a search team looking for me."

Patrick grabbed a piece of fresh cut pineapple, placed it in his mouth, and said, "I have no doubt that there is," before chewing and swallowing it.

She turned to face him and inquired, "Then why do this, Patrick? Why risk going back to prison?"

He sipped from his glass and then placed it on the table he had temporarily assembled for their brunch.

"Because you're worth it, Saamyah." He gazed deep into her eyes so to speak to her soul, "You always have been."

Saamyah broke his intense stare, sipped from her glass, and then turned to look back out to the water. Her body twitched when his fingers began to trace her bare arms.

"You should try eating something," he advised.

Saamyah ignored the hungry burn in her belly as well as the fresh seasonal fruit, homemade muffins, and hard boiled eggs before her. "I'm not hungry."

Though frustrated, Patrick evaded the opportunity to fight. He knew that in time she would eat, he just had to be patient.

As he indulged alone in the meal he had prepared for them, he watched her watch the water. He silently wished he was a reader of minds, if only for a moment, so that he would know what she was thinking—even if it was all evil.

"You're NOT listening to me!" Bryan exclaimed, momentarily forgetting he was speaking to his superior officers.

Captain Brown rose from her seat on the corner of Lieutenant Duncan's desk. "Russell, it's not that we are not listening. It's just that your argument is not sound."

"I agree," Lieutenant Duncan stated in support as he swiveled in his chair behind his desk. "Given your history with Cambell, I believe you are operating in your emotions not with your skills as a detective."

Bryan shook his head in disagreement. "Not true. That is NOT true." He paused to calm himself before continuing. "I told you yesterday that she had an early morning interview and promised me she'd call before and after the meeting."

"Yes, you did," Captain Brown confirmed, "but you also shared that she did call you."

"Only when she arrived. She left me a message only when she arrived. I never got a call when she left."

Captain Brown shrugged her shoulders. "She could have forgotten."

"Even if that were true, Captain, where is she now? I've spoken with Bryce. She didn't report to work yesterday and she is not here today." He paused to let them both ponder what he had said before asking, "Have either of you heard from her? Has she called in?...I've been to her place multiple times and have gotten no answers. And all calls go straight to voicemail."

Silence fell in the room and Lieutenant Duncan finally spoke, "Russell, perhaps-"

"No...No more listening to either of you. Something does not feel right about this...In fact, it didn't feel right from the moment Saamyah told me about the interview...I just wished I had..." His voice trailed off as a knot grew in his throat and tears filled his eyes. He turned and stepped away from them to collect himself.

"She's been missing for twenty-four hours," Bryan finally said. He wiped his eyes and looked at Lieutenant Duncan and then Captain Brown. "At least issue an APB...It is what we would do even if she was not an officer of the law."

The office fell silent a second time and Captain Brown was the first to break it in concession. "Okay."

She exhaled loudly and confessed. "I'm not completely sold on the theory, but I would rather err on the side of caution...So, okay." She grabbed her folder from the desk and walked to the door, commanding, "Get a team together and go see what you can find out down at the marina. Report back to me what you discover."

Her hand firmly gripped the door handle as she contemplated the worst possible outcome. She turned to meet Bryan's eyes then Lieutenant Duncan's. "Reach out to her emergency contact...In the event that this matter does go awry, someone in Texas should know of it before hand." With that, Captain Brown opened the door, stepped out of the office, and left her capable officers to shoulder the burden.

Astonished to see Saamyah emerged from isolation, Patrick stopped short of entering his study and secretly watched her move about the room. She delicately ran her fingers across the mahogany desk, walked them along the rotating globe, and finally pranced them over the keys of the laptop. Expecting the system to be secured, she tried her luck anyway and struck the space bar to find that the screen was locked. Saamyah was mildly disappointed.

She picked up a photo, smiled, and placed it back on the desk. She picked up another, outlined the faces behind the glass, and placed it back on the desk. Exhaling slowly to suppress her sorrow, she walked over to the bookshelf. She dragged her fingertips across the spines of several books until she stopped at a beloved title. She pulled the book from the tight enclosure, opened it at the book mark, and began to read the highlighted text.

Patrick gradually entered the room reciting, "I loved her simply because I found her irresistible…Once for all, I knew to my sorrow, often and often, if not always, that I…loved…her…against reason, against promise, against peace, against hope, against happiness, against all discouragement that could be." He stopped behind her.

Saamyah unhurriedly closed the book and carefully worked its way back into its place on the shelf. "You always had a liking for Dickens."

Talking to her back, he corrected, "My brother more so than I."

She turned to face him. "All the same considering you memorized passages."

Patrick stared deep into her eyes and elucidated, "It became a favorite the day I met you."

Saamyah broke their intense gaze and shared, "David said those very words to me."

"Not surprising. We both loved you…I just meant it more."

She laughed halfheartedly and looked up at him. "No, you were the coward… Always too cowardly to do what you knew to be right, always too cowardly to avoid doing what you knew to be wrong."

Patrick smiled, pushed her hair from her face, and gently stroked her cheek. "I see that the story of the lone orphaned boy is still yet your favorite." He grazed her lips with his and whispered. "Prayerfully, you will get your happy ending, too."

He turned and walked away. Before exiting the room, he stated, "You're free to read whatever you like, but do not touch my laptop again…Dinner is at 7."

"Are you a cop?" The man called out to Bryan as he watched him scrutinize the waters and the boats moored to the pier.

"Why do you ask?"Bryan asked, taking notice of the man that stood on his deck winding several feet of rope around his triceps and hand.

"You have that look about you…Like a cop."

Bryan flashed his badge from afar and corrected, "Detective actually. I'm here looking for my partner." He returned his badge to his back pocket while asking, "You mind answering a few questions?"

He shrugged.

Bryan walked down the dock towards the stern where the man stood. "Noticed any un-familiars as of late?"

He dropped his rope into a bin and then locked it shut. "Not since a day or so ago. A pretty lady came looking for this newbie that was docked a few yards down."

Confused, Bryan inquired, "Newbie? I thought Olivia Bartlett lived on these waters…in her boat."

He shook his head. "I know nothing about a Bartlett and I have been living on these waters for years. I have seen a lot of people come and go, but Bartlett does not ring a bell…That partner of yours came by looking for that newbie." He paused for a moment. "I believe he said he was from Arkansas…No, Texas…Hell, I don't know; somewhere further out west."

Concealing his worry, Bryan asked, "By chance did you get his name?"

He shook his head. "No, no name. He was never around much to get one…But, that boat of his was something of a dream though. He told me that he and his fiancé where planning a life on a remote island in the Caribbean."

"What?"

"He and his fiancé-"

"No, I get that part," Bryan interjected. "What island?"

He shrugged. "Beats me, but I am certain they are partway there by now. They left some time ago."

"FUCK!" Bryan turned and yelled in frustration. "I knew it. I fucking knew it." He grabbed his cell phone from his hip, quickly punched in a number, and held it to his ear.

"Duncan, it's Russell. I'm at the marina and it doesn't look good. Saamyah's car is still parked here, but she is nowhere to be found…I received intel from an informant… We are going to need aid from the Coast Guard. Call me on my cell."

"Saamyah," Bryan heard the informant whisper.

Bryan turned to face him and asked, "You know her?"

The man shook his head. "No, but the name sounds familiar." He pondered for a moment—thinking hard on where he saw or heard the name. Then he remembered and uttered, "Saamyah Anne."

Alarmed by the red flag, Bryan probed, "Excuse me?"

"The name of the boat…Her name was *Saamyah Anne.*"

"I've got to go," Bryan stated, stepping in the way from which he came. "Thanks for all your help, Mr…"

"Saunders. Eric Saunders."

Bryan nodded, thanked him again, and dashed toward his vehicle.

Patrick offered her a glass of wine, but she refused it nudging the glass away. "I don't drink.

"You do tonight," he forcefully insisted, offering her the glass a second time.

Saamyah took the glass and sipped the beverage trying her best to hide her disdain for the taste of alcohol.

"Good girl," he approved. "Have a seat. Dinner is almost ready."

Saamyah went to sit on the cushioned seat at the table and obediently sipped her wine as she watched Patrick prepare their meal to the soft symphonic tunes humming through the surround sound. Shortly thereafter, a plate of mushroom stuffed chicken, homemade mashed potatoes, and steamed asparagus was presented to her. After praying over her food, she sliced her chicken with her fork and knife and placed the morsel in her mouth.

"Do you like it?" Patrick asked, taking a seat across from her.

Saamyah took a sip of her wine and then responded, "You still know your way around the kitchen."

He smiled. "Yeah, mom taught me well, but I am sure you would agree that David was the better cook."

Saamyah did not respond. Instead, she took another bite of her chicken and satisfied her intense hunger in silence.

Perturbed by her lack of conversation, Patrick grabbed the bottle of wine from the center of the table and moved to fill her glass.

Saamyah shook her head and grabbed her glass. "No, I can't drink anymore. I'm already feeling lightheaded."

Patrick took her hand and held it and the stem of the glass simultaneously. He began to pour more wine while affirming, "We are having sex tonight, Saamyah. Whether you like it or not, it is going to happen." He released her hand and placed the bottle back in the middle of the table. "Now, it is my hope that the former rather than later occurs, but that is up to you and this bottle of Chardonnay."

Saamyah blinked back the tears that began to swell in her eyes and took a long a sip from her wine glass.

"Good girl," Patrick approved once again.

Several bites later, Saamyah wiped her mouth with her napkin and placed it on the table. She took the finally swallow from her glass and then leaned back in the cushioned seat.

"I hope you left room for dessert. I made your favorite."

Saamyah shook her head and closed her eyes. "I'm stuffed, but thank you."

Patrick wiped his mouth and placed his napkin on the table. He slid across the curved, cushioned seat to close the space between them and gently stroked her face. His lips touched hers in a kiss, but it broke when she feebly nudged him away.

"Stop, Patrick," she pleaded.

Saamyah could feel the wine relaxing her body to the point of defenselessness. She took a few deep breaths to gain her energy and felt a warm wave envelope her body. When it passed, she opened her eyes and saw Patrick staring at her with desire in his eyes. She sat up in her seat and grabbed Patrick's thigh when a vertigo spun the room.

Saamyah giggled. "I am so intoxicated right now."

Patrick smiled and placed his hand on top of hers. He turned her head to face him and kissed her. His mouth tasted hers when she kissed him back and a soft moan escaped him. Their kissed deepened and he fervently planted a trail of kisses on her neck.

"Wait, stop, stop…" Saamyah protested. Too weak to fight him, she backed out of his embrace. "Please, Patrick…Don't…Don't do this to me." She searched the eyes of the man she once loved and hoped that the love he once had for her developed a guilty conscience over his intent.

He ignored her request and took her hand. "Come."

Saamyah slowly rose to her feet and followed him to the open floor. She was enveloped in the warmth of his body as he slowly swayed her to the soft music. Her arms found a resting place around his neck and his around her waist.

Patrick danced her in small circles all while caressing her bare back, feeling the softness of her skin. Captivated by her sweet scent, he placed lingering kisses on her shoulder and then neck. With the yearning to advance the encounter, Patrick took her hands from around his neck and led her to her bedroom.

Saamyah felt his solid, heavy body press her against the cool wall. Despite the distraction of his tender kisses, she felt his hand slip under her dress and tug at her panties. Her hands gripped his and she pleaded for him to stop.

Patrick moved to cover her mouth with his in hopes to silence her pleas and extinguish her fight, but she frantically moved her head to avoid his lips. Saamyah's petitions accompanied the pull of her underwear from his grip, and frustrated him more.

He grabbed her wrists, pinned them above her head and warned, "Saamyah, this can be as good or bad as you want it to be. It all depends on how much you fight it."

Saamyah closed her eyes and took deep breaths to stop the spinning of her head. When the dimly lit room was stilled, she opened her eyes and requested between breaths, "Patrick…please…please let me go."

Patrick responded with a kiss on her lips and continued to kiss them until she returned the gesture. He released her hands and moved his down to grope her breasts. When she opened her mouth, he dipped his tongue in it to taste it.

Saamyah bit down hard on his tongue and released it only when he shoved her into the wall.

"Shit," he murmured behind the hand that covered his mouth. Patrick glared at her in anger as the taste of blood filled his mouth. While he recovered from his injury, Saamyah attempted her escape. His hand grabbed her wrist and his might swung her in the direction of the bed.

Saamyah missed the bed by a few inches and fell to the floor. Her outer thigh hit the wood first, then her elbow and remaining body. She winced in pain and cried in defeat. When Patrick walked to her, she beseeched, "Patrick, please…please…"

Patrick yanked her to her feet and shoved her down to the bed. When she sat up to flee, he struck her face with the back of his hand.

Saamyah fell back onto the bed, covering her warm throbbing cheek. She first heard him free himself, and then felt him grip her thighs and pull her body closer to his hips. The tear of her underwear was followed by the abrupt thrust into her body. Saamyah gasped at the agony that accompanied the plunge that widened her body.

Patrick buried his face in the nape of her neck as he pushed deep into her warm firmness. Overwhelmed with ecstasy, Patrick enveloped her thighs in each of his forearms and pulled her body down on him with each of his moves. Every thrust sent a wave of pleasure through his groin that traveled throughout his body. He groaned aloud at the delight her body gave his.

Saamyah firmly gripped the sheets, bracing herself for each thrust that violated her body. She arched her back to cope with the pain that the tranquil effect of the alcohol did not subside. Between her cries, Saamyah prayed that the nightmare would soon end.

Patrick's loud moans masked the sound of her soft sobs as he felt the advent of his climax. He lifted his head, released her legs and took each of her hands in his. Their fingers intertwined, Patrick pressed her hands against the bed as he hurriedly moved inside her. Feeling his orgasm at the peak of his manhood, he released her hands and firmly held her hips.

Saamyah held the air in her lungs as Patrick exploded in her body and whined his pleasure. When he collapsed on her in exhaustion, she released the air she had trapped in her lungs and wept to herself.

The sound of her distraught cries finally softened his heart. After regaining his bearings, Patrick kissed her neck, her cheek, and her lips between pants. He wiped her wet face and looked into her teary eyes. In the dim moonlit room, Patrick could see her deeply rooted anguish and, immediately, he was overwhelmed with guilt. Despite the years of wanting her, wanting her body, and wanting her to hurt, he did not feel avenged as he thought he would, now that he had taken it.

"…I'm so sorry, Saamyah." He moved to kiss her, but she turned her head to avoid it. Patrick rested his head on hears and whispered in her ears, "…All…All I ever wanted was a chance to love you." With that, he slowly slid out of her body, stood to adjust his clothes, and walked out of the room.

Saamyah erupted into a loud cry. Inebriated, frightened, and in agony, she was confused as to how she was to emotionally feel. She pressed the bottom of her dress down between her thighs and turned on her side. In a fetal position, she wept herself to sleep—the familiar comment ringing in her ear.

*** *** ***

Saamyah blinked her eyes open to the bright sun shining on her face. Struggling to collect her thoughts, she was immediately reminded of the night before by the wet pillow, bruise on her thigh, and pain between her legs. With a migraine throbbing at her temple, she slowly slipped out of the bed and move cautiously to the bathroom.

After brushing her teeth, Saamyah placed a hot, wet towel on her face, trying her best not to aggravate her bruised cheek. She moved the cloth down to the front and then back of her neck. Returning the cloth to the towel rack, Saamyah picked up her brush and slowly ran it through the tangles in her hair. As she detangled her knots, she relived the previous night's events.

Despite wanting to forget, Saamyah could not force out of her mind the final words Patrick spoke to her. There was something oddly familiar about them. In a daze, Saamyah thought long and hard in an effort to recall the origin of the statement. When she finally remembered the individual who had professed those very words to her, she dropped her brush onto the floor and walked out of the bathroom.

She found Patrick at the kitchen counter slicing vegetables. He looked up at her and smiled, saying, "Good afternoon."

Saamyah feebly smiled and moved to slowly slip between him and the counter. She looked into his eyes and then dropped them to the top button of his shirt. Her trembling fingers touched the button and began to loosen it. Her body jumped when Patrick dropped the knife onto the counter and gently gripped her hands. Saamyah yanked her hands from his grip and looked up into his eyes. She saw nothing in them, and fear and nervousness overcame her. Her fingers loosened the first button, then the second, then the third, then the fourth, and, finally, the fifth. After inhaling and exhaling slowly, her trembling fingers pushed back the garment to reveal the tattoo of the sailboat with the words 'Saamyah Anne' across his heart.

"Oh, my g-." Saamyah gasped covering her mouth. She instantaneously remembered the tattoo's symbolical promise: *"When we marry, I will purchase a boat like this one and it will sail us around the world...You, me, and our babies."*

"Saamyah," he said, raising his arms to hold her. "In time, I was going to tell y-"

She shoved his body from her screaming, "GET AWAY FROM ME, DAVID!"

The throbbing pain at her temple made her nauseous. Saamyah grabbed her abdomen and leaned forward. "...I'm...I'm going to be sick."

"Saamyah, please let me help you," David pleaded stepping towards her.

"NO!" She screamed at him, bracing herself for the vertigo that crept up on her. After it quickly passed, she took a deep breath she added, "Just... just stay away from-" Saamyah rushed to the sink and emptied her stomach's contents. She felt David touch her back to sooth her and she forcefully pushed him away.

David watched her turn on the water to rinse her mouth and wet her face. His heart went out to her as she cried. "Saamyah, please let me-" David begged as he walked to her.

Saamyah grabbed the cutting knife from the counter and swiftly pivoted to warn him, "I said stay away fr-"

David gripped the knife after he unexpectedly walked into it.

Saamyah gasped and released the knife, "Oh no...I'm so sorry...David, I'm so sorry."

Blood spewed out of his mouth as he tempted to say her name, "Saa...Saamy..." He slowly pulled the knife out of his body and released it to the floor. Applying pressure to his wound with one hand, he grabbed Saamyah's arm with the other as he fell to his knees and then on his back.

Saamyah lowered herself to her knees next to him and cried. "David...I didn't mean to, David."

David smiled at her through his pain. Touching her face, he gurgled, "...I'm...I'm sorry, too..."

As he apologized, memories consumed his mind of him shoving his gun and credentials into Patrick's torso on the eve of the undercover operation. David challenged him, "If you want things between us to be as they were, then prove it." He glowered into his identical twin's eyes and commanded, "You make sure she dies, even it means you have to kill her yourself."

David had groaned in agonizing misery. Hindsight now 20/20, he regretted the ultimatum he cornered Patrick with. David realized, now that he was suffocating in his own blood, that he had only his pride to blame for not letting her go, his jealousy for keeping them apart, and his rage for killing his only sibling.

"...Please...please forgive me," he petitioned aloud of Patrick's spirit and then of Saamyah's heart.

Saamyah burst into tears at his request. She thought it unjust for him to ask her to forgive all that he had done to her and all that he had taken her through. However, she considered the request believing that forgiveness was a relief more for the victim than the offender.

Saamyah took his hand and held it. She stroked his head and nodded hers saying between sniffles, "Yes...Yes, I forgive you."

David smiled and then grunted causing more blood to spill from his abdomen. "Tha...Thank you."

"You're welcome."

David tightened his grip around the hand that held his. "I love you, Saamyah," he whined looking deep into her eyes. He coughed up blood and then affirmed, "I do...I...I always did."

"Shhhh," Saamyah soothed him while gently stroking his head.

"I...I love you," he affirmed once more.

Saamyah nodded and acknowledged, "I know."

"...Please, say it..." He groaned and then slowly panted, "I...I know he had...y-your heart, but...but please...let me have this."

Though overwhelmed with so many emotions, Saamyah stifled the urge to erupt into another to cry. David's request was one that she had not fulfilled since the death of her parents. But knowing that it would be his last before he left the earth, Saamyah gazed at him and obliged, "...I...I love you."

David triumphantly, but weakly smiled. "Th-thank...you." He closed his eyes and exhaled with his last breath, "Thaaank yoooou..."

Saamyah leaned forward and erupted into an agonizing cry. The thought that both Barnes men had drawn their last breaths in her arms devastated her. Exhausted by the intensity and pain, she rested her head on his shoulder and fell into a deep sleep.

*** ELEVEN ***

Saamyah slowly opened her eyes and found herself in a cool, dimly lit room lying in a bed she did not know. Disoriented, she made the effort to sit up, but the pain at her temple and the IV in her arm prohibited her. Afraid of the unknown, she panicked and began to call out into the dimness for help.

"Saamyah, Saamyah. It's okay, it's okay," a male voice said, rushing to the bed. He turned on the lamp beside the bed and took a seat at her side.

"Bryan?"

"Hey, yeah, it's me."

Saamyah threw her arms around his neck and squeezed him tightly as she sobbed.

"Sssshhhh. You're safe now," he assured her as he held her close. He gently rubbed her back and repeated, "You're safe."

Once her cries quieted, Bryan released her and slowly removed her hands from around him. He stood and announced, "I'm going to let the nurse know that you are awake."

Saamyah immediately grabbed the tail of his shirt. "NO, please. Please don't leave me." She began to cry again. "...I'm so afraid."

Bryan took his seat again and assured her, "Not afraid, but maybe anxious to be alive…You were unconscious for several hours, Saamyah."

"No…No, it's fear." Saamyah corrected and reaffirmed as she relived her most recent memory. "…Patrick...David…" She uttered and then began to hyperventilate.

"Saamyah, Saamyah, calm down. You're going to make yourself sick." He wiped the tears from her eyes, and coached her breathing. "I'm here and I am not going to allow anyone to hurt you. Okay?...Patrick is dead. He cannot hurt you anymore."

"I need to get home. Can I go home?"

Bryan pushed back her hair and replied, "I don't know. Let me go get the nurse so we can find out."

Saamyah slowly released his shirt and intently kept watch on the door long after his exit. As she awaited Bryan's return, her mind drifted to thoughts of Patrick—David—Patrick and the secret they both had parted the world with. She pondered their meticulously calculated switch the day of the undercover operation and the moments preceding the identical twin's death.

David had loved her and, just as he had done in previous undercover operations, had confessed it multiple times. He did so so that she would be confident in his love for her in the event that either of them had fallen in the line of duty. Only, in that instance, it was Patrick—not David—that had expressed his heartfelt emotions. Transfixed on the task at hand, Saamyah failed to notice the difference. And, due to her lack of involvement or presence in the memorial or funeral services, the truth was never allowed an opportunity to unveil itself.

Tears fell from her eyes as her heart ached at Patrick and David's demises. She attempted to soothe herself with the reminder that their ruins had followed their desire to exterminate her. Unfortunately, that truth gave her no freedom. Saamyah knew that her lack of courage and honesty attributed to their plights. She truly loved Patrick more and, just as David had revealed while in temporarily confinement, Patrick—in his death—had proved that he was the brother who loved her the most. Patrick had died so that she could live.

At the distant sound of footsteps and familiar voice, Saamyah quickly wiped her eyes. She vowed to leave the tragedy at the hospital upon her release and, just like Patrick and David had done, go to her grave with the secret…Two people had died on the day of Patrick's death several years ago. For the first time, Saamyah realized that the second person was not her.

As promised, Bryan returned with the nurse and seated himself back at Saamyah's side. He took her hand and held it firmly.

"Hi, Ms. Cambell. My name is Sue. May I call you Saamyah?"

Saamyah nodded. "May I go home?"

"Thank you and I hope so, but that is up to the doctor." She walked over to check her IV and then took her wrist in her fingers to check her pulse. "You came to us severely dehydrated. How do you feel now?"

"What answer would permit me to go home?"

The nurse released Saamyah's wrist and gave her a look of concern. "The truth," she simply replied.

Saamyah looked away and did not respond.

"Mr. Russell."

Bryan shifted his gaze from Saamyah to the nurse after she called his name. He understood the meaning of her gesture when she nodded toward the door.

"He can stay," Saamyah allowed, gripping Bryan's hand tighter when he started to rise.

"As you wish." The nurse looked at Bryan then Saamyah and informed her, "Upon arrival, there was evidence of a sexual assault. So, a rape kit was performed and the test results corroborate the bruises on your body."

Saamyah did not confirm the speculation or the test results.

"Please, Saamyah, help me help you," the nurse beseeched. "There are a slew of officers waiting to take your statement, but I first have to get through these preliminary health questions."

"Saam-" Bryan started.

"Mr. Russell," Sue spoke, stopping him.

Bryan nodded in deference to her.

"A gamut of tests is being run now, but I recommend that you test again in three months for HIV. Are you currently on birth control?"

Saamyah sat stoically in the bed and spoke to nothing she said or asked. Instead, she allowed the fresh tears that fell from her eyes to convey all that she thought and felt.

The nurse gently stroked Saamyah's forearm in an effort to soothe her. "I will speak to the doctor and see if you we can get you out of here. I will give you an emergency contraceptive to take with you." With that, the nurse exited the room.

Saamyah burst into a heartfelt cry and Bryan moved closer to enclosed her in his arms. He held her firmly as she buried her head in his chest and cried.

That evening, DeVaughn knelt at the bedside in Bryan's master bedroom and stroked Saamyah's hair just as he had in her youth every time she fell ill. He feebly smiled when her eyes fluttered open.

"Hey, babe sis," he whispered.

Saamyah saw the man that closely resembled her father and weakly smiled back at him. "DeVaughn."

"How are feeling?"

"...I'm tired...head is...killing me...so cold..." She closed her eyes and began to drift back into a deep sleep.

DeVaughn placed his hand on her forearm and gently shook her. "Saamy- geeez, you are burning up." He looked at Bryan who stood at the door. "Her body is fighting something. How long was she at sea? What did they give her at the hospital?"

Bryan shrugged, stammering, "I...I...don't know...maybe fluids—I think...I believe two or three days...I...don't know."

DeVaughn turned from him, frustrated with his answers. He scanned the contents on the nightstand and immediately noticed the unopened emergency contraceptive. His sorrowful heart dropped at the implications and worry overcame him.

"Saamyah, wake up?" He shook her more forcefully. "Why haven't you taken this?" He held the box to her face when her eyes squinted open.

"DeVau-." She turned on her back and drifted off to sleep.

"She has been vomiting a lot. Haven't been able to keep anything down," Bryan answered for her.

Ignoring him, DeVaughn yanked back the comforter. "Saamyah, wake up. You need to take this." He placed his arm behind her neck attempting to sit her up. "Ugh, you are really burning up." He gently released her and paced the floor.

Bryan began to worry. "What's wrong?"

DeVaughn stopped in mid-step and looked at him. "I don't know. Something has spiked her temperature and triggered a migraine." He paused to match her symptoms to possible causes and effective remedies. When none was immediately found, he opted for an old-school therapy. "Do you have a soaking tub?" He asked Bryan.

"What?"

"A soaking tub! Do you have a soaking tub?!"

"Yes...Yes, in my bathroom—the...the master bathroom."

DeVaughn nodded. "Okay, in my suit jacket, on my keys is a set with pink silicone covers. Use them to get into Saamyah's unit. Look in her bathroom, bedroom, and kitchen for a sumatriptan succinate injection kit."

"A what?"

"A medicine kit...It will probably look like a cosmetic bag and in it will look something similar to an EpiPen. Bring it and a change of clothes for her."

Bryan felt uneasy about what he had no knowledge of and what was about to transpire, but he left the room to do as he was instructed.

Once Bryan left, DeVaughn ran cold water in the large tub and made several trips to the kitchen to obtain ice from the refrigerator's ice maker. Moments later, Bryan returned to the room with the kit and a change of clothes in his hand.

"Thank you," DeVaughn simply stated as he retrieved it from him. He left the room to place the kit on the bathroom counter. Afterwards, DeVaughn walked to the bed toward Saamyah.

"What's going on? What are you doing?" Bryan asked, finally breaking his silence as he watched DeVaughn gather Saamyah in his arms and lift her from the bed.

Glaring at Bryan, DeVaughn warned, "No matter what happens do NOT come into this bathroom."

Bryan opened his mouth to protest, but DeVaughn stopped him by reaffirming, "Don't."

Bryan swallowed the knot that replaced the words stuck in his throat. He said nothing more as he watched DeVaughn carry Saamyah, dressed in the attire he had purchased at the hospital, in the bathroom and closed the door with his foot. Seconds later he heard Saamyah's shrieking cries.

Childhood memories flooded her mind as she attempted to fight DeVaughn off her. The frigid water stabbed her skin like knives and she screamed in pain.

"GET OFF ME!...GET OFF OF ME!...LET ME GO!...STOP IT!...STOP IT!...AARRRGHH!...I HATE YOU! I HATE YOU!"

DeVaughn held her down by her hands into the freezing water and ignored her wailing legs that splashed water and ice cubes around the room.

"Saamyah, calm down. You are only making it worse. You are only making yourself worse."

Saamyah stared deep into his eyes and cried, "Please...DeVaughn...Please..."

He simply shook his head.

Overwhelmed with many emotions, Saamyah burst into a horrid sob until the sharp pain at her temple quieted her. She groaned in misery and ultimately allowed the fight in her to flee.

"Sshhhh...Just relax," he softly breathed to her as he knelt to the floor and pushed her wet hair from her face.

DeVaughn released her arms when he observed the struggle leave her body and she acclimated to the cool temperature of the water. Soaked, he rose from the wet floor and carefully made his way across it to the linen closet for a towel. En route back to the tub, he grabbed the injection kit.

After giving her the shot in her thigh, he gently kissed her forehead, and reminded her of how much he loved her. He then placed the kit on the counter as he walked toward the bathroom's exit. When DeVaughn swung open the door, he found Bryan, with red, teary eyes, standing immediately outside it.

Patting himself dry with the towel, DeVaughn directed, "Please keep an eye on her...I have to step out to make some calls."

Bryan nodded and allowed DeVaughn to walk past him before he rushed to Saamyah's side. He kissed her cold, trembling lips then knelt to the wet floor next to her.

"Bryan," she whispered.

"I'm here," he assured, stroking her wet hair.

She opened her eyes and lifted her hand to touch his face. He shuddered at the feeling of ice against his skin. Bryan's heart went out to her when he considered her entire body submerged in ice water. He took her hand from his face, kissed it, and then held it.

Bryan was able to fight back his own tears to be her strength but found it impossible to continue to watch her suffer. "Are you ready to get out?" He asked.

Saamyah nodded.

"Okay," he acknowledged and began the process of removing her from the tub, drying her off, changing her clothes, and nestling her back in his bed.

DeVaughn reentered the condo. When he saw Bryan walk from his master bedroom, he asked, "Where is Saamyah?"

"Resting in bed," Bryan answered.

DeVaughn exhaled in frustration, tucked his phone in his back pocket, and headed down the hall with intentions to wake her.

Bryan side stepped to keep him walking further down the hall. "Please, just let her rest."

"Move, Bryan," DeVaughn ordered.

"Look—she has done everything you have requested. She's taken the pill, the shot, the…the inhumane ice bath. Please, just let her rest."

DeVaughn peered deep into eyes and commanded once more, "Move."

Bryan sensed the volatile threat behind DeVaughn's command, but he could not bring himself to comply. His heart ached from the torture he had born witness to thus far, and could not bear to witness anything more.

Though furious, DeVaughn could not help but admire Bryan's courageous fight for Saamyah. However, he felt it ill-timed and inappropriate. "Bryan, you seem like a nice guy, but, then again, I don't know you and I don't know the dynamics of your relationship with my daughter…and, frankly, I really don't give a damn. But you will never, and I mean NEVER, interfere with my dealings with her."

"She is not a child, DeVaughn," Bryan started.

DeVaughn turned and began to walk away in frustration.

"More importantly, she is not your child," Bryan continued in an attempt to correct him.

DeVaughn pivoted to face the ignoramus that knew far less than he would ever admit. "The state of Texas recognized me as her legal guardian the very night our parents died. So, yes, she is my child." He closed the space between them then warned, "Don't you ever forget that."

Bryan nervously swallowed the lump in his throat and backed out of DeVaughn's personal space. He raised his palms to his shoulders and conceded, "Look, DeVaughn, I think this conversation is taking a turn for the worst. Emotions are running high and tempers are flashing hot…Why don't we both cool it…I will grab a couple of beers and then we can both cool it."

DeVaughn stared blankly into his eyes allowing his anger to subside. He then nodded and went to take a seat on the leather sofa. While he closed his eyes and exhaled loudly, he sunk deep into the cushion. When DeVaughn opened his eyes again, he saw

Bryan standing before him with an opened bottle. DeVaughn took it while saying, "Thank you," and sipped from it long and slow.

Bryan drank from his own bottle before he sunk in the seat next to him. "So, has Saamyah always been this strong-willed?"

DeVaughn sipped from his bottle and answered, "From the moment she was conceived." He took another sip before continuing, "Four pregnancies and she was my mother's only c-section." Chuckling, he added, "Her labor was actually induced because she was a week past her due date. And, when that was unsuccessful, they went in to get her."

Bryan shook his head and drank from his bottle as he watched DeVaughn placed his half empty one on a coaster positioned on the coffee table in front of them.

"She makes it impossible for me to get close to her," Bryan confessed not allowing the silence in the room to linger.

DeVaughn leaned back into the cushion and closed his eyes. "I guess I am to blame for that...I never allowed dating to be a priority for her."

"No, it's more than that...It's like she's holding onto something from her past that won't allow her to love or be loved."

"She's been through a lot, Bryan...She's been through a lot and has seen a lot. Because of that, she chooses not to love because she is afraid to lose those she loves."

Bryan finished his beverage and placed the empty bottle on the coffee table. "I know; she's told me about her former fiancé."

"The romanticized version I'm sure."

"What does that mean?"

DeVaughn rubbed his tired eyes. He contemplated unveiling his family's skeletons to a stranger he had just met, but ultimately opted to keep the skeletons closeted.

"Let's just say that nothing with the Barnes brothers ever occurred by chance," DeVaughn finally responded after opening his eyes.

Bryan tried his best to piece together the fragments of past and present conversations. "Was Saamyah always a target?"

"Let her tell it, it was true love and I was being the overbearing and overprotective father."

"And how would you tell it?" Bryan encouraged, ignoring DeVaughn's reticence.

"That she was marked from the moment I decided to medically practice on the wrong side of the law, even more so when I made the decision to resign."

"I don't follow," Bryan confessed.

Though apprehensive, DeVaughn finally offered, "Silence is a damning thing when lives and freedoms depend upon it...My silence provided a comfortable life for my siblings and me, but it also made me an accomplice to several malpractices...My resignation from that practice put my entire family at risk, especially the most vulnerable of the pack—Saamyah."

"And she wasn't prior to your resignation?"

DeVaughn sat up to finish his beer and then placed the empty bottle back on the coaster. "If anything would have happened to me, my brothers would have seen to it that she was taken care of."

Bryan presumed that the brothers that he spoke of shared a life of crime and not DNA. Before he could ask him the clarifying question, DeVaughn looked at his watch and said, "It's getting late and I have surgery tomorrow."

"Of course...I have a guestroom. Would you like to lie down for a while? What time is your flight?"

"That's very generous of you. I have an open ticket. So, I can take the last flight out tonight or the earliest tomorrow."

Bryan nodded. "The guestroom is down the hall, first door on the left. Please make yourself at home."

He watched DeVaughn rise from his seat and disappear into the darkness of the hallway. Bryan then double checked the security of the door, threw the bottles in the recycling bin, and made his way to the master bedroom. After changing his damp attire and slipping quietly into the bed next to Saamyah, Bryan wrapped his arm around her waist, and snuggled close to her warmth. He lightly kissed her temple lightly and inhaled the scent of her hair until he fell asleep.

Saamyah slowly walked down the dimly lit hallway and into the kitchen to see her brother add sugar to his coffee.

"Hey," she greeted slightly above a whisper.

DeVaughn looked over his shoulder to confirm the voice he heard and replied, "Hey." He turned back to stir his coffee. After placing the spoon on the counter, he turned to face her, and leaned against the counter. Before sipping from his mug, DeVaughn asked, "How are you feeling?"

Saamyah dropped her eyes and shrugged. "Okay, I guess...Feeling a little groggy from all the medication..." Her voice trailed off as she watched DeVaughn take another sip from his mug, place it on the counter, and turn again to face her. He folded his arms across his chest and tried to discern the person who stood before him.

Anxious of the silence, Saamyah rambled, "Thanks for coming...I know that you are still upset with me and...and aren't really speaking to me at the moment...I also know it couldn't have been easy for you to get away on short noti-"

"What are you doing, Saamyah?" DeVaughn interjected after he grew tired of her meaningless talk.

Bewildered, Saamyah asked, "What do you mean?"

"Here? Your life? Your future? What are you doing?"

Saamyah exhaled in disbelief and turned from his gaze. "I'm living my life that's what I'm doing."

DeVaughn shook his head in dissent. "No, you're not. You're ruining it. In fact, you're throwing it away."

"DeVaughn-"

"No," He stopped her, dropping his arms and shrinking the space between them. "This is ends now. You're coming home." He started out of the kitchen and Saamyah trailed him.

"But, I have my assignment."

"FORGET your assignment, Saamyah." He yelled, facing her. "This has never been about the assignment. You and I both know that. I just went along with this venture because I was tired of fighting you." He paused to cool his temperament. "You can work anywhere in any position with your credentials."

"I need this…I need to-"

"To what? Get away from me?"

"This isn't about you."

DeVaughn laughed half-heartedly. "Don't play mind games with me, Saamyah. I'm not one of your perps."

Unable to deny the truth, Saamyah looked away.

"You have one week."

"I'm not leaving."

"You are and it's not a request." He turned to walk away.

"Stop treating me like a child!"

"THEN DAMN IT, STOP ACTING LIKE ONE!" He retorted so close to her face that she could see the veins protrude from his temples.

Saamyah flinched in fear. She had not seen her brother this angry or having raised his voice as loudly as he had just done in a long time. Tears swelled in her eyes as she reasoned, "DeVaughn, please try to-"

"No! You don't get to take me through this another time, Saamyah…This is it—and I mean it."

Saamyah sensed the heaviness of his heart when his voice cracked. Because of that she could not respond. Instead, she watched him try to wipe the stress and exhaustion from his face.

With his back facing her, DeVaughn confessed, "I'm tired of wondering if you are going to live one day to the next; if I am going to get a call requesting I come identify your corpse…" He turned to face her. "I'm tired, Saamyah Anne. I really am."

"DeVaughn, this is who I am. This is my career, my life, my-"

He held up his hand and shook his head to stop her.

"Do you hear yourself? This is not you. The lying, deceiving, manipulating-"

Saamyah angrily chuckled at the attack of her character. "…Well, I guess we are cut from the same cloth," she replied in defense.

He shook his head in dismay. "This job, this…this place has changed you…The woman I raised would never speak to me as you just have or…or put herself in so many compromising positions."

Injured by the innuendo, Saamyah inquired, "What does that even mean? Compromising positions?...DeVaughn, I gave myself to one man and was raped by another. That does NOT make me a compromising woman."

She turned to walk away to keep from screaming profanities at the man who has been her father longer than she had known her biological one.

"Do not play on my words, Saamyah Anne. You know what I mean."

Furious, she turned and faced him again. "You want to know what I know, Doctor Cambell?" She smugly inquired and waited for a response. When none was given, she continued, "I know that every decision has been made for me from the moment I was born. If it wasn't Mom and Dad, it was you, Trévion, and Christian…Just once—ONCE—I wanted to have control of my own life. But even in the times that I thought I did, you were somewhere redrawing the blueprint of my life."

"I gave up my life for you—not Trévion, not Christian—you. So, if I had to modify your plans to ensure you remained on the straight and narrow, then so be it. I earned that right—damn it."

"And what good did any of it do me?…Look at me, DeVaughn. I mean really look at me…I am broken and have been for quite some time. And no amount of coming of age groups, violin practices, riding lessons, or therapy sessions have been able to fix me…You deprived me of the one thing I needed most."

Furious with the ingrate before him, DeVaughn retorted, "And what was that, Saamyah?"

"A family that sees me."

DeVaughn huffed. "So, I don't see you?"

"You don't and you're not now. That is why it is so hard for you to believe that what happened to me is not my fault…I followed all the rules. I followed everything you taught me. I said no, I screamed, I fought back and guess what, DeVaughn? It didn't work—none of it worked."

"No, you didn't do everything I taught you. I emphatically told you to stay away from Patrick Barnes, Saamyah, and you didn't listen...You lied to me and you lied to yourself. So, yes, this whole damn mishap is partly your fault. YOU, not me, put yourself in this compromising position."

"I did not ask for this!" Saamyah began to cry. "To be abducted and raped...what woman wants that, DeVaughn?"

Her tears softened a portion of his heart, but much of it remained hardened by the fact that he could not protect her from the traumatic experience that had almost taken her from him forever. It angered him to no end, and he struggled to manage such an erratic emotion. "Saamyah-"

"Was it her fault, too?"

"Who?"

"Dinah, who was viscously raped by the man who lusted after her or-"

"Oh, here we go. Saamyah, stop-"

"OR Tamar who was brutally raped by her own brother— King David's beloved son?"

"Saamyah, stop! Don't dare pitch the Bible against me when I am trying to talk to you."

"Why not? You did every chance you could to berate me as a child."

"Saamyah, that was different and you know it. I-"

"Yes, I know...You had three children to raise and yourself to put through medical school... You always did what you had to do so that our family could survive." She stared deeply into his red, tired eyes and bitterly spoke, "But, damn it all to hell, if we are not still paying for the sins of our beloved brother."

DeVaughn struck her face with an open hand—something he had not done since she was 16 and foolishly decided to abscond to Mexico with a few girlfriends.

He watched her hold her cheek with one and push back her hair with the other. When their eyes met, DeVaughn blankly stared back into the eyes of the seven-year-old girl he altered his life and jeopardized his freedom for. Behind her tear-filled eyes were the many memories that plagued their family; the memories that

Saamyah desperately tried to forget and, when she could not forget them, she ran away from them. He also saw pain, much of it he had caused and much of it he had allowed to come to her. For the first time in a long time, DeVaughn actually saw her and was lost for words. His heart sank, but he could not bring himself to apologize, as an apology did not seem fitting at their moment of discord.

"You have one week," he reminded her, and then pivoted to collect his personal belongings.

After inhaling deeply, Saamyah exhaled with courage, "I will leave when I complete my assignment and not a moment sooner."

DeVaughn stood at the door with his back towards her. He considered vocalizing a response that would inevitably ignite another spirited exchange, but his exhaustion held his tongue. So, in lieu of a second familial squabble, DeVaughn unsecured the door, opened it, and then slammed it closed behind him after he exited.

*** *** ***

"Thanks again for pressing your way. I know that you have been through hell in the last week," Maurice spoke to Saamyah in appreciation after the last student departed the lecture hall.

She dropped her eyes to avoid his gaze. "I take it you and Bryan spoke."

"There is really nothing that he and I don't discuss."

Saamyah lifted her eyes to meet his and smiled. "Brothers in arms."

Maurice smiled at the description of their relationship. "I'd like to think so. Although, he, at times, believe that the entire world is against him...It makes it difficult to discern where his loyalty lies."

Saamyah nodded in concurrence. Diverting the subject, she stated, as they walked out of the lecture hall, "I hope that I didn't terribly bore your students."

Maurice laughed as he closed the door behind them after they exited the room. He then placed his hand on her lower back to guide her to the elevator that would take them to his office. "Hardly. I am certain that your presentation was a reprieve from the monotony of my lectures—especially for the guys."

Saamyah blushed and tried her best to hide it. She pushed her hair behind her ear and stated, "They are good kids."

"They are," Maurice confirmed, dropping his hand to push the button for the elevator. "But today is the first time in a long time they were all attentive."

Saamyah smiled. "You're too kind."

"I'm only telling the truth. You should really consider teaching."

Before she could object to his proposal, the elevator doors opened, and Maurice allowed her to enter first. He entered after and selected the twelfth floor.

"Just think about it, Saamyah. There are several adjunct opportunities and you have quite a gift—a gift that could shape and mold the minds of the future."

Saamyah rolled her eyes at all the flattery. Smiling, she finally said, "I'm not saying yes, but I will think about it."

"Excellent."

The doors opened and Saamyah exited first and awaited Maurice's guidance.

"I just have to grab a few things and then we can be on our way." Maurice unlocked his office door, opened it, and flipped the light switch before he permitted Saamyah to enter first.

Saamyah stood watching him transfer items from one bag to another. When he began to frantically search for something, she placed her tote in the chair in front of her and offered her assistance. "What are you looking for?"

"My phone," he replied as he looked under folders, papers, and books.

"What does it look like? I can help look."

"No, that's okay. I think I left it in the lecture hall. Let me run back down there to get it…I'm so sorry, Saamyah, I know that it's already late."

She shook her head. "It's fine. Go get your phone."

He started out of his office with his keys in his hand. "Okay, I'll be right back and then I will walk you to your car."

"No problem… I'll go to the restroom while I wait for your return," Saamyah said while following him out.

Maurice pushed for the elevator and the doors immediately opened. He stepped in then turned to instruct her, "The faculty restroom is down the hall and to the right." As the doors closed, he added, "You will need the key. A spare set are in my bag on the-"

Saamyah laughed at the mechanical interruption when the elevator doors closed and walked back to the office. Once there, she saw two bags—one on the desk and one in the chair. She quickly rummaged through the one on the desk and, when no keys were found, she moved to the one in the chair.

Making his slow descent to the first floor, Maurice remembered the duffle bag he had in his chair. He immediately jumped to press the button to the next floor in an effort to catch an elevator back up.

"Come on, come on!" He impatiently hurried.

Saamyah unzipped the black duffle bag and began pulling out its contents in search for the keys. In addition to the dark clothing, she pulled out a black ski mask and an address book. After scrutinizing the mask, Saamyah placed it on the desk and quickly thumped through the book of familiar names.

"What the…" her voice trailed off and Saamyah placed the book on the desk.

Though fearful of what she would discover next, Saamyah's curiosity compelled her to reach into the bag once more. When her hand grasped a glass bottle, she brought it to light to determine it was cologne—*L'Homme De Tes Rêves*. In an immediate panic, Saamyah dropped the bottle of cologne and watched it bounce off the chair, hit the floor, and roll into a corner. She quickly grabbed the address book, snatched her tote from the chair, and ran to the elevators.

"Come on, come on," she rushed as she frantically pressed the elevator button.

The elevator was taking longer to arrive than she was willing to wait, so Saamyah opted for the stairs. Walking as fast as her pencil skirt and heels would allow, she placed the address book in her tote and searched for her cell phone.

"Bryan, it's Saamyah," she announced on his voicemail while pushing open the door and rushing down the first flight of stairs. "Listen, I'm on Miami's campus. I need you to meet me at the station right now...I-"

The call dropped.

"Arrrgh," she growled while trying the call again.

"Saamyah," Maurice called out once the elevator doors opened. "Saamy-"

He walked into his office and saw the contents of his duffle bag on his desk. He rummaged through the nearly empty bag to ascertain all that she had discovered. Searching under the clothes she had placed on his desk, he noticed that the address book was missing.

"Fuck!" He yelled in frustration.

Maurice retrieved his extra set of keys from the zipper enclosure in the bag that sat on his desk. He then walked out the office door, closed it behind him, and rushed to the elevators.

Saamyah continued to race down the stairs while making several attempts to get a call out. When the phone finally rang again, she left a voice message saying, "Bryan, it's Maurice. It's been Maurice all along. I have proof, just meet me at the station right-"

The call dropped again.

"Damn it!"

She repeated the call multiple times until the phone rang again.

"Hello."

"Bryan! Thank God you answered."

"Where...you?...I...hear you."

"Bryan, just get to the station. Call Lt. Duncan, find a judge who is still up at 11 o'clock at night, and get a search warrant to search-"

The phone rang in her hand. She looked at it perplexed and answered it.

"Bryan?"

"Saamyah, just tell…where…and I…come…you."

"NO! Just get to the sta-"

The call dropped and, just as she tried the call again, the door to exit into the parking garage swung open. Saamyah froze with terror when she saw it was Maurice.

"Give it to me," he demanded.

"Maur-"

"GIVE IT TO ME NOW!"

Saamyah handed him the phone.

"And your firearm."

"I don't have it."

"Don't lie to me!" He yelled.

"I'm not…I don't have it. I secured it in my vehicle."

"Give me your bag," he ordered.

Saamyah did as she was commanded and watched him rummage through her things. Once the truth was confirmed and he placed the address book in his back pocket, he said, "Let's go."

"Where?"

"Don't worry about where." He clinched her triceps and walked her to his truck. Once there, he opened the passenger door and obtained a pair of handcuffs from his glove compartment. He cuffed her left wrist and then clipped the second cuff to the handle of the front, passenger door.

"Is this really necessary, Maurice?"

"Get in the car, Saamyah."

Saamyah awkwardly maneuvered into the vehicle, closing the door with the swing of her arm. She watched Maurice walk and climb into the driver side. He then lifted his armrest and entered a code to open the metal safe. After retrieving his gun and securing it behind his back, he closed the safe and the armrest.

She jumped in fear when he reached over her but was calmed when she realized he was only retrieving her seat belt. He placed hers on and then his own.

"There is really no point in securing my safety if you have plans to kill me. I would much rather be comfortable and take my chances going through the windshield."

Maurice did not respond. Instead, he started the ignition and proceeded out of the parking garage. Shortly after surfacing above ground, Saamyah's phone rang.

"Bryan," Maurice answered.

"Maurice? What the hell is going on? Where is Saamyah?"

"Meet me at the lot of the old abandoned mill—the one we used for tactical training earlier in the year.

"What?! What for?!"

"Just do it!... And no boys in blue or she dies before your last good-byes."

"How do I know you haven't killed her already?"

Maurice dropped the phone in his lap and yanked Saamyah's hair hard enough so that Bryan could hear her cry out. "Does she sound dead to you?" Maurice asked after retrieving the phone.

Trying to remain calm, Bryan finally reasoned, "Look, Washington, whatever your vendetta is I am sure this has nothing to do with her. Please just let her go and we can settle this as men."

Maurice scoffed. "As men?...Meet me at the mill. You better make it in two hours or she dies." Maurice ended the call before Bryan could respond and drove toward the interstate that would take him to the countryside.

"Why are you doing this?"Saamyah finally asked thirty minutes into their silent ride on the open road.

"Doing what, Saamyah?"

"All of this? The rapes, the murder, my abduction?"

Maurice did not immediately respond, but when his silence broke he inquired, "Are you asking me for a motive?"

"I'm asking for the truth." When he failed to respond, she hesitantly asked, "Is killing me a part of the plan."

"You were never a part of the plan. That is why you were warned to stay out of it."

Saamyah had flashbacks of the brutal attacks that threatened her well-being. The attacks gained familiarity as she remembered that they were prompted by her involvement in the Miami Beach case. She stared at him in astonishment, "That was you?"

When he did not answer, Saamyah put the final pieces of the puzzle together herself. "It was you. Wasn't it?" She exhaled in disbelieve as she recalled a lot of the facts about the case. "…The entire time…The…entire…damn…time."

Saamyah turned to sit back in her seat and stared out the front window. As she thought more about his betrayal and her naiveté, the tears fell from her eyes. Breaking her silence, she confessed, "I thought we were on the path to becoming friends." She looked at him. "Was I wrong to think that?"

"Yes," he replied falsely in an effort to stop her from tugging at his heart's strings. "You couldn't walk away, so, I used you to progress my plan."

Saamyah burst into a heartfelt cry. She later turned her back against him, rested the side of her head on the seat, and watched as they drove further into darkness. While watching, she pondered the last three months of her life and everything that DeVaughn had told her days before. Once again, he was right. She had made a mess of her life and exercised poor judgment time and time again. If she was to survive this night, it was indeed time to return home—return to the safety, security, and shelter of her family.

Saamyah realized that the smooth ride on the dark roads had lulled her to sleep when she opened her eyes to an empty parking lot. She looked at the time on the dashboard and it read 1:11 A.M.

"Where are we?"

Maurice placed the vehicle in park and turned off the engine, but left the keys in the ignition. "Enough of the questions, Saamyah?"

Saamyah's phone rang and Maurice answered it. "Russell, you're late."

"I'm coming from the marina, Washington. It is damn near impossible to get to the mill in under two hours, and you know it."

Maurice ignored Bryan's subliminal suggestion that he was being unreasonable and calmly responded, "My instructions were clear as were my consequences. Were they not?"

Fighting the urge to yell a host of expletives at him, Bryan simply said, "Look, I am about 20 miles out. So, I should be there in about 30 minutes; probably less if I can maintain my current speed. I just need you to be-"

Maurice ended the call and dropped the phone is his lap. He looked at Saamyah and explained, "It appears that your boyfriend is going to be late."

Lacking the courage to look him in the eyes to see the truth, she looked passed him to see out the driver-side window. She then stated above a whisper, "So, I guess you are going to kill me now."

Maurice did not confirm nor deny her statement. Instead, he turned to look out the front window and asked if she had to use the restroom.

Saamyah swallowed the knot in her throat while pondering her answer. She feared it was a ploy to take her deep into the fields and shoot her. "Please, Maurice, please don't do this. Think of your wife. Your baby…I'm sure whatever Bryan has done he can make amends."

Maurice exhaled loudly and asked again, "Do you have to use the restroom?'

Saamyah wiped the tears from her eyes with her free hand and nodded her head as she answered, "Yes."

"I'm going to un-cuff you because you have been cooperative thus far, but, Saamyah," he turned in her direction to peer deep into her eyes, "don't give me a reason to kill you."

"Okay."

Maurice took the keys out of the ignition and exited the truck. Closing the door behind him, he walked to Saamyah's door. He slowly opened the door to keep from hurting her wrist and methodically removed the handcuffs. After carefully inspecting her hand and wrist for bruises, Maurice gently massaged the cuff imprint on her skin.

Saamyah noticed the level of care in which he used to comfort her and knew with certainty that exterminating her was never a part of his plan.

"How did he hurt you, Maurice?"

Maurice lifted his eyes to meet hers. "He stole something from me."

Saamyah searched his eyes for clarity, but, when none was found, she gently touched his face and encouraged, "Tell me what it is. I can help you get it back."

Maurice took her hand from his face and feebly smiled. "Even if you could, Saamyah, it would never be the same."

"Maur-"

"When he arrives, I want you to take my truck and leave…There is a good chance that he and I won't leave here alive."

She shook her head in dissent. "No, there has to be a better way to resolve this. There-" Saamyah stopped when Maurice turned to walk away.

"I will show you to the restroom."

Saamyah descended the vehicle, closed the door, and followed him.

Moments later, Bryan slowly crept into the familiar lot and immediately noticed Maurice's truck. He parked his vehicle a few yards away and climbed out calling both his and Saamyah's names.

"I guess your private tour is over," Maurice told Saamyah inside the mill after hearing Bryan call out to them. He moved to descend the steps, but Saamyah stopped him by grabbing his arm.

"Maurice, wait." She paused, searching for the appropriate words to change his mind. "This doesn't have to end this way. Neither one of you have to die.

"I either die honorably tonight or disgracefully after trial."

Saamyah nodded in deference. "I don't understand what he did, but I understand why you did what you did to me."

Maurice nodded and spoke, "Please forgive me." He then kissed her cheek and added, "Good-bye, Saamyah."

Saamyah said nothing in return. Instead, she followed him out several feet behind.

"WASHINGTON!" Bryan called out while trying to find an unlocked entrance. "Washington, where are you?!"

"I'm right here," Maurice announced, coming around the corner with his firearm pointed in Bryan's direction.

Bryan raised his hands, "Washington, what the hell are you doing, man? What the hell is going on?"

"Slowly put your weapons on the ground."

"Where is Saamyah?" Bryan asked slowly removing the gun from his back and placing it on the ground.

"And the one at your ankle," Maurice ordered.

Bryan did as he was commanded.

"Now, kick them both to me."

Bryan kicked both firearms towards Maurice and asked, "Washington, please, where is she?...Is she okay?"

Maurice placed the gun he held behind his back and shortened the distance between them. He patted Bryan down to confirm that he had discarded all his weapons. He then punched Bryan in the abdomen and watched him ball over in pain. "That's for the many years of being an asshole," Maurice spoke.

"And this," Maurice began as he punched Bryan in the face, "is for Rachel."

Bryan fell to the ground from the unexpected blows and struggled to breathe through the pain. He watched Maurice shake the tension from the hand he had struck him with, and prepared for another blow to his body.

Overwhelmed with rage and hatred, Maurice kicked Bryan in the torso and again in the chest. He finally retrieved his firearm from behind him and pointed it at Bryan's head saying, "And this…this is for the night I saw you fucking my wife."

Maurice tightened his hold on the grip in preparation to pull the trigger, but stopped when another gun was fired. He lowered his weapon when he realized that he was the target.

"He's had enough, Maurice. You've made your point. It's over," Saamyah said while still pointing Bryan's firearm at Maurice. She tried her best to ignore Bryan's groans as she attempted to diffuse the situation.

Maurice touched his shoulder, scrutinized the blood on his hand, and faced her, saying, "He literally had everything a man could possibly want, but still wasn't satisfied until he had my wife."

Maurice raised his weapon back to Bryan's head, but before he could pull the trigger, he felt several bullets penetrate his chest.

Though the tears that swelled in her eyes blurred her vision, Saamyah could see Maurice drop his firearm and fall to his knees. He looked at her with apologetic eyes, exhaled for the last time, and fell forward. She then fell to her own knees and wept into her hands relentlessly.

Saamyah shivered from the coolness of the interrogation room.

"Are you okay?" The female officer asked.

"Just a little cold," Saamyah answered rubbing her biceps with each hand.

"They should be here shortly, but I will talk to someone about turning off the air."

"Thank you," Saamyah replied, watching the uniformed officer walk out of the room.

When the officer returned moments later, she was accompanied by homicide detectives. They took seats across the table in front of her and flashed their badges. Saamyah acknowledged their introductions with a nod and braced herself for a series of questions.

Almost two hours of reliving the details that had led up to as well as the specifics of her nightmare, Saamyah exited the room and walked down the long corridor emotionally, mentally, and physically exhausted. Her eyes burned because of sleeplessness, but she still was able to read the 5 A.M. hour on the clock that hung above the exit. In deep thought, she almost collided with an opening door.

"I'm so sorry," the officer said. "Are you okay?"

Immediately revived by her near frontal lobe accident, Saamyah assured, "Yes, I'm fine. Please, don't worry about it."

Inside the room, Bryan lifted his head at the sound of a familiar voice. He saw Saamyah standing at the door engaging in conversation with the officer who had left the room for their break. "I'll be back," Bryan told the detective as he rose from his chair.

"Saamyah," he called out, watching her side-step the door and the officer to continue in her departure.

"Saamyah, wait." Bryan hurried after her.

Ignoring the voice she knew all too well, Saamyah walked toward the exit as if she never heard it.

"Saamyah...Saa-" He grabbed her arm once he was within reach.

Repulsed, she turned around to face him yanking her arm out of his grasp. "What?!"

Taken aback by her harsh inquisition, Bryan simply said, "Nothing, I...I just wanted to thank you for what you did."

She stared intensely into his eyes and asked, "What exactly did I do, Bryan?"

Bewildered, he reminded her, "You saved my life, Saamyah."

"No, Bryan, I actually took one...It just so happened that it wasn't yours," she corrected.

"Saamyah, don't-"

"No, Bryan, you don't." She turned to walk away, but changed her mind when she believed he was walking away from the incident unscathed. She turned back to face him and asked,

"What the hell is wrong with you? Are you some kind of sociopath who just does and takes whatever he wants?"

Bryan started to answer, but was interrupted.

"His wife, Bryan?...His wife?!...He was your partner. He was your FRIEND. YOUR BROTHER."

"...I...I...I didn't know," he lowly stammered.

"Know what? That she was married? That he was your partner? That he caught you?!" She awaited an answer, but, when none came, she confessed, "It still amazes me that he did not kill you both in the act."

Bryan moved towards her and touched each of her arms with each of his hands.

"DON'T!" Saamyah exclaimed. She forced his hands off her and shoved his chest to move him out her personal space. "Don't you fucking touch me!...You disgust me!"

Tears fell from her tired eyes. "I will never forgive you for this, for what you forced me to do, for any of it..." Saamyah pointed an accusatory finger at him and said, "It should have been you that died...It should have been you," before dropping it.

Deeply pained by her cruel words, Bryan choked, "So, why didn't you let me?... If you feel so strongly about it, Saamyah, why didn't you let me?"

"Because someone had to live a life of guilt and shame....So, don't thank me—I only chose you to spare Maurice."

When Bryan said nothing in response, Saamyah bid him farewell and continued in her route to exit the building and meet her ride back to the university's campus for her vehicle.

*** *** ***

Several days later, Saamyah sat at her desk and stared blankly into an abyss. As she spoke, she ignored the eyes that Andrew held on her.

"I still can't believe that I missed it," she finally concluded.

"Not just you, we all did," Andrew uttered after she apprised him of the Miami Beach case's fatal end.

Though his eyes were affixed on her, Andrew, too, sat at his desk gazing into void. He was in immeasurable awe of all that she had divulged. Separating truth from lie, Saamyah's confession quashed not only the rumors that swarmed the department, but also his own speculations.

"...Hell, even I was convinced that Russell was the perp...Evidently, that was Washington's intent. He knew that all roads would lead to Russell and, without adequate manpower, the department would not have bothered with a detour."

"Yeah...That was until I came along and devastated his carefully considered plot," Saamyah surmised. "...But still yet, I missed it..."

Andrew exhaled loudly overwhelmed in astonishment. With little left to console her, he finally offered, "...So often, Saamyah, we find the devil in the details."

"...Yeah...I suppose you're right..." Saamyah breathed, recalling Maurice's departure of the police force prior to SCD's inception and the mandatory transfer of all sexual assault matters. As she reflected on the calendar of events, Saamyah speculated that his resignation followed after calculating the risk of duplicitously working the Miami Beach case as both an investigator and a perpetrator.

Her thoughts then drifted to Maurice's personal relationship with Bryan. He had intimate knowledge of Bryan's comings and goings, one (or many) of which included trysts with his wife. Apparent now, Maurice had not been oblivious to Bryan and Robyn's adoring gazes, loving touches, and lingering kisses. Undoubtedly, to Saamyah, they were all innocent and attributed to their common loss; it is how they comforted each others' hearts just like she and her brothers did in their times of sorrow. However, unbeknownst to Saamyah, Maurice had knowledge of more and discerned differently. He meticulously feigned ignorance and maintained his composure to advance his plan for the ultimate revenge—Bryan's life, for his wife.

"It will be a while before the department recovers from this," Andrew conveyed, breaking the silence in the room.

"Assuming it recovers at all," Saamyah proposed as she emerged from her meditative gaze.

"I pray that it does; though it may take a while with no help from the media." He exhaled loudly in aggravation and attempted to update her in her absence. "Since the incident, this place has been a circus with a pool of reporters baiting officers with defaming allegations and-"

A light knock on the door interrupted Andrew.

"It's open," Saamyah called out, awaiting the visitor's entrance.

Lieutenant Duncan entered the room to first set eyes on and greet Andrew, "Bryce."

"Lieutenant," Andrew greeted in return. He rose to excuse himself so that he and Saamyah could have privacy, but stopped when she rose and touched his forearm.

"Promise me something," she started in a whisper.

"What is it?" He whispered in return.

She looked beyond his blue eyes and petitioned his compassionate spirit, "Promise me that you won't hold this over him."

Andrew squinted at her. "Who?"

"Bryan…Believe it or not, he feels inadequate next to you and much of it is attributed to what you know of him."

Andrew dropped his eyes and sighed. Bryan's and his professional relationship had been a tumultuous one for years and Andrew did not expect it to improve because of this cataclysmic event. If anything, upon Bryan's return to the office, the relationship would sour more. That was unless Andrew made a conscience effort to rise above Bryan's arrogance, cynicism, and selfishness. Indisputably, Saamyah's request demanded much from him.

"Please," she softly pleaded.

Andrew met her eyes again and replied, "Of course."

She smiled then stretched and folded her arms around his neck. "Thank you."

He wrapped her arms around her waist and responded, "You're welcome."

Upon releasing her, Andrew walked out the room closing the door behind him. Saamyah smiled feebly at Lieutenant Duncan and walked to her desk to continue packing the banker's box.

"My prodigal child has returned," Lieutenant Duncan spoke, walking to her. He took in the various boxes around her and added, "Only to leave again."

"Yes, I am leaving," Saamyah confirmed as she placed more items in the box. "I assume you are here because you've received the request for early release—it's only a few days, Lieutenant."

"No... I mean, I received it, but that's not why I am here, Cambell."

Saamyah ceased packing and beseeched, "Please, don't ask me to stay."

Lieutenant Duncan laughed halfheartedly and assured, "I wouldn't dare. Although, as I told you on your first day, you are more than welcome to."

"And just as I told you on my first day, 'no-'" she started.

"'Thank you. I am not interested in a new law enforcement officer opportunity; I am just here for the change in scenery,'" they finished in unison.

Saamyah laughed and wipe the lone tear that fell from her eye. "I'm sorry I gave you hell."

Lieutenant Duncan shook his head in dissent and offered, "Just kept me on my toes...You're a damn good detective, Campbell. You're going to do well wherever you go and whatever you pursue."

"Thank you," Saamyah responded.

He nodded and then cleared his throat. "Listen, I wanted-"

"Oooh no. No drawn out good-bys or farewell happy hours or parties."

Lieutenant Duncan laughed, "I wouldn't dare...But, seriously." He paused to find the words.

Saamyah stepped from behind her desk. "What? What is it, Lieutenant?"

He exhaled loudly and shared, "Detective Washington's widow will arrive shortly…She has made several requests to speak with you."

Saamyah lowered her eyes and her head follow. She walked behind her desk again and began to place more items in the box. "I know and I've denied every one of them…Thanks for letting me know."

"I didn't know that, Cambell. You were out for a while and I wasn't sure what the status of things were for you." When Saamyah said nothing in return, Lieutenant Duncan added, "I thought today, your last day, would be okay…Would you like me to stay and oversee-"

"No," she interjected waving off his suggestion with her hand. "It's okay. The last thing a grieving widow needs is someone hovering as she questions her husband's assassin."

Lieutenant Duncan nodded. "…I'm really going to miss your fire. The office won't be the same without you."

Saamyah smiled, walked to him, and gave him a hug. "And I am going to miss you hazing me; my days won't be the same without it."

They laughed. "I'll let you get back to it," Lieutenant Duncan said before walking out the room.

The smile remained on her face even as she walked back to her desk and placed folders in an empty box. When there was another light tap on the door, she walked to it asking, "What happened? Did you forget to tell me how wonderful I-" Saamyah stopped short of her jest when she saw Robyn Washington on the other side of the door.

The two women stood face-to-face speaking nothing with their mouths, but saying everything with their eyes. Saamyah took in the same woman she met weeks ago glowing and vibrant, now dull and depressed. Her long locks were pinned in a high, lifeless bun and her once gleaming, chocolate skin was now dreary and pale.

Ashamed by what Saamyah knew, Robyn dropped her puffy, red eyes and greeted, "Hello, Detective Cambell."

"Hello, Mrs. Washington." Saamyah greeted in return.

The sting of Saamyah's salutation could be seen in Robyn's nervous disposition. She tried her best to recover, but nothing could escape Saamyah's judgmental eyes that pierced through her flesh and penetrated her soul. At that moment, Robyn no longer felt the few inches in height she was over Saamyah. Instead, she felt she had shrunk double in size.

"May I come in?" Robyn finally found the courage to ask. "I came to-"

"I know why you're here," Saamyah interjected. She stepped aside to allow Robyn to enter and watched as the casually dressed widow looked about the office. "I was not expecting you, but am willing to talk as I pack." Saamyah closed the door and walked to her desk to continue placing items in the box.

"Thank you," Robyn whispered as she set her large tote in Andrew's chair.

Robyn retrieved the framed picture of the two familiar faces that sat at the edge of the desk. Andrew's wife looked as effervescent as she remembered. Her fingers trembled as she outlined the faces of her former friends. Hindsight now 20/20, she surmised that her strong ties to Bryan attributed to their faltered friendship. When the tears escaped her eyes and landed on the glass, she gently wiped them away, and set the frame back on the desk. "I really did love my husband...I still do."

"I'm sure you do," Saamyah affirmed without looking away from her task.

"We were both in a lot of pain from the loss of Rachel— Bryan and I," Robyn stated, beginning her ramble as she felt the need to explain her wrongdoing. "...I guess a part of me always felt guilty for introducing them. Rachel ached from his infidelity and then, later, Bryan ached from her sudden death...All the heartache could have been avoided had they never met."

"And, let me guess, this heart-wrenching ache compelled you and Bryan to find solace in each other, right?...To hell with the living, innocent parties..." Saamyah huffed and added, "Such the classic tale of betrayal."

Saamyah met Robyn's eyes and inquired, "Did you at least wait until your soror was in the ground before you consoled her husband?"

Robyn did not answer.

Saamyah's eyes dropped to Robyn's womb. "Are you certain of whose child you are carrying?"

Again, Robyn did not answer.

Saamyah always prided herself in her failure to pass judgment, but the current circumstance and the casualties surrounding it, turned her from the Biblical principle. At that moment, she loathed Robyn and found her to be a soul not worthy of salvation.

A pregnant silence grew in the room until Robyn broke it confessing, "I hold no malice against you for taking him from me."

Saamyah closed the desk drawer she was in and looked in Robyn's direction. "Excuse me?"

Robyn turned to look at her and rephrased, "I said that I am not angry with you for killing my husband—the father of my child."

Saamyah scoffed, "And you are certain he is the father?"

Robyn did not entertain her indignant inquiry.

Saamyah walked to her and stopped when she was only inches apart from her. Any closer and Saamyah would have been tempted to shove her into the wall behind her. "You killed your husband the first time you stepped out on your marriage. YOU did, Robyn, NOT me." She turned and walked back to her desk. "He was dead long before I pulled the trigger," Saamyah added matter-of-factly.

Taken aback by Saamyah's callous words, Robyn asked, "Have you no remorse for what you did?"

Saamyah looked at her, "I have been feeling remorseful for the last several days. When did your feeling of remorse kick in, Mrs. Washington?...Before the sunset on your adulterous affair or after you learned of the monster you drove your husband to become?"

Robyn shook her head in dismay. "You're such a bitch."

Saamyah laughed halfheartedly. "You fucked your husband's partner, a man he considered a brother, and I'm the bitch?!" She recalled in a rage, "Your husband assaulted, raped, and killed because of what you and Bryan did!...Oh, yeah, there is definitely a bitch among us, but it sure as hell isn't me." Saamyah halted her scornful words before her message developed into a hurtful rant.

"How dare you stand in judgment of me?! Yes, I may have stepped out on my marriage, but YOU killed him. NOT ME...You had a choice, Saamyah, and you chose to kill my husband!"

"Choice?!...What choice did I have, Robyn? Or better yet, what choice did you afford me? It was either your husband or your lover..."

Saamyah paused to temper her rage with a deep breath. After exhaling, she added, "I'm not sorry about the choice I made. Trust me, the state would have executed him just the same."

Robyn sobbed and Saamyah's hardened heart could not bring her to comfort her. Instead, Saamyah took a seat at her desk and contemplated their spirited exchange.

Once she calmed herself, Robyn moved her tote to the floor and took a seat in Andrew's chair. She then confessed, "I regret my part in this—I do...But Maurice was not without fault. He was no saint."

"I'm not of the habit in speaking ill of the dead," Saamyah simply told her.

Robyn continued despite Saamyah not wanting to discuss her late husband's shortcomings. "I never was a priority to him; it was always this job...his advancements...degree...and teaching..."

Bewildered, Saamyah asked, "And you were a priority to Bryan?"

"He made me feel like I mattered...Even if it was only for a few hours."

Disgusted by Robyn's desperation, Saamyah rose from her seat saying, "Well, I hope those few hours were worth all this to you." She then walked out of the office, slamming the door behind her.

*** *** ***

A creature of habit, Saamyah opened and closed each cabinet and drawer in the kitchen checking for anything that could have been left behind during the pack. She also peered into the microwave, stove, and was in the midst of inspecting the refrigerator when there was a knock at the front door.

"It's open," she called out, expecting it to be either her brother or the condominium community's property manager.

Bryan opened the door, stepped in, and closed it behind him.

Astonished, Saamyah uttered, "Bryan."

"Hey."

"Hey," she replied. Saamyah closed the refrigerator door and walked out into the open space to meet him. "I...uuuh....came by your place earlier, but you weren't home."

Bryan dropped his eyes and confessed, "I was home." His eyes met hers again and explained, "I just wasn't ready."

Saamyah sensed sorrow in his voice and it made her uncomfortable. Good-byes were always a challenge for her, but this one was indeed more challenging than others. "I understand."

A quietness fell in the empty room until they both broke it by saying each others' name. They chuckled lightheartedly in unison.

"You go first," Bryan allowed.

Saamyah took a deep breath and wiped her eyes. "I'm going to miss you, Bryan...Despite everything, I really am."

After wiping his own tears, Bryan closed the space between, held her face, and kissed her lips. With his forehead gently pressed against hers, he whispered, "Please, don't go."

"Bryan..." Saamyah turned her face from his.

Bryan used his hand to turn her face back so that her red, teary eyes could meet his. He then took each of her hands in his and held them against his chest so that they could feel his racing heart.

"Saamyah, I love you more than anyone woman I have ever loved in my life... Please, stay...stay here with m-"

"Bry-"

"Marry me, Saamyah."

Bewildered, Saamyah searched his eyes and asked, "What?"

Bryan released her hands and slowly descended to one knee. From his loungewear pockets, he pulled out a black velvet box, opened it to unveil a platinum diamond ring, and repeated, "Saamyah, please, marry me."

Saamyah's heart raced as raging emotions enveloped her. The strongest of them was agony; agony caused by the reality that of all the times he could have proposed to her, he chose to do so just before she walked out of his life.

Due to his ill-timing, Saamyah was unable to discern if Bryan's proposal was prompted by his love and longing to enter into a life-long covenant of commitment and fidelity, or his selfish desire to keep her close. Either way, Saamyah was uncertain of the man that knelt before her. Their short-term association had revealed that he was a man of questionable character. Bryan had lied, cheated, and manipulated for his own selfish gain; and reputations, lives, and unions have been destroyed because of who he was and what he had done.

Along with this litany of doubts, Saamyah had recalled that Bryan had once before impulsively proposed and wed his late wife. That matrimony was encased in heartbreak, scandal, and death. All of which Saamyah knew she could do a lifetime without.

She gently closed the velvet box and whispered, "I'm so sorry, Bryan, but I can't marry you."

Bryan closed his eyes and bit his quivering bottom lip to prevent a flood of emotions erupting in a cry. Though his eyes were closed, he could visualize Saamyah bending towards him for a kiss and then walking to the door.

"Saamyah, wait!"

Against her better judgment, Saamyah stopped at the door, turned, and waited for Bryan to reach her. The stroke of her hair with his hand and the tender touch of his lips on hers sent a cool chill up her spine.

His free hand he held her face close to his and he sobbed on her lips, "I love you, Saamyah."

Saamyah removed his hand and said, "Good-bye, Bryan." She then opened the door, walked out, and closed it behind her.

Bryan pressed his back against the door and slid down it until he reached the floor. He bent his knees before him and propped an elbow on each. Bryan then gripped the box with both hands and released a heartfelt cry.

Saamyah noticed DeVaughn leaning against the front of the rented SUV. She had opted for a rental so that her personal vehicle could be shipped back to Texas ahead of her departure.

Though she knew that her red eyes were an obvious tell of her weeping, Saamyah wiped her face dry before she walked past her brother.

Not quite the reaction DeVaughn was expecting for a woman who had just accepted a marriage proposal, he scrutinized his little sister and ascertained that something had gone amiss.

"Are you okay?" He asked her.

"Yup," she quickly responded, walking past him to the passenger door. "Let's go," she said before climbing into her seat.

Befuddled, DeVaughn walked to the driver side, climbed into his seat, and blankly gawked at her. She had put on her dark sunglasses to conceal her eyes, but she could not hide the tears that fell from them.

"Saa-"

"I'm fine," she interrupted him, staring straight ahead out the front windshield to avoid eye contact.

"No, Saamyah, you're not," DeVaughn disagreed.

She wiped her face and responded, "Well, I don't want to talk about it."

DeVaughn exhaled loudly with frustration as he turned and looked out the driver's side window. Silence fell between them allowing time for DeVaughn to be reminded that his days of commanding her to act were long over; he was learning to "see her." Nonetheless, he was still troubled by her unspoken pain. So, DeVaughn decided to share a moment of truth with her. He turned to look at her again and stated, "Saamyah, I don't know him like you know him and I probably never will. But, I do know that Bryan is the only man that has ever fought me for you."

DeVaughn turned her face to his, removed her sunglasses, and looked deep into her tearful, red eyes. "He came to me, babe sis." He grabbed her hand and elaborated, "He came to me and asked me for your hand."

Saamyah's heart was moved by the revelation, but it still was not enough to sway her decision. So, she took back the sunglasses her brother held, placed them back on her face, and looked out the passenger window. "Let's go home."

DeVaughn silently conceded and secured himself in the seat with the safety belt. After starting the ignition, he backed the vehicle and attached cargo trailer out of the parking lot and began the drive that would leave the last three months of Saamyah's life in the rearview mirror.

Made in the USA
Middletown, DE
17 October 2022

12931647R00250